THE GLASS WOMAN

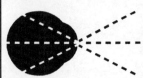

This Large Print Book carries the
Seal of Approval of N.A.V.H.

THE GLASS WOMAN

CAROLINE LEA

THORNDIKE PRESS
A part of Gale, a Cengage Company

GALE
A Cengage Company

LIBRARY OF CONGRESS CIP DATA ON FILE.
CATALOGUING IN PUBLICATION FOR THIS BOOK
IS AVAILABLE FROM THE LIBRARY OF CONGRESS

ISBN-13: 978-1-4328-7390-5 (hardcover alk. paper)

Published in 2020 by arrangement with Harper, an imprint of
HarperCollins Publishers

Printed in Mexico
Print Number: 01   Print Year: 2020

To my two sons, Arthur and Rupert.
I love you more than books.

Jafnan er hálfsögð saga ef einn segir.
A tale is but half told when only one
person tells it.

Icelandic proverb, from
The Saga of Grettir the Strong

PROLOGUE

The day the earth shifts, a body emerges from the belly of the ice-crusted sea. Bone-white fingers waving, as if alive.

The men and women of Stykkishólmur stumble into the cold air, cursing as the tremors shower tufts of turf onto their heads. But the sight of the arm, beckoning them towards the frozen water, freezes them in their tracks, half-finished words left unspoken, mouths agape.

The men surge forward, scrambling over the wrinkled hillocks of solid seawater. It is hard work. He struggles among them, cradling the throbbing wound in his side. His tattered breaths rip from him with every jolt of his sealskin boots on the ice.

Behind him, safe on snow and frozen soil, people are watching. He can feel them weighing his every step — hoping for the ice to give way.

9

He remembers carrying the heavy body in the winding sheet, weighted with stones; remembers his wound paining him as they scraped through the snow and smashed the ice with long staves before sliding the body in. The sea had swallowed it immediately, the flash of white vanishing into the darkness. But the knowledge of the body stayed, like the blood-spattered scenes at the end of the Sagas: those age-old, heat-filled stories, which are told to children from birth and fill every Icelander with an understanding of violence.

Six days ago, he had muttered a prayer over the black water, and then they had laboured back to the croft. The ice had crusted over the hole by moon-down, and by the time the pale half-light of the winter sun seeped into the sky, the snow concealed it. Weather masks a multitude of sins.

But the land in Iceland is never still. The grumbling tremors or the sucking of the waters must have dislodged the stones, and now the body has bobbed upwards and broken through the cracks in the ice. And here it is. Waving.

He slips and falls heavily, grunting as the smack of the ice throbs through his side. But he must carry on. He heaves himself upright, gasping at the pain. The ice creaks

10

under his boots. Beneath him, the black water gulps, endless and hungry. He eases himself forward.

Gently. Gently.

The earth shudders again — no more than the shaking of a wet dog, but it throws him to his knees. The world reduces to grating, shifting sheets of ice. He lies face down, gasping — waiting for the *crack* that will echo like a shattering bone. It will be the last noise he hears before the sea swallows him.

The ice stills. The world stops shivering. Silence settles.

He pulls himself to his knees and the two men alongside him do the same.

They exchange a look, eyebrows raised, and he nods. The ice groans. Underneath, the dark current seeps, like a secret.

'Hurry!' one of the people on shore calls. 'Another quake will take you!'

He sighs and scrubs his hands through his hair.

'It would be best left,' says one of the men, who is tall and black-eyed, as if he is formed from the same shifting, volcanic rock as the land.

The third man, light-skinned and red-haired, like a Celt, nods. 'Until the spring. More light, the ice will thaw.'

11

He scratches his beard, then shakes his head. 'We must get it out now . . . *I* must get it out.'

The taller of the men scowls, his dark eyes blackening further. 'Go back,' he says. 'Don't risk yourselves.'

But now the other men shake their heads too.

'We stay,' says the taller man, quietly.

The crowd on the shore still watches: ten people, but their excitement and whispering make them seem more. They are muttering in huddles, mouths hidden behind mittened hands. Their words make grey clouds of sound in the cold air — poison circling like a miasma.

They are near the water now; the ice crackles under their boots. He holds up a hand. They stop.

He lies down on his stomach and eases forward. Less than a hand-span beneath him, he can see the gulping black sea. In front of him, the white-shrouded shape bobs in the water. The frozen fingers beckon him invitingly.

The ice grinds its teeth.

He jabs with the scythe and, with a rush of exultation, feels it catch on the cloth. He heaves. The body floats closer, pale hand flapping towards his face. He flinches. Then

12

the material rips and the scythe tears free. The body bobs away.

'Leave it,' growls the dark-haired man.

He stretches out with the scythe again. His cold muscles shriek in protest, and his arm judders with the effort. He jabs hard, and the metal point stabs through the sheet. He winces, as though the cold metal has punctured his own flesh, then closes his eyes, breathes deeply, and stabs again. The blade sinks into the meat.

The other two men hold him as he starts to heave the body from the water. Slowly, a dark shape emerges and flops out onto the ice.

'I'm sorry,' he rasps.

They carry the heavy parcel over the sea-ice, back to land.

He tries not to look down at where that dead hand trails across the slush and ice, like the fingers of a child, balling snow ready to hurl. Smoke from the fires in the nearby crofts sends a black scrawl into the icy air — dark runic scribbles against the villagers' excited white breath.

As the men near the shore, the people surge forward, fluttering like eager carrion birds, jostling to be the first to gorge on this unexpected feast.

■ ■ ■ ■

PART ONE

■ ■ ■ ■

Long shall a man be tried.
Icelandic proverb, from
The Saga of Grettir the Strong

Part One

RÓSA

Rósa sits in the *baðstofa* of the croft that newly belongs to her and her mamma. A biting plume of wind shafts through the gaps between the turf wall and the tiny window, which is made of pale sheepskin, shorn of wool and stretched, until it is thinner and more translucent than the expensive paper imported from Denmark.

She shivers as the wind plucks at her tunic, but still she huddles closer to the opening to catch the fading light, tugging her shawl about her shoulders.

She dips the quill into the precious pot of ink.

My dear Jón Eiríksson,
I write to beg your mercy and understanding, my husband. Your apprentice, Pétur, arrived today, with your kind gift of three woollen dresses and bade me to

17

join you in Stykkishólmur. I wish to be a
dutiful wife in this, our new marriage,
but I regret I cannot join you

Rósa stops, bites her lip and pulls the
shawl more closely around her. Then she
scores out *cannot* and writes *will not.* Her
hand wobbles and she presses down so hard
that the quill snaps, spattering ink over her
words.

Her eyes sting. She growls, balls up the
paper and hurls it to the floor.

'Pick that up, girl,' her mother wheezes,
from the opposite bed. 'Are we richer than
Niord to waste good paper and ink?' A rattling cough bubbles from her chest.

'Sorry, Mamma.' Rósa smiles, teeth gritted, then picks up the paper, smoothing it
over her knee. 'I cannot think . . .' She feels
her mouth crumpling, and bites the inside
of her cheek.

Her mother smiles. 'You are nervous, of
course. Your husband will know that, no
matter what you write. I remember when I
wed your father . . .'

Rósa nods mutely, a sudden stone in her
throat.

Sigridúr's smile fades. She pats the bed
next to her.

'This is not like you. Sit. Good. Now, what

18

troubles you?'

Rósa opens her mouth to answer, but can find no words for the crushing panic she feels at the thought of leaving her village to live with this stranger, whom she must suddenly call 'husband'. When she thinks of him, she cannot picture his face, but only his hands: strong and sun-darkened. She imagines them pulling on oars, or wringing a chicken's neck.

Suddenly Sigridúr clasps Rósa's hands. 'No more of that!' For a moment, Rósa wonders how her thoughts were so plain to see. Then she looks down at her hands and realizes that, without thinking, she had begun to trace the *vegvísir* on her hand.

'No runes!' Sigridúr hisses.

Rósa nods and clenches her hands into fists. 'I know.'

'You cannot *know*. You must remember. Your husband is not like your pabbi was. He will not blink and pretend not to see what is under his nose. You must quote nothing but Bible verses and hymns to him. No runes. No Sagas. You understand?'

'I am not a fool, Mamma,' Rósa whispers.

Sigridúr's expression softens and she strokes Rósa's cheek. 'Do not fret. If his prayers become tiresome, you must wait until he's asleep, then beat him over the

19

head with his Bible and lock him outside in the snow.'

Despite herself, Rósa smiles.

Sigridúr snorts and adds, 'For *the huldufólk* to feast upon.'

Rósa rolls her eyes. 'Mamma, please. Not even in jest — you've said so.'

'Don't fuss,' Sigridúr says. 'There is no one to overhear us.' She pauses and her eyes flash. 'Besides, the *huldufólk* prefer to eat children.'

'Mamma!'

Sigridúr holds up her hands. 'I must laugh while I can, my love. Marriage.' Her mouth twists. 'And to a man from so far away.'

Rósa feels her panic rising again and crushes it. 'Remember, Mamma, the new turf on the roof, the big stove. Peat to burn — it lights much better than manure. And Jón will trade with Copenhagen for wood for you when the ships arrive. Imagine *wood* to line the walls, Mamma. Furs instead of homespun. You will be warm all winter. In time, you will fight off this infection.'

'Your pabbi taught you to argue, that is certain. And to be a fisherman's wife. Such a waste.'

'He is not simply a fisherman.'

'Yes, *goði* is not a title to snivel at. I know he grows barley on his home farm and does good trade with the Danes. I heard his speech, just as you did. A pretty picture he painted. But people say —'

'Rumours, Mamma, and we will pay them no mind.'

'They say Jón's first wife —'

'Overblown stories.' Rósa's voice sounds harsh, even to her own ears, but it distracts her from the prickling sensation in her hands and feet whenever she imagines being alone with this man. Three nights ago, she had dreamed that her new husband was lying on top of her, but he had the head and shoulders of an Arctic bear. He leaned forward to kiss her, but opened his jaws wide and roared. The meaty stench of his breath had made her gag and she had woken retching. She worries that the dream is an omen and she has tried time and again to write to Jón, delaying the time when she must travel to Stykkishólmur. But then, when she listens to her mother's wheezing, she knows her decision is right. Sometimes, when she closes her eyes, she sees not Jón's face but another man's — a face more familiar than her own. A hand reaching out to brush the hair back from her forehead. But she quashes that thought too, and says, 'We won't talk of Jón's first wife. It's jealous gossip, aimed at frightening me. You said so

21

yourself.'

Sigridúr nods slowly, looking down at her hands, which are blue-laced with cold. 'But, still, Stykkishólmur is four days' hard ride away. The land is cruel, especially after the hard winter we had last year . . . They say there are ice floes in the sea that have not melted for twelve months. And why does he want *you*?'

'Such a compliment, Mamma. You must stop, or my head will grow too big for the croft.'

'Hush!' Sigridúr grins. 'I think the world of you, but . . . Why not a girl from his own village?'

Rósa has worried at the same question herself, but now she reaches across and clasps her mother's cold fingers. 'I must be irresistible.'

Sigridúr smiles sadly. 'Your pabbi would have known what to do.'

'I miss him too.' Rósa embraces her, closing her eyes and inhaling the sour smell of wool and sweat that reminds her of her childhood.

Rósa's father, Magnús, the Bishop of Skálholt, had died nearly two months earlier. It had started with stomach pains, but within a month his belly had swollen as if he were heavy with child.

The village had whispered, of course, that it was the work of some witch with a grudge, peeved perhaps that he had banned all runes and the casting of spells, where previous bishops had openly read from the Sagas and the Bible alike. Magnús had treated the rumours with contempt: he had denounced them from the pulpit and had threatened to have the gossips thrown from the church. It smothered the hissed rumours, but didn't stop the illness raging through his body. He was dead before the Solstice, leaving little in the way of money or goods for his wife and daughter. Magnús had sold the lavish croft with its glass windows and wood-lined walls, giving the money to the upkeep of the church. He had chosen to live instead in a small, cramped, turf-roofed building, like his flock.

Riches feed the body but devour the soul. Better to live humbly, like Christ.

During his lifetime the villagers had been generous: in addition to the weekly tithe, they had given ale and mutton enough to keep the family well fed and create the illusion of prosperity. But it had taken Rósa very little time after her pabbi's death to see that their situation was desperate.

Soon, her mamma had developed a cough

that bubbled like a sulphurous marsh with every breath. Rósa lay in the *baðstofa* at night, listening to the fluid filling Sigridúr's chest. She remembered Pabbi's lessons about the four humours: too much water in the lungs could leave a person drowning in their own body.

She watched her mother shrink and wheeze, curling into herself like an old woman: grey-skinned, with eye-sockets like caves. Rósa's desires for herself withered and her life sharpened to a single purpose: help Mamma to survive.

On the first Sunday of July, a month after Magnús's death, Rósa had gone to church with the intention of praying for guidance. She and Mamma had eaten the last of their *skyr* that morning and were too proud to beg.

On the way to the church, she had passed Margrét, who was using a stick to scratch lines in the ground outside her croft. She turned at Rósa's footsteps, then quickly scuffed out the lines with her shoe. 'Just a Bible verse.' She grimaced, her chin jutting aggressively, and tucked her grey hair into the threadbare cap where it had come loose.

'Which one?' Rósa couldn't help asking. It was no secret that Margrét couldn't read or write a word and was envious of Rósa's knowledge. She had been scratching out a rune, no doubt.

'Ten Commandments,' Margrét snapped. 'In pictures. Enough of your smirking, Rósa. I saw that young man of yours.'

'Young man of mine?' Rósa thought she could feel heat rising to her cheeks.

'Don't play the fool with me. He's off digging turf on a Sunday instead of going to church. You'll have to keep Páll in line if you want him to make a good husband.'

'Then you must look for the girl he means to marry and tell her so. Perhaps you will find her when you go to church, Margrét, instead of making *patterns* outside your croft.'

Rósa didn't wait for her to respond, but quickly walked on. She scanned the fields for Páll, but couldn't see him. Neither was his one of the dozens of faces that turned to hers, then away, whispering, when she walked into the church.

The building was hot with bodies as the villagers crowded to welcome the newly appointed bishop, Olaf Gunnarsson. They fidgeted as he spoke.

Suddenly, Bishop Olaf was speaking Rósa's name, the daughter of the great Bishop Magnús. He beckoned her up to the wooden

25

pulpit as everyone stared; she could imagine
them judging how thin she had grown. As
soon as he let her go, she darted back to
her bench, taking a deep breath only once
the eyes of a hundred villagers were no
longer upon her.

But as she looked up once more, she had
the feeling that someone was still watching.
She glanced to her left and there he was: a
stranger in the village where she knew
everybody's name.

He was a huge man: the muscles in his
arms stretched the material of his tunic. He
was dark-skinned, as if he spent much of
his time outside. His heavy beard hid too
much of his mouth for her to read his
expression.

She dropped her gaze. When she looked
up again, he was still staring.

After the service, the stranger left quickly.
Rósa didn't have to ask to find out who he
was because everyone was full of talk: Jón
Eiríksson was a rich fisherman, farmer and
merchant from Stykkishólmur. A self-made,
powerful man. Since the death of the chieftain in the area, he also acted as *goði,* deal-
ing with many legal and church matters
from his own croft — there was no church
building in his tiny settlement. He had been
travelling south to buy a new cow and had

stopped at Rósa's village. The Skálholt church buzzed with talk.

Old Snorri Skúmsson's white beard quivered with excitement. He leaned in close to Rósa — she could see the red veins that spidered over his nose. 'He's given out that he is here to welcome Bishop Olaf and pay his respects, but of course he's not fooling anyone.' Snorri sniggered. 'His wife died and now he's after a new one — everyone has been talking of it. We all saw him staring at *you,* Rósa. And you won't be staying in the church now, with your pabbi gone — a good thing. Women reading — pah!'

Rósa recoiled. Was bad breath a sign of rot on the inside? But she forced a smile. 'Your daughters are much older than I am. Perhaps you should seize this chance for one of them.'

Snorri gaped as Rósa curtsied, then ran outside and down the hill before he could reply. Mamma would be proud of her. Pabbi would have been less so.

Again, she scanned the hills and fields for the familiar set of Páll's shoulders, but he was nowhere to be seen. The rest of the villagers filed back to their crofts, some calling to Rósa as they passed, then turning back to their neighbours to mutter. Rósa clenched her jaw and forced out a greeting.

27

It had been like this ever since Pabbi had died: the whispering and speculation. Sometimes Rósa felt as if she were standing naked in a blizzard, every soul in the village pointing as she shivered.

Then Hedí Loftursdóttír came and pressed a clump of moss into Rósa's hands. Her face was pale and her light blue eyes darted left and right. 'For your mamma. It will help her cough.'

Rósa nodded and smiled. Perhaps some people still felt compassion for her. But before she could draw a breath to thank Hedí, the girl had run away, head down, as if Rósa carried some terrible disease.

The sky was a wide blue eye above her. When it paled, near midnight, the sun would skim below the edge of the horizon, then resurface in a blink, shedding a milky half-light.

In the distance squatted the upturned tabletop of Hekla. It spat smoke and ash into the sky, sometimes spewing out black rocks and lava to entomb the land and people for miles around. Hekla was known to be the open door into Hell. All in Iceland feared it, and many would rather die than live within sight of it. But Rósa could not imagine living anywhere else.

It would mean leaving her mamma. And Páll.

Rósa flexed her fingers, squeezing the soil beneath, and smelling the black dead-ash promise the mountains made anew each day: *we will remain.*

Something comforting in that relentless obstinacy. No more thoughts of ghosts and spirits. No more thoughts of leaving.

Two days after the church service, there had been a knock on the croft door. Rósa had known who it would be — no one ever knocked in Skálholt.

She hadn't mentioned to her mamma anything about the service, or about the broad-shouldered stranger, and when she heard the knocking, Rósa froze.

Sigridúr stirred and coughed, then gave the door a dark look, as if the wood were to blame for waking her. 'God's teeth!' she mumbled. 'Open the door, Rósa, would you?'

Rósa pretended to be absorbed in her knitting. Another knock. She remained motionless, and Mamma, still coughing, gestured at the door.

Rósa sighed, set down her work and opened the door. In the sudden glare of light, all she could make out was a tall,

29

bearded figure.

'Komdu sælar og blessaðar.' Jón's voice was deep.

She shielded her eyes from the light. *'Komdu sæl og blessaður.'*

From her bed, Sigridúr had snapped, 'If it's traders, shut the door. We've sold both cows and all the sheep we can spare. I've nothing else I want to be rid of.'

'Mamma, it is a visitor,' Rósa hissed. 'A *man.*' Then she turned to the broad figure in the doorway and smiled. 'Forgive us. Mamma is wary of strangers, since Pabbi's passing. But you are Jón Eiríksson, *goði* of Stykkishólmur.'

He gave an awkward duck of his head that she supposed was a bow. 'Indeed. May I come in?' The flash of white teeth in his black beard softened his face.

She returned his smile, despite the hammering of her heart.

Sigridúr pursed her lips and struggled to sit up. 'You must take us as you find us. My husband died some months ago and —'

'I am sorry.'

Sigridúr gave a curt nod. 'Your wife died too, folk say.'

He sighed. 'Two months past.'

'So soon? And I heard you buried her in the middle of the night, then went out fishing the next day. As if your wife cost you no more grief than a dog.'

Rósa gasped. *'Mamma!'*

'It is the truth. Look at his face.'

Jón clasped his hands together, as if in prayer. 'I buried her alone, it is true. I didn't . . .' He sighed, scratched his beard. His face was weather-beaten, his mouth had deep grooves at the corners, and there was darkness in his eyes, like a slammed door.

'My wife was suddenly unwell. It was . . . distressing. She was from near Thingvellir and had few friends in my settlement.'

Rósa held up her hand. 'I apologize. Mamma grieves still and . . . We feel Pabbi's loss keenly every day.' She gestured at the sagging turf roof and the broken beams, which would need imported wood to repair them. He was too polite to look directly at these signs of their poverty, but he nodded in sympathy.

'But you should not feel you must explain,' Rósa continued. *'All have sinned and fall short of the glory of God.'*

'Indeed.' His expression brightened and his voice was warm.

Sigridúr snorted. When Magnús was alive, she had been more reserved, but since his death she had cared little for the opinions of others.

31

But Jón seemed not to take offence: he puffed out his cheeks, then exhaled. 'Like any man, I have enemies, keen to spread rumours. But, believe me, I mourned my wife. It pained me that I could not help her.'

Even Sigridúr had the manners to hold her tongue.

He turned to Rósa. 'Bishop Magnús was a virtuous man. A good man with a good family.'

Sigridúr's scowl returned. 'As you see.'

The weight of silence rested between them.

Sigridúr didn't take her eyes from Jón's face. 'Rósa,' she snapped, 'fetch food and drink for our guest.'

Rósa went through the cowhide curtain to the pantry, where she could still hear them. The shrillness in Sigridúr's voice made her flinch.

'You would be best to visit Margrét — she has sheep and daughters both. I'm sure she'd trade either for a few ells of home-spun, or their weight in dried fish.'

Rósa scooped some *skyr* onto a plate, poured two cups of ale and hurried back to the *baðstofa*.

Sigridúr's lips were pursed. 'I am weary.' She indicated the door. 'Thank you for your visit. *Bless.*'

Jón bowed. '*Bless*. I'm sorry to have troubled you.' He turned to go.

Rósa glared at Sigridúr. 'Won't you stay? We have *skyr* and ale —'

'Thank you, no. *Bless*.' He ducked through the little doorway and was gone.

As soon as he left, Rósa rounded on her mother. 'What possessed you to be so rude?'

'You are not a cow that he can offer a trade for you.' Sigridúr narrowed her eyes. 'You may wilfully ignore what others say, Rósa, but a woman listens to wisdom if she wants to live to old age. They say he cut the hand off a merchant who cheated him. And that he had a man in his village burned for witchcraft. And his wife —'

'His wife died of a fever, Mamma. The rest is gossip.'

'Only a child could be blind to the darkness in that man.' Sigridúr sank back onto her bed, coughing. 'It's all over his face. His wife no sooner dies than he's on the hunt for a new one.'

Rósa's mind hissed the same thought, but she knelt, taking Mamma's hands. 'It would be a good match.'

'Nonsense. Your brain will rot. Think of your writing. Besides,' Sigridúr grinned, '*you* are too willful to be a wife.'

'I will try to be . . . obedient. And mar-

33

riage will not stop me reading or writing.' Rósa's voice faltered, as she thought of the scraps of parchment she had hidden under her mattress, which contained scribbled thoughts about a new Saga: a little like *Laxdaela Saga,* except this time the heroine would not kill or die for love. Surely her husband would not grudge her the chance to write occasionally. Even Magnús, who had despised anything associated with the old ways, had scoffed at the belief that writing stories or poems could be a form of witchcraft. He had also believed that, as he lacked a son, his daughter should be taught to read and write, despite the mutterings of the villagers when they saw Rósa curled up with a quill and parchment.

Sigridúr stroked Rósa's hair. 'Bless your innocence. A man like that would set fire to your feet if you wrote a single word. Besides, keeping a croft, you would have no time to do anything other than sleep and eat. And I would never see you. No. I'll hear no more of it. You'll stay here.'

'Jón is wealthy —'

'So was Odd of the *Bandamanna Saga,*' Sigridúr muttered, 'and he carried misfortune with him too.'

Sigridúr persuaded Rósa that it could not

34

happen: he was too old, too odd, his home too distant. Besides, the man went through wives like cloaks.

But the late summer threw down early snow, which breathed cold over the village. Their evenings were spent huddled around the fire, burning precious tallow candles for extra warmth, stitching clothes that were more patch than cloth. Hunger shifted in their bellies and clawed at their guts. It would be yet another hard winter.

When Sigridúr's cough worsened, and every breath sounded as if a swamp were squatting in her chest, Rósa began to have nightmares that Mamma had choked to death during the night, or starved, or died from the cold. More omens, perhaps.

She found a large, flat stone and used a stick with charcoal from the fire to draw out the protective *vegvísir* symbol, which she placed under her mamma's straw mattress. The rune was only truly effective if drawn in blood on the forehead but, mindful of whispers, she hid the stone and hoped it might offer some net of protection around Sigridúr.

Even as she did it, Rósa knew that the real answer lay within her grasp: food and warmth would bring her mother back to full health.

But every time Rósa thought of Jón's face, she shivered.

In the end, it was Páll's pabbi, Bjartur, who forced the decision.

Páll had been Rósa's closest confidant from childhood — his pabbi was Mamma's cousin. Her earliest memories were of wrestling with Páll in the long grasses, or of him pelting her with snowballs. When they were older, they had lain on their bellies on the hillside, side by side in the sunlight. His eyes and thoughts, his very smell were as familiar to her as her own skin.

When they were sixteen summers, Rósa took to seeing Páll more often: she left the croft early and returned late. The two of them often walked over the hill, out of sight of the spying eyes of the village.

Magnús had become increasingly severe about Rósa spending time with Páll. 'It isn't fitting. You're no longer children.'

'You are seeing harm where there is none,' insisted Rósa, when Magnús wouldn't relent.

'And *you* are ruining your chances of a good match,' bellowed Magnús. 'Ignorant girl! You know how people talk.'

'Let them! Anyone would be a fool to think there is harm in my friendship with Páll. A poison-minded fool!' Rósa spat the last word, and Magnús reeled, then turned and walked to the door.

He stopped there and said, very low, his back still to her, 'Many fathers would have beaten their daughters for less. Remember that, next time you call me a fool.'

Rósa had spent the night alternately sobbing and raging, and nothing Sigridúr could say calmed her.

The next morning, she had woken early and crept out to see Páll as usual. Despite her fury with Magnús, she found herself saying to him, 'I must see less of you in the coming months.'

'Oh?'

'My pabbi says . . .' She uprooted a grass stalk. 'He says I must spend more time alone.'

'Doing what?' Páll smudged the ink on the parchment and cursed under his breath. Rósa poked him with a toe.

'He says . . .' Rósa hid her face in her hands. 'He says I must prepare to marry.'

'Marry?' Páll sat up, smiling quizzically, as if it were some joke. 'Surely old Snorri Skúmsson is too much sought-after for you to have any hope there.'

Rósa laughed, but the sound emerged as a sob.

Páll's smile faded. 'So I am to see less of

you because you are to marry?'

Rósa nodded. 'Someone from . . . I don't know where. Pabbi is talking of . . . He says I must make a good match. Someone . . . powerful.'

Páll blinked and Rósa was suddenly dry-mouthed.

Finally, Páll said, 'Well, no doubt you will be like Gudrun from *Laxdaela Saga,* and men will be killing each other for your love.' He used the quill to flick ink across her face.

Rósa wiped it away, then used her finger to smear it across his cheek. 'Don't waste ink, you scoundrel!'

He grinned. 'No waste when it makes you laugh.'

They said no more about marriage and, after some time, she fell asleep with her arm across her face. She was wakened by a tickling sensation on her stomach. She reached down to brush away whatever insect was bothering her, and discovered that her stomach was bare — her dress had ridden up while she was asleep — and her skin was covered with letters where Páll had written on her.

She sat up. 'What are you doing?' she snapped. 'How will I wash these off?'

'I . . . I don't know.' Páll was red-faced and wouldn't meet her eye. 'Your dress

38

moved and I — I thought you would laugh, and then I . . . You're just — And I couldn't —' He turned away.

She leaned towards him, smiling. 'You're a fool. Soak your tunic in the stream and I can wash the ink off. There's your payment for drawing on me: you will be cold and wet.'

She had expected him to laugh, but he got up without looking at her and then returned a short while later, his tunic soaked.

She squinted up at him. 'Well? I cannot rip it from your back.'

He swallowed, then slowly lifted his arms and peeled it off.

She stared. When she had last seen his body — when they had last swum together, the summer before — his arms and stomach and chest had been very much like hers: the flat planes of a child. Now his chest had broadened, while the digging and hefting of peat had made hard slabs of muscle under his skin.

When Páll held out the wet tunic to her, she found she couldn't move to take it.

'Here,' Páll murmured.

Rósa shook her head: the letters could stay and he should put on his tunic. But he must have misunderstood her, because he closed his eyes and inhaled, then knelt next to her and began wiping her skin with the tunic.

Rósa jumped and gasped at the cold.

'Am I hurting you?' Páll asked. 'Should I stop?' He looked at her face. His blue eyes were fathomless and deep, his expression utterly serious.

She shook her head. Then she lay back and closed her eyes.

He worked carefully, one letter at a time, the cloth marking an icy trail, which left the surface of her skin stippled with cold. After a long time, when the sun had dropped in the sky, and Rósa had begun to shiver, Páll stopped.

'Finished,' he whispered. Then, before she could move, he leaned forward and pressed his lips to the skin of her navel. A single moment of heat. Rósa jumped and drew a sharp breath.

Páll recoiled, as if she had slapped him. 'I'm sorry, I shouldn't have —'

'No! I didn't mean —'

'I'm sorry, Rósa. Please forgive me.'

And before she had found the words to tell him he didn't need to apologize, that she wanted him to kiss her again, Páll had jumped to his feet and backed away from her, as if she might scald him.

For the rest of that summer, he had

40

treated her like a stranger. He barely met her eye, and if she spoke to him, he grunted in response. When Sigridúr asked Rósa what had happened, Rósa didn't know how to explain. All she knew was that, before, seeing Páll had been like looking at the familiar and beloved mountains that surrounded her home. Now, meeting his eyes was like staring into the open mouth of Hekla. When she looked at him, her whole body burned.

Magnús also noted the separation between them: he smiled and patted Rósa's head, as if she were a child. 'Sensible girl. That was never any sort of future.' When Rósa raised her eyebrows, Magnús continued, 'It wouldn't do. A bishop's daughter and a crofter's son?' He laughed. 'I made you for better things. You'll be a match for some fine *goði* somewhere. Hólar to the north, perhaps. Or even Copenhagen.'

'I want to stay here.' The words were out of Rósa's mouth before she had even formed them in her head. 'With you. I want to help you in the church. Here, in Skálholt.'

Magnús had laughed again but, when Rósa had been adamant, he had finally agreed that she need not marry and could stay at home.

After Magnús's death, Páll had come to the

41

croft more often, shyly offering strips of dried mutton or sacks of manure for the fire. Over time, he smiled at her again, teased her. Slowly, it seemed their friendship was returning to what it had once been. Rósa finally felt able to look at Páll again, to meet his eyes without fear.

Once he brought to the croft a large block of peat which he must have obtained from a trader, although Rósa could not imagine how.

When she asked, he grinned. 'Believe me, you would rather not know.'

'You *stole* it? Then take it back.' She shoved it towards him, but he held her wrists lightly with one hand and laughed. 'Your mamma needs it.'

She stopped struggling, but left her wrists in his hand. 'I won't burn stolen peat.'

'Your mamma will. Besides, I didn't *steal* it.' He took her hands and squeezed them, smiling. 'A greedy rogue wanted ten loaves. I gave him the bread, and he gave me the peat, happily.'

'But . . .' She tried to ignore the jolt of his skin on hers. 'Wherever did you find the flour for ten loaves?'

Páll chuckled. 'I am generous. The crust of the bread will fill his belly, while the inside of each loaf is packed with good hay

42

for his horses.'

'*Páll!*' She laughed. The trader had almost certainly deserved it and the peat would help to dry the air in the croft, which would soothe Mamma's cough.

Páll continued to bring food and fuel. Slowly, Rósa began to hope that there might be a future for her with him. Perhaps she and Páll between them could keep Mamma alive through the winter, until the warmth of spring began to heal her.

At night, when the darkness surrounded her, Rósa lay on her bed and remembered again the feeling of Páll's lips on her, his body close to hers. The heat of him.

But then, one day when Rósa was out on the hill, searching for bog bilberries, she heard the squelch of footsteps behind her.

Rósa did not turn. 'There are very few, Páll. You should go back and help your pabbi — he will rage if he finds you have neglected your work.'

'Indeed I will, and have done for weeks, though my son pays me no mind.'

Rósa gasped. 'Bjartur! *Bless.*' She bowed her head in greeting, hoping he would continue on his way, but he continued to stand, arms folded.

'Your eyes will freeze if you stare so,' Rósa said finally.

43

Bjartur scowled. 'Mind your tongue, Rósa. And keep away from my boy.'

'Good day to you, Bjartur. May the fair weather continue.'

His lip curled. 'Always above yourself. You're poisoning Páll —'

'I will tell him —'

'You will *tell* him to stay away from you.'

'He is a man, and may command himself.'

'Ah, but he does not. *You* command him. Tell him to stay away.'

'You cannot order me —'

'I can and I will. You're unruly and selfish, and you've been allowed to tread your own path for too long. Must I spread word in the village that what they whisper is true, that you've bewitched my son? Shall I tell people that they should search your croft for runes and other writing?'

Rósa forced herself to return Bjartur's baleful glare. 'You would not . . .' But her voice shook.

Bjartur stepped towards her. Though her guts were roiling, Rósa stood firm.

'Have you looked at Páll, these past months?' he growled. 'Truly *looked*?'

Rósa blinked. 'You are trying —'

'The boy is exhausted. Thin as a broom-handle.'

'I . . .' Rósa dropped her gaze. 'I had not

44

noticed.'

'No,' Bjartur sneered. 'You have been too full of your own thoughts and plans to see that my son starves himself to fill your belly.'

'I — I will tell him to eat and rest.'

'Tell him to keep away. You're poison to him.'

Rósa prayed that Bjartur would leave, but he took a step closer. He smelt of bitter turf and sour sweat.

'The *goði* from Stykkishólmur seeks a wife. Direct your simpering smiles at him.'

Rósa's jaw dropped.

Bjartur turned his palms towards the sky. 'A wealthy man, he'll send coin and food for your kinfolk.'

Rósa ignored the trembling in her legs and drew herself up to her full height. 'I am not a fool, Uncle. Your self-interest —'

'You could save us all from grief, Rósa. It will be a hard winter, and many will die.' He hawked up phlegm and spat upon the ground. 'Think on it.'

He turned and trudged back down the hill. In the stoop of his shoulders and his limp, Rósa saw the ghost of what Páll might become. If he survived.

Jón stayed for nearly three weeks, trading in the surrounding area, watching. Watching

45

everything. He refused the offers from various villagers, usually those with daughters of marriageable age, to share their roof as shelter. Instead, he made a little camp on the hillside, in spite of the cold nights.

Rósa passed him daily on her way to collect water from the river. She didn't smile and wave a giggling greeting, like the other girls, but walked with her head down. The feel of his eyes on her made her skin itch.

Again and again she went over Bjartur's words of warning on the hillside. Perhaps he had been right. Perhaps her marriage to this rich man would be better for everyone. But no! Why should she marry a stranger? Why should she leave everything behind?

Then, one night, Sigridúr coughed so violently that her handkerchief came away freckled with red, and Rósa knew that the decision had made itself.

The next morning, when she saw Jón trudging over the fields to the church, she took a deep breath, called a greeting and hurried to walk alongside him.

Jón stopped and turned to her. 'It will be another grim winter.'

She looked at the grass. His cold blue eyes made her insides coil. Not quite fear, but the feeling made her shift from one foot to another.

'You must miss your pabbi. He was a good man.'

'Thank you. He was. You knew him?'

'I met him briefly at the Althing. His dedication to God and his care for his people were remarkable. Some bishops are greedy, but your pabbi was humble.'

She nodded.

'And he would be proud of his daughter, I think.'

She forced herself not to reply. Women should be quiet and biddable.

He smiled and looked at her through narrowed eyes. 'You are the epitome of humility, Rósa Magnúsdóttir.'

His gaze on her was like a touch. She found herself looking at his hands: the thick veins like ropes, the strong fingers. Her own hands trembled; she clutched the wool of her skirt.

'Does it please you to be obedient?' Jón murmured.

She measured her words. 'Pride is a sin. God says, *Do not be haughty.*'

He stepped closer to her. 'You are a fine woman.' His body radiated heat and Rósa squirmed, but forced herself to smile and meet his gaze. As they walked, he described Stykkishólmur's beauty until she could almost taste the salt and hear the puffins.

47

She made admiring comments. Mamma had told her that men needed adoration.

His manner became easier. He smiled as he itemised his wealth: the linen sheets, the abundance of bread and meat, the large peat fires that warmed the kitchen and *baðstofa* all day. 'I have every comfort that might be dreamed of,' Jón said. 'It is a good life, only solitary. The Bible tells us that women were created for men, *bone of my bones, flesh of my flesh.*' His eyes were dark blue, impenetrable. He reached out and touched her cheek, then rested his hand upon her shoulder. It was hot and heavy.

Rósa's breath was tight in her chest.

Jón took her hand between his own. Her fingers disappeared. He looked down at her wrist. 'Such delicate bones. Like a bird.' He opened out her fingers and intertwined them with his. 'I would care for you, Rósa. You understand?'

She nodded, wide-eyed.

'I would send food to your kinfolk in Skálholt.' He squeezed her fingers. She gasped. He leaned in close to her ear. 'Say yes to me,' he whispered.

Rósa sighed and closed her eyes. The darkness inside her widened its jaws but she ignored it and fixed her face into a smile.

■ ■ ■ ■

Sigridúr was furious, of course. 'Your pabbi nurtured your mind, taught you to read. Will you waste that in a life of drudgery? Stoking fires and beating washing until your body breaks? Aim at the bishop, if you must marry.'

Rósa set her jaw. 'This is for the best. You will have meat and —'

Sigridúr wheezed. 'You will be far away across the country. And there's a coldness in that man.'

'Hush, Mamma. He is . . . good.' The more Rósa said it, the more she believed.

'Marry someone young. From Skálholt.'

Unbidden, Rósa thought of Páll's smile, his kiss, which had lit up her whole body. A sudden memory of him, aged twelve, chasing after her. She had stumbled and he had fallen, laughing. When she turned to him, her own laughter seemed to come from his chest, his from her mouth. The memory ripped through her now, leaving her momentarily breathless.

And yet when a stone is caught in a rushing river, what choice does it have but to move?

When she next saw Jón, Rósa dropped her

49

gaze and smiled meekly. They discussed scripture, and when he talked of the instruction for women to be silent in church, she nodded. She showered him with praise.

They sat next to the river and he put his hand on the back of her neck. He must have been able to feel the pounding of her heart — her whole body shook with it. When they stood, she peered down to look at her reflection, but beside his huge bulk she was less than a shadow, pale as a ghost. The surface of the water flickered, she disappeared, as if something had swallowed her.

It took a week of silent glares and growling stomachs, and a fire that kept dying overnight for want of peat to burn, before Sigridúr grudgingly agreed to the match. When she gave her blessing, Rósa's eyes stung and her knees were shaking.

Jón visited to thank Sigridúr, and to say that he would travel west to Stykkishólmur after the wedding — the herring were plentiful in September, the hay must be harvested, and he should attend his people as *goði,* giving out food and counsel. 'Forgive me, Rósa. My work and my people have claims on me.' His mouth was a flat line and he squeezed Rósa's fingers.

She swallowed. 'Of course. You are a great man.'

Jón's face relaxed. 'I will send my apprentice to bring you home. He will care well for you on the journey.' He stroked the palm of her hand.

She had to force herself not to flinch. This was her future: this mountain of a man, with the stern face and crushing hands. She nodded, unable to force any air past the jagged stone in her chest.

Rósa found Páll out working, shifting squares of turf on a roof. She tried to look at him through unfamiliar eyes and saw that, although he was lean and looked weary, his shoulders had broadened and his arms were hard with corded muscles.

She closed her eyes and exhaled slowly.

Páll turned when she called his name, but he didn't climb down.

'I hear you are to marry.' His face was hard, his voice flat. 'I wish you joy.'

'I wanted to tell you —'

'It is not my concern. Marry, if you like.'

He turned his back and slashed viciously at a piece of turf to square it. The sun glinted off his hair, accentuating the trace of red. She had tugged at the reddish hairs in his beard when it first grew, calling him a *Vestmannyar,* from Ireland. He had laughed, his breath warm against her hand.

51

'Won't you come down?'

'I must finish this roof.'

'I . . . Let me explain —'

'Nothing to explain. Only . . .' He clenched his jaw and, for a horrible moment, his voice shook. Then he coughed and said brusquely, 'I thought you were set on church life. Here.'

'I . . .' She sighed. 'I'm sorry, I —'

'Don't.' When he looked at her, his eyes were the blue of a glacier in midwinter.

After a long silence, she turned and walked away.

Behind her, she could hear Páll grunting with exertion as he shifted the squares of turf.

The marriage ceremony took place on the first day of September, in the jaundiced pre-evening light. The dark church was crowded with most of the people of Skálholt, craning their necks and muttering.

Rósa shrank under their hard eyes and whispered words, and pushed her hands into the dress Jón had bought for her, white linen, shot through with strands of red silk. When sunlight caught the silk fibres, Rósa's body was picked out in fire. In the right pocket, Mamma had placed a wooden cross that had once belonged to Magnús; in the left was a stone, which she had pressed into her hand that morning.

Rósa had frowned at the symbol on it. *'Ginfaxi?'*

'Courage in battle.' Sigridúr had grinned. 'And victory when wrestling.'

Now, under the eyes of the villagers, Rósa clutched the cross and the stone, squeezing them until her hands ached. Her blood pounded in her ears, but she could still hear snatches of the gossip around her. She heard the word *witchcraft* and tried not to roll her eyes. The villagers were happy enough still to use runes, but envy meant it suited them to be suspicious of Rósa and Sigridúr. She could also hear them murmuring about Jón. She heard *first wife,* then tutting and stifled laughter.

A finger of sweat traced the length of Rósa's spine.

If Jón heard any of the snatches of gossip, he didn't show it. He stood next to his apprentice, Pétur, whom Rósa hadn't seen before.

Pétur was slimmer and darker than Jón: his skin was like the bronzed buckskin of Pabbi's empty coin purse, and there was a coiled stillness about his body, which made Rósa think of the pictures of wolves she had seen in books about those lands to the east.

53

His eyes were brown, but in the few beams of orange light from the tiny, high windows — expensive glass, imported from Denmark — they glowed almost amber. They locked on her, and Rósa's breath caught. Then the corners of his mouth tugged upwards and his face softened.

Sigridúr nudged her daughter. 'They say he's one of the *huldufólk.*'

'And they *say* a woman writing is witchcraft,' Rósa muttered.

'He was found on the hills as a child. As though he'd grown from the earth. He looks it too, with that dark hair, those eyes.'

Rósa risked a quick smile. 'One of the *huldufólk* would have made off with the children by now.'

But it was true: Pétur looked darker and harder than any Icelander Rósa had seen, as though he was somehow formed from the volcanic soil itself.

Sigridúr gave a wheeze. '*Huldufólk* or not, he's a pretty fellow. Now *that* would be a marriage choice.'

'You are past marrying age, Mamma.'

Sigridúr snorted.

Rósa kept her eyes fixed on Jón's face. He smiled at her, grey eyes brightening from slate to sky. She felt the iron fist loosen around her chest.

When she had entered the church, Rósa had searched for Páll's reddish-blond hair. She had allowed herself to imagine he might grin at her; even if he didn't, even if he scowled, just seeing him might give her strength. When she realized that he hadn't come, it was like a physical blow. She had lost him. Truly lost him. She pressed her hands to her stomach and forced herself to breathe through the pain.

She straightened her back, pressed her mouth into a fixed rictus. Around her neck was a leather cord, on which dangled a tiny glass figurine that Jón had offered to her that morning as a wedding gift. It was cold, like frozen water, and shaped into the perfect form of a woman: tiny hands clasped in introspection, gaze meekly lowered. Rósa had gasped: glass was costly and rare, and she had never before possessed anything that had no purpose other than to look beautiful.

'I had it from a Danish trader,' he said. 'Beautiful. Fragile. Humble.' He touched her cheek. His hand was burning on her skin. 'It made me think of you.'

A woman made of glass and stillness: perfect but easily shattered.

Rósa squeezed the figurine until her hand ached. Later, she would find that the glass had left a purple imprint of itself on her palm.

The bishop's voice was deadened by the dark, fuggy interior of the church, the air heavy with the warmth of too many breathing bodies.

After the words of blessing had been spoken, Jón looked at her and reached out, as if to stroke her cheek again, but let his hand drop to his side.

She exhaled slowly — she hadn't realized she had been holding her breath.

He travelled back to Stykkishólmur that afternoon, no wedding feast, not even a night in Rósa's bed — though she was thankful she didn't have to endure Mamma snoring in the bed opposite hers while she lay with her husband for the first time.

It would be Pétur who returned in three weeks to take her to her new life.

Skálholt, September 1686
It is late but still light. In the morning, they will leave, she and Pétur, travelling north-west; Rósa will become someone else. She finds herself remembering *The Saga of Eirík the Red,* in which Gudrid journeyed to foreign lands, only to find that all who accompanied her were plagued by illness and that her travels were marked with death. Gudrid sought out a seeress and they sang ward songs for protection.

Now, in the pantry, Rósa mutters the words in some attempt at protection, as she stuffs linens into a sack to take with her.

'Sun knew not
what temples she had,
Moon knew not
what power he possessed,
Stars knew not
what places they had.'

She fumbles over the linens and drops them. Her hands are shaking.

Sigridúr has drunk too much *brennevín* and is snoring softly on her bed when Rósa returns to the *baðstofa*. Pétur is warming his hands by the fire. He fixes her with those eyes, dark bronze in the gathering gloom. At first she thinks he is scowling at her, but then she sees that he is staring at the glass woman, which dangles from a leather cord around her neck. Perhaps he disapproves of the expense. Rósa tucks it inside her dress.

He raises his eyebrows, then turns back to the fire. 'Have you seen the sea before?' he asks.

'Never. Shall I like it, do you think?'

His smile seems mocking, as if he finds something about her amusing. 'Some take to it and some don't. But I think Jón has chosen you for reasons other than your strength at the oars.'

'Oh.' She stares at the fire. She is no innocent: she knows what men expect.

The silence between them shifts. Rósa smooths her skirts: they are linen and silk, another gift from Jón.

'Your family must miss you when you are trading.' Then she remembers Mamma's tale: Pétur was discovered on a hillside as a child. She feels a blush creep over her

58

throat. 'I mean —'

'I have no family.'

She looks down at her lap. The linen scratches her skin. 'I am sorry for you.'

'You must not be,' Pétur says. 'Jón is better than a family.'

'You call him Jón?'

'Should I call him *Master*?' He studies her face; she looks at her hands. 'When you wrestle your life from the hands of the sea, the waves are your master.'

'You believe in . . . sea spirits?'

'Some things go beyond our understanding.'

Pétur uses the poker to shift the peat. The orange glow flickers over his face and he looks, for a moment, monstrous. Earlier, she had watched him crouch by the river and impale a trout on a fishing spike.

Now, he leans towards her. 'You must have heard the rumours — I am one of the *huldufólk.*' The sharp angles of his cheekbones and his dark eyes make him the very image of one of the grinning elves.

He laughs and Rósa jumps.

'Superstitions are ungodly.' Her hands are sweating. In her skirt pocket, the runestone Mamma had given her is warm against her skin.

Pétur raises a mocking eyebrow. 'Ah,

Rósa, such piety! You may even win over my own dear pabbi.'

'Your dear *pabbi*?' He'd said he had no family.

Pétur leans in closer. He smells of sweat: a sharp, animal odour. 'I believe what any Icelander believes,' he says. 'Some answers are given in the Bible. Others are not.'

'And . . . Jón?' Rósa holds her breath.

'Jón is an Icelander. But the blood and the heart may tell us different truths.' He watches Rósa until she looks away.

'What of the *prestur*? He likes my husband?'

'Egill? Best to stay away from him. Jón will tell you the same.' Pétur gazes morosely into the fire.

After a moment of silence, except for the crackling fire and Sigridúr's snores, Rósa asks, 'Will I have a maidservant?' She imagines, briefly, a mouse-haired, hazel-eyed girl like herself.

But Pétur shakes his head. 'The croft is not so large that you will need help.'

The likeness fades; Rósa feels a stab of loneliness.

Pétur looks up, his eyes suddenly hard in the firelight. 'Besides, you should keep apart from the people of Stykkishólmur. They are full of nothing but sly gossip.'

She opens her mouth, then, seeing the burn in his gaze, shuts it.

They set off early the next morning. The sky has been filled with pale light for hours, but even the farmers are asleep, the cows and sheep still drowsing in the fields.

Pétur holds Rósa's stirrup while she clambers atop the mare, a beautiful chestnut beast, comically shaggy in her thick winter coat. Rósa has not ridden since she was a child; she feels awkward in the saddle and grips the mane tightly.

'Do not worry.' Pétur smiles at her nervousness. 'She is a fine mare. Sturdy, strong and full of courage. Wait until you feel her *tölt*.'

Rósa's confusion must show, because Pétur chuckles, his face light and animated.

'See, I will show you.' He swings himself into the saddle of his own dun mare and digs in his heels. The mare walks, trots, then changes her gait to high-stepping strides, which are so smooth that Pétur hardly shifts in the saddle.

He circles the mare back to Rósa, grinning. 'The *tölt*. It will cover the ground and is comfortable — the horses can sustain it all day. You try.'

Rósa presses her heels against the mare's

61

sides and the horse springs forward into the smooth, high-paced gait. Remembering riding a trader's horse as a child and bouncing in the saddle, like a sack stuffed with wet rags, Rósa laughs. 'It feels like flying.'

Pétur whoops, a strange, inhuman sound, and kicks his horse to catch up, but hers is faster. She gallops up the hill, the wind whipping tears from her eyes.

Birds are flushed from the long grasses ahead of her: two ravens flap skyward, then circle overhead, shrieking. Rósa feels a chill: the carrion birds make her think of Hugin and Munin, Odin's twin messengers of Thought and Memory, who deliver word from the dead. She shakes off the thought and urges her horse onwards.

It is only when she reins in her mare at the top of the hill that she sees it: Skálholt lies far behind. She has left, without even realizing it. Her little croft is a smudge of brown against the green, no bigger than her thumbnail. Somewhere, in the scattering of crofts, Páll will be rising for the day. Will he sense, somehow, that she has gone?

Overhead, the ravens circle and caw.

Pétur reins in next to her. Expecting mockery, she rubs her eyes with her sleeve and turns her face away.

'You can return, briefly, if you wish,' he

says, gently. 'I will wait.'

She shakes her head. 'I have said my farewells.' She pushes away the image of the downcast slant to Páll's shoulders when she saw him last. 'Let's go on.' And she turns her back on Skálholt and looks to the cloud-hooded mountains ahead.

Pétur kicks his mare on. 'You are stronger than you seem, Rósa. *Eigi deilir litur kosti.*' Appearances can be deceptive.

She shrugs off the compliment — or perhaps it is an insult — and keeps her eyes fixed on the grey clouds in the distance. 'What is my mare's name?'

'Hallgerd. And mine is Skalm.'

'Good strong names.'

'There is much to be told by a name, Rósa.'

Is he trying to flatter her? She is nothing like a rose. 'Pétur' means *stone.* At first, it had seemed a fitting name: hard, jagged and unrelenting. But now she considers his laughter, his kindness at her grief. He is right: appearances can be deceptive.

She is so lost in thought that she does not notice the large rock until her mare veers sharply left to avoid it. Rósa falls. The grass is soft and it does not hurt, but her face is hot as she scrambles to her feet.

'Are you injured?' Pétur dusts off her skirts.

'I am well, only . . .' Tears sting her eyes and she swallows hard.

Pétur picks a sprig of heather from her hair. 'The land does not want to release you. This brave piece of heather has martyred itself so that you will stay.'

She cannot help laughing, and wipes her eyes.

'Here, keep it in your pack,' he says. 'It will remind you to watch your step. I carry a knife to remind me.'

'To watch your step?'

'No. To remind me that there are many ways to silence a chattering woman.'

Her stomach drops and she backs away. He chuckles, then takes her hand and helps her back into the saddle. His hand is strong, his grip hard.

'They say a fall bodes a good journey,' he says.

'You use proverbs from the Sagas. I did not think . . . I imagined it would not please a religious man, like Jón.'

He fixes her with those strange golden eyes. 'Jón is not a zealot.'

'So Jón approves of the old ways?'

'Talk is one thing. Witchcraft will see you burned.' He yanks the reins, his face rigid as his horse wheels away and canters off.

She examines the broken boulder that caused her fall and realizes that it marks the spot where Jón Arason and his two sons were beheaded after the civil war nearly a hundred and fifty years ago. Arason's execution had taken seven blows of the axe. Rósa looks at the black soil beneath her feet and wonders if, deep in the earth, the richness of the man's lifeblood might still pulse.

She mutters a blessing for him and squeezes the runestone in her pocket.

In the days after his execution, Arason's followers had hunted down his executioner and poured molten lead into his throat. *Blood for blood.*

Overhead, the ravens wheel and shriek, always searching for the dead.

The rest of the day passes in a blur of wind-flattened grass and snow-hunched mountains that grapple with the horizon and shift their shape with every step.

When the sun reaches its zenith, the land broadens. It is greener and tamer here. The horses saunter drowsily, heads low to the ground, snatching mouthfuls of grass, which is webbed by rivulets of water. An exposed spine of stones, ten times the height of a man, juts upwards, as if the earth has done battle with itself and ripped off its skin.

Pétur sees her staring. 'The ancient ones used to think the ground here was alive. Every time there is an earthquake, even now, the landscape changes. Pieces fall away or rise up. Whole hills are engulfed.'

'Whole hills? *How?*'

He gestures at the ragged stone teeth. 'The earth moves and the rock cracks. The land breaks open. Fire and melted rock bubble up, like blood. When the ground sleeps again, these scars remain.'

'Where *are* we?'

'Thingvellir. It is where the Law Council meets.'

She exhales in awe. 'The Althing?' This is the place, then, where laws are passed, and where men and women have been tried and burned or beheaded for casting spells or reading runes or spreading sickness.

In her pocket, the stone throbs, like a beating heart.

Rósa searches for a blackened patch of soil, which might mark the place where bodies had crisped and burned, but the tangle of grass, water and rock stretches off into the distance, insolent with life.

She closes her eyes, sure, for a moment, that she can hear a raw-throated scream in the distance. But it is only a raven — the

66

bird can imitate almost any call. It flaps overhead, shrieking like a man on fire, then gives a gurgling chuckle.

Rósa is suddenly cold and weary. 'Will we stop to eat?'

Pétur shakes his head and passes her some dried fish from his pack.

She would like to argue that she is exhausted and aching from the time in the saddle, but the obstinate set of his mouth silences her.

As she chews, she notices the far-off figure of a man on a black horse. Pétur leans across and grasps Hallgerd's reins, pulling the mare towards a cluster of birch trees. 'You look weary. Here, the trees will provide shelter.'

'Shelter from what?'

Pétur does not reply, but squints into the distance, his mouth hard.

Rósa doesn't protest: she must try to be mild and biddable.

They eat in silence while the horses graze. Rósa gazes in wonder at the knot of branches surrounding them: trees not much taller than her own head. 'I have never seen so many trees before.'

He puts his fingers over his lips. Then he whispers, 'Jón says that in other lands there are clusters of trees called forests. They stretch up like mountains, blocking out the light. The soil beneath is always in winter.'

Rósa hears a branch crack as the horse-man rides past the stand of trees. Pétur waits a moment for the hoofbeats to recede, then his face softens. 'In Stykkishólmur they say that years ago, when the Vikings arrived, the land was covered with thick forests, but the men felled the trees and the soil was washed away. The land never recovered and never forgave them. Now, every farmer must work from dawn until dusk to scratch hay from the dead soil. And if he does not show gratitude, the earth devours him.'

Rósa shivers. The mountains rear large and black, their sides striated with huge vertical clefts, as if some giant of old had plunged an axe into the rock.

The hoofbeats of the black horse fade. 'We were hiding,' she mutters.

'No. I felt compassion for your woman's weariness.'

'You are . . . I do not believe you.'

'Lying is a mortal sin. You are brave. Remember why I carry a knife.' His eyes are narrowed, his voice flat.

She grips Hallgerd's thick, greasy mane for courage. 'Don't threaten me! I will tell Jón. And are you a Catholic, to speak of mortal sins? It is forbidden to . . .' She trails off at his expression. 'You are laughing at me.'

He holds up a hand in apology. 'I am not laughing *at* you. But Jón had not warned me you had such a temper.' He tilts his head to one side, mouth curled into a smile. 'Or perhaps he does not know.'

Then Pétur digs his heels in; Skalm trots away.

She flaps her legs against Hallgerd's ribs until her mare catches up. She gives him a withering look and he laughs again, kicking his mare forward.

Her unease grows when they ride late into the evening and he shows no sign of stopping at any of the settlements or scattered crofts they pass. In fact, he veers away from any blink of light in the blanketing grey of falling night.

Rósa's chin lolls onto her chest and then she starts awake. Unable to bear the bone-burning exhaustion, she demands, 'Are we to sleep in the saddle?'

'We can stop, if you must.'

'And sleep out in the cold?'

'The horses will keep us warm, and I have blankets.'

He is teasing her, surely. But, in the fading light, his face is as severe as ever.

'Is there a settlement nearby?'

He shakes his head. 'A day to the east is the closest.'

She takes a breath to quell her growing hysteria. She will not sleep out in the open air, where there are foxes and rats and the marrow-gnawing cold. 'I would like a bed.'

'We will sleep outside.'

Louder, her voice sharp: 'I need a bed!'

He growls, then gives a tight nod. 'Very well. There is a croft on the other side of this hill. We will be there before dark.'

'Why did you not say so before?'

When they reach the croft, he tells her to wait ten horse-lengths back, by a small clump of birch saplings. He knocks on the door. An old man shuffles out. He and Pétur confer in low voices, then the man nods and Pétur returns to Rósa.

'We sleep in the barn. The horses too.'

'With the *animals*?' Rósa's voice is high-pitched.

'No animals. They are all out in the open, as we should be in this weather.'

'Did you ask him for a bed?'

'We are sleeping in the barn, Rósa. Come, this way.'

The man, who has been watching their exchange, calls, 'Tómas!' and Pétur walks back to him. The man gestures at the *baðstofa,* but Pétur shakes his head and

70

points at the barn with its sagging turf roof. In the end, the man nods but disappears into his croft, then emerges with two woollen blankets. Pétur walks to the barn, pulls open the rickety door and leads the horses inside.

Rósa stalks after him into the dark fug. 'He would have allowed us into his croft. And he called you Tómas?'

'The horses can sleep against the bales of hay. We will lie alongside them.'

'Why did he call you Tómas?' She wrinkles her nose. 'This barn smells foul.'

'Sometimes folk in outlying crofts have no outhouse.'

'So they use the *barn*?'

'Sleep outside, if you prefer.' Pétur has already encouraged both horses to lie down and has settled himself under a blanket next to Skalm. He turns his back on Rósa and his voice is muffled by the horse's mane. 'We will rise with the light, so you should fall asleep quickly, wherever you do it.'

Rósa scowls. Pétur's breathing has already lengthened and deepened. She huddles under the blankets, and pillows her head against Hallgerd's warm neck. The mare grinds her teeth with contentment and gives a huffing sigh.

Rósa lies rigid, blinking into the darkness,

her blood thrumming in her ears. Pétur seems to be asleep. She presses her hands against her belly and curls around herself. She imagines she is stone or earth, but still, on every breath, she is aware of the soft rise and fall of her flesh, the brittleness of her bones beside the growling, deceptive creature in the shape of a man.

She remembers the smooth ease with which he had lied to the man who owned the barn, the lightness of his laughter.

And as sleep drags her down to its swampy depths, she remembers something else: Jón's first wife, Anna, had come from a settlement near Thingvellir.

Near Thingvellir, September 1686

Rósa dreams of Páll. He reaches for her and brushes his fingers over her cheek. She leans into him, but cannot reach him: all she can feel is the pulsing fingerspan of air that separates them. When she looks up at his face, it is not Páll, but Jón. He moves his hand down to her throat, squeezes and releases her neck, pushing air in and out of her lungs. She tries to claw free, but Jón's broad body is suddenly a sculpture, made of the blue ice from the belly of a glacier. He lurches at her, clawed hands stiff with frost, beard rimed with snow. His voice is a funnelling wind as he howls and twists in fire. When his blackened hand clasps her shoulder, she screams.

'Hush, Rósa!' Pétur grips her arms and shakes her. 'You will wake the farmer. And you're terrifying the horses.'

She sits up and rubs her eyes. Both mares

73

are now standing rigidly in the corner, their nostrils flared, their muscles shuddering under their thick coats.

Rósa is trembling. 'Was I calling out?'

'And thrashing and screaming — it was like holding a fish.'

The hands she felt upon her must have been Pétur's. Rósa shivers and rushes outside. The cold air scrapes against the exposed skin of her hands and face — winter's bite is looming. She squats behind the barn and relieves herself: pissing inside would be repellent. She leans her head against the cold wood until her breathing steadies enough for her to return inside. *Not an omen, Rósa. Only a dream.*

They travel in silence. The land is black-toothed and raw, occasionally stippled with rough scrub and coarse, yellowed grass. The haunting desolation stops her breath in her throat. In the distance, the mountains look like gathering storm clouds. There is an old belief that each mountain contains a spirit, and perhaps this accounts for the itch between Rósa's shoulder blades as they move into the craggy landscape. There are a thousand eyes upon her, peeling off her skin, staring into her soul. She incants the warding verses in her head, then mutters the Lord's Prayer under her breath. Pétur glances at her, his dark eyes inscrutable in the fading light, and she flushes.

She would like to ask if he, too, can feel the eyes upon his skin, but when she studies his face, the slow-dropping shadows have cast him in a sulphurous light, sharpening the planes of his cheeks and the hollows of his eyes. He looks dark and beautiful and her words die on her lips.

As evening approaches, the sky fades to tarnished steel. The occasional birch tree claws skywards. There is a tale that one of the *huldufólk* haunts the roots of birches and turns the golden leaves into treasure to tempt greedy travellers. The last thing they see is the precious metal turning back into a pile of leaves. Meanwhile, the elf man sits on their chest and feasts on their soul.

It is a warning against avarice. Rósa wonders if she would feel anything if a creature began to gnaw at her soul. But marriage to a wealthy man is not the same as selling her soul out of greed, surely.

The further away from Skálholt she travels, the more everything blurs, as if the darkening land is casting a veil over her thoughts.

Towards evening, she becomes aware that they are changing direction, riding north-east, towards a ridge of snow-topped mountains.

The land closes around her, like a fist. 'I thought Stykkishólmur was to the west.'

'We must find a croft to sleep in.'

'Thank you.'

'It is for me, not you — I cannot endure your lamentations about the cold.' He winks at her and she flushes. 'Besides,' he continues, 'we will arrive in Stykkishólmur tomorrow so you should sleep tonight. I cannot deliver you exhausted. Jón's rage is best avoided. You must learn how to please him.'

She turns away from him and looks at the mountains, then puts her hand to her throat, where the glass woman chills her skin. Sometimes she feels as if the leather cord is strangling her.

'There are four crofts this way, in a place called Mundarnes.' Pétur points beyond the rocky path ahead.

'That would be . . . Thank you.'

After a short silence, he says, 'It would be . . . easier if you called me Tómas away from Stykkishólmur. People like to gossip in these parts.' His face is tight, watchful.

She senses that her answer will dictate whether or not she sleeps with a roof over her head. 'Very well,' she says stiffly.

■ ■ ■ ■

Just before the sun takes its brief dip below the horizon, they reach a bundle of four crofts, packed tightly as a clenched fist.

Pétur raps on the door of the nearest. When a young man opens it, Pétur bows and asks if he might beg a bed for the night with his new wife. They are travelling west and have misjudged the distance, he explains with a laugh.

Lies flow from his mouth like water. Again, twisting unease knifes in Rósa's gut. The young man has the flat, plain face of a labourer. He nods along with everything Pétur says without speaking a word — perhaps he is a little simple.

Then the man says, 'What is your name?'

Without faltering, Pétur replies, 'Tómas Agnarsson.'

'Is that so?' The man narrows his eyes. 'You look very like what I've heard of Jón Eiríksson's man, Pétur. There is much talk of *him* in these parts.'

Rósa's blood jolts. The man is anything but simple. A cruel smile tugs at the corners of his mouth.

Pétur doesn't blink. 'Many people look alike.'

77

The smile broadens on the man's flat face. 'Not like you, they don't. You look like a foreigner, not even a Dane — too dark. One of the *huldufólk,* you are.'

Pétur's smile is hard. 'Take care. Superstitions will light fires under your feet.'

'You're a foundling child. Egill might have taken you in as his son, but you cannot name your true pabbi. It is certain you are no *prestur*'s boy. You have the look of an outlander — a savage. Everyone in these parts has heard of you, Pétur, enough to know you on sight. Why do you give a false name?'

'You would be wise not to pry.' There is a dangerous edge to his words.

The man rubs his hands. 'Ah, that would be the Anna Olafsdóttir matter? I heard it ended badly. Nasty state of affairs.' His broad face sharpens, and when he smiles, he reveals small, pointed teeth, like a rodent's. '*Sickness* took her, was it?' His mocking laugh rebounds off the hills around them.

Rósa's throat constricts.

'We will sleep elsewhere.' Pétur turns away.

But the flat-faced man follows, a swagger in his step. 'This is the new wife then? Look at her — wide-eyed, like a lamb. She doesn't

78

know what she's married.' He laughs and calls to Rósa, 'Get away while you can.'

Pétur grabs the man by the neck and slams him against the wall of the croft. He struggles, but Pétur draws a knife from his belt and slowly levels it so that the point of the blade rests against the man's gulping throat.

'It seems to me,' Pétur growls, 'that your face needs reshaping. Your mouth is too big, your ears too small. And your nose is so long it is no wonder you stick it into other people's affairs. So I will help you.'

The man's throat bobs as he swallows.

Pétur's voice is a raw hiss. 'Shall I shorten your nose?' He brings the blade upwards. 'Or perhaps the problem is your eyes.' He moves the blade to within a hair's breadth of the man's left pupil. 'Or does your throat trouble you?' He rests the knife edge against a hammering vein in the man's scrawny neck. 'It troubles me. Too noisy.'

'I — I didn't mean . . .' The man's desperate eyes flick to Rósa, who is frozen in horror. 'Forgive me, mistress, I am sure you will be happily married. I —'

'Quiet!' Pétur's voice is steel. 'Remember, *engi er allheimskr ef þeg ja má.*'

No one is stupid if he can keep silent.

The man gibbers another apology and

79

then, when Pétur releases him, stumbles inside the croft, rubbing his neck and coughing.

Pétur sheaths his blade in his belt and grabs Rósa's arm. 'Come. He may have brothers. And the neighbours will have heard.'

'But the dark —'

'Damn the dark! We must leave.' He yanks her arm, pulling her away from the croft, and bundles her into her saddle.

As they gallop away, she looks over her shoulder at the lights from the fires burning in the crofts, then back at Pétur, whose face has shifted and juts savagely, like the fierce stones at Thingvellir.

Rósa grips her horse's mane and blinks at the endless void of darkness ahead. It is like riding off the edge of a cliff.

■ ■ ■ ■

PART TWO

■ ■ ■ ■

True is the saying that no man shapes his
own fortune.
Icelandic proverb, from
The Saga of Grettir the Strong

PART TWO

RÓSA

The next morning, Rósa and Pétur reach Stykkishólmur.

He had driven them onwards through the night, until Rósa was drowning in exhaustion. He wouldn't rest, and refused to answer her questions about the flat-faced man's words. The stranger's mocking laughter had whirled in her mind. *Anna didn't die of sickness? And Pétur is Egill's son?*

Eventually, she had lain forward along Hallgerd's neck and let the mare's movement lull her into a restless doze, full of images of blood dribbling from the gash in an eyeless man's throat, then of lambs lying down and placing their thin white necks on chopping blocks.

She wakes with the smell of salt sharp in her nostrils. 'Where are we?'

'Home.'

They are on a hill. Like the gods of old,

they have an aerial view of the remote tiny world below. Behind them stretches a lava field: what was once red liquid rock has frozen and blackened while still bubbling, then smothered itself with moss, but it still has the simmering appearance of shifting liquid, as if the land were a boiling sea of green. Above them, a mountain yawns into the sky, incisors scraping the surface of the clouds and breathing cold air from the snow-covered skull. A wisp of smoke puffs lazily from the gaping jaws.

Pétur nods towards it. 'Drápuhlídarfjall. Do not worry. It only threatens eruptions. Sometimes there is more smoke, sometimes less, but never any explosion. And we are standing on Helgafell. It is talked about in ___'

'*Laxdaela Saga*. So Gudrun Ósvífrsdóttir . . . ?'

'She is buried at the foot of the hill, yes. We will pass her grave.'

Rósa feels a thrill of excitement: she spent her childhood in awe of the fierce Saga woman, who married four times and urged men to kill each other for love of her.

'There is a tale that if you climb Helgafell, starting at Gudrun's grave, and you don't look back or speak a word, you will be granted three wishes.'

84

'Surely the *prestur* doesn't permit such superstitions?'

Pétur turns those golden eyes on her. 'The *prestur* dislikes it.' There is a twist to his mouth at the word *prestur.* 'But all old sayings have something in them.'

'I won't tell the *prestur* you said so.'

'You should not speak to him at all.'

In a settlement of fewer than thirty souls, how can he expect her not to speak to the *prestur*? 'You dislike him? But the man in Mundarnes, he said —'

'That Egill was my pabbi?' He purses his lips. 'I lived in his croft for a time, but that is not the name I would use for him.'

'But if you grew up with him? Why —'

'Prying again? The curious child gets burned fingers.'

She twists her fingers in Hallgerd's mane. Women must not speak their minds: the Bible tells them to be silent, submissive, respectful. She is no Saga heroine. No Gudrun Ósvífrsdóttir.

'I . . . Forgive me.'

Pétur gives a tight nod, then urges his horse forward. 'Jón will be waiting.'

As the horses pick their way down Helgafell, Rósa looks back. Stykkishólmur is edged with mountains: like a cupped hand, they protect the village or shield it from pry-

85

ing eyes. Rocks jut out of the greenery: the bones of the soil, scrubbed clean by years of over-harvesting and tree-felling. The grey carcass of the earth peeping up, indecent and raw.

The land flows towards the beach, where there is a scar of black sand, and then the rumpled surface of the sea, which Rósa hasn't had a chance to take in, so dazzled has she been by the savage beauty of the landscape. The sea is a dull blue near the shore, fading to a smoky mirror in the distance. Islands are scattered over the surface, thousands of them, like rocks thrown by a petulant troll.

As they draw closer, Rósa notices what she has missed before: some of the small mounds of grass near the coast are the roofs of turf-covered crofts — at least ten of them — which are built into the hills so they seem to have grown out of the land. They look bigger than the crofts in Skálholt and, from a distance, are hump-backed, huddled and separate. Rósa is used to crofts rubbing shoulders and even, sometimes — because of the shortage of wood — sharing walls.

'The crofts are very widely spread.'

He nods. 'We dig ourselves into the hills. In the winter, the snow cuts us off completely. Each croft is like one of those

86

islands out there.'

Rósa's stomach lurches at the thought of being snowed in with Jón, a stranger, and Pétur, who lies about his name and holds knives to men's throats.

Pétur directs them towards the largest croft, set fifty horse-lengths up the hill, separate from the others. A hundred paces from it stands a large turf-roofed barn, and there are several smaller buildings within a stone's throw of the door. It faces out towards the sea. On the other side, there is a little stream, where she will be able to wash clothes and gather water for cooking. In Skálholt, washing clothes had meant trudging to the Hvítá or Tunga.

As they turn up the path towards the croft, there is a shout from behind them. Rósa sees a dark-robed man standing with both arms raised. His thin face is fish-belly white. He strides towards them, tapping a staff on the ground.

'Keep still and quiet,' Pétur mutters.

Rósa nods and casts her eyes down. The skeletal figure stops by Pétur's mare and clutches the bridle with his bony claws. His black robes show him to be the *prestur*.

'This is the new one?' His voice is a wind-dried rasp.

Pétur's tone is flat as a blade. 'As you see.'

The old man stares at Rósa. She fixes her own gaze on Hallgerd's mane and digs her fingers into its warmth.

'She is thin,' he says. 'Will she last the winter?'

'She may, if we can keep her from your poison, Egill.'

'Watch your tongue with me, boy, or you will regret —'

Pétur gives a bark of laughter. 'Watch my tongue with *you*? Do you imagine yourself the *goði* now?'

Egill turns to Rósa. His eyes are blood-shot, as if he is drunk, but his voice is clear and sober. 'Be careful, young woman. Your husband may look honest, but underneath he is a devil. And Anna was —'

He is cut off as Pétur boots his mare forward. She knocks into Egill, who sprawls on the soil. Pétur grasps Rósa's reins and both horses break into a canter. Egill's shouts follow them. His words are lost in the wind, but his rage is clear.

When they are out of earshot, Pétur pulls the horses to a halt. His breath comes in gasps, as if he has been running. Rósa's heart hammers in her throat. 'He — he spoke of Anna. What —'

Pétur leans across and pulls on her arm, dragging her close enough to smell the sweat on him, to see the wild urgency in his eyes. 'No questions about Anna. Not to me, not to anyone in the village, and especially not to Jón. He is a good man. Believe that. No matter what you may hear.'

'I . . . I will try.'

Pétur squeezes her hand. The gesture leaves her breathless. Then he turns his mare and they ride up to the single croft, which crouches alone and exposed on the hill.

Jón is waiting outside; he must have seen them approaching from a distance. He wears a clean tunic, and his dark hair and beard shine where he has splashed water on them. His expression is grim. 'What words of wisdom from the old man?'

Pétur flashes a warning glance at Rósa, then gives a tight smile. 'Egill requires your position of *goði* — and you are a devil.'

Jón grins. 'Well, I shall not be *goði* once he has made a bonfire of me. But, then, if I am a devil, it will hinder the burning.'

Rósa gasps, but Jón laughs. 'We joke, Rósa. Egill will scorch his own fingers before he can singe a hair on my head.'

Jón's laughter fades as he stares after Egill. 'Still, we must be careful. He is never as brave without Olaf standing beside him.

Who knows what he might say then?' He turns to Rósa. 'Forgive me, Rósa. Welcome!' He holds out his arms, and leans forward as if to lift her from the saddle, then stops and bows instead.

She dips her head in confusion. 'Thank you.' Who is Olaf? She daren't ask.

'Look how meek she is, Pétur. Shy as a bird! But do you like your new home, Rósa?' The sweat glistens on his neck, where his skin meets his tunic.

'It is very . . . beautiful.'

'Good. You will be happy, though I must spend hours away from you.'

'I . . . Of course.'

'Already obedient! Your pabbi raised you well. Come closer.'

She dismounts, bows and holds out her hand. He takes her fingers and kisses them. She tries not to recoil. His paw-like hands scrape against her skin.

'Your journey wasn't too difficult? The path can be rough at this time of year, until the rain.' He squeezes her hand. 'I hope this winter will be better than last — mine was the only croft that suffered no damage. Egill was spitting with rage. But you will be safe here.'

She would like to tell him that she is weary and wishes herself at home. She wants to

90

say that Pétur made her ride through the night, and that yesterday evening he threatened to use his knife to gouge out a man's eye.

But she forces a smile. Her jaw aches. 'Thank you.'

His eyes brighten, as some tension within him uncoils. Within his giant hand, her own hand sweats.

'And your mamma?' he asks.

'Better. The moss tea Pétur brought has helped her cough, and she has a peat fire, so the air is dry. We're grateful, truly.'

He waves a hand in the air, as if shooing flies. 'Enough. Now, you will eat. Pétur will see to *dagverður* for today.'

Next to her Pétur, who has stood silently observing, raises his eyebrows. The two men watch her. She hears the expectation in the silence.

'No,' she says. 'I will prepare *dagverður* for all of us.'

Jón presses his fingers into her palm. 'So biddable,' he says. 'Come.' They leave Pétur waiting outside, while Jón shows her what she has married.

Before today, she imagined being led into the *baðstofa* to perform her *duty* — a word that summons vague, blurred images of naked bodies and the shivering promise of

91

pain. She tenses, waiting for her husband to kiss her. She will not pull away. She must kiss him back.

But Jón doesn't stop in the *baðstofa:* he shows her the four beds — short, but wide enough for two people. The room has an open stove and the air is bitter and thick with smoke: all this is familiar, if larger than the cramped Skálholt croft. Above, where she is used to seeing turf and roots, there are rows of tightly packed wooden boards, which form a ceiling. And there is a ladder. She reaches out and rests her hand on a rung.

'Leave that!' Jón's tone is sharp. 'This way.'

He leads her through an archway to the large kitchen. She has never seen one before. It has a low table, a stool, and the luxury of a raised stone *hlóðir* for cooking, instead of an open fire. Jón studies her face, as if waiting, then steps closer. A muscle pulses in his jaw. He looms over her, sweating.

She swallows. 'The croft is . . . very fine.'

'God rewards obedience. I have always thought it fitting that respect is rewarded, while defiance is punished.'

Rósa's mouth is dry. But she cannot help asking, 'You have a loft?'

'Pétur and I made it together. I admire

the foreign way of building upwards. When I travelled to Denmark on a merchant ship to trade two gyrfalcons —'

'*Two?*' Gyrfalcons are more precious than gold.

'The Danes paid well, in cloth and cows. When I saw the houses there, and in the Scottish isles, I knew I wanted a loft space. Somewhere quiet and private.'

'May I see it? The loft space?'

His expression is suddenly watchful. 'The room is kept locked.'

'May I look — briefly?'

His face is hard, as if she has asked something indecent. 'It holds my farm papers and other private things of no interest to a woman.'

'Pabbi taught me to read and write. Perhaps I may help you — and I have never seen a loft.' She smiles expectantly, then turns to the ladder.

'Stop!'

She freezes.

He scratches his dark beard, then says, more softly, 'The Bible tells us that wives are subject to their husbands.'

'Why —'

He holds up a hand. 'You said your mamma is well? She enjoys the meat I send? No need to thank me again. It is easy to be

93

generous to such an obedient wife.'

Her mouth hangs open. He presses his fingers under her chin and she hears the soft click of her teeth.

He smiles coldly. 'This way.' He takes her hand and pulls her to the pantry, crammed with barrels of *skyr,* and the storeroom, rafters weighted with drying cod.

'I will teach you how to gut and dry the fish, Rósa. And we are harvesting the hay now. Can you use a scythe?'

She nods, imagining the gasp of the grass as the scythe slices through it.

'Good,' he says. 'You will help us, once you have brought *dagverður.*'

She nods again, her jaw aching. The list of tasks is dizzying: washing, cooking, cleaning, mending, gutting, reaping. And those locked rooms up the ladder . . . Exhaustion threatens to engulf her.

Jón continues: 'We also have a barn, and a pit-house for storing fishing and farming equipment. It is kept locked. Stay away from it.' When her eyes widen, he adds, 'I lock it against cord thieves. Besides, many of the tools are sharp.' His hand upon her shoulder is heavy; he squeezes. 'We are far away from the other crofts — no one would hear you cry out, if you were bleeding.' His face is impassive, as if he is talking about the

94

weather.

She forces herself to nod. She feels like a marionette she had once seen in a trader's cart, with no voice of her own, only the ability to nod or shake her head, senselessly, as her master dictates.

Jón loosens his grip on her shoulder. His tone is suddenly brisk. 'You will sweep every morning. You will bring food — *dagverður* at noon, and *nattverður* after sunset. Pétur and I take our meals in the fields or upon the boat.'

Her legs are trembling. 'Will you eat in the croft today?'

'The hay needs harvesting but we will eat together now.'

She shivers and tugs her shawl around her shoulders. 'I am not hungry.'

'You will eat now. With me.' A muscle pulses in his jaw. 'Tomorrow you will bring *dagverður* to the summer field, on the hill. Simply cross the stream behind the croft and follow the track.'

'And am I to take my other meals . . . ?'

'As you wish.'

Alone, then. She draws a shuddering breath and thinks of Mamma. Of Páll. She knots her fingers together to keep her hands steady. 'I want to . . . please you.'

'Do as I tell you, and I will be pleased.'

95

For a moment, it seems he might lean across and kiss her, but instead he takes her hand and presses his lips to the palm. His mouth is hot and wet.

She resists the urge to snatch it away, then turns to cut thick slices of the dark rye bread while he watches. She can hear him breathing. Her heartbeat thuds in her throat.

They sit and eat in silence — Jón watches her every mouthful. The bread is like ash on Rósa's tongue; she nearly retches, but forces herself to swallow. Jón rips into his bread and chews methodically, devouring three chunks. While he is still finishing his last mouthful, he rises, wipes his hands on his tunic and says, 'I will return late. Do not wait for me. You will sleep when it is dark. You must care well for yourself. Your life is important, now you are my wife.'

Then he turns and walks out the door.

Once the sound of his footsteps has faded, she leans her head on the low table. The wood is reassuringly solid. She closes her eyes and clenches her teeth to stifle her tears. Her husband is a good man: everyone tells her so. And yet, when he collects his scythe, he walks down the path to the barn, not towards the pit-house, where he had claimed his sharp tools were kept.

For a moment, Mamma's voice is as clear

as if she were standing at her shoulder. *Foolish girl, what did you expect?* What would Páll have said about her husband? He would have made some joke, but she cannot summon his voice, can barely imagine his face. His features are blurred; he belongs to another life.

She touches the glass woman at her neck. If she had seen another woman with such a prize, Rósa would have imagined her husband must love her very much.

Rósa sighs and presses the cold glass to her forehead. Her skin burns.

She sits in the kitchen and watches the shadows shift as the sun drops in the sky. Her muscles are rigid and her legs ache from the enforced stillness but, somehow, she cannot bring herself to move. It is as if a thousand eyes are watching her, as if the weight of Jón's hand is still on her shoulder.

Eventually a grainy grey dimness seeps into the croft. What if Jón returns after all? What if he wants to share her bed? She clutches her tunic with both hands and presses it against her legs, as if she could seal herself off.

The shadows press in on her. She hears a footstep behind her, jumps and whirls around. No one is there. She is alone, still. Outside, the wind scrabbles against the walls of the croft and, in the distance, the sea sighs. It is as if the rest of the world has ceased to exist. Her eyes burn from straining to peer into the gloom and she forces herself to stand and light a candle. The flame makes the darkness leap up and, for a moment, Rósa is convinced she sees a pale face in the corner, staring at her. She gasps and nearly drops the candle, but when she looks more closely, the shape is not a face but a rolled-up blanket.

She pulls it around her shoulders. Still, her muscles will not stop shaking.

As she tugs the blanket tighter, Rósa's fingers brush against something dry and crisp. She holds the candle close to the blanket and sees, caught in the weave of the fabric, a tiny brittle head of latch herb, tied to a thread.

Surely not . . . Not here. She peers more closely. Definitely latch herb. If it was dried in the shadows, then tied to a silken thread to be worn around the neck, it would open any locked door. But the very existence of such a necklace would be enough to raise an accusation of witchcraft.

Again Rósa hears a footstep behind her and whips around, stuffing the blanket and the herb beneath the kitchen bench. But, once again, there is only darkness and the wind. She retrieves the blanket and carefully pulls the latch herb free. Thinking of the loft and the pit-house, she puts it into her pocket. But then her hand brushes against Pabbi's wooden cross. She draws the herb out again and rips the leaves from the stalk, then throws it into the glowing embers of the *hlóðir*.

When she brushes the hair back from her face, her cheeks are wet, although she doesn't know when she began to weep.

Exhausted, she sits at the table and waits for her husband to return.

When she wakes, it is morning; the croft is hushed and still. She blinks and rubs her eyes, then springs upright. Had Jón returned and found her asleep? He will be furious.

She hurries through the kitchen and out onto the hill. There, coming up from the pit-house, are Pétur and Jón. She drops her gaze to the ground and curtsies.

He takes her hand and pulls her upright. 'You look tired, Rósa. I told you to rest.'

'I . . . I rested,' she whispers, not daring to ask where he slept.

'Bring our food to the field today. Don't forget your other duties.'

She nods, remembering the endless list of tasks.

'Come, Pétur,' he says, and they turn and walk back down the hill.

After the men have disappeared from sight, Rósa trudges back to the croft and allows her fixed smile to fade. Her cheeks ache.

'Courage, Rósa.' Her words hang on the empty air like dust motes.

The croft creaks in the wind. She peers into the dark recesses of the *baðstofa,* to where the ladder stretches up into the yawning space above. Then she remembers Jón's hand on the back of her neck, warm and weighty. She shakes her head and turns back to the kitchen.

She hacks four chunks of the dense, hard bread, and spreads each piece thickly with some grease from the storeroom, which she thinks is rancid butter, but when she touches it experimentally with her tongue, it tastes fishy.

Whale fat.

She recoils and investigates the other shelves of the storeroom. Mostly dried fish and strips of dried mutton, but there are some bowls of *skyr* and a jug of beer. She also finds a leg of smoked mutton. She cuts thick chunks of meat from the bone and lays them on the bread: white fat, glistening jelly and all.

She loads everything into a wooden pail, but the little package looks a pitiful amount for two grown men. She cuts more bread and layers it with *skyr.*

Still not enough.

Perhaps if she can impress Jón, he will not scowl at her so. She rummages through the storeroom until she finds a pot of something solid and yellow. Again, it looks like butter which has melted and solidified. She shaves a little off with the knife and lets it dissolve on her tongue. It tastes like sunlight. She has to stop herself gorging on it in great spoonfuls. She has read of honey being exchanged illegally — any trade must be done with the Danish alone — although she has never tasted it before. She slathers it generously on the last two pieces of bread.

Then she wipes the board clean and stands in the squeezing silence, tapping her knife against her teeth. The sun isn't quite at its zenith; she has some time. A slippery newborn curiosity pulls her into the *baðstofa.*

The beds are large, but the blankets are made of the same thick wool as those in Skálholt. She holds a blanket to her face and inhales.

Could she leave now? Take one of the horses and ride home before the snows? But

101

no. She would be returning to watch Mamma starve and sicken and die. Rósa bites her lip until she tastes blood.

She perches on the edge of the biggest bed, then lies down. Her marital bed. Again, that urge to run. She closes her eyes and exhales into the smothering silence, then turns to look at the wall, wondering if Anna had stared at the same boards. Had she felt scared too? She shifts closer to the wood, traces the outline of the grain, runs her fingers over the whorls. As she moves, she hears a rustling sound, as if her weight has moved something under the mattress. She lifts the corner and sees that, underneath, there is a sheet of paper with a large, looping sign on it. She reaches out for it, disbelieving. But, yes, it is written on the paper: the runic symbol for assistance . . . a cry for help. Rósa studies it, her thoughts whirling.

Why?

Suddenly the wood above her head creaks — as if under the pressure of a moving body.

She bolts upright and stuffs the paper back under the mattress, her heart vaulting in her chest. 'Who's there?'

The floorboard creaks again. Rósa strides to the base of the ladder. 'Hello?'

A yawning square of darkness stares back,

102

unblinking.

Nothing. No one. Silence.

Blood beating in her ears, she climbs. The black mouth swallows her, and she can see only shadows. She leans in close: a bulky metal bar is attached to the door handle, as if in warning.

She pushes on it but it doesn't move. She shoves her shoulder against it, heaving with all her weight, but the door might as well be a rock. When she presses her ear to the wood, it is warm — as if it is still part of some living, breathing life from a far-off land, where trees creak in the breeze.

Then she hears the whispered whistle of a breath, carefully repressed.

She scrambles down the ladder, falling over the last rungs and scraping her knees — one of her stockings rips, but she ignores it. She runs through the *baðstofa* and tumbles into the warmth of the kitchen, where she stands, doubled over and gasping for air. As her heartbeat slows and her breathing steadies, the silence of the croft closes in on her once more. No sound from above.

Fool! She scolds herself and tries to laugh, but her mouth trembles and the sound emerges as a sob.

Then something on the floor catches her

eye: mixed with the dirt and the straw there are some wisps of blonde hair, fine as a spider's silk. Rósa picks them up and twists them between her fingers. The hairs are long and straight; she brings them close to her face. They are stained with a brownish rust, which flakes off onto her fingers.

Blood.

Rósa recoils and throws the hair into the *hlóðir,* where she had stuffed the latch herb the night before. She is pushing it into the flames with the iron poker when she hears it again: a breath or a whisper behind her. She drops the poker, which clatters onto the floor, but Rósa doesn't care.

She snatches up the basket of food and runs towards the fields, not daring to look over her shoulder. There is a moving, breathing creature in the croft. A rat, perhaps. But a rat heavy enough to make the boards creak?

Seabirds wheel and scream overhead. Rósa shakes her head. She must have imagined the noises in the croft: her tired brain has conjured sounds from thin air.

She squeezes the glass woman for comfort. It is cold and bloodless.

Gradually, her breathing slows. She focuses on the rippling musculature of the fields, the protuberant bones of the mountains and the blank gaze of the sky.

Down at the bottom of the hill, the little village buzzes with life. Women bustle back and forth between crofts, calling to each other; two men are holding a sheep between them and attempting to tether it. The animal bucks and both men fall; a watching child roars with laughter, then runs away when the men shout and raise their open palms in threat. But then the child stops and points. Straight up the hill. Directly at Rósa. And, one by one, like flowers turning to the sun, the villagers angle their pale faces to stare at her.

Rósa lifts a hand in greeting.

As one, every single villager turns away and resumes their tasks. Not one person even glances back at her. It is as if she has been transformed into some mountain spirit.

Then there is a shout from her left. Rósa jumps and turns.

Two women stand on the path, skirts snapping in the wind, hands raised in greeting. They smile and Rósa's stomach unclenches. She must have imagined the villagers' strange behaviour.

One of the women before her is white-haired beneath her cap, and leans heavily on the arm of the other, who is, Rósa sees, also well past youth: she has a smattering of silver in her hair, but she is tall and broad, and there is a bright intensity to her gaze.

'*Sæl og blessuð!*' she calls. Her voice is light, sing-song.

'*Sælar og blessaðar,*' Rósa replies.

The old woman mumbles, '*Blessuð.*' She has a face like rumpled knitting and her mouth is a badly darned sock, the slash of lips barely visible.

The younger woman beams. 'I am Katrín Sigúrdsdóttir. This is Gudrun Pétursdóttir. You are Rósa?'

Katrín has very light blue eyes, which could make her look hard and cold, but an open smile softens her face.

'Yes. Rósa Magnúsdóttir.' She smiles shyly. 'I arrived only yesterday.'

'Was the journey hard?'

'It was long and I am a little tired.' Rósa reminds herself that she mustn't seem too morose. She gestures at the mountains and the sea. 'It is so beautiful here.'

As if she is half a field away, Gudrun shouts, 'You're very young, child. Thin too.' She turns to Katrín. 'The girl looks as if a strong gust will carry her away. But Anna was thin also. Jón likes 'em all bones beneath —'

'Gudrun!' Katrín snaps.

106

Gudrun's mouth twists sourly and she mutters something incomprehensible.

There is an awkward silence, which Rósa breaks. 'I am twenty-five.'

'Twenty-five and not married until now? But you are not particularly ugly, although my eyes are cloudy. Is she very ugly, Katrín?'

Katrín tuts. 'Not at all. Forgive Gudrun. She thinks that each winter she survives grants her the right to be even ruder.'

Gudrun grunts. 'I say what every soul will be thinking.'

'Remember that those appear wisest who stay silent.' To Rósa, Katrín murmurs, 'Gudrun likes to stir the pot. If you ignore her, she'll lose interest.'

Gudrun shouts, 'Stop mumbling, Katrín!'

'She is also a little deaf. So you may say anything you please about her, as long as you whisper.'

Rósa smothers a giggle. 'Forgive me, but I must take this food to Jón.'

'Are you not going to welcome us into the croft?' Gudrun cries. To Katrín, she mutters, 'I thought this one might be different.'

Katrín says, 'For pity's sake, Gudrun, hush. Perhaps we may visit when Jón is fishing.'

Rósa's chest tightens. 'He does not like people in the croft?'

Katrín's eyes are suddenly anxious, as if she is trying to warn Rósa of something. 'He likes to keep his home private.' She reaches out and squeezes Rósa's arm — Rósa could almost weep at the sympathy in that touch, the feeling of being unexpectedly understood.

Katrín looks at her through narrowed eyes, as though reading her thoughts. 'You haven't looked after a croft yourself before? No time for rest.'

Rósa's throat aches too much for words. She nods.

Katrín smiles. 'You must come to the village and bring your mending. We often knit together, while the men are out on the sea or in the fields.'

'Jón won't like that either,' grumbles Gudrun. 'And shouldn't you be staying away from the wife this time, Katrín?'

Katrín glances sideways at the older woman, then mutters to Rósa, fast and low, 'You must come and find me, if you notice anything strange. Promise you will do that. There is darkness in being alone here.'

Rósa backs away from what sounds almost like a threat.

Suddenly Katrín freezes: her eyes are fixed on the glass woman at Rósa's throat. Her mouth hangs open, as if someone has struck her. Rósa tucks away the ornament.

Gudrun snorts suddenly, breaking the silence. 'Well, at least if you read and write, you won't cause trouble by scrawling on stones like An—'

'Did Pétur bring you here?' Katrín cries, falsely bright.

Rósa nods, but instinctively clutches the runestone in her pocket.

Gudrun leans in close. 'Egill grieves that he could not tame Pétur, but I have told him many a time, you cannot break the devil.'

'I do not think Rósa needs to hear —'

'Put Pétur before the Althing and have him strung up, I say. He's a violent beast. Why Egill should still care for him, after everything —'

'Gudrun, enough!' Katrín rubs her temples. 'Rósa must take Jón his food and we shall make her late. It was a joy to meet you, Rósa. *Bless.*'

'*Bless.* And you, a joy.'

Katrín leads Gudrun away, the older woman still mumbling, the words lost in the wind.

Rósa walks up the path to the field, counting her steps to still her thoughts.

Stykkishólmur, September 1686

Rósa hurries along by the grey sea, watching puffins diving from the cliffs into the water below and surfacing, beaks crammed with tiny fish. A ptarmigan flares up from the grass at her feet, wings thudding in the air, like heartbeats. Her own frantic heart thrums in her chest.

She sees the men, at last, in the middle of a hayfield. Jón raises his hand and beckons her over; she waves back vigorously. She will tell him what the women said and about the noises she imagined in the croft: they will laugh, and his amusement will chase away the seeping fear lodged in her stomach.

But what if he realizes she has climbed the ladder? As her husband and *goði,* he could have her flogged for disobedience.

She picks a path down one of the gaps between the tall grass stems. It brushes her skirts and hisses as she passes.

Jón lays down his scythe, his smile wide and open as he indicates the field. 'A crop to be proud of — yes, Rósa?'

Here, with a smile on his face, eyes bright with sunlight and joy, he looks as mild a husband as any woman could wish for. Rósa almost leans into him, almost says, *I heard strange noises. Why is the loft locked?*

But under his searching gaze, her mouth feels stuffed with linen. She swallows. 'You work hard,' she manages to croak.

He nods. 'Most folk don't seed the big fields — they keep them for grazing sheep, then rely on dried fish through the winter. But as a boy I was always hungry and sickened by the dried fish. It's like sea-brined tunic — endless chewing!'

Rósa smiles at the apt comparison.

Jón's eyes brighten. 'Stykkishólmur was poor, everyone sickly and living from hand to mouth. I worked from dawn until dusk farming, and spent nights at sea, catching more fish than all the other boats together. I tilled the soil with dung until I could grow barley, and I nurtured my herds until they were the largest for miles. And then the gyrfalcons — they are worth thirty cows each, more, if a king from another land desires one.'

'It is . . . marvellous.' This time the

admiration in her voice is unfeigned.

He waves away her praise, but flushes, suddenly boyish. 'I will not see people starve. I allow them certain freedoms, where other *goðis* flog and tax their people to death. But I am no tyrant . . . although there are those who would paint me as one.'

'Egill?' she murmurs, remembering the black-cloaked figure.

Jón scowls. 'And Olaf, Egill's lackey. They call me a villain.'

Pétur grunts. 'Egill is so crammed with dung it clouds his vision — everything looks like shit to him.'

Despite herself, Rósa giggles.

Jón smiles at her with new warmth. 'Farming is unforgiving work. The soil is mostly ash and sand. But it is worth the sweat. Otherwise our jaws cramp from chewing dried fish.' He scatters a handful of sulphurous black soil into the breeze. 'You like the fish?'

'I like it well enough.'

'Ha! It is a sin to lie.' But he is beaming and he looks much younger. 'It's disgusting. I am glad when we have mutton.' He leans in conspiratorially. 'As a boy, I trapped rats to avoid eating the fish.' He chuckles. 'Look at her eyes, Pétur! You will not have to eat rats, Rósa.'

'I have never been rich enough to be particular about food.'

He touches her fingers. 'Wait until you taste the hay, Rósa. Like sunlight. My sheep and cows are the strongest for miles — Danish traders pay double. Here.' He snaps the golden head and lays it on his palm. 'Eat it.'

He cannot expect her to eat hay like one of his sheep. She stares at him. He looks back, unblinking. Slowly she puts the grass head on her tongue. It is like a spiked beetle, clawed legs scrabbling at her throat. Jón keeps watching her, until she chews, then swallows.

He raises his eyebrows. 'Well?'

'I can taste . . . the sun and the sea in it.' She tries not to cough.

Jón claps his hands and laughs, like a child. 'Pétur! Pétur, come here. The hay — she loves it.'

'She will be a cheap wife, if she likes the sheep fodder.'

They laugh. Rósa's throat feels as though it has been scraped with a blade.

Jón insists on giving her a scythe. He is a different man from the one who glared and forbade her to venture into the loft. He holds her hand gently and shows her how to sweep the scythe in wide arcs, swinging back and forth, building a rhythm so that

113

the blade slices through the stalks, like butter. She can feel the length of his body pressed against her back and legs; it sends a confusing heat through her.

Pétur follows, tying bundles of hay with a longer stalk, then leaning the sheaves against each other to dry, ripen and gather richness from the sun.

As they walk, Jón lays his hand upon her arm, puts his hands around her waist. When he touches her, she freezes, her whole body humming, like a wind-scoured shell. She exhales slowly and closes her eyes, but she cannot make sense of the jumble of sensations and the roiling in her gut.

Jón seems not to notice her confusion. He exclaims in delight when he unwraps the *dagverður,* although he tells her she must be more frugal tomorrow.

'We mustn't eat everything, or we'll be forcing down dried fish all winter.'

In her chest, Rósa feels the fist of fear unclasp. Jón smiles at her and laughs with Pétur. Still, when her husband reaches out to brush the hair back from her face, her own laughter dies and her breath is tight in her throat.

A muscle in his jaw pulses, but he allows his hand to drop to his side, then turns away.

Rósa whispers an apology, which hangs

114

on the air between them.

Pétur collects his scythe to continue reaping. Jón squints and looks out at the sea. Rósa searches desperately for something she might say that will chase away the darkness on her husband's face.

But instead she finds herself saying, 'I met two women, while I was walking.'

'Who?' Jón's voice is like a whip.

'Gudrun and Katrín.' Rósa twists a stem of hay around her fingers, pulling it tight until her fingertips sting.

'Gudrun is a troublemaker, and I wouldn't trust Katrín as far as I could . . .' His hands are clenched into fists. 'They are not suitable company for the wife of the *goði*. You should not speak to them — they have upset you.'

Rósa twists the hay tighter. Her fingertips turn dark red.

Jón takes her hand and unwinds the hay. His fingers are rough, his big hands shaking with restrained strength. 'What is it?'

'They said . . . They said —'

'*What* did they say?'

She flinches at the iron in his voice.

Jón sighs again, and rubs his hands over his eyes. 'Rósa, I have a whole field to harvest. What did they say?'

'They said that . . . you will not allow

115

anyone into the croft.'

'I cannot have the whole settlement in my home.'

She bites her lip hard to stop it trembling. He reaches out and pulls her lip gently from between her teeth. She finds herself frozen, waiting for his hand to move.

'You will not invite the women back.' His voice is soft, almost tender as he strokes her cheek. 'Will you?'

'But how am I to find companionship?'

'Look at me, Rósa,' Jón says, his voice laced with steel.

She pulls her gaze away from the sea, which stretches endlessly into the distance, and focuses on the chipped flint of his eyes. 'I have seen gossip corrode a person. You must understand . . .' He sighs. 'Anna . . . I warned her. She should have listened.'

When she says nothing, he leans in closer to her. She edges away.

'Rósa, a life in the church would have meant an existence of solitary prayer and study. I thought you would be content —'

'I am content. It is simply . . .'

'What else can be the matter?'

'No matter, except . . .'

'What is it?' he growls.

'I . . .' Her voice is tight and high. 'I thought I . . . heard something.'

116

'*Heard* something?'

'It sounded like — Well, I thought I heard *something*.'

Jón swallows, audibly. 'Where?'

'The loft. But the door was locked, so I didn't —'

'You didn't go in? I forbade it, Rósa! You gave your word.'

'I didn't go in! But —'

'*But?*'

She flinches. 'I was frightened. I thought an animal might be trapped.'

He gives a sudden laugh, startling her. 'Ah, yes, a rat, perhaps! We will go back to eating them, if their scrabbling scares you.' His laughter is hollow, his eyes sharp and watchful. 'You didn't go up the ladder?'

Mutely, she shakes her head.

He pats her hand. His skin is cold. 'Rats!' His jaw is rigid and his laughter doesn't touch his eyes. 'Rats can be vicious. They might have hurt you.'

Under her dress, Rósa's legs tremble.

He picks up his scythe. 'Stay away from the loft. Rats are dangerous.' He turns away. 'I will return after dark and we will eat *nattverður* together. You would like that, yes?' She can feel his gaze upon her, like a touch.

She keeps her head down, but risks glancing at his face: all the child-like mirth has gone. His lips are pressed into a thin, pale line. He clenches the scythe with white-knuckled hands and attacks the hay.

She runs back down the hill and fills a pail with water from the stream. For the rest of the afternoon, she cleans the croft with noisy urgency, filling the air with the sounds of sweeping and scrubbing and her own panting breath. It had been cleaned recently, but already a fine film of dust had gathered on the scrubbed wooden table. Seeds from the hay fly from the blankets like fleas when she shakes them out.

Her husband's world follows her everywhere, it seems.

She walks down the path to the barn, telling herself that she must tend the animals, but when she passes the pit-house, she stops. Pabbi used to scold her for her curiosity. It would lead to trouble one day, he'd warned.

The door to the pit-house is locked, and when she tries to peer through the gaps between the wall and the window, she can see nothing but darkness. The back of her neck itches but, when she turns, no one is there. Only the village at the bottom of the hill, with its bustle of bodies. As she watches the people going about their business, she notices that, every so often, they will stop and glance up the hill, shading their eyes from the glare of the sun. As if they, too, are searching for something. She watches them for some time, but the busy chatter and commotion make her feel more alone than ever so she traipses back to the croft to continue her tasks.

So far north, darkness eases itself through the sky early, leaching the light from the air and gradually turning everything a monochrome grey. Rósa only realizes how dark it has become when, in the middle of scrubbing the floor, she stands and bangs her head on the table. The night has brought fingers of cold and, rubbing her head, Rósa lays down her cloth and lights the tallow candles, warming her hands in their meaty flame. The smell makes her stomach gripe — she has hardly eaten since the bits of bread she sneaked while making *dagverður* for the men. She slices a thin sliver of bread, smears it with honey and eats with her back against the *hlóðir*. The warmth of the bread reminds her of the hay fields.

Rósa goes to the door of the croft and peers out. No sign of Jón. Nothing but the blank darkness, the closing hand of the night.

Quickly, she lights a taper, then hurries through the croft to the ladder. She climbs awkwardly, holding the flickering taper in one hand, careful not to quench the flame with a sudden movement. When she reaches the door, she holds the taper close to the lock, then reaches out and pulls on the metal. Her hand shakes, the flame trembles, her breath is noisy in her throat.

The lock won't move. She examines the hole where a key should fit, then presses her fingers against it. Perhaps if she could find a broken spoon or some other piece of metal, she might be able —

There is a sudden noise, a rustling, then footsteps and the rumble of voices; Rósa freezes, then realizes that the noises are coming from down below, from outside.

Jón!

She blows out the flame; sudden darkness swallows her and she must scrabble her way down the ladder in the pitch black, heart clattering, blood ringing in her ears and her hands slipping on the rungs — where are the rungs? — and then she is in the *baðstofa* and running through to the kitchen and the voices are closer as she lights a candle, then sets out the mutton and the *skyr* and the bread. She drops the bread and has to brush the dirt off it, so that, when Jón and Pétur

120

walk into the kitchen, she is wide-eyed and breathless, holding out the loaf like a shield.

'There is no more meat. I'm sorry, I had thought . . . This is not enough. I will walk to the settlement tomorrow, and see if one of the other women will trade some mutton for bread or fish.'

A hot pulse thrums behind her eyelids.

Jón shakes his head. 'This is enough for now.' His gaze travels over her hot cheeks and heaving chest. 'Are you unwell, Rósa? Has something happened?'

She shakes her head vehemently. 'I will get more meat tomorrow. Perhaps Katrín —'

'No!' She jumps at the steel in his voice. 'No,' he repeats softly. 'I won't have you knocking on doors, trading food, like some Danish sailor. Pétur will slaughter a sheep.'

'I am used to trading with other women. And I would like to explore —'

'You'll grow to know the place soon enough. It is full of gossips, without you encouraging them by knocking on doors.' Jón gives a quick, taut smile. 'You have everything you need. If you want meat, you shall have it. You will be happy.'

'But . . .' She clutches her skirts and draws a breath. '. . . I would like the company, not to gossip, of course, I would not say any-

121

thing about you, but only —'

'*Enough!*'

His gaze is iron. 'You will do as I say, Rósa.'

She nods. She is so weary. A tear splashes onto her hand; she dashes it angrily away.

He squeezes her fingers. 'No need for tears.' He drinks some *brennevín,* then takes a savage bite of his bread and chews noisily, staring at his plate. 'You are tired, Rósa, so not yourself. But I forgive your curiosity. It is natural. I understand. And I will not be angry as long as you do as I say.'

And that is when it hits her, like a fist in her guts: a sudden and visceral longing to be curled in her cramped home in Skálholt, huddled under a blanket with Mamma. They used to laugh at each other's icy toes. Hungry and cold and content.

As if he senses her thoughts, Jón says, 'Pétur is to travel inland tomorrow, to trade. He will also go to Skálholt to see your mamma and give her more food. You can write her a letter, telling her you are happy and safe. I have paper and ink.'

A strange peace offering. Rósa doesn't ask if she can accompany Pétur, although she would happily endure that terrifying ride to be back at home with Sigridúr.

But she must stay, be a good wife and

obey her husband if she wants Mamma to survive the winter.

Rósa feels like a trout she had seen Pétur impale upon a fishing spike when he fetched her from Skálholt: she may flap and flail, but she cannot work herself free.

She stands stiffly, clears and washes the plates in the bucket of water from the stream, then tiptoes through to the *baðstofa*, where she pulls off her woollen dress, tugs on her night shift and crawls beneath the knitted blankets.

The bed has absorbed the chill of the dark. Rósa shivers and waits for Jón to slide in next to her. She counts her rapid breaths, which sound as if they belong to someone else; she twists the corner of the blanket and resists the urge to chew it, as she used to when she was a child. Silver moonlight spills through the tiny sheepskin window and fills the room with sharp shadows. Anything could be lurking in the darkness behind that slick of gleaming light. Her teeth chatter.

Noises from the kitchen. The rumble of male laughter, loose with drink.

She squeezes her eyes shut and pulls the blanket so it covers all but the very top of her head. Then she takes the tiny figure of the glass woman and curls around it, holding it close to her chest, as if cradling her own throbbing mind.

She slips into a gritty unconsciousness, where everything is made of shadow and sounds are like snagged fragments of wool. She is herself, and yet, at the same time, she knows she is Gudrun from *Laxdaela Saga*, torn between her two lovers. Jón grasps one hand, Páll the other, and as she strains to escape Jón's grip, she finds herself pulling him closer. She cries out, but when she opens her mouth, no sound emerges and then, when she chokes, she vomits up stone after stone, each one inscribed with a runic symbol. She kneels to gather and hide them from Jón, but then his hand is under her chin, forcing her to look him in the face, and when she meets his eye, his mouth twists into a snarl.

'Anna!'

Rósa bolts upright into wakefulness, clawing at her throat, where she can still feel the pressure of Jón's fingers, can still hear his growl of Anna's name.

The bed next to her is cold and empty and the slash of moonlight from earlier has faded; the croft is muffled by the night. There are no noises from the kitchen. The men have gone, somehow, somewhere. Out to tend the animals?

Suddenly she remembers the piece of paper she had found, with the strange runic symbol on it. She slides her hand under the mattress, but her fingers clutch empty air. She sits up and lifts the mattress, peering into the space and patting with her hand. But there is nothing.

Strange. Her mind playing tricks on her again? She had been so very tired when she arrived.

Rósa sighs and lies down, but as she does so she hears a noise overhead. A definite *creak,* as if under the pressure of a soft-soled shoe. Rósa holds her breath, not daring to move or breathe. Another *creak.* She exhales unevenly and stuffs the blanket into her mouth.

There is the scratch of the lock, then footsteps coming down the ladder.

Rósa squeezes her eyes shut and holds her breath again. The person — whoever it is, if it is indeed a living person — is standing in the *baðstofa.* There is silence for the space of five thunderous heartbeats, then a gust of air as someone passes Rósa's bed. The footsteps stop next to her head and Rósa attempts to exhale, to breathe evenly, to seem to be sleeping. After a moment, the figure continues into the kitchen and then out into the night.

Rósa lies rigid and counts the tug and push of each breath in her lungs. After fifty, she staggers upright, bolts into the kitchen and vomits into the cooling ashes of the *hlóðir*.

She leans her head against the stone until her breathing steadies. Then she stumbles back into the *baðstofa* and lies down to wait for Jón. He does not come, and she squeezes her eyes shut and lies shaking, counting her heartbeats.

When Rósa finally opens her eyes, pale early-morning light is seeping through the gap between the sheepskin window and the horse-skin curtain. She must have slept, in spite of her terror, and now it is late. Jón will be furious. He must have come in at some point in the night — but when? Dry-mouthed, she remembers the footsteps overhead, the figure that had stood over her, the rush of air as someone — *something* — strode past her.

How can she ask Jón about it? She remembers the way his hands had clenched into fists the day before when she mentioned the loft. Or will he look at her with pity, as if she is a fanciful child?

She sits on the bed, pressing her palms

against her closed eyes, then forces herself to stand, to breathe, to tug on her clothes, to walk into the kitchen.

Jón is at the bucket, splashing water from the pail over his face and arms. His unclothed chest and back are thatched with brown hair, like the pelt of an animal.

Rósa flushes and looks at the floor. 'Forgive me,' she croaks, 'I must have overslept. I thought I heard . . .' She raises her eyes, searching his face for any hint that the noises might have been his footsteps. That he might have been watching her while she slept.

His expression remains blank. 'It is early still.' There is no trace of the previous night's irritation in his voice. But where had he slept? Not at the table? Mixed with her relief that he hasn't touched her is the worry that perhaps there is something about her that he finds repellent.

Around his neck is a leather cord, holding a tiny ornament made of glass. It is similar to the glass woman he gave her, but is one of the saints, she thinks, like people of the Catholic faith used to wear. It is not the sort of ornament that a *goði* should have. Jón notices her staring and raises his eyebrows, as if in challenge. Rósa looks away.

He takes her hand, pulls her towards him

127

and presses a kiss onto the corner of her mouth. She holds her breath and stands utterly still. His beard scratches her cheek; he smells of the mutton-fat soap.

'I will finish the hayfield today. Bring *dagverður* at noon and we will eat together. You would like that, yes?' He strokes her cheek.

Her skin itches. 'Yes,' she whispers.

'You won't need to feed Pétur.'

'Oh?'

'He left for the south before sunrise. I sent him with supplies for your mamma. There was no time for a letter, but he will tell her you are happy here.'

His words knock the breath from her, but she manages to murmur, 'Thank you.'

Perhaps she could pass a letter to a merchant, travelling south. Again, the longing strikes her to climb aboard a trader's cart and journey back to Skálholt.

Jón reaches out, puts two fingers under her chin so that she has to look him in the eye. There is an odd intimacy in his work-roughened fisherman-farmer's fingers so close to her throat. There is possessiveness too: he studies her face, then his gaze travels down her body. She quivers like a rabbit, stripped of her skin. She waits for his hand to move down to her breast or to encircle her throat. He sighs and his fingers trace a burning path down to the hollow at the base of her neck, where her pulse frantically flutters.

Thoughts of fleeing dissolve under his touch. He would hunt her down and haul her back.

He smiles. His teeth are large. 'It must seem so strange. I know that. But you will be happy here. The Bible tells me to honour you. And what does it say wives should do, Rósa?'

'Obey,' she whispers, thinking, *What about love?*

'And you are obedient.'

She forces herself to nod — a tiny inclination of her head, which increases the pressure of his fingers under her chin.

'Tell me you are happy, Rósa.' He is steely-eyed, unsmiling.

'I am . . . happy,' she mutters.

He runs his thumb over her bottom lip, then lets his hand drop. 'You will be a good wife.'

The door bangs as he leaves, and the croft slumps into a pensive silence.

Rósa stands shaking. It must have been Pétur she heard last night, in the loft room — perhaps he was fetching papers for the journey south. But why would he stand over her, watching her? She turns to the ladder, but she cannot make herself climb into the gaping mouth of the darkness above.

Instead, she finds the mutton-fat soap and scrubs the table. She sweeps the floors. She rubs whale oil into the wooden doors and rafters until they gleam; she washes and scrubs and sweeps until not a speck of farm dust remains in the croft. Then she finds the rye flour and makes more bread. Pétur must have slaughtered a lamb before he left: the legs hang from the rafters in the store-room. They are dry now, but there are dark pools on the straw where they have dripped blood.

She will make a *lifrarpylsa* for Jón. She chops the liver, mixes it with oatmeal and stuffs the mixture into the stomach sack of the lamb. Then she boils some water and drops in the *lifrarpylsa*, where it bobs and bubbles until nearly noon, filling the croft with the bitter smell of cooking offal. Throughout it all, she hums, to cover any other noise — real or imaginary.

When she takes the *lifrarpylsa* to Jón, he exclaims in wonder and devours it, wiping the fatty juices from his beard with his sleeve. When he smiles at her like this, it is hard to imagine the man whose presence feels like iron bars encircling her. Perhaps she has imagined all of his threats — or perhaps his words have been kind all along, and she has twisted them somehow into something menacing.

But sometimes she will look up and see her husband watching her, and something in his expression makes her want to wrap her arms around her belly.

Still, he has not lain with her, has barely touched her. At night, he leaves the croft and walks down the path to the barn. Rósa lies alone in the dark. When she closes her eyes, she imagines she may be invisible, as if she is slowly being rubbed into translucency.

The more time she spends around this huge stranger, the more distant Jón seems. When he walks past her in the croft, she shrinks into herself, flinching from his animal heat. One morning he notices, then takes her hand, uncurls her clenched fist and presses his lips to her open palm. It is a gesture of such intimacy and tenderness that it takes her breath away. He smiles at her, then walks outside and up to the fields, leaving her standing in the doorway, staring after him. She almost calls him back, but the words die on her lips.

On the third morning of Pétur's absence, she waits until Jón has gone to the fields,

131

then runs down the hill to the village.

The crofts are larger than those in Skál-holt, and dug into the hillside, so it seems they are hiding. She pauses, before walking among them, then takes a breath and fixes a smile on her face. These are her husband's people: she must impress them, and then Jón will see that he need not keep her away from them. She glances back up the hill, towards the fields, but he is out of sight and the swell of fear in her chest subsides a little.

The first croft she comes to is silent, the door ajar. She peers inside. In Skálholt, it would not have been unusual for strangers — travelling merchants or pilgrims visiting the church — to call at some of the crofts, but Rósa reminds herself that she doesn't know the customs here. She is wavering on the doorstep when there is a cry from behind her.

'You!'

She whirls around to see a huge man, even bigger than Jón. His face is red and fleshy, his eyes tiny gimlets.

'You're the new one,' he growls, folding arms like mutton shanks across his broad chest.

'I . . .' She takes a step backwards. 'Do you live here? Forgive me, I was —'

'Prying,' interrupts the man, sourly. 'Like

132

the last one. And look where that got her.'

'I meant no harm.'

'So *she* said. Didn't stop the sickness, though, did it?'

'Olaf! Leave her be.' Katrín is suddenly between them. She puts her hands on her hips and scowls at Olaf, who glowers back at her.

'Is this the courtesy you show to our *goði's* wife?' demands Katrín. 'What will Jón say when he learns you've been threatening her?'

'Not *threatening*,' mumbles Olaf. 'She was poking about in my croft and —'

'I'll remember that,' snaps Katrín, 'next time you want chickweed for blisters and I find you *poking about* in my croft. Come, Rósa.'

Katrín takes her arm, and Rósa leans into her as they walk away.

'Thank you. I —'

'Does Jón know you are here?' Katrín's eyes are wide.

'No, he is in the field. I —'

'Then you must go back to the croft. Now!'

'But I thought I might visit —'

Katrín places her hands on Rósa's shoulders. 'Come to me some other time. Now you must go.'

133

'But I —'

'Look, people are talking. What if they tell Jón you were here?'

Rósa looks over Katrín's shoulder and sees a small crowd gathering. They whisper to each other. Someone laughs: a harsh sound, like shattering glass.

'Go now,' Katrín says urgently. 'I will talk to them, try to keep them quiet this time. But you must be more careful. Go!'

Katrín pushes her away, and Rósa stumbles as she runs up the hill, breath tight in her chest, skin tingling with the sensation of being watched.

Halfway up the hill, she stops and bends double, trying not to sob. She dare not turn to see if the villagers are still watching her. She can picture their hard-eyed stares — the same look Olaf had worn when he talked about sickness. But the expression on every face hadn't been of hatred: it had been of revulsion and fear, as if she were some venomous snake that had been placed in their midst.

She has to force her legs to move, has to force herself to return to the darkness of the croft. And she cannot make herself venture further than the kitchen. She huddles next to the *hlóðir,* drawing breath after shuddering breath deep into her lungs.

Outside, the wind moans. Overhead, the boards creak and sigh. Rósa presses her hands over her ears.

By the time Jón returns, later that day, she has compelled herself to stand and to prepare the food. She can barely look at him, and waits for him to accuse her of disobedience, waits for him to say that he knows she has been to the village. But Katrín must have kept the villagers silent, because Jón says nothing to her, other than speaking of the hay and the sheep.

At night, the croft exhales: time is measured in silences. For five nights, Jón waits until she feigns sleep before he comes to bed, loose-limbed and sour-breathed with drink. She lies cold in the darkness, confused and frightened. When she falls asleep her body is curled into a ball; she wakes in the same position, her muscles aching from remaining still.

Does she repulse him? Is there something wrong with her face, her body, her smell? She fears his touch, but she cannot stand this strange isolation. She feels like the hard, transparent ornament that hangs around her neck.

Perhaps he is nervous of her, although why, she cannot think — he has been mar-

135

ried before, after all. Or does he think that *she* does not desire *him*? Does he wait for some sign from her? Her thoughts hum in the darkness as he snores next to her. On the fifth night, she turns to him in bed.

'Mamma knew a woman in Skálholt. She was married, but had no children.'

'Did she not?' The drink has made his voice slack.

'No, she . . .' Rósa bites her lip. 'She thought it a sin to . . . lie with her husband.'

'She did?' Jón's words are sharper. He is suddenly alert. 'The Bible tells us lust is a sin.'

'But,' she swallows, 'did not Adam ask God to create Eve as . . . as a companion?'

Tentatively, Rósa reaches for his hand and lays it on her cheek. There is a catch in his breath as he touches her. She presses her lips to his palm; he moves his hand, slowly onto her shoulder, then to her breast. Something inside her shrinks from his touch, which is cautious and tickles unpleasantly. She forces herself not to cringe as he moves his hand to her stomach, then under her shift.

He kisses her. His mouth, large and wet. His lips, rubbery and slack. The drink is sour on his breath. His eyes are tightly shut. He kisses her harder and rolls on top of her,

136

hitching her shift up over her hips. He is heavy. Rósa pushes against him so that she can breathe. He uses his legs to prise hers apart.

It stings when he enters her. She gasps and clamps her jaws. His movements are violent; she closes her eyes and counts in her head. The cold glass figurine on the cord about his neck taps repeatedly on her chin. But after a little shaking and grunting and shuddering — his eyes closed, his face twisted, as if in agony — it is over. He rolls off her and, almost immediately, falls asleep.

She lies still, staring at the black shadows and the silver flood of moonlight. From between her legs, a tiny gush of fluid, like the contents of a handkerchief. She rolls away and it remains between them, the sludge of a contract signed with her blood. In the morning, she will strip the bed and soak and scrub the sheets in the stream.

But, in spite of the pain, she feels a swell of victory. Perhaps he will be kinder to her now; perhaps he will love her as a husband should, now that she truly belongs to him.

That night, Rósa dreams of Páll. His body is on top of hers, but she cannot feel anything. As he moves, she tries to kiss him, but her lips, too, are numb. She wraps herself around him, pulling him closer, but he fades away to air and she is left feeling hollow, like a discarded eggshell.

Rósa wakes early, in the mother-of-pearl half-light before dawn. The bed next to her is empty, as usual. She pads into the kitchen, pulling her shawl tight against the chill, a sting between her legs with every step. She doesn't realize she has been holding her breath until she sees the empty kitchen: Jón has already left. She should make bread; she should burn the wool from the sheep's head and put it in the whey. She should darn the socks he has laid over the stool, a gaping hole in one heel.

She slumps next to the *hlóðir* and huddles close to the warmth. Then she takes the perfect, untouched glass woman from around her neck. The tiny, transparent face is so humble, so flawless. Was the figure based on a real woman, or did the man who had crafted it imagine this perfect creature?

Rósa sighs and shoves it into her pocket. She had hoped to feel *some*thing. Love? Contentment? Some new power over her husband? Instead, the transaction has made her feel small and soiled, like a spoon used to scoop the slippery innards from a dead animal.

Still, Jón is keeping Mamma and Páll

138

alive. And he doesn't beat her, hasn't hurt her. Perhaps that is enough. Perhaps a contented marriage is only a matter of becoming resigned to the shape of one's own discontent.

The nights fall into a pattern: Jón drinks enough to become slack-faced and smiling, his easy speech slightly slurred. When they go to bed, he sometimes falls straight to sleep, snoring. Those nights are better: his face, as he sleeps, looks younger, more open. In the muted half-light, she sometimes thinks she might feel . . . *something* for him. A certain tenderness, brought on by proximity. And she feels safer on those nights and often falls asleep soon after him; she doesn't listen, breathlessly, for sounds from the loft room.

But on the nights where he climbs atop her, his face is as blank and closed-off as the locked room above. He says nothing to her but, after he has finished, presses a kiss onto her cheek or her breast, then climbs off her and walks out into the night. Sometimes he returns in the early hours and slides in next to her, his skin cold and smelling of the sea, his breath sour with *brennevín.* On those nights, while he is gone, Rósa has to keep her pillow pressed over her ears to prevent herself hearing noises from the loft. Twice, she has fallen asleep, then woken to the stir of air as a body passed close to hers, walking out of the *baðstofa*. Once, she woke, her breath tight in her throat, certain that someone was standing over her, watching her. She clenched her jaw and lay absolutely still; she could feel the heat from a body close to hers; she could feel the rake of someone's gaze on her face, her hands, her body. She didn't move.

Eventually, she must have fallen asleep, and when she opened her eyes some time later, the croft was dark and silent.

She doesn't tell Jón any of this. She doesn't know which would be worse: his anger at her questions, or his contempt at her childish imaginings.

When Rósa gazes out at the sea, it no longer looks beautiful, like some escape to a distant land from the Sagas. Instead, it seems like an enclosing ring of iron.

Sometimes, while she is washing clothes at the stream, Rósa sees a distant figure, which might be Gudrun or Katrín or some other villager, watching from afar. Occasionally, they come closer and speak to her, but there is something skittish in their movements

140

and expressions; their words are guarded.

Katrín had promised she would find a way for Rósa to visit her, hadn't she? Or had Rósa dreamed that too? Increasingly, she finds herself scoured by the whirlwind of her thoughts and is no longer sure she can trust her own senses. She considers going down to the village again, but then she remembers Olaf's snarling face and stands frozen in indecision on the hillside, gripping the runestone in her pocket so hard that her hand aches.

Once, she sees Jón moving among the people. She watches him walk down the hill to the village. Someone notices him, and a ripple runs through the villagers, like the wind sifting through wheat: as one, they all freeze and lower their eyes to the ground. Even the children stop playing and run close to their mammas' skirts. Then Jón is among them. Even from this distance, Rósa can sense the anticipatory hum that moves through the people as he walks past them. Occasionally, he stops to pat a child's cheek, or to speak to one of the women. He is huge: his great shoulders and meaty hands make the women and children seem even smaller. Rósa feels a stirring within her as she watches her husband: from so far away, she can imagine that he is offering them

141

comfort or kind words.

Then Jón walks back up the hill, and the people scatter to their crofts, like startled birds taking flight.

Rósa turns back to her croft too, her loneliness a slow-forming ice in her gut.

After a week of solitude, Rósa feels close to screaming. She must see someone, talk to someone. She will go down to the village again, after she has done the washing. No matter if Jón is angry, she cannot be alone any longer.

She is arranging the bedlinen over the rocks near the stream to dry and practising what she will say to Jón if he sees her in the village when two women approach. They must be her age, or thereabouts — both have small children with them. They whisper between themselves and giggle. They stop ten horse-lengths away, then one pushes the other forward. The woman stumbles a little and hisses at her friend, who laughs in response and pushes her forward again.

Rósa calls out a greeting.

Both women jump and one of the children scuttles behind its mother's skirts.

Rósa raises her hand. 'I am Rósa. Jón Eiríksson's wife. His . . . new wife.'

'We know.' The fairer woman pushes her

cap back on her head and squints at Rósa. Her expression is guarded. 'I am Nóra. This is Clara.'

Rósa knows her smile is too wide but she cannot help herself. 'I have been . . . And Jón . . . I thought you might run away, like everyone else. It is as though I have the sweating sickness.' Her laughter sounds high-pitched.

An unreadable look passes between the two women. The darker-haired one, Clara, says, 'You would *like* company, then?'

'Hush, Clara!' says Nóra. 'Remember . . .'

Both women stare at her, large-eyed, as if ready to bolt.

Rósa's smile trembles. 'I would be glad of company. I do not bite.'

They blink at her joke. 'Keep to yourself,' says Nóra, gently. 'It is safer.'

Clara elbows her and hurriedly adds, 'You must have plenty of food and a warm croft. I am surprised you come out at all.'

'He does not want her to wander, like —'

'Hush, Nora!'

'Oh, hush yourself, Clara! We cannot be expected to pretend —'

'Anna?' Rósa tries to keep her voice light. 'You speak of Anna?'

Both women look at the ground, at the stream, at their splashing children, anywhere

143

but at Rósa.

'Did you know her well?' Rósa presses. 'I heard, in Skálholt . . . Traders said that — that Anna went mad with loneliness?'

They exchange glances. Finally Clara mutters, 'Katrín knows —'

'Clara, hold your tongue!' Nóra barks, real fear in her eyes.

Clara kicks at a stone. 'She changed. Anna. She was . . . At first — Ask Katrín.'

'For Heaven's *sake,* Clara, hush!' Nóra pulls at her arm, turning back towards the village. 'We must go,' she says to Rósa. 'So much to do. You must understand. Come, children.'

They gabble a hurried farewell, and Nóra tugs at Clara's hand. Ushering the children before them, the two women scurry down the hill, Nóra scolding all the way.

Rósa catches some of the words; most are to do with food.

Perhaps that old man, Egill, is right, and her husband has bought the people's silence with food. But what can have been so terrible about Anna? Rósa cannot help thinking of the noises she has heard above her head and, for a moment, it crosses her mind that Anna might still be up there. Perhaps Jón has shut her away and only allows her out at night. But such thoughts are madness, surely.

She thinks of how Jón's eyes darken at the mention of Anna's name and how something in his face slams shut.

Rósa presses her palms to her eyelids and counts, slowly, until her breathing settles. She must talk to Katrín.

The next day Rósa lingers by the stream. She has no clothes in need of washing so has rubbed dirt into one of Jón's tunics. She sees Katrín from a distance, but the older woman notices her and stops short, then makes as if to turn back down the hill.

Hurriedly, Rósa places the hood of Jón's tunic over a rock, then tugs so it catches and rips. Jón will be angry, but at that moment Rósa doesn't care. She makes a show of struggling with the tunic, mutters an oath and pulls harder.

Down the hill, Katrín is watching.

Rósa throws up her hands and wades into the stream, soaking her skirt, boots and stockings, but still the hood won't budge. Briefly, she wonders how she will save the tunic if Katrín does not help.

Then, to her relief, Katrín calls, 'Can you free it?'

'No! It is stuck.'

Katrín hesitates, then trudges up the hill.

'Let me help,' she puffs. 'You lift the stone and I'll pull.'

Katrín heaves while Rósa pushes the stone. For a moment, she thinks the tunic isn't going to shift but suddenly it comes free. Katrín whoops as she stumbles backwards, arms flailing, then trips and falls forward, boots and skirt in the stream. She laughs. 'Well, my boots are clean now.'

'I'm sorry,' Rósa says, and reaches out to take Katrín's hand.

Soon they are both sitting on a rock, dabbling their toes, gasping at the icy chill.

'How do you like Stykkishólmur?' Katrín asks.

'It is not the welcome I had hoped for.'

'It must feel very strange.' Katrín smiles sympathetically. 'And forgive me for sending you away from the village. I was thinking of your safety.' She pauses, as if weighing something in her mind. Then she takes Rósa's hand. 'We should like to see you, Gudrun and I — and the other women. Gudrun is not as fierce as she seems. It is hard to be poor, when Jón is so wealthy.'

'But he provides for the settlement.'

Katrín opens her mouth then shuts it and nods.

Rósa pulls at a thread on her tunic. Katrín seems so kindly — it is almost like sitting next to Mamma. 'Was Anna lonely, too?'

Katrín's smile fades. 'Anna was . . . different from you. She was strong, in many ways. Of course, that brought its own problems.'

'With Jón?'

Katrín shivers. 'That wind. It will be winter soon.'

Rósa bites her lip, recalling the rumour that he had buried Anna alone and so quickly after her death.

Katrín squeezes her hand. 'There are some things you would be better not to know. Seeds, once planted, are hard to uproot.'

Rósa waits for more, but Katrín's tone shifts. 'You must find company when Jón is not here. At the right time, when Olaf will not see you. Or Egill. Then you will be happier, I think. Nóra and Clara are kind. You spoke to them at the stream yesterday?'

'They seemed pleasant, and I — I would like —'

'Of course you would. We all know how lonely it can be when the men are in the fields or out at sea. And Jón is away more often than most.'

Rósa nods. She feels a crushing weight in her chest whenever she thinks of returning to the croft, the silence of her thoughts — and those noises. Still, she forces a smile.

147

'You are all married, then?'

'Yes. But my husband and Gudrun's died many years ago.'

'I am sorry.'

'A fishing accident. A storm and some rocks. It happens here, from time to time. The sea swallows men whole. We didn't find the bodies, only some wood from the boat.' Katrín looks at the sea, so flat and peaceful now, with its smattering of islands and scattering of birds.

Rósa almost places her hand on the older woman's arm, but stops herself, unsure: she has never had a female companion. She says, 'You must have been . . .'

Katrín inclines her head. 'I was. It shattered my soul.' Her eyes are bright with tears. 'But I had no time to mourn. The land does not forgive idle hands, and that winter was hard. If I had wept in my croft, I would have starved — my daughter, Dora, too.'

'Skálholt was the same. We were never short of food while Pabbi lived, but my mamma would have wasted away this winter, if I had not . . .'

Katrín gives a tight smile. 'You exchanged yourself for food. No need for shame, I would have done the same. The winters were hard here too, until Jón brought the traders.'

148

'How did you survive?' Rósa asked.

'I gathered wool. I walked around the boundary walls in the snow, and collected stray tufts. I spun and knitted all winter and we lived — just.'

'Your daughter was lucky.'

'Perhaps. For a while. She is . . . gone too, now. The snow . . .'

Katrín's mouth folds and, for a terrible moment, Rósa fears that the older woman will begin to sob, and that she herself will say something foolish or callous. She places a tentative hand on Katrín's shoulder.

Katrín wipes her eyes, then peers at Rósa. 'When I first saw you, I thought you were nothing like . . . But there's *something* . . .' She cocks her head to one side. 'I wonder if he's noticed.' Before Rósa can ask what she means, she stands and brushes off her skirts.

'I would like to talk more.'

Katrín holds up her hand. 'We have spoken too long already. I would not risk you. You must go now. But . . .' She pauses. '. . . you are growing thin. You cannot —' Her mouth twists. 'Remember that my croft is not far. Don't risk yourself, but . . . I'd not have you weeping and starving.'

Rósa's smile is tight. 'I . . . rarely weep,' she lies.

'Good. I'd thought he'd crushed the spirit

149

out of you already.'

Rósa waits.

Katrín seems to weigh her words. Finally, she says, 'You remind me of — Let Anna's fate be a warning to you.'

Rósa shivers. 'But Anna died of a fever?'

Katrín takes her hand. 'Do as he bids you. Or, at least, let him see you doing so.' Before Rósa can ask any more, Katrín mutters, 'I must go.' She picks up her basket of washing, which is still dry, and walks down the hill. Rósa watches her and, for a moment, she cannot catch her breath.

How can she be more careful than she is already? There had been real fear in Katrín's eyes when she spoke of Jón. And something else . . . A tightening around her mouth that spoke of rage.

Rósa feels as though she is on the lip of a volcano and must balance on the precipice, ignoring the heat, while the lava bubbles beneath her.

She should take her husband's meal up to the field, but she cannot bear the thought of sitting next to him, smiling, talking about the hay and the sea, and pretending that there is no shifting darkness in the silence between their words.

So she hefts her own basket, and in spite of the height of the sun, urging her to the field, she does not fetch Jón's food. Instead, she sets off up the hill, searching in the grass until she sees it: a little wooden cross. Anna had died on a summer's night, so the rumour went, and Jón had buried her immediately.

Had he wept as he did so? She has not asked him about Anna. She can voice none of the questions whirling in her mind.

She examines the cross. Something is scratched into the wood. Rósa squints. *Proverbs 12:4.* No doubt a verse about dutiful wives proving a blessing.

Rósa marches down the hill to the croft and finds the Bible in the *baðstofa,* next to where Jón sleeps. She flicks through the grubby, well-thumbed pages until she finds it. As she expected: *An excellent wife is the crown of her husband.* Then she reads the other half of the verse: *but she who brings shame is like rot in his bones.*

She snaps the Bible shut and places it on the bed, then paces back and forth, walking through to the kitchen and then the storeroom, trying to steady her breaths.

She finds a quill and ink, and starts a letter to Mamma, but she does not know what to say: she has never lied to Sigridúr before. She crosses out line after line, then folds the piece of paper, with its blots and scratched-out suspicions, into a tiny square and hides it in a gap between the wooden boards.

Then she pauses, standing in the silence, ears straining for a sound from above. She remembers her ridiculous suspicion earlier: that Anna was still alive, shut up in the loft. Madness, surely. Suddenly she is filled with a hot rage: against her husband, against this place, against this suffocating silence.

Rósa strides to the ladder and pulls herself up, rung by rung. She slaps her hand against the locked door of the loft room, which rings with the sound — as if the dead trees are singing.

'Who's there?' Her voice echoes in the gloom.

All in your head. Fool!

Rósa is about to descend again when she hears it: a sound like an exhalation, half suppressed, as if the croft itself is breathing. A chill needles Rósa's skin — the hairs on her arms stand to attention. Some age-old animal instinct tells her to run.

She ignores the trembling in her legs, and rattles the door handle, pushing her weight against the solid wood. Nothing. No movement. And then, when Rósa presses her ear to the door, no noise except the gasp of her own panicked breaths and the blood thud-

152

ding in her ears.

She slumps back and covers her face with her hands. No one is there. Nothing and no one. Even a ghost would have been company. She squashes the thought — Pabbi would be horrified.

Another sudden sound — like the snap of linen sheets in the wind.

Rósa bolts upright, then scrambles down the ladder and out of the croft. Cold air stings her face. She leans on the wall, clinging to the stone so tightly that it sinks sharp teeth into her skin. The pain is a relief. The pain is real.

She rubs her eyes. Her hands are shaking. She is weary, so weary. That is why her mind is conjuring these noises. Except . . . she hears them. Truly, she could swear she hears them.

She looks at the rumpled face of the sea — wind-darkened and sullen today.

Rósa feels she will never become used to the *size* of it, the overwhelming feeling that even as it encloses her in an icy fist it also stretches endlessly away into an unguessed-at number of lands and infinite other lives, each full of its own troubles.

But there is no escape. Every heartbeat feels like the tightening of a rope, binding her to this body, this place.

153

She cannot even write to Mamma — what could she say? That her husband is cold and strange? That she fears the croft is haunted? That she hopes it is haunted, for if it is not, she is losing her mind?

When she takes Jón his *dagverður,* part of her wants to fling her arms about his neck and cling to him: he is solid and sweating and real. She resists the urge. If he pushes her away, she will be truly alone.

'Do you believe in ghosts?' Rósa asks him.

Jón's expression darkens. 'Why?'

'I read a passage in the Bible earlier and —'

'The devil distorts our understanding of God's Word. What passage were you reading?'

'I cannot remember.'

'Perhaps it was the disciples meeting with Moses and Elijah, long after their deaths. But that was a *transfiguration* — a vision Jesus granted them. They were not ghosts. Don't be foolish, Rósa.'

Rósa stares at her hands in her lap. 'But as the spirit doesn't ascend to Heaven until Judgement, might some spirits be . . . wakeful? If they were unhappy?'

'Who has filled your head with such corruptions?' Jón's eyes are wild now. 'Was it Katrín? I have told you to stay away from her. The woman is poisonous.'

'No! Not Katrín. I — I simply thought of —' Her vision blurs.

'Ah.' His expression softens. 'Your pabbi? What a brute I am. Here, stop weeping.' He presses a linen cloth to her cheeks, and seems so contrite that she thinks she must have imagined his savagery.

He dabs at her tears. 'No talk of ghosts, Rósa. Your pabbi would not approve. You sound like a child! I cannot have a child for a wife.' His smile is rigid.

She looks out at the sea, blinking the heat from her eyes.

He turns away from her then, and goes back to hefting the bundles of hay. His face is like a desolate rock.

With a creeping nausea, Rósa remembers the chill she had felt when walking over Anna's grave earlier. As if something had *infected* her. She presses her fingers against her throat, counts out the flurry of life, then shudders.

'You are cold,' Jón says. 'You should return to the croft, before you catch your death.'

She starts. He presses a kiss into her cheek; her skin crawls.

As she trudges down the windswept hill towards the croft, which squats like a hunched beggar against the bleak weather, Rósa takes with her this knowledge: if ghosts do not exist, she must be going mad.

The feeling of being tugged apart at the seams intensifies — Rósa can feel the yank of hysteria tightening around her chest on every breath. She focuses on small tasks: gathering the scraps of wool caught on the beams of the barn, carding and spinning — she drags the spindle outside, as if sunlight can shield her from the dark, gasping presence in the croft — or is it in her mind? She can no longer tell.

She starts letter after letter to her mother, but she cannot write more than one or two lines: *Things are so very strange here. I wish I could return to you. I think of you often. Sometimes I hear noises and I remember the stories you used to tell me of* draugar, *those spirits of the dead who drive the living mad, then drink their blood . . .*

Each time, she crumples the paper, or folds it into a tiny square and hides it beneath the bed or between the cracks in the wood where Jón will never find it. She will finish the letters, one day, and she will send them south with a trader. She needs only to find the right words.

She cannot stop herself weeping at odd

moments; her hands shake as she writes. Perhaps if she could speak to someone, if she could see Katrín . . .

After seven days, she says to Jón, 'I would like to have help in the croft.'

He is back from a day out on the sea, and his face is grey with cold and weariness: he seems carved from rock. He has been rubbing his fingers over his eyes and yawning, but at her words, he bolts upright, alert.

'Why? You do a fine job — the croft is clean, the clothes are washed and mended. You prepare the food with skill.'

She rubs her chapped fingers. 'Still, I would like company.'

He encircles her wrists with his thumb and forefinger and squeezes, his hand huge around hers. Rósa thinks of the strength that must rest within them, these hands that wield oars and the scythe so easily; these hands that dug his first wife's grave.

She swallows nervously, frees herself and puts a hand into her pocket, gripping the glass figurine as if it will give her courage. 'You are away so much.'

'I am away less than I should be,' he growls. 'I *should* travel to Denmark to trade. Rósa, I stay here this winter because of you.'

She looks at her feet. 'You can leave me

here,' she whispers. The thought of wintering alone is horrifying, yet she might be able to breathe without his eyes upon her. The noises might stop. 'Go to Denmark.'

'I *cannot,*' he barks, and she flinches.

He takes a breath. His fisted hands are trembling. 'Come, Rósa. I don't like leaving you, but I must provide — you see that. You were alone much as a child. I thought you would not mind the solitude.'

She thinks of long summer days spent playing with Páll.

'I admired your poise when we first met. You seemed happy, so self-possessed. I chose you for better things than idle chatter.'

He watches her silently, until she nods.

He shifts a little closer and takes her hand again. 'You may read the Bible, of course. I know you will not let your duties slip.'

She thinks of the endless knitting and sweeping, cooking and mending. And she thinks of the Saga of her own that she had started a lifetime ago in Skálholt. But the thought of writing is impossible with this compression of her thoughts. Her world is constricting to the tiny compass of her body: the shift of her breath, the thud of her heart.

'This solitude should strengthen your faith. This time with God is a gift. You must be grateful.' His voice has taken on the commanding tone of the *goði*.

She wants to remind him that the Bible says it is not good for man to be alone, but disagreeing with Jón, she is discovering, is like shouting into a blizzard.

On Sabbath days, she stands on the hill, watching the people of Stykkishólmur as they pray and worship. Sounds wash over her. She is like the grass: present but invisible. The people from the settlement avoid looking at her, keeping their eyes fixed on Egill, as he stands at the pulpit, then on Jón when he speaks afterwards.

She remembers Egill's warnings when she arrived, that Jón is a devil, that the people have no love for him. It has crossed her mind that she might visit Egill and question him, but there is something predatory in the old man's gaze.

Egill preaches his dry and terrifying sermons on the open mouth of Hell, which waits at the top of Mount Hekla for all souls who sin. Afterwards, while Jón addresses the people on secular matters, telling them what food to expect and where they should fish, Egill stands apart from the congregation. He is gaunt, and his face has the taut, hungry look of a carrion bird. Olaf stands

159

beside him, meaty arms folded across his barrel chest. They scowl at Jón as he leads the people in a final prayer for good harvests and dry weather.

After the service, Rósa forces herself to walk near to where they stand and draws a breath to speak but can find no words. The two men stare at her, coldly.

'You continue to look thin, child,' Egill says. 'And unhappy.' He smiles.

She opens her mouth to answer, but then a strong hand is on her elbow and Jón is at her side.

'Come, Rósa.' His face is tight. 'You are tired. You must rest.' He puts his arm around her shoulders and pulls her in close, as if he is embracing her. It is like being pinioned by a rockfall.

Rósa resists, then allows herself to be pulled away. As she turns, a smirk creeps over Egill's face, like a crack in an ice sheet.

When they are back in the croft, Jón holds her hand and leads her to her bed.

'Lie down. If the services tire you, you should stay in the croft.'

'They do not tire me.' She tries to sit up but he pushes her shoulder until she is lying down.

'Well,' he says, 'if you must still come to the services, then you will stay close to me.

A good husband should care for his wife. I wouldn't like Egill to upset you.'

'I —'

'Rest now, Rósa. Close your eyes.' He watches her until she does so. 'Rósa, you know you are fortunate to have this life, these riches. Yes?'

His grip on her hand tightens. She clenches her jaw, then nods.

'Good,' he says. 'You must write to your mamma, telling her of your good life here, how you are content with me. She will be happy to hear it.'

Rósa's stomach jolts and her eyes snap open. He is smiling at her and his voice is silken as he says, 'You would like to make your mamma happy?'

Rósa's mouth is dry; she swallows. Jón grips her hand more tightly. Her bones crackle. She whispers, 'I will . . . write.'

'Good.' He grins, his face lightening. 'Give me the letter and I will send it south with a trader.' He releases her hand and pats her cheek, then turns and strides from the room. After he has gone, she stretches out her hand. It is pale and bloodless, like the limp body of a strangled creature.

One morning, after Pétur has been gone for ten days and Jón has left early to go out on the boat, Rósa rises from her bed and decides that she cannot endure another moment alone in the croft.

She will go down to the settlement again. She will visit Katrín.

She sets off early down the hill, towards the distant huddle of crofts. She will be back before sunset. Jón need never know she has disobeyed him.

As she runs down the path, she glances back over her shoulder. The croft looks peaceful: the wind gusts birch leaves around the door — whirling gold glimmers in the autumn sun. The beauty makes her catch her breath. She reminds herself that the sunlight will fade and the leaves will rot. And then her husband's croft will look like the unquiet burial mound that it is.

There is a saying that the resting places of the unsettled dead often appear beautiful from the outside. *Draugar* haunt places that they loved in life, or where there is unfinished business: the ghost of Thorgunna in *Eyrbygg ja Saga* rose again and again because her bedding hadn't been burned upon her death. Who knows what tasks Anna might have left undone?

Rósa shakes her head, and turns away from the croft, running down the hill, away from Jón and from the version of herself she doesn't recognize.

The rearing mountains and the sharp smell of the black and red soil fill her with a giddy lightness, making her fears of these past weeks ridiculous: there are no ghosts. She will explain to Katrín how she thought she heard breathing and movement in the loft. Katrín will tell her that only fools believe in *draugar:* there are no spirits that drive people insane, then devour them.

Katrín must have seen Rósa approaching; she runs out of her croft before Rósa has even reached the bottom of the hill.

'Rósa!' Katrín clasps her in a quick embrace and immediately Rósa feels more human.

She had begun to feel like she was fading, as if she herself were turning into a *draugr.* Now, for the first time in days, she smiles. 'I hope I am not intruding?'

'You are very welcome. But Jón?'

'He . . . does not know I am here. He is fishing. Please do not —'

'I am no simpleton.' Katrín clasps Rósa's shoulders. 'I shall not say a word. And the others can also be trusted, for that at least.'

Rósa feels a wave of relief, but it turns to alarm. 'The others?'

'They'll be glad to see you. Just pay no heed to Gudrun's sharp tongue.'

Before Rósa can protest, Katrín leads her inside the fuggy gloom of the croft, where four women sit around the open fire, knitting. Rósa has met three of them already: old Gudrun, with her blank eyes and whiskery face; Nóra and Clara, whom she saw at the stream with their children. The little ones are playing, tumbling on the floor like puppies, their mothers uttering sharp warnings about the heat of the fire, and protesting when they tangle the wool.

The fourth woman is younger, very near to Rósa's own age, she guesses. She has skin the colour of *skyr* and hair so pale it is almost white. Her eyes are the lightest blue — they seem almost opaque. She is breathtaking and Rósa finds herself smiling. The woman scowls. Rósa flushes and turns to examine the croft.

It is small, a similar size to Mamma's, although, like Jón's croft, the walls are lined with wood. There is no separate kitchen, simply a narrow *baðstofa,* which serves as a space to cook, live and sleep. A doorway opens into the pantry: there are barrels on the floor, and dried fish hangs from the rafters. Despite the dimness of the room and its size, it feels lighter and less oppressive than Jón's.

Katrín holds Rósa's hand as she makes

the introductions, her touch warm and steadying. 'Gudrun you have met already. And Clara and Nóra.'

'Yes. *Bless.*' Rósa curtsies and the women giggle a little.

Katrín tuts. 'Your fine manners turn them into children.' Clara and Nóra smother their laughter and return Rósa's curtsy.

Katrín indicates the pale beauty with the cold gaze. 'And this is Audur.'

Rósa curtsies again and says, *'Komdu sæl og blessuð.'* Somehow, the more formal greeting seems appropriate. 'You are as beautiful as Gudrun from *Laxdaela Saga.*'

Audur's eyes remain blank and humourless. 'Does your husband know you read the Sagas?' She does not curtsy.

Katrín glares at her, then seats Rósa and passes her a mass of wool. 'Untangle this,' she murmurs. 'It will keep your hands busy.'

Rósa sees that her fingers are shaking. Gratefully, she sets to work freeing a smooth skein from the snarl in her hands.

The croft is hushed, each woman weighing the silence.

Finally, Katrín says, 'We will have snow early, this year.'

'Nonsense!' Gudrun cries. 'The air is mild still. Look at the sea — no darkness on the water.'

'You cannot see past your own nose.' Katrín snorts.

'Insolent girl! I always smell bad weather, and this year I do not.'

'Who is to say your nose does not fail, along with your eyes and ears?'

Rósa expects Gudrun to be affronted, but both women are smiling. Perhaps they often needle one another so.

'I shall knit you a shawl to keep you warm this winter, Gudrun,' Katrín says, 'so that you will not freeze, even if your weather-telling nose has lied.'

'Do not trouble yourself.' Gudrun sniffs. 'I may be dead before the spring. Starved.' She blinks her milky eyes at Rósa. 'If only Jón would grant an old woman more meat . . .'

'Well, then, I will knit you a shroud,' Katrín's grin widens, 'and you will not have to trouble Rósa with matters that do not concern her.'

'Heartless woman!' Gudrun splutters. 'Rósa may give me meat, if she wishes. Anna often did.'

'Once!' Clara chimes in. 'She gave you meat *once,* towards the end, and she probably cursed it first.'

Katrín stiffens, and there is real heat in the glare she shoots at Clara, who drops her

166

gaze and snaps an oath at her child, then pulls a chicken bone from his hand to stop him jamming it into his ear. The child howls and, as Katrín helps Clara with him, she hisses something at her. Clara looks chastened.

Then Audur calls, above the child's clamour, 'I hope you are contented in your marriage, Rósa.' She gives a thin smile.

Rósa bows her head. 'I am.'

'Why does she whisper so?' Gudrun complains.

Audur's voice grows mocking. 'She is quiet because she wanted to stay in the church with her pabbi.'

'I have always loved reading in solitude,' Rósa murmurs.

Audur gives a high-pitched, serrated giggle. 'You have your solitude now.'

'Audur!' Katrín's tone is sharp.

Rósa raises her chin. 'I am lucky to be able to read, I know.' She cannot help adding, 'Most women cannot.'

Audur colours. 'And do you want children? They are rarely quiet.' She indicates the red-faced pair by the fire, both of whom are now crying as they fight over the chicken bone.

'God grants children when He wills it,' says Rósa, clenching the wool in her hands.

No one in Skálholt would have dared question a *goði's* wife so. Rage rushes through her. 'You would know that, if you read your Bible.'

Angry spots of colour stand out on Audur's cheeks. 'Anna longed for children also. Two years, but no sign. No wonder she started —'

'Audur! Enough!' Katrín snaps.

Rósa bites her lip and stands, ready to leave, but Katrín pushes her back onto the bench. 'Come now, my croft seems small all of a sudden. Nóra, Clara, the children must roll around outside, away from my fire.' Then Katrín turns to Audur. 'Gudrun must go to the outhouse. Audur will take her.'

Audur grimaces, then helps Gudrun from the croft.

Once the other women have gone, Katrín smiles kindly at Rósa. 'Audur has a sharp tongue. I will scold her for her rudeness, but you must not be upset.'

Rósa blinks until she can speak without her voice shaking. 'What have I done to offend her? And how does she dare to ask such questions?'

'It is no secret that Audur wanted Jón's wealth for herself.' Katrín grins. 'I suppose he did not want her bitterness to turn all his milk to *skyr.*'

Rósa manages a faint smile. 'Thank you.'

Katrín offers Rósa a plate of food. 'Eat. If you faint from hunger, I will have to answer to Jón.'

'Jón tells me so little of the village. He only orders me to stay away.'

'He finds it hard to trust,' Katrín says carefully. 'People who have known darkness carry it with them always. Pétur is the same.'

'Yes, I saw how Egill . . . I cannot imagine them —'

'As pabbi and son?' Katrín gives a wry chuckle. 'Neither could the settlement. Egill believed he was doing good, but there's a type of love that smothers. Pétur shamed Egill, then shunned him. It is a poison that seeps between them now.'

Rósa runs her finger over the plate. 'And Anna was unhappy?'

Katrín purses her lips. 'Not at first. She was . . . At first, she was like a wash of sunshine.'

'But not at the end?'

'Some people need love more than others. Anna was . . . so young. So affectionate. And she was so happy to be away from Thingvellir. She used to sit and talk to me while I knitted. She reminded me of my own Dora.'

Rósa thinks of the stories the traders told,

of the woman who walked over the hills at night, shouting curses to the wind. 'Jón changed her?'

Katrín nods and blinks, and Rósa cannot bring herself to push the matter, although she wants to ask about the noises, wants to tell Katrín that, in the dark, the groans and sighs of the loft make her want to crack a hammer against her skull, just to stop the sounds.

Katrín passes Rósa another piece of bread. 'Anna changed Jón too. He is not the man he once was. Best to obey him — or seem to. He is not violent but . . .' She touches Rósa's hand. 'You should do as he says. Please, Rósa.'

Rósa swallows, tight-chested.

As she stands to go, Katrín embraces her, then kisses her cheek. 'You are sensible and will keep yourself safe. I know it.'

As Rósa walks back up to the croft, the sense of compression is almost unbearable. It is like walking into an icy sea, knowing that the darkness and the cold will press the air from her lungs so that she will have to open her mouth to take a breath. And, as the water fills her ears, her nose and her mouth, no one will rescue her, even if they do hear her final, bubbling scream.

Stykkishólmur, October 1686
Pétur returns in the middle of a crisp, sun-spangled afternoon. He has been gone for nearly two weeks, and Rósa has watched Jón grow increasingly fretful, scanning the horizon and muttering about harvests and fish.

Then one day Pétur reappears — silently, as though he has emerged from the earth. One moment, Rósa is watching the clouds scudding across the sky, the next there is a voice behind her.

'You will go blind if you stare at the sun so.'

She whirls around. Pétur is grinning, not three arms' lengths from her. How can she have failed to hear him?

She pats her cap: she must look like a windswept fishwife. 'You startled me.'

'Forgive me. A lifetime of trying to escape being seen has taught me no other way than

171

to creep.' He turns to the sea. It is silver today, and radiates the first promise of winter's waiting ice.

'Is my mamma well?' Rósa asks.

'Her cough is gone. She wanted me to give you this.'

Pétur presses a kiss to her cheek. His face is rough and he smells of grass. Rósa gasps and pushes him away. He laughs and holds up his hands. 'I only pass on a gift from your mamma. She said you would be furious and that you would shriek and slap my face. I said you were too gracious to do that. It seems I was right.'

Rósa's rage is tempered by the faintest glow of amusement: she can imagine Mamma cackling as she persuaded Pétur to kiss her — it is a sign that Sigridúr is well.

Pétur bows again. 'I am sorry, Rósa. You must tell Jón of my insolence. He will cuff me soundly about the ears.'

Despite herself, she smiles. 'I shall not say a word.'

'Sensible woman.' He winks at her and, when she starts, pretends not to notice. 'Is Jón on the boat?' he asks.

'No. In the field, ploughing.'

'I'll take him the *dagverður*. But I need your help, Rósa. Will you walk to the field, wave to him and tell me when he has turned to plough the other way? Then he will expect you, and I can surprise him.'

Rósa cannot help laughing: his bright, guileless excitement is contagious.

Pétur hides behind the croft wall while Rósa strides up to the field. She sees Jón from a distance, calls and waves. He wipes his forehead with his sleeve, waves back, then continues ploughing. Pétur knows her husband so well — she pushes down a surge of what feels, ridiculously, like envy.

When Jón has turned the plough the other way, Rósa beckons Pétur from behind the wall. He starts up the hill, and, as he passes, gives her shoulder a pat. For a moment, she is left breathless.

Pétur runs up the hill, soft-footed as a stalking cat, following Jón for ten paces or more before finally leaping upon him, whooping. And, instead of growling and rebuking Pétur, Jón lets out a gust of laughter, a rich, deep sound she has not heard from him for two weeks, playfully pushes Pétur to the ground, then pulls him up and claps him on the back. Even from this distance, the delight on her husband's face is as clear as water.

Rósa remembers the laughter she used to share with Mamma, who knew her better than anyone in the world — except, perhaps,

173

Páll. The familiar longing to leave clutches her. Once the winter snows fall, all travel will be impossible.

She squeezes the cold glass woman in her pocket until her hand throbs. Then, suddenly decided, she runs down the hill towards the settlement.

She arrives at Katrín's croft, panting, and is about to knock on the door when it swings open. Katrín looks at Rósa's poised fist. 'I hope you were not planning to insult me by knocking. Come, come.'

Katrín pushes a bowl of unfamiliar green leaves towards her. Rósa tries to refuse, but Katrín thrusts it into her hands. 'The flesh is melting from you. These will strengthen your blood. I'm too old to carry you up that hill. Eat!'

'I have not been hungry,' Rósa says, lamely, taking a mouthful of the leaves. They are bitter, but delicious, and somehow warming, though they are raw. As soon as she begins to eat, she cannot stop. Katrín goes outside to pick more leaves twice, watching every mouthful and smiling, as if Rósa is her own starving daughter.

'Anna loved these too.' Katrín leans forward and takes Rósa's hand. 'You must tell me if you feel unwell. Promise you will tell me?'

Rósa feels a sudden horror. 'The leaves are —'

'Of course the leaves are good. But you are so pale. Jón's croft . . . Is there anything strange, which makes you feel unwell?'

Rósa swallows, thinking of *draugar.* 'What do you mean?'

'What have you seen?' Katrín's tone is sharp.

'Nothing. I —'

'Tell me, Rósa. You must. If something dangerous is —'

'It is nothing, or my imagination. I have heard noises.'

'When? Where?' Katrín leans forward, her eyes large and urgent.

'At night, mostly. From the locked room. It is all in my head, I am sure.'

'Locked room?' Katrín's hands tighten around the bowl.

'Yes, in the loft. I am . . . He has forbidden me to go into it.'

Katrín sits back, her face tense. 'The loft has never been locked.' There is a silence, then Katrín stands. 'I will go this moment, and look.'

'No!' Rósa gasps. 'No, you mustn't. Then he will know I've told you!'

Katrín sits again, but her mouth is tight, her jaw clenched.

Rósa whispers, 'What do you think . . . ?'

'I don't know.' Katrín's face is bloodless. 'Eat. Please. Now.'

Rósa sits and forces herself to eat. As she chews, a chill wind squeezes itself between the wooden boards. The leaves turn into a tasteless mulch that sticks in her throat. Quietly, she puts the bowl down. 'Pétur has returned. He seems happy.'

Katrín stirs, as if waking. 'Good news. Trade must have been brisk — plenty of Danish merchants. Many Icelanders will have nothing to do with Pétur.'

'Because he was a foundling?'

Katrín nods. 'Some believe he is a demon. Or that one of his ancestors was a pirate who raped women and murdered children. People see Pétur and think violence must stir his blood.'

'Surely not!' Rósa protests, and yet she remembers the way her guts churn when she looks into Pétur's copper eyes, which seem lit from within when he is angry and when he is joyful. There is a ferocity about him that makes her nerves hum.

'Pétur ran away once,' Katrín says. 'But Egill sent Jón to fetch him, and Pétur chose to stay with Jón when he returned.'

'Egill *wanted* Pétur to return? But Pétur told me Egill was a brute —'

'Egill still thinks of Pétur as his own, no matter the bad blood between them.'

'What happened?'

Katrín shrugs and looks down at the fire. And, just as when she asks questions about Jón, Rósa feels she is being told only half of the tale.

'Gudrun says Pétur is a monster,' Katrín murmurs. 'She is terrified of him.'

Rósa's skin prickles. 'And you? Do you fear him?'

'Of course not.' She looks away.

'And Anna? Did he ever hurt Anna?'

'I . . . No.' But then Katrín clamps her mouth shut and a little muscle twitches in her jaw.

Rósa examines the thickening skin on her own work-roughened hands — they look like the hands of a stranger, a much stronger woman than herself. They look like the hands of a woman who isn't scared to speak her thoughts.

Katrín puts her calloused hand on Rósa's. 'Not everything is a tale from the Sagas.'

Rósa smiles. 'I have read too many stories, I know.'

'I too. And now listen to us! No wonder men do not like women reading — if more of us did it, they would be washing our clothes in the river while we feasted at the

177

Althing. Think of Freydis in *Eírík's Saga,* chasing away barbarians and threatening to cut off her breasts.'

Rósa tries to laugh and, gradually, the shadow in the room subsides. But time scythes past, and soon she must return to the lonely croft on the shoulder of the hill because her husband will be waiting.

Rósa runs up the hill, but she is late: a chink of orange light from behind the horse-skin curtain and a rumble of voices tell her that Jón and Pétur have already returned.

She is about to rush into the croft — he will be angry that she is not there and that there is no food prepared, but then she stops and listens. Jón's voice is a low growl of frustration. She presses her ear to the door.

'You should have tried harder,' he says. 'Nothing? No reports?'

Pétur's voice is low and meek. 'I didn't ask directly. It would raise suspicions. Would you rather I'd —'

'No, no. Of course not. You did well. Forgive me, I —'

'I know. But you have nothing to fear.'

'Unless . . .' Jón's voice is darker. 'The land is full of pockets. What if —'

'Ridiculous!' Pétur's voice is hard. 'Far more probable Danish traders —'

'You have said Denmark many times. And I have told you that circumstances do not arrange themselves to comply with our wishes.'

There is a silence, as if each man is waiting for the other to speak.

Rósa holds her breath, but the silence continues. It occurs to her that they may find her standing with her ear pressed to the door. She ducks into the light and warmth of the kitchen. Jón and Pétur stand on either side of the table.

Expecting a scolding and an inquisition, Rósa gabbles, 'I was looking for wool scraps. In the barn. I will prepare the *nattverður*.'

'No need,' says Jón, without taking his eyes from Pétur. 'You will eat alone. We must go to the boat. We will be out until morning.'

'The boat? Now?'

'Pétur heard a rumour of a shoal of cod.'

'But it is night!'

'We know the waters.' Jón clasps Rósa in a quick, tight embrace, and she can feel his heart thudding. His breathing is laboured. 'Come, Pétur.'

The door bangs behind them, leaving a warm, empty silence. Rósa leans against the *hlóðir,* mulling over their words. What had he to fear? And why were they speaking of

179

rumours and Danish traders? Pétur said he had heard nothing. But Rósa could have told them, quite assuredly, that whatever they were saying about Jón in the south would not have been recounted to Pétur.

She sighs, looks at the loaf on the table and decides she cannot bring herself to eat. Instead she sweeps the floor. She is not fool enough to believe they would go out on the boat now. They are avoiding her. They want to talk. But why abandon her? Why not sit in the *baðstofa* or the loft?

She holds her breath, listening to the rustling and sighing of the croft. They say Anna went mad before she died. Did she imagine noises, too? Is this what madness feels like?

Rósa pinches herself hard, then bites her lip until she tastes copper. She fetches paper, a quill and ink.

Dearest Mamma,
I am glad you are well. Everything here is strange. There are odd noises and I feel I am in danger somehow. But perhaps it is only my imagination running wild. Jón is

Rósa sighs and crosses out everything, except *I am glad you are well.* Then she folds up the sheet of paper into a tiny square and kneels to stuff it between the boards under the bed with the others.

Her hand closes on something cold and sharp under the bed. She recoils, then reaches with tentative fingers and grasps the object, pulling it out into the light.

A knife. The metal is dull, as if it has lain unused for many months, and when she peers more closely, she can see brownish stains on the tip of the blade. Like rust, but richer in colour. She scrapes one of the marks with her fingernail and it flakes off easily. She tastes metal and realizes she is biting her lip again.

Rósa's mouth is dry, her heart juddering in her chest. She leans her head against the door, then takes the little glass woman out of her pocket. Cold. It is always cold, no matter that her skin should warm it.

■ ■ ■ ■

PART THREE

■ ■ ■ ■

The nights of blood are the nights of most
impatience.
Icelandic proverb, from
The Saga of Viga the Glum

JÓN

South of Mundarnes, December 1686

The past cannot be buried beneath a frozen sea. I became the man I am today long before that pale hand waved above the water's surface. I would like to imagine that time is a fishing cord, that I might press along it, feeling for the moment when a wrong decision tethered me to the rock that would one day sink me. And yet, try as I may, I cannot find the moment when that rope began to fray.

Sometimes I wonder if God hears my grief. Prayers fall like pebbles from my lips, and still the Lord is silent.

Even the Creator cannot unmake the past.

I crouch in a ditch, seven days' hard walk from Stykkishólmur. My sealskin boots are sodden; the sour stench of manure and fear burns my throat. There is a croft not fifty paces from where I squat, yet I will not

185

move until darkness falls. Then I will creep to the barn and hope to find that the sheep have left a little grain and water. I will huddle against their warm bodies and hope for oblivion.

But I mustn't rest long. I know the men will have begun their chase. I can imagine them, if I close my eyes, hot-breathed wolves on a scent. I need to live for three days longer. Then they can catch and kill me; it won't matter.

I rest on my heels. The mud sucks and shifts under my weight, releasing a pungent gust. My eyes water. Before I fall asleep, my head on my chest, I mutter a prayer, although I no longer recognize my own voice.

The nights stretch out, torturous and cold; I drift in and out of sleep. Ice crawls into my belly, feathering my bones. I dare not sleep too deeply in case I wake with a knife at my throat, or don't wake at all.

When I open my eyes, a pale winter light is swelling on the horizon. I must not be seen. I crouch in the ditch again. My fate awaits me to the south, but travelling by daylight makes the gap between my shoulder blades itch. Journeying at night brings its own risks: the earth in Iceland is a restless beast, never still, always ready to swallow unsuspecting travellers.

The sun rises, like God's all-seeing eye. I wrap my arms around myself and try to say, 'Amen.'

Instead I hear, in a rasping whisper, 'Anna. Anna. Anna.'

Finally, I heave myself from the ditch and force myself onward.

Overhead, a gyrfalcon soars, sharp-eyed hunter, riding the wind. I remember when I first trapped two fledglings to sell to Danish traders. I had watched the female for weeks, while she sat on her nest, warming her eggs. She eyed me warily at first, but soon grew used to my presence and gradually, day by day, I was able to creep closer.

When the chicks hatched, I waited while she filled their shrieking beaks with fish; I watched as they fattened and feathered. Then, one cloudy day, while the mother was wheeling through the leaden sky, I climbed the rockface to the nest.

The birds fluttered their budding wings and screeched at me as I reached out and closed my hand around one, then the other and placed them in the sack on my shoulder. They were soft and warm-bodied and, as I lifted them, they struggled against the confines of my fingers, thrashing with their talons and battering their sharp little beaks against my skin. I took care not to squeeze too tightly.

Even the liveliest spirit can be tamed, but death has no recourse.

I keep walking south, though I am losing all sense of where I am, or how far I must go before my task will be complete. I have always navigated by the sun and the stars, but now the heavens themselves are turned upside down — the sun sweeps low across the horizon and the land is often in cloudy darkness, or a still and gloomy dusk. The seeping wound in my stomach throbs. My skin burns in the chill air and my legs are like loose sails, shaking with every gust of wind.

But that hand beckons always at the corner of my vision, dragging me down, promising silence and peace beneath the frozen earth.

RÓSA

For the next five days, Rósa barely sees her husband and Pétur. They are fishing, they say, and certainly the storeroom is filling with cod, which Rósa must clean and hang to dry in the wind. The men do not even return to the croft to sleep.

'We sleep on the boat,' Jón says. His eyes slide from hers and he turns away.

'The nights are long,' Rósa replies, shrinking from the memory of the wind buffeting the groaning croft. Sometimes she climbs the ladder at night, feeling her way through the dark until she presses her hand against the locked door. She has tried prising the lock open with a knife, jamming the blade into it until the rasp of metal on metal sets her teeth on edge. She still wakes to the sound of footsteps passing her bed; she curls around her stomach and squeezes her eyes shut.

189

When she catches sight of her reflection in the stream, she barely recognizes the thin, pale girl staring back from beneath bruised eyelids. But she can't tell her husband that, like a child, she is afraid of the dark.

'I would like you . . . next to me.' She reaches out to take Jón's hand.

He shakes her off. 'I cannot let the settlement starve to please you, Rósa.'

Some nights Rósa lies awake, thinking of the knife beneath the bed. It pulls her hand towards it, like a lodestone. In the darkness, she reaches out and runs her finger along the blade. Such a simple thing, a knife. It has one task and one alone.

Occasionally, she takes a breath to ask Jón about it: she will mention it carelessly. *I found a knife. You must have dropped it,* she will say. And then what will he do? What will he ask her? What will happen to that sharp blade?

When her husband looks at her, she compresses her mouth into a fixed rictus.

One day, the wind picks up; the water is a sour and surly metal, and clouds darken the horizon.

Jón returns home late that night, grey-skinned and cold. He barely looks at her but shovels food into his mouth in silence.

Rósa takes a breath. 'A storm is coming.'

'I can read the weather.'

'Then you will be at the croft tomorrow? You will stay here tonight?' Despite his coldness, her heart lifts.

But he shakes his head. 'We must bring the sheep and cows into the barn and will rise early to fetch the last of the hay in, before the rain. I will sleep in the barn.'

She inhales sharply and he looks up, then reaches across, puts his hand to the back of her neck and clasps it gently, but she can feel the coiled strength in his grip.

'You do not object?' he murmurs.

She shakes her head.

'Good.' He pulls his hand away to continue eating. When he has finished, he brushes his cheek against hers and leaves to find Pétur.

After he has gone, the silence in the croft expands. Rósa can hear the thudding of her blood in her skull. What if she hears more noises? She cannot suffer another night spent hiding her face under her bedlinen, imagining the cold metal of the blade under the bed.

She sweeps the *baðstofa,* banging the brush against the benches, as if the noise of mundane activity will ward off any malevolent presence. She wonders which bed Anna lay in as she died. There is a tradition of cutting a hole in the wall next to the body for the removal of the dead, so that their spirit will not find the door and come back to haunt the croft as a *draugr*. Rósa can see no sign of any hole: the wooden boards are all intact.

There is a scuffle from the loft room overhead.

Rósa starts and calls out but there is no reply. Her blood sings and she puts her hands over her ears. Still, the thought of Anna's presence is smothering. Rósa throws down her brush and strides out into the cold.

No stars today. Helgafell and the other mountains clamp around the land and the sky, swallowing the huddled crofts.

Rósa's teeth chatter, but she would rather the cold than the noises.

A memory flickers: watching the aurora lights in Skálholt with Páll. Frost layered the ground, so they wrapped their arms around one another and huddled against the bodies of the sheep for warmth. At once, Rósa wonders why she hasn't thought of it before and runs the hundred paces to the barn, shivering. She will wait with the horses. When the men bring the sheep and the cows in, she can say that she will help to settle the animals.

The barn is draughty, but the horses radiate warmth. Rósa can hear them contentedly munching hay in the gathering darkness, shifting their hoofs restlessly and snorting dust from their nostrils. Friendly, familiar noises. No madness here.

Rósa wraps her arms around Hallgerd's neck and scratches the greasy mane just in front of her withers. Hallgerd grinds her teeth and rests her chin on Rósa's shoulder, wiggling her top lip in an attempt to caress Rósa's back. She grins. This is how horses befriend one another. She presses her face into Hallgerd's hot neck and breathes in the rich scents of grass and horse-sweat.

Suddenly, Hallgerd's neck stiffens. Every muscle is alert and her ears prick forward, concentrating intently on some sound outside the barn.

A boot thuds on the pathway.

Pétur and Jón!

But the men would have the sheep and cows with them, and Rósa cannot hear the animals. Hallgerd does not relax and begin to chew her hay again, as she would if it was a noise she recognized. Instead she and Skalm bolt forward, knocking Rósa to one side. Rósa falls painfully on her wrist but she springs up, every nerve alive. Both

193

animals are now rigid at the far end of the barn, staring at the doors, ears pricked, nostrils flaring.

Rósa's instinct is to hide, to cower behind the horses and wait for the danger to pass, but she forces herself to creep towards the doors. All is silent. She holds her breath and opens one of the doors. A cold wind funnels against her face, and a snowflake — the first she has seen in Stykkishólmur — melts on her nose.

No more footsteps. No shadows.

Rósa closes her eyes. Enough foolishness. She must return to the croft. Jón made it clear he did not want or need her help with the animals. She will write another letter to Mamma, and this time, she will send it south.

As Rósa walks up the path to the croft, the snowfall thickens and the wind sighs and plucks at her tunic.

It is when she is passing the pit-house that she hears another noise — not a footstep this time but the rumble of a voice. She stops dead.

She rarely thinks of the pit-house any more. It squats, dark and chill, fifty paces from the croft. She has never seen Jón fetch anything from within. It is simply an empty building, sag-roofed and surly, that would probably collapse on top of her if she opened the door.

But tonight a glow emanates from inside. And susurrating whispers.

Who would break into her husband's pit-house? Vagrants from the hills? Anyone honest would come to the croft, not hide in the pit-house, like an outlaw. More noises contrived by her own mind. She stifles a sob. She must find Jón.

She spins around to run up the hill to the field, then crashes straight into someone and is knocked sprawling.

'Forgive me.' The voice is deep, male. The hands that pull her up are strong around her wrists.

'Let me go!' she shrieks.

'Rósa!' the man exclaims.

Rósa screams and kicks out at the attacker, who will not release her wrists, who somehow knows her name and keeps repeating, 'Rósa! *Rósa,* hush!'

The door of the pit-house bursts open, and two more male voices join the chorus: 'Rósa! What is it? What is the matter?'

And the nightmare gains intensity, for somehow Jón and Pétur are there. The world compresses and Rósa feels like the startled horses: muscles rigid, poised to flee.

Jón and Pétur wrench the man away from

her. There is a scuffle and the thud of fists on flesh. Pétur howls and clutches his arm. Jón curses. He lights a torch. In the flickering orange glow, the stranger is dragged to his feet, and Rósa sees the face and surely it cannot be, but it is.

Páll!

Even in the shadows, she can make out his wry grin as he wipes the blood from his lips.

'A fine welcome, Rósa.' He winces and massages his ribs. 'Your husband's man punches hard. I will not breathe easily for a week.'

Pétur is bent double, cradling his arm and groaning.

She rounds on Páll, who is still rubbing his jaw and holding his sleeve to his lip to staunch the blood. 'Why are you here?' She wants to embrace him, but perhaps he will disappear, and she will find herself clutching the air and trembling. 'How did you — ?'

'You *know* him?' Jón cuts in, his voice steel.

'Yes, Páll was . . . is . . .' She rubs her eyes. 'We grew up together,' she finishes lamely.

'We were like siblings — is that not so, Rósa?' He loops an arm around her shoulders; her whole body hums with life.

196

She nods mutely. *Siblings.*

Pétur straightens, though his face is tight with pain; his injured hand hangs limp. With his good hand, he holds the flickering torch closer to Páll's face. '*You!* I saw you a week ago. In Skálholt. You were asking about Rósa. And you questioned me.'

'Questioned you?' Jón rounds on Pétur.

Pétur shuffles his feet. 'Only about the farm. He is barely more than a boy.'

'A boy who has *followed* you here,' Jón says. 'A boy who has travelled more than a week on foot and with traders, because of what *you* told him.'

'I told him *nothing*!' Pétur's voice is raw; his injured hand trembles.

'You said *something* undoubtedly,' Jón growls, through gritted teeth. He turns to Páll. 'We are preparing for a bitter winter, and I do not have time to host you, forgive me. You will return to Skálholt tomorrow. There may be a trader's cart.'

Páll's face falls and Rósa cannot prevent herself interrupting. 'I will look after him, Jón. It will take none of your time. I will —'

'*You* will be silent!' Jón's voice is like a slap.

Rósa recoils. Páll draws a sharp breath. She can feel his body brace.

Please don't! Please. She stares at his face

197

and he glances at her, then gives a tight nod.

'I mean,' Jón continues softly, 'that you have many duties. You will exhaust yourself, *elskan.*' The endearment is loaded with menace.

Rósa is about to protest, but Páll interrupts, with forced brightness, 'I shall be no trouble. I repair roofs, but work is scarce in Skálholt. I came here to work for you, learning how to fish and how to trade.' He is lying, she can tell, but he smiles at Jón with the charm that used to convince the women of Skálholt that he had not raided their hen-house though his sleeves bulged with eggs.

Jón scowls.

'I am a fast learner,' Páll says smoothly. 'I can put my hand to any task.'

'I have Pétur to help me.'

'But you have so many to provide for, now you are sending food to Skálholt, too. There is little enough to go around there. My neighbours Snorri and Margrét are eating enough bread for five people between them. Fattening themselves for winter while I go hungry.' He slaps a hand against the flat muscles of his stomach.

Why are you lying? For a moment, Rósa dares to hope that Páll might have followed her to rescue her. But then she frowns: even if he truly had pursued her here, he couldn't take her away from her husband. The thought is a child's dream, drawn straight from the Sagas.

'So you come begging for more?' Jón says. 'I send enough to Skálholt.'

'I'm no beggar. I would like to learn a trade. And you are the most skilled and powerful man I know.'

Rósa almost smiles.

Pétur glowers. 'Learn some other trade, back in Skálholt.'

Páll's grin doesn't waver. 'I have heard of your skill too, Pétur. Come, let me stay. You will gather twice the food for this winter with my help. You will barely know I am here. I will be your shadow, except . . . a shadow that catches fish.'

Jón and Pétur smile reluctantly, and Rósa allows herself to breathe. *Please. Please!*

But then Jón sighs and rubs his beard. 'I cannot —'

Rósa steps forward, trembling, and touches Jón's arm. He freezes. 'He has travelled far, Jón.'

He looks at her hand.

She tightens it on his arm. 'We *cannot* send him away.'

'I must.'

'But,' Rósa clutches his tunic, 'would you send my own blood into the cold? What if the snows . . . ?' She blinks back tears.

Jón closes his eyes and rubs his temples with his fingers. 'I . . .'

'Jón!' Pétur gives a warning growl.

Rósa takes a breath, then presses her body against Jón's. The thud of his heart makes his muscles tremble, as if in rage. 'Please, Jón. I ask so little of you.'

Jón sighs and turns to Páll. 'I may need some help. Pétur's arm pains him.'

'It is nothing.'

'You may stay two days. You will sleep in the barn with the horses.'

'Jón!' Rósa cries. 'He must stay in the croft.'

'Do not test me, Rósa,' Jón says.

'Jón!' Pétur snaps, his lips pressed into a thin line. He nurses his hand still, as though he is cradling a wounded creature.

Jón allows himself to be pulled to one side. The hiss of the men's angry whispering thrums through the dark. Rósa hears the words *injury, foolish, madness.*

Páll peers at her. 'Are you well, Rósa? You look thin.'

'And *you* look dirty.'

He chuckles. 'Skálholt has not been the same without you to insult me.'

I have missed you too, she thinks. She hadn't known how much. It is as if she had lost all feeling in a limb and learned to ignore its awkward numbness, but now the sensation is returning: wholeness bubbles through her. She glances at Jón. She must not smile at Páll so in front of him.

'How is your pabbi?' she asks lightly.

'He is well.'

'I am surprised he could spare you.'

Even in the half-darkness, Rósa sees his eyes flinch from hers. He has not told his pabbi then, or has left Skálholt in defiance of Bjartur's wishes. Rósa does not know whether this should make her happy or wary.

The men are still arguing, Pétur gesturing wildly.

Páll scrubs his hands through his hair. 'I am to return to Skálholt, then.'

'My husband is very private . . .' She trails off. How to justify Jón's strangeness?

A jagged breeze scoops past them. Rósa shivers and pulls her cloak more closely about her.

'Here, take mine.' Páll starts to untie it, but Rósa shakes her head. She judges her every movement with Jón's scowling eyes.

Páll's gaze is fixed on her face. She knows what he is thinking: not so long ago, he would have wrapped his arms around her to warm her. She would have leaned into his body until the shivering stopped.

He takes a step towards her, but she gives a single shake of her head; he stops, and Rósa exhales. The pain of keeping him at a distance is lessened by the exultation that he had listened to her. She has become so used to being invisible and mute.

Jón is gesticulating at Pétur, who is trying to flex his arm, but drawing sharp breaths with every attempted movement.

Jón gives a savage growl, then strides back to clap Páll on the shoulder, teeth clenched in a smile. 'Well, Pétur is an invalid, so I need help. You will sleep in the barn?'

Páll smiles and claps Jón on the back in return. 'A barn will be luxury after so many nights sleeping in chilly caves.'

Pétur hangs back, tight-jawed, his arm folded across his chest.

Jón gestures for Pétur to show Páll to the barn. He nods. 'Follow me.'

Páll flashes a quick smile at Rósa and is gone.

'Return home, Rósa,' Jón says. 'You are cold.' He lays a hand on her back and pushes her towards the lonely croft on the hill.

'I would like . . .' she begins.

But Jón has already turned away.

She drags herself back to the smothering

warmth of the empty croft and curls up on her bed.

Páll is here. Páll! She can barely believe it, has to pinch her leg to check she hasn't dreamed it. She draws out the cold glass woman and the runestone Mamma gave her. She clutches the stone until it seems to draw the heat from her body, until it feels like a heart, throbbing with warm life.

But along with her excitement is the creeping knowledge that she must be even more careful now. Jón will be watching them.

The day after Páll arrives, Rósa wakes to find that the men have gone out on the boat early — even Pétur, with his damaged arm. She remembers how, as he had tried to flex his fingers, he had gasped, then drawn his sleeve back to reveal muscles that were oddly bunched and twisted. Surely that injury couldn't have been caused by the brief scuffle with Páll. Pétur had looked at his arm with lip-curling loathing and, when he caught her staring, scowled.

She looks out to sea. Páll's presence is like sudden sunlight on the horizon. Even the creaks and groans of the croft do not jolt through her like alarm calls: she climbs up to the darkness of the loft, and the rustling she hears behind the door seems, for a moment, reassuring, like an old wound that no longer pains her but reminds her that she is alive.

Rósa tries again to write a letter, but gets no further than *Dear Mamma.* What could she say? That Páll has arrived, and the sight of him makes her blood sing in her veins? That last night she dreamed she returned to Skálholt with him? That the scrabbling from the loft has become a familiar madness? That she feels as if she is turning into someone else, as if Anna's ghost is filling her lungs with every breath?

She walks the hundred paces to the pithouse but, like the loft, it is locked — a bulky padlock hangs on the door: a solid iron bar with a complicated mechanism beneath. She has never seen such a thing, except on the church coffers in Skálholt where the relics were kept. Pabbi had traded the lock with a Dane.

She looks over her shoulder, draws the runestone from her pocket and smashes it against the lock, hard. It remains solid and unyielding.

She trudges further down the hill and peers out to sea. Among the scattering of islands and the broken rocks, a tiny boat bobs.

Páll. His smile. His warmth. But in two days he will return home.

The air is metallic and heavy with the threat of snow. She stares at the grey clouds, willing them to unload upon the hills, so that Páll will not be able to leave. But the clouds stay distant, cold and full.

Shoals of cod and herring skim the peninsula, and, for two days, the men row out on Jón's boat, Pétur working one-handed. They return after dark, blue with cold, smelling of salt and fish, but triumphant. They heave the nets into the storeroom and scatter the glistening bodies as if they are spilling treasure.

She has had no chance to speak to Páll alone — as soon as she tries, either Jón or Pétur calls him away. Páll gives her an apologetic smile and leaps to do their bidding.

Jón must be pleased with Páll, because the two days pass and still her husband allows him to remain. Rósa dares not ask what Jón plans, or how long he will let Páll stay.

Jón does not invite him into the croft, and Rósa goes down to the beach more and more often, scanning the water for a sign of the boat.

On the sixth day, after she has watched them row away, Katrín trudges across the sand. She stands ten paces away.

'Look ahead. Jón will be watching. People wonder about your guest.'

Rósa looks at Páll, sitting in the boat. He flashes a smile at her. Jón frowns and Rósa wills Páll to turn away. 'His name is Páll,' she mutters. 'He's my mother's cousin's son. Jón is allowing him to help.'

'Strange,' murmurs Katrín. 'Such a change in Jón . . . It will have the villagers whispering witchcraft.'

'Jón would never believe them! And I would say . . .'

'Hush, I was jesting.' Katrín folds her arms and gives Rósa a measuring look. 'But men are jealous creatures and your face is an open book. Take care Jón does not see that look.'

'Oh.' Rósa flushes and turns back to the sea. The boat is a dot in the distance. Overhead, frenzied birds wheel and call, eager for easy pickings.

Katrín's eyes are creased with concern. 'You look thin and tired. Weary people make mistakes.'

Rósa would like to confide in Páll, but she remembers Katrín's words, about how she must be careful, how her face is easily read. So she avoids Páll's eye, and when he speaks to her, she mutters monosyllabic responses.

He frowns in confusion, then anger.

On the seventh evening, Jón brings Páll into the kitchen and asks Rósa to feed them all. Páll behaves like a man she has never met: he laughs with the others, his easy familiarity mirroring their brusqueness.

Jón catches her watching and smiles. 'He is a fine young man. Puts me in mind of myself ten years ago. He will go far.'

Is *this* why Jón is allowing him to stay? As an apprentice, of sorts?

That night, the men go back out to the barn to sleep, and Rósa sits in the kitchen, staring at the table.

Suddenly there is a figure in the doorway. Rósa jumps, then sees it is Páll.

'Should I return to Skálholt?'

'I . . . Why would you?'

He walks into the kitchen and stands in front of the stove. 'You do not want me here. And I don't wish to make you un-happy. I will leave.' He turns to go.

207

'No!' She stands and grabs his hand, without thinking. He turns, his face suddenly a handspan from hers. 'Please stay,' she whispers.

'Then you must stop glaring at me so.'

She sighs. 'I don't want Jón to become . . . suspicious.'

His face softens. 'Suspicious of what?' He moves a step closer. 'We have done nothing.'

She nods. She dares not look up at his face, his eyes. She thinks of Katrín's warnings. But Páll's hand slides up her arm, over her shoulder and around the back of her neck and she cannot help leaning into him. His face is so close she can feel the heat of his breath as he exhales —

There is a *bang* from outside the croft, and Rósa jumps away from him, as if dropping a hot pan.

Páll's eyes are wide with alarm. He starts to speak, but Rósa puts a finger to her lips, then picks up a cloth as Jón walks into the croft.

'Ah, Páll,' he says, his eyes darting back and forth between him and Rósa. 'You must help with the sheep. Pétur's arm pains him.'

'Of course,' Páll says.

Jón waits, watching him, and when Páll doesn't move, he growls, 'Go on, then.'

Páll goes out into the dark, leaving Jón

and Rósa alone. Jón walks very close to her and she freezes. His massive bulk makes her think of the stories of Arctic bears.

'You are a sensible woman, are you not? A good wife.'

'I hope so.'

'And good wives know when to stay silent.'

She nods. Her throat is dry.

He takes her hand and kisses her fingertips, one by one. 'I am fortunate to have found a woman I can trust absolutely.'

She says nothing. His hands are rough. Calluses from the fishing cords, from the scythe. Calluses from wielding a knife.

He steps closer to her, pressing the length of his body against hers, wrapping his arms around her in what should feel like an affectionate embrace but pinions her arms to her sides. Her heart batters unevenly in her chest.

'Look at me,' he murmurs.

She raises her eyes to his.

'What were you talking of with Páll?'

Her mind whirrs. 'Only about when we were children.' She swallows. 'We used to go from one croft to another, begging for *skyr*.'

'You were hungry?'

She nods.

'Ah, well, you aren't hungry now. I provide

everything you need, do I not?'

He kisses her forehead. She stays very still and waits for him to release her.

After Jón has left, Rósa sits in the darkness of the croft, remembering the feel of Páll's hand on her neck, reliving the moment to smother the noises from above and the voices in her head.

Rósa sees Páll less and less as the men spend more time preparing for the harsh winter ahead. He joins Jón and Pétur to sleep in the barn with the sheep, cows and horses; the animals must grow used to being inside before winter. Jón and Páll take turns to separate sheep that have locked horns in frustration and, after seven days, Jón tells Páll that he may stay for the winter. Rósa's heart flips in her chest and she smiles at Páll, until she notices Jón staring at her. She lowers her gaze and returns to gathering stray tufts of wool.

Later, when darkness has settled around the croft and Rósa sits alone in the *baðstofa*, waiting for sleep, she hears a scratching of metal on wood. She bolts upright, heart hammering, then realizes that the sound is coming from outside.

She wraps a shawl about her shoulders and steps out into the gloom, quashing thoughts of some spirit risen from the sea. She stumbles, twisting her ankle in the dark, and gasps. The pain is real. Everything else is just stories.

The scratching again, and a figure crouched low, next to the window.

'Who's there?' she hisses.

The figure turns and stands: it is taller than a woman should be, and broader. It towers over her and she opens her mouth to scream.

'Rósa!' It is Páll.

She crumples forward and stifles a sob. He reaches for her, lifts her before she falls and holds her against his chest. 'Forgive me, I didn't mean to startle you.' His voice is muffled by her hair and she feels him press his lips to her forehead.

'I . . .' She finds she cannot speak. His fingers move across her cheek tentatively, as if he is touching something impossibly fragile.

She pushes him away. 'Jón?'

'In the barn. Pétur with him.'

'You must go back. It is too dangerous.'

'To talk to you? To comfort you? Jón could not protest at that. He is no monster.' He takes her hand between his.

She closes her eyes. She cannot tell Páll that her husband's every glance sets a hum of fear across her skin. Páll will ask what Jón has done to terrify her, and she will have to reply that he has done nothing, nothing at all. But that sometimes, when she looks into his eyes, it is like staring into the depths of the river Hvítá, which used to drown people with indiscriminate brutality: women and children would disappear, and the river would rush remorselessly onwards, its churning waters unchanged.

Instead, she says to Páll, 'People gossip in the village. And Jón is mindful of his reputation. I would not have him send you back to Skálholt.'

He sighs and drops her hand. 'You must find a way to see me during the day, then. Out in the open.'

She nods, aware that she is agreeing to dip her toes into the churning waters.

Páll leans forward and kisses her cheek. She gasps, but before she can speak, he has turned to walk down the hill to the barn. From the set of his shoulders, she knows he will be laughing: he has always enjoyed danger.

After Páll has stayed for nearly two weeks, Jón introduces him to the villagers: he addresses them at the end of a church service on the bare bone of the hill outside the

croft. They crane their necks as Jón introduces Páll: 'My new man. Blood relative to
my wife.'

Páll smiles as Jón claps him on the back.
Pétur hangs back, his jaw hard.

Jón stands tall, staring at the villagers.
'Remember, the Bible tells us to be obedient. We must obey our God and listen to
those who have authority over us. Indolence
is a sin. Gluttony is a sin. Lust is a sin. Idle
gossip is a sin. God tells us to go forth and
to sin no more, for those who sin will burn
in the fiery pit of Hell for eternity.'

There is a sighing and a rustling from the
congregation, like birds fluffing their feathers before settling in to endure the cold.

Afterwards, Katrín passes close to Rósa
and murmurs, 'That was a warning.'

'To me?'

'A warning to all of us to remain obedient
and keep our distance.'

Something black, flapping in the breeze,
catches Rósa's eye. She looks up and, like a
raven, shadow-feathered and glint-eyed,
Egill sits on a distant rock, his gaze fixed on
her. Olaf, his lackey, stands behind him.
Olaf is as broad as he is tall; his face is the
puce of liver sausage, his arms, like shanks
of mutton, folded across his broad chest.

Olaf leans in close to Egill and mutters

something. Egill nods. Both men continue to stare at her.

When they are not out on the boat, Jón and Pétur spend the days schooling Páll. There is plenty to be done, what with ploughing the fields and the endless task of caring for the sheep. There are lambs to be weaned, ewes to be dipped and the wool to be clipped from around the tail, ready for mating. They show Páll once, then leave him. Rósa suspects it is a test, but it allows her to spend time with him, in the open, as they had decided. It allows her to drink in the sight of him and imagine, for a moment, the life she might have lived.

Páll struggles with the ewes: wrapping his arms around their heaving bodies, barely managing to clip a finger's width of wool before the beasts break free.

After both his tunics have been ripped, Páll growls, 'This is impossible.'

Rósa is patching his tunic, where a horn has torn the wool. 'Let me help.'

'Be serious. There must be someone else Jón can find to do this. Some men can have the whole fleece off in three breaths.' He clutches at a ewe. She dodges him and charges past, knocking him over yet again.

Rósa tugs the thread tighter. 'Jón dislikes

outsiders.'

Páll grins. 'Every Icelander dislikes outsiders. But I have seen no illegal English merchants in these parts, no stranded Basque whalers for him to massacre.'

'How can you laugh at such a thing?' Rósa thinks of the village where the whalers had become stranded; on the instructions of the village *goði,* the people had slit the throat or sliced open the stomach of every man, then rowed the bloodied bodies far out to sea. The corpses of dead whalers washed up on the western shores of Iceland for weeks. 'Jón is not a villain, as that *goði* was.'

'Of course he is not.' Páll's smile is uncertain. 'That is why I jested. Jón is a good man, surely. And the village leaders often distrust outlanders.'

Rósa purses her lips and stops sewing just long enough to glance over her shoulder. The men are out of earshot, down the hill. 'Jón mistrusts nearly everyone.'

Páll stands and brushes himself down. 'Why did he marry *you,* then, Rósa from Skálholt? And his first wife was from elsewhere too, was she not?'

'Near Thingvellir.'

'And I'm more of an outsider than a villager. He allows *me* to stay.'

'Pétur's arm. You work hard and . . .' Rósa

215

pricks her finger and winces. Jón seems to prefer outsiders, trusting strangers more than the villagers.

'Does no one from the settlement ever come up here?' Páll asks.

'He goes to their homes every week to pray with them and offer advice. But he does not like them to visit the croft.' She puts her bleeding finger into her mouth.

'Why?'

She feels a surge of irritation. Doesn't he know how dangerous it can be to ask questions? 'They have the *prestur* too. Jón is their *goði,* not their nursemaid.'

Páll smiles. 'It does not baffle you that your husband was chosen as *goði* when he wishes to spend his time alone?'

She sets down her sewing and looks at the barn doorway, where a rectangle of sea is perfectly framed. It promises other worlds, far away. But for Rósa the ocean might as well be a depthless picture upon a wall.

Páll nudges her boot with his toe. 'More fool Jón to trust the craftiest egg-thief in Skálholt. Oh, come, Rósa, I thought that might make you smile.'

'I am trying to patch your tunic without stitching the sleeves together.'

His grin fades and his gaze drops to her mottled skin and swollen knuckles. She

216

resists the urge to sit on her hands.

He leans towards her. 'You work hard.'

She keeps her voice brisk, keeps stitching. 'There is much work to do.'

He nods. 'And have you friends here?'

'There is a woman. Katrín. She is . . . kind. But I am busy.'

His warm gaze settles on her face. 'You always liked to hide behind books. Do you ever think of them? And your writing?'

She smiles thinly. 'No time for books here, Páll.' She thinks of the scribbled scraps of writing she had brought with her from Skálholt. But people have been burned as witches for writing poetry: she imagines Jón's rage if he found them. She had held her writing over the *hlóðir,* but hadn't been able to burn it; instead, she had stuffed her words, along with her letters, into the gaps in the floor.

Now Páll says, 'And do you miss reading?'

She clenches her jaw. She misses everything about her old life: the reading and writing, the long days of freedom. 'I miss Mamma.' Again, the tug of longing to return to her, or at least send a letter. But she would have to write a list of lies, or Sigridúr would be tramping over the freezing mountains, risking her own life in her rage.

'Sigridúr was well when I saw her last,'

217

Páll says. 'The moss tea has done her the world of good. She has meat now, every day. And warm clothes.'

Rósa reminds herself of it every time she wants to run from the croft and hide in the hills.

Páll sits next to her on a bundle of hay sheaves. He smells of sheep and sweat. 'They say Jón's last wife died of loneliness.'

She fiddles with a loose thread and stitches it back in. She can't look at his face. 'You cannot *die* of loneliness, Páll.'

He looks at her for three breaths, then rises to try to capture a ewe.

Rósa holds the glass woman in her pocket, running her fingers over the perfect, smooth lines.

Over the afternoon, time stretches, and Rósa forgets everything except the barn, the animals and Páll. He turns to smile at her every time he releases one of the shorn animals and she smiles in return. They could almost be back in Skálholt.

Occasionally, Rósa holds a hoof, or strokes a flank. It becomes a rhythm: the weight of the ewe between them, the warm, greasy wool coming away under the sharp metal, then the ewe struggling to right herself before they finally release her.

Rósa watches his face until her eyes sting; she laughs at his jokes and, when he puts a hand on her arm, she allows the weight of her body to rest against him.

It is only when a dark shadow falls across the doorway, cutting off the rectangle of light, that Rósa sees Jón staring at them, his arms crossed over his chest. She has no idea how long he has been watching, but her stomach jolts and she recoils from Páll.

'The sheep are nearly shorn,' she says.

Jón walks deliberately slowly into the barn and, standing very close to her, says, 'You shouldn't be here, Rósa. You might easily be hurt.'

Rósa shoots a frantic glance at Páll, who is about to speak. When he catches her eye, he nods and closes his mouth. Rósa exhales.

Jón looks the ewes over and gives Páll an approving clap on the back. 'Fine work. We will be glad to have you this winter.'

Rósa turns away to pick up her sewing, still shaking. If she closes her eyes, she can still feel those moments with Páll's hands on hers, his arm alongside hers, his laughter uncurling in her ear. She runs the memories through her mind again and again, like fiddling with perfect pearls on a fragile thread.

The next morning she feels, for the first

time in weeks, as though she can breathe. Páll will be here this winter. The thought is like a flicker of light in the gloom.

So she is unprepared, when she is scrubbing the tabletop, for Jón to appear in the kitchen and sit on the bench. He should be in the field, but he watches her, tapping his forefinger against his lip.

His gaze makes her cheeks burn. She offers him a timorous smile, but his eyes are flint. Finally, he says, 'Do you know your Commandments by heart, Rósa?'

She doesn't pause in her scrubbing. 'All Christians do.'

'And you obey the Commandments?'

A finger of sweat creeps down her spine. 'I hope so.'

He leans forward. 'Tell me the Commandments, Rósa.'

She wipes the hair back from her forehead with her wrist. 'Honour the Lord; keep the Sabbath; honour your parents; do not blaspheme or be covetous; do not steal or commit murder or — or adultery . . .' Her eyes flash to his face, but he is impassive.

'And?' he murmurs.

Her mind scrabbles. 'Do not bear false witness.'

'Yes.' He stands and walks over to her, slowly. 'Do not deceive, Rósa. So, I ask you again, do you keep the Commandments?'

'I . . .' Her mouth is dry. He is so broad. His body emanates heat, and she finds she has leaned backwards until the wall is hard against her spine.

'Deceit may take many forms, Rósa. Hiding your thoughts, for instance. Or hiding other things.' She blinks at him, thinking of yesterday, when he must have seen her body close to Páll's. Or perhaps he knows of her conversations with Katrín, her disobedience in going down to the village. A man in Skálholt once beat his wife to death because he suspected her of disobeying him. Not a soul protested when they heard her scream.

'I am not hiding anything.' She cannot hold his gaze.

He nods slowly, then leans forward and puts his mouth very close to her ear. 'You will write to your mamma. Tell her you are well. I will send the letter.'

Her stomach turns to water. He raises his eyebrows and she whispers, 'Thank you.'

He smiles and pats her hand. Then he is gone. As she watches him striding up the hill, she cannot stop her hands trembling. As soon as he is out of sight, she runs to the bed and crouches down.

No letters. They are all gone. Her stories too. The stories that could be evidence of witchcraft; the stories that could see her burned.

And then her unease turns to horror.

No knife.

JÓN

When I was a child, I imagined *evil* to be some dark force — a cloven-hoofed and horned beast eager to lead man into temptation. I imagined a creature like my pabbi, sunk in his cups: bloat-faced, spitting threats and violence. But life has taught me that darkness resides in every human heart, a tiny smudge of sooty smut on even the whitest of souls. And I must admit that the same stain marks my humanity, as it does the soul of every man and woman.

With my every breath, I have fought that festering kernel of darkness, which rots within my spirit, growing with each thought.

Now, after everything that has passed, I am alone in my cave, near Thingvellir. I curl into my own body, shuddering, and I remember.

I have lived in the same croft all my life.

223

When I was a child, it was a pinched and draughty place. The walls crumbled and the turf roof seemed always on the point of collapse — exposed roots snaked from the soil, revealing the rotten skeleton of the broken beams beneath.

My pabbi traded the food that should have filled our bellies; he swigged ale all day and gulped *brennevín* at the first sign of darkness. He was a fisherman, and we also had a small field. But he left the boat to rot on the beach. What crops he planted withered from lack of water or were smothered by the weeds he allowed to rampage.

We were thin and dirty. The greedy *goði* taxed us on what little food my pabbi could produce. The people of Stykkishólmur avoided us, as if our poverty were some infection. We were but a step away from the vagrants and exiles who were left to beg by the roads until they were murdered by the cold and buried by the snow.

I felt a burning shame on looking at Pabbi's drink-softened features, his slack jaw and bleary eyes, his drunken animal twitches. And I despised the cries from inside the croft when he beat Mamma, dull, hopeless calls, wordless, and without expectation of response. They were always cut short when he threw her onto the bed and clamped his hand over her mouth, then used his bulk to crush her, while he yanked up her shift. I watched through the gaps in the turf, helpless.

She made no sound, beyond the rhythm of her breath, which matched his thrusts. Her eyes were fixed and blank. At last, he would groan like a bull in pain, then collapse onto her. She would lie silent and unblinking, then ease herself from under him, tug down her skirts and return to patching his clothes.

I used to dream that I was not his child. I spent days staring across the sea, waiting for my true father to arrive — a brawny Danish trader. He would drown the drunken impostor who masqueraded as my father.

Mamma and Pabbi both died of sickness when I was fourteen summers. He killed them both — an infection from rotten fish he had stolen from another man's net. The smell of it had turned my stomach and I had refused to eat it, as had Mamma. Pabbi cuffed both of us about the head, spat, 'Ungrateful savage,' then threw me from the croft. After I had gone, he forced Mamma to eat the foul-smelling flesh and, drunk as he was, ate it himself. I returned under cover of darkness. They lay in the *baðstofa*, groaning; the room stank like a midden.

Pabbi was sprawled on the floor, spattered with his own shit and vomit. I ignored his groans and resisted the urge to kick him as I stepped over his writhing body to go to Mamma, who was barely moving on the bed.

Her breathing was shallow, her mouth crusted with sour vomit. As I drew closer, she hunched over and retched, bringing up green, rank-smelling bile. I tried to encourage her to drink, but she brought everything back up, time and again.

Her eyes were large and frightened. She had spent her life being hurled about and pummelled by a tyrant. Nothing and no one had ever saved her, and this time would be no different.

I held her hand as her last breath grew chill against my cheek.

I felt too hollow for tears. I shut her eyes and kissed her cooling lips.

'Jón.' Pabbi's voice was an agonized rasp. He held his hand out for the pitcher of water, which was just out of his reach.

I watched him dragging himself towards it, breath tearing from him.

At the last moment, just as he was about to clutch it, I kicked out and smashed it. The water sloshed onto the floor. Pabbi gave

226

a low moan and tried to suck some moisture from where it seeped into the earth beneath him. His mouth filled with dirt and he retched.

He looked up at me, eyes burning. 'Water.'

I watched him, paralysed by horror at my own lack of pity.

His expression changed. 'I'll whip you . . . until you bleed . . . you miserable wretch. *Water!*'

Heart pounding, I shook my head. Alongside my rattling fear was a rising euphoria. He couldn't touch me now.

His lips curled back in a snarling rictus. 'Should have drowned you . . . years ago . . . useless whelp —' His words were cut off as he coughed and vomited, then collapsed, face down, into his own mess.

I couldn't help it: I smiled. My poor dead mamma would have felt safe, if she could have seen this. Perhaps if she had known that the man who had tormented her for years was no more than a bag of rotting flesh, spitting curses, she might have smiled too.

I fetched his *brennevín* from the pantry and sat down. At the sight of the bottle, his eyes lit up. He licked his lips. I drank. As the clear, sour liquid loosened my thoughts, I felt the stirring of something more intoxi-

227

cating than the alcohol.

For a long time, Pabbi wept, dry, hacking sobs, as he tried to struggle towards me, towards the drink. Then he fell silent, the only sign of life the snorting of his breath against the earth floor.

As darkness dropped from the sky, like a stone, even that noise quieted.

I leaned in close to his face. 'I hope it pains you,' I hissed.

RÓSA

After the disappearance of the letters and the knife, Rósa creeps around the croft, avoiding Jón's gaze. When he catches her eye, she shrinks. She feels the compression of her own spinning thoughts on every breath. Once again, she tries to write to Mamma, but she rips up the paper and burns it: reading her thoughts is like cracking open the mind of a madwoman.

The long, lonely hours while the men are on the boat are punctuated by the odd creaks and flutterings from the loft. At least when the men are in the croft they drown the noises.

The day after the knife and the letters disappear, she is standing at the door of the croft when she sees Páll walking towards her. Jón and Pétur are in the barn, but still she shakes her head and waves him away. Páll doesn't stop until he reaches the croft

229

and holds out the corner of his tunic, where there is a jagged hole.

She tuts. '*You* did this, with a knife. On purpose.'

'Slander! I didn't use a knife.'

'But —'

'I used a nail.' He steps closer.

She exhales slowly, as if breathing through pain. 'Jón will —'

Páll's grin fades. 'You fear him.' His voice is suddenly hard.

'I . . .' She can't bring herself to deny it.

'Yesterday when he came to the barn you *flinched*, Rósa.'

'I —'

'Has he hurt you?'

'No, never, it is simply . . .'

Páll narrows his eyes. 'He has threatened you?'

'He —'

'If he has threatened you, I'll kill him.'

Rósa puts her hands over her mouth. 'No! No, you cannot.' She imagines Páll striking her husband, imagines Jón brushing him off, like a bear cuffing a wolf about the head. Then Pétur would hold Páll down and Jón would take the knife and —

'No! I . . . Would you . . .'

Páll looks at her, waiting.

'If I were to leave, would you . . . You

230

would come with me?'

'Leave? But —'

'Not because I am frightened of Jón, but I miss Mamma and . . .' She trails off, helplessly, willing him to understand.

He nods slowly. 'I would do whatever you needed me to.' He leans into her and rests his forehead against hers for the space of two shuddering breaths, then turns to go.

Rósa watches him walk away, then stands staring at the empty space where he had been. The wind whips her hair around her face. The air scrapes over her skin with the promise of the coming ice and the winter snows that will enclose her if she does not leave soon.

Somewhere behind her, a raven caws. A single raven is a bad omen, they say.

The next morning, when she sees Gudrun by the stream, Rósa could almost weep with gratitude. The woman is rude, but even Katrín admits that she can predict the weather with uncanny accuracy.

Rósa calls a greeting and helps Gudrun to draw a bucket of water. 'Will the snow come early this year?'

Gudrun squints at her. 'The winds are tricksters, who can say? I smell sudden storms — not good weather for travel.'

Rósa forces her voice to remain level as she picks up Gudrun's bucket and offers to carry it to her croft. Gudrun smiles and clutches Rósa's arm with her bony claw as they walk down the hill. 'Nice to see a wife of Jón's with manners,' Gudrun wheezes. 'Anna would sooner have spat on me than helped me.'

'Katrín liked her, I think,' Rósa ventures.

'Ha! And Katrín calls *me* blind! Even when Anna lost her mind, wandering the hills, gibbering like a madwoman, Katrín claimed it was a fever.'

Rósa feels a chill. 'What did Anna say?'

Gudrun narrows her eyes. 'Things she imagined. Better not to listen to the rantings of a lunatic. Madness is a sickness.'

Rósa nods, dry-mouthed, and when she returns to the empty croft, she can almost hear Anna whispering. Or is it a noise from the loft? Or in her own mind? She presses her hands against her skull and curls up with her back to the wall. Once the pounding in her head has ceased, she climbs the ladder and puts her lips to the door.

'Who's there?' she hisses. 'Anna?' But there is no movement, nothing but the thud of her blood in her ears.

Even the ghosts have deserted her now.

■ ■ ■ ■

That evening, Jón sets down his spoon and asks Rósa if she has written to Mamma yet.

She flushes and shakes her head.

'You must. Tell her how well you are.'

'I will write soon,' Rósa whispers.

'Are you certain you have not written already?' Jón stares at her for too long, and her skin crawls. As he reaches into his tunic pocket, she knows what he must have. Still, it is a shock when he spreads them out on the table: one letter after another — fifteen in all. Each filled with blots and scribbles and pools of ink where she has wept onto the paper. He opens them in turn, his large fingers tracing over her words. *Doubt . . . Danger . . . Something monstrous . . . I do not trust him . . .*

Her heartbeat clamours in her ears.

Jón places his hand on hers. 'It is hard to know what to write, when you have so much to tell.' His voice is soft, his tone silken. 'But your mamma doesn't need to have every detail to share with the neighbours, does she?'

Mutely, Rósa shakes her head.

He gestures towards the scraps of the Sagas. 'You shouldn't put yourself in . . .

danger.' Jón takes a step towards her and laces his fingers with her own. Her hand feels tiny in his. Her skin is so thin and pale, her veins blue underneath.

He squeezes her fingers. 'Your mamma needs to know you are happy — you *are* happy, aren't you, Rósa?'

She nods again.

'Good. I took the liberty of writing to her for you, as you struggled to find the right words for her.'

Ice water trickles down her spine.

'I sent the letter south with a trader this morning. I do not think there will be more traders for some time — I expect heavy snow. A blizzard. But I will keep you safe here.' He embraces her and kisses the top of her head. 'So you need not worry about what to tell your mamma. And she will spread word of your happiness to her neighbours, *elskan.*'

As he pulls her close, the handle of the knife in his belt presses against her stomach. She glances down. It is, unmistakably, the knife from under the bed.

Two nights later, when Pétur and Páll are out on the boat, the night is pierced by a desolate howling.

It is Jón who hears it first. He creeps from

the barn into the croft and wakes Rósa, pressing a hand over her mouth. 'Sssh!' he hisses, his eyes wide and wild.

'What?'

'It sounds like a fox, except . . .'

The sound is uncanny. It is the bawl of a desperate child when the air is being crushed from its lungs.

He beckons her and she pads from the *baðstofa,* pulling on her shawl.

Another howl tears the darkness, as though the earth is being eviscerated. Rósa snatches up her knitting needles — a child's imagining of a sword.

Jón clasps his knife, the blade now clean and gleaming. He is white-knuckled and grim. Rósa's desire to run is almost overwhelming. She wishes for Páll's presence — even Pétur's harsh sarcasm would feel like protection. But both men are far out to sea so Rósa finds herself in the dark, alone with her knife-wielding husband. He makes her go in front of him and she keeps picturing the blade in his hand. They tread over the ground where she remembers seeing Anna's grave. She imagines Jón carrying his wife's body out at night and digging, then lowering it into the earth and covering it with soil.

He had told everyone she had died of a fever.

Rósa stifles a sob and forces one foot in front of the other.

They follow the screams. As they draw nearer, the noise sounds increasingly like a child being savaged. Rósa has her knitting needles pressed so hard into a palm that, days later, she will be able to trace the imprint of the wood on the whorls of her skin.

In her other hand, she grips the oil lantern, holding it high over her head, as Jón has instructed. The light wavers, no matter how she tries to steady her hand.

Behind her, she can hear the huff of Jón's breathing. If she ran, how quickly would he catch her? She would have to drop the lantern and they would both be running through the dark. When she fell, he would be upon her.

As they near the boundary wall, they can hear rasping breaths — a demon? A spirit come to tempt them? Rósa tries not to think of the *huldufólk*: they will eat your heart in front of your eyes. The stories make grown men tremble.

The groaning howls are loud and high-pitched.

Rósa stops.

'Come, Rósa.' Jón's voice is terse. 'More light.'

She holds the lantern higher and the light picks out twin round mirrors of polished obsidian in the darkness.

Eyes.

A ghoul: a spirit, wailing. Rósa's heart leaps. But no! There is the scrabble of tiny paws battering the ground, an animal's desperate, panting panic.

'Steady.' Jón uses a lilting tone that calms the horses if they are skittish.

The light picks out the grey-brown coat, fading to winter-white, the delicate, vulpine face and the sharp white teeth in the snapping jaws. An Arctic fox pup, perhaps three months old. It has tried to scramble over the wall, but a rock has fallen on it, trapping its hind legs. It blinks at Rósa and she feels a clench of connection with the frantic creature. Suddenly she feels that her fate is somehow tied to that of the animal: if only she can free it, she will survive.

It throws back its head and screams, but in a voice like that of no animal Rósa has ever heard: the pain and crushing compression of the rock force its tone to the pitch of a tortured human. Rósa's blood freezes and momentarily slews to a halt.

'She's a beauty,' Jón breathes.

237

'A fishing cord?' Rósa whispers. 'I can wind it around her muzzle so she can't bite when you free her.'

'That pelt will be worth a fortune.' Jón raises the knife.

'No!' Without thinking, she puts her hand out, as if she is shielding her own skin and bone.

Jón grunts. 'Step away, Rósa. The pup is suffering. And that pelt will buy a whole herd of sheep.' He lifts the knife higher. The muscles in his arm and back are bunched. Rósa's stomach churns as she places her hand on his shoulder.

'But, Jón . . .' She swallows. 'You could — We should free her.'

He shrugs off her hand. 'She'll limp away and be ripped apart by ravens. This is a kindness.'

'But . . .' Rósa imagines the wild freedom of the open; she pictures the creature running for safety, returning to its pack.

'The leg is broken, the chest half crushed,' he says. 'Better a quick death.'

The fox pup snarls, legs flailing, paws battering a frantic, helpless beat.

Jón hefts the knife and takes a breath.

Rósa steps in front of her husband, in front of the blade. The metal is cold against her throat. She swallows.

238

'Move!' Jón hisses. And is it her imagination or does he increase the pressure on the blade?

Rósa shakes her head. She can feel her pulse in her chest, in her skull, in the tips of her fingers. Any woman who defies her husband should be punished. The slightest movement from him would cut her off, like a clipped length of wool. She imagines the icy metal, the struggle for breath, the burst of her blood.

'God's teeth, Rósa! *Move!*'

'No,' Rósa says, her voice flat and steady, as if she is certain, as if she is unafraid. 'I will not.' Then she reaches out, clasps the cold knife and pushes it to one side. While Jón gapes, she creeps towards the fox, trembling hand outstretched. Elation and fear bubble through her.

The fox's eyes are wild. It snarls and there is an acrid tang of sweat and blood and shit, summoning sharp images of the outhouse and used menstrual rags.

Rósa sinks her fingers into the dense pelt. The fur is soft and chill as meltwater. The dark eyes fix on hers. She will free it; they will both escape.

For a moment, Rósa allows herself to imagine turning and, taking Jón by surprise, snatching the knife from his hand and press-

239

ing it against his neck. She imagines how his eyes would widen, how his face would crumple, how he would beg and beg and —

Suddenly, Jón pushes her to the ground. He straddles the fox; there is a flash of steel and he slits the animal's throat. Hot blood splatters across Rósa's cheeks, over her tunic and shawl. She cries out, trying to clutch the creature's gaping throat, but Jón holds her back, one-handed. She struggles, but it is like fighting an avalanche. She collapses forward, gasping. Jón releases her and drops the knife. It is an arm's length from her hand. It would take only a moment to seize it. But no. No. You cannot fend off a landslide with a knife.

When she can bring herself to look up again, the fox pup has slumped to the ground, lips drawn back in a rictus of snarling fear, eyes still bright, but frozen.

Jón puffs as he lifts the stones and pulls the animal free. He doesn't look at her. 'Help me open the stomach. We'll keep the heart and liver. Leave the guts for the scavengers. Nothing wasted.'

Rósa silently obeys. The whiteness of her hands against the darkness of the blood and entrails is mesmerizing. Hands belonging to another woman? Crimsoning hands, capable and sure. She helps Jón to pull back the skin

240

and draw out the long ropes of the viscera and the stomach. It is hard, slippery work, not like the tiny innards of the fish, which slide out like perfect little jellies.

When it is done, and they have scattered the bowels away from the boundary wall, they trudge home, towards the pale dawn that slices through the darkness.

Jón hefts the fox as if it is a sack of oatmeal, or an unwieldy block of peat for the fire. Its coat gleams: the beautiful rare pelt, for which Danish traders will pay a fortune. Coin that will buy more food. Coin that will keep Jón as *goði*. Coin that will silence any whisperings.

Rósa slouches behind, dragging the lantern, clutching the knife, trying not to look at the fox's eyes, half open, glazed and already clouded. Trying not to imagine the clasped fist of the heart in the chest, still warm.

Jón swings the body into the barn, then strips off the skin with a tender focus, pausing occasionally to stroke the fur.

Rósa sways and nearly falls, imagining the cold blade shaving her own flesh from her bones.

Jón grunts as he separates the legs from the body. 'Go to bed, Rósa. You look ill.' The knife flashes in his hand.

241

Rósa's throat aches too much for speech. Only once she is out of earshot does she allow the sobs to escape. She bunches her fingers against her mouth to stifle the sound, but it bleeds out into the half-darkness. She crouches by the croft wall, leaning her forehead against the cold stone.

She cannot stop picturing that moment, when she had stood with the knife against her throat, when she had defied him. She had felt the strength in her own body, the hardness of her muscles, as she had stood staring at Jón. How much strength would it take to plunge that blade into her husband's throat? Rósa shakes her head to dismiss the image, but it reels through her brain, time and again. And yet, each time, just before the knife embeds itself in her husband's flesh, he reaches out with one hand, pins her down and she becomes the helpless fox pup under his hand as the icy metal opens her.

JÓN

Near Thingvellir, December 1686

The wind is cold, even in my cave, and I haven't eaten in days. Still, it barely matters, as long as I have energy enough to lift my knife. Besides, times past have taught me that fury, not strength, will drive a blade through flesh. And I have rage enough for ten men.

I wrap my cloak more closely about myself and watch the waxy sunlight moving over the grasses. Darkness will arrive soon.

After Pabbi died, I dragged him from the croft, dug a shallow hole on the hill and rolled his body into it. His head struck a rock and the side of his skull smashed, like an egg.

That was the only time I wanted him alive again — to feel that rock.

I covered him with the lightest scattering of soil, leaving his fingers exposed. For the

243

next week, the nights pulsed with the yips and cries of feasting foxes.

That first night, I crept back to the croft, swept every trace of Pabbi's mess and vomit from the floor, then curled up on the bed behind Mamma. I clasped her body, her cold flesh cooling my skin. I tried to weep, but no tears came, only a dry, hacking noise, like vomiting.

The moonlight scythed through the pock-marked walls, like God's ever-seeing eye, and I begged for absolution. For being too small, too weak, too gutless.

When morning came, Mamma's hair and skin were rimed with frost. When I tried to move, my limbs felt like the frozen earth beneath me. My joints crackled.

I forced myself to stand upright, to fetch a cloth and water, to rinse the mess from Mamma's mouth, to wash her blue fingers, praying all the while.

Then I picked her up and carried her outside — the empty husk of her skin and bones — and laid her by the stream while I began to dig. It was heavy work, and before long I was sweating, my limbs shaking. Still, I knew I must make the hole large enough that foxes wouldn't be able to reach her.

The voice from behind me made me jump. 'I am sorry.'

I spun about. It was a woman from the settlement. Her face was sombre as she looked at Mamma's body. I recalled her name — Katrín. She was never among those villagers who giggled and whispered, but had smiled kindly at me, when Pabbi was not looking. Mamma had once told me that, when I was a babe, she had helped to care for me until Pabbi had refused to allow anyone into the croft.

'She was a good woman.'

I nodded, chest too tight for speech, and continued to dig.

'You should bury her away from the stream.' The woman's voice was clear and she wore that same kindly smile.

I shook my head. 'She loved to watch the water.'

'The ground here is full of rocks.' Katrín pointed.

'No matter.' I set my jaw. 'I will bury her here.'

'It is not only the rocks. She will . . . So close to the stream, her body will . . . It is not clean . . .' Katrín pressed her fingers against her eyelids. Her voice was rapid and low. 'The stream. If you bury her here, her body will poison us all.'

I felt savage, weightless, cold. 'What of it?'

Katrín narrowed her eyes. Then she took

a large rock and began digging.

We worked in silence, my mind whirling. Was she so careless of the lives of the villagers that she would watch them die? Was I?

We dug and dug. Finally I threw down my spade and turned on her. 'Why do you help me?'

She set down her rock and wiped her hands on her tunic. Her gaze was steady. 'You look as if the wind might snap you. Grave-digging is hard work.'

'But you said Mamma's body will . . . Her body —' My throat felt raw. I clenched my jaw, then hid my face in my hands.

Katrín sat beside me and laid a hand on my shoulder while I wept.

Afterwards I sat, empty, staring at the blank stretch of the sea.

She turned to me. 'You are angry. Your anger hurts you?'

I nodded silently.

'You would like others to feel that pain.'

I nodded again, more slowly.

'Then,' she said, 'we will bury her here. Everyone will feel your grief.'

She picked up her rock again, and began to strike at the soil.

I clutched her wrist. 'We must bury her away from the stream.'

Katrín inclined her head. 'That hill is

246

beautiful. I will help you dig.'

The soil was looser and the grave was quickly finished. Still, we were both sweating heavily. We lowered Mamma's body in together, slowly, tenderly.

Before I scattered the soil, Katrín called, 'Stop! Look at the sea.'

I wiped my forehead and looked out at the horizon, where the sea was indistinguishable from the sky. Both were endless and old as the earth. The sea whispered — silver and savage and cold.

'She will be near water always,' Katrín said.

'Thank you,' I whispered. I asked again, 'Why do you help me?'

The reflection of the sea in her eyes made Katrín's expression uncanny, as if she could see some other, secret, world beyond this one.

'Your mamma was a good woman. You will be a good man. I know it.'

After I had buried my parents, I cleaned the croft and washed my clothes. I walked down to the village daily but the people stared at me, lips curled in revulsion.

I set to work alone, repairing Pabbi's fishing boat — it took weeks of foraging on the beach for driftwood, even though the boat

247

was only a small, two-oar vessel.

At night, I studied the Bible and used a stick to scratch out lines in the dirt, teaching myself to read and write by the verses I already knew from church. I practised writing phrases and numbers, only going to bed when the fish-oil in the lamp ran out, then rising before first light to work on the boat again.

I might have starved if Katrín hadn't brought me fish and *skyr* every day. When I refused, she poked me in the ribs. 'I'll not watch you work yourself to a skeleton. Looking at your bones puts me off my own food.'

Her rough humour made my eyes sting.

The other villagers did not say a word to me but watched from afar, squint-eyed and sour.

One day, when Katrín brought me food, I gestured to the watchers. 'Do they think I will harm you?'

'Perhaps.' She gave a wicked grin. 'Although not one would lift a finger to stop you, even if you leaped upon me and cut my throat.'

I blinked. 'They despise you too?'

'I am well liked. But these people, Jón — whispering warms them in the dark winters. They would watch their own grandmammas drowned by a merman for the sake of a good story.'

'My misery entertains them?'

'Your misery is not unusual. Find me a family where a pabbi has not drowned, or a babe has not died.'

I remembered that Katrín, also, had lost a husband to the sea and a daughter to the land. I nearly reached out to take her hand, but stopped myself.

'If I am no different,' I said, 'why do they stare?'

'This land will kill you, if it can. We Icelanders are forged of different metal from the soft foreigners — even the Barbary pirates did not stay long. Have you ever known a Danish trader to winter here from choice?'

I shrugged. How did this concern me, or the people's morbid curiosity?

'We seem strong, Jón, all of us, but we are like grass — we bend so the wind will not break us. *You* are like the sea: you surge forward again and again. See yourself now. Your parents are dead, your croft is falling apart and your boat is riddled with holes, yet you don't stop.'

I spread my hands. 'I don't want to die.'

'You want to *live*. You want a better life than the one you were given.'

The sea hushed on the sand below.

'You offer hope, Jón. You show them that life can be more than survival.'

Through the next three months, Katrín fed me, while my nights were lived upon the boat, and my days spent working the fields. That autumn, I caught enough fish to begin trading and I sowed grass seed, in the hope of harvesting hay, rather than thistles, from the land Pabbi had neglected.

By the following year, many of the women relied on me for food. Their own husbands had drowned or disappeared into the hills years ago. Stykkishólmur was a place of women, children and feeble old men. The village was in search of a leader: the old *goði's* greed had smothered the people. But gifts of food, I discovered, ensured people's loyalty.

My reputation grew. I took little in return for the fish, only asking that whatever driftwood was found on the beach should come to me. I lined the walls of the croft with wood; later, I added boards over the *baðstofa,* creating the loft.

Later, Anna's behaviour forced me to add doors and locks, costly but essential.

My first dealings were modest. I traded with farmers in the neighbouring settlement, and after three years of hard work, I acquired a small flock of sheep and supplied the people with milk, *skyr* and wool. After trading the two gyrfalcons, I gained both riches and a reputation with the Danish traders: they visited Stykkishólmur often, and I was able to provide for the people — *my* people, as they began to seem.

Katrín thought it odd that I did not expect more from them, but I said, 'There is no need to demand more.' And, at that time, it was true.

My whole life, people had whispered about me behind their hands, or sneered openly. Now they bowed and curtsied, and called me 'Master'. I kept them at a distance and demanded they ask permission before entering my croft. Sometimes I saw them flinch as I passed, and it made me walk taller. Perhaps I could have smiled at them, but I did not.

When the stale-breathed old chieftain died, the village was unanimous: they wanted me as *goði,* the man to whom they would pay taxes — though I never demanded that they do so — the leader to whom they tied their fate. I was recognized as a generous *goði* and a merchant of standing, my name known through much of Iceland.

And at night, when I lay down to sleep, I tried not to think of all the parts of myself that I must keep hidden to survive.

Darkness has fallen in the cave; the last thin skein of sunlight unspools over the horizon. The sky is alive with stars. I hold my hand in front of my face and flex my fingers, then wrap them around the handle of my knife and squeeze, as if I am wringing the last tatters of breath from some newly dead thing.

Enough. It will be enough.

■ ■ ■ ■

PART FOUR

■ ■ ■ ■

When the storm abates, the waves roar.
Icelandic proverb

RÓSA

A thickening rime of frost glitters on the earth and Rósa is increasingly confined to the croft, sometimes with the men, sometimes without. But even when she is alone, she feels eyes upon her. She starts to dream that Jón is standing over her, cloaked and hooded, a knife in his raised hand. In the day, she watches him talking and laughing with Pétur and Páll, with a crushing sensation in her chest and around her skull.

It grows colder still. Beneath bulge-bellied clouds, the ground groans.

One night, the snow falls in great white sheets; the air is opaque and tangible within the wall of ice. In the morning, when Rósa steps into the blizzard, she cannot catch her breath. The snow is flung from every direction. It falls downwards, as snow should, but it also seems to rise up from the ground, so that the cold clasps her nose and mouth, leaving her gasping. Where the ice touches, it burns.

She slams the door and takes shelter in the kitchen. She is alone. The men are in the barn and she is entirely cut off. She holds her breath, listening to the muffling silence of the blizzard. The roof moans under the weight of the snow, and the light that usually seeps through the thinly stretched sheepskin windows is muted. The fragile lantern flame flickers.

Rósa bolts upright: the men must be trapped in the barn with the animals. She imagines the hot bodies of cows and sheep, confined in sudden darkness, under the groans of the bulging roof: they will be wild with panic.

Páll!

She takes a lungful of air and hurls herself headlong into the snow again. It is stifling: ice in her nostrils, gusts of wind snatching her breath, cold serpenting into her flesh and burrowing into her bones. She knows what Mamma would say: 'Ullr, the snow god, is having a tantrum.' Rósa shakes her head to dispel the thought. Only God controls the weather.

But if that is true, then perhaps He is in a fury too.

She staggers through the drifts, sinking up

256

to her waist. She trips, falls, heaves herself upright, skirts weighted with ice, and forges onwards. The barn is dim through the unyielding wall of snow.

Then she hears a voice on the air, bellowing, *'Rósa! Rósa!'*

She surges forward. Great drifts of snow tower in front of the barn. She can see a tiny chink of darkness where the men have tried to open the door, but they haven't been able to shift the snow more than a finger's width. She starts to dig at the wall of white with her hands and feet, throwing it to one side.

'I am here!' she gasps.

'Hurry!' The voice sounds fearful.

As Rósa clears the snow, she sees, with horror, a ribbon of red snaking from under the barn door. It mingles with the white snow, turning into a lurid pink slush.

She digs faster and harder until, finally, she is able to yank the door open enough to squeeze through the gap, into the fuggy darkness.

A single oil lamp forms a circle of light. The air is thick with a coppery stench. Rósa can hear ragged panting and a moan of pain. Pétur and Páll are hunched over Jón's body, which is curled in the straw: foetal and bloody.

Pétur presses his hand against Jón's side where there is a wound that lays his entrails bare. She claps her hands over her mouth, remembering her desire to hold the knife, to stab him. It is as though, by wishing for it, she has made this happen.

Jón is still conscious. 'By your face, I am a dead man.'

Pétur's eyes are pleading, as if he expects Rósa to perform some sort of magic. 'A ewe,' he chokes, his voice raw. 'She panicked. Jón tried to hold her. I told him to let go.'

Rósa gapes at the corrugated rents in his flesh.

The blood plumes from his body and his eyes are glazing. She thinks of the fox again. Would a hunter decide it was a kindness to end his suffering?

Pétur's voice cuts through her thoughts. 'Rósa. *Rósa!* The wound. Quickly!'

Of course! She hurls herself into the snow, wades across the yard and searches around the *baðstofa* until she finds her sewing basket. What is the right thickness of needle, the right strength of thread to stitch a man together?

Briefly, she imagines sitting in the kitchen and letting the snows bury the croft while, out in the barn, Jón slowly bleeds dry.

Sweet Jésu, what am I becoming?

She stumbles back to the barn, pulling her tunic up around her nose and mouth so she can breathe. Her tears mingle with the snow.

When she finally reaches the barn, she expects Jón to be dead. Perhaps, for a moment, she hopes for it. But no: he is still wheezing. There is more blood and the other men are pale, trembling.

She works quickly, threading the needle and pressing the skin together. Jón moans, but she doesn't stop. Underneath her fingers, a man's torso — whole and intact — emerges. The stitching is large and ungainly, but the bleeding stops, except for a whisper, which she smudges away with the hem of her tunic.

'Good work,' Pétur mutters.

Jón is unconscious now, mouth slack; his skin is the translucent white of frozen petals, blue tracery of veins visible underneath. She presses her head against his chest, listening to the frantic *whump-whump* of his heart. She is relieved — at least, she thinks she is.

Outside, the snow plummets in a thick shroud; the world is silent as a tomb. They lift Jón between them — Rósa supports his lolling head — and struggle to the croft.

The sharp splatter of cold flakes makes him writhe and moan.

'Hush,' she murmurs, as she would to a feverish child. 'Hush.'

That night, they take turns to sit with him; the hours are punctuated by his whimpering. Outside, the snow covers their tracks, obliterating the path they made to the barn and burying the frozen drops of Jón's blood.

In the morning, they are all grey-faced. Jón's skin is slick with sweat; his breathing is rapid and shallow. Rósa examines the wound: it is red and angry.

He groans, and a string of spittle spills from the corner of his mouth. Pétur wipes it away with the corner of his tunic. A brisk gesture of everyday love, of the sort Rósa has seen between mothers and their grubby-faced children.

Pétur sees her watching and raises an eyebrow, then curls his lip. The expression makes him look more monster than man.

She swallows. 'Katrín has angelica.'

'He doesn't have a *cough,* Rósa.' Pétur's scowl deepens. 'Katrín's weeds will not help him.'

'He can't stay in the *baðstofa.* The air from the kitchen is foul — just look at the smoke.' She indicates the spiralling soot, a black reflection of the snow outside.

260

'Where, then?' Pétur demands.

'The loft?'

'The locked room?' Pétur shakes his head.

Páll is frowning. 'What is a *loft*? And why is it locked?'

'He stays here,' Pétur says.

Rósa sighs and piles more fuel onto the fire to quell the convulsive shivering that is racking Jón's body. As the peat burns, the smoke thickens. Soot and ash spiral through the air.

The first time Jón coughs, he howls, and a stain like rich wine spreads across his tunic. Pétur dashes to his side and presses his hand to the wound. Jón moans and, as the smoke billows, coughs and cries out again.

Rósa does not take her eyes from Pétur's face. 'So much smoke will kill him.'

Pétur shuts his eyes, then opens them. 'The loft, but . . . He will be furious.'

'Would you prefer him alive and angry, or dead?'

Pétur gives a bark of laughter, then gazes at her. The expression in his golden eyes is unreadable. 'He thought you such a little mouse, Rósa, when he married you. Help me carry him.'

Between them, they manage to heave Jón up the ladder, where they rest him on the ledge, slumped like scythed hay. His breath-

261

ing is shallow but Rósa's large stitches have held him together — a stuffed doll, bulging at the middle.

Pétur draws a key from a pouch at his hip as carelessly as he might produce a knife. Rósa is open-mouthed. He turns to Rósa and Páll. 'I will take him in now.'

Rósa shakes her head. 'No, you must —'

'*You* must go back down the ladder.'

'The croft is mine —'

'The croft is Jón's. He is your husband, who told you to stay away from the loft.'

Páll steps forward, half smiling. 'What is this, Pétur? Why —'

'You would do best not to ask questions. It is safer. For everyone.'

Páll puts his hand out. 'But wait —'

'It is safer,' says Pétur. 'Believe me. Some things it is better not to know.'

Páll looks about to argue, but Rósa sees Pétur's body brace; she remembers Mundarnes and the man who had challenged him. She remembers the knife against his throat.

'Páll, come down with me,' Rósa murmurs.

He doesn't respond. His gaze, still fixed upon Pétur, is hard and cold.

Rósa puts her hand on Páll's arm. 'Come with me. Please.'

262

He gives a brief, tight nod, and they descend the ladder, while Pétur waits.

When they are back in the *baðstofa,* they stare at one another, listening to the sound of the door swinging open almost silently, on well-oiled hinges, and the grating sound of Pétur dragging Jón's body over the floor above their heads.

Páll spreads his hands. 'I don't understand —'

'I know,' Rósa hisses, then presses her finger to her lips.

They listen to the shuffle of footsteps, the creak of the floorboards and the sound of muffled whispering. The noises are straight out of Rósa's tormented dreams, and she has to stop herself placing her hands over her ears.

Eventually, Pétur climbs down the ladder. He walks straight past them and into the kitchen, then tips some water into a pot and sets it on the *hloðir.*

He turns to Rósa. 'The wound needs cleaning. You must have moss. Where is it?' He speaks as if nothing out of the ordinary had just happened, as if there is not a secret room over their heads, as if he had not just growled a threat at them.

Rósa blinks, then passes Pétur a pot of pale green fronds, which he empties into the pan. She almost reminds him that Katrín would have more moss and other herbs besides, but the set of his jaw silences her.

For the rest of that day, Pétur keeps Páll and Rósa separate. Every time he climbs the ladder, he makes Páll come up after him and sit outside the loft room while he tends Jón. He tells Rósa to stay in the kitchen.

Rósa listens for voices when Pétur is in the loft: she can hear whispering, but nothing to distinguish one voice from another. For a moment, she allows herself to imagine that Anna is indeed up there, and has been all this time. What would that mean for Rósa? What happens to an unnecessary second wife, once the first has been revealed?

In the late afternoon, Pétur descends the ladder again.

'The animals need feeding,' he says tersely to Páll. 'You will come with me. Rósa, we will need to eat when we return.'

She looks down at her hands and nods, minutely. Páll sighs and stands. Out of the corner of her eye, she watches them pulling on layer after layer of cloaks and blankets. Every time Pétur moves his arms, the keys in his pocket jingle, until he is wearing so many layers that their sound is muffled.

Then he opens the door and the storm roars into the croft. The wind is like a physical punch and the cold air compresses Rósa's chest. Within the few moments it takes the men to walk outside and shut the door, she is shuddering uncontrollably.

She huddles near the *hlóðir* and counts sixty heartbeats, then moves quickly to the ladder. The door at the top looks the same as it ever did and is locked, of course. Pétur wouldn't have been so careless. When she presses her ear to the wood, she can hear Jón's laboured breathing, but no other sound. She waits for whispering, or footsteps, but there is nothing.

She sighs and goes down the ladder. It is when she is walking back to crouch next to the warmth of the *hlóðir* that something on the floor catches her eye. Something gleaming in the straw. She picks it up and, for a moment, thinks she must have finally slipped into madness because . . . It cannot be, surely. And yet . . .

Keys! She shuts her fist around them and closes her eyes. She daren't let herself hope. But now she is turning and putting one hand after the other on the rungs of the ladder, and now she is putting one of the keys into the lock and it fits — it fits! — and now she is turning it and pushing against the door, and the whole croft is watching her and she holds her breath and the door swings open and the cold air gusts out with a foetid, primal stink.

Rósa hesitates: the black space gapes in front of her, and the loft is filled with Jón's harsh breathing. It is hard not to imagine his eyes upon her as she steps into the room. She moves like a sleepwalker, shuffling through the shadows, arms outstretched, heart hammering.

Jón is laid by one wall, his hands clasped across his stomach where the ewe's horn tore through him. His skin is waxen, his breaths rapid, and his body seems shrunken, somehow: his muscled legs and arms are concealed beneath a blanket, and in sleep, there is something soft and childlike in his features. She crouches next to him. He stirs and groans, and Rósa bolts upright, ready to run if his eyes open. But, although his eyelids flutter, he doesn't look at her. Instead, his mouth opens, as if he is trying to speak. He coughs and Rósa notices that his tongue is dry, his lips cracked. Quickly, she dips the corner of the blanket into the moss tea and presses it to his mouth. He sucks on the cloth, like a nursing babe. Rósa dips the cloth in again and again, and he opens his mouth, although his eyes remain shut. Slowly, she reaches out and strokes the hair back from his forehead.

Finally, his breathing steadies and deepens. His mouth closes. Rósa sets the jug back on the floor and wipes her cheeks, which are wet. She hadn't realized she was crying.

Shakily, she stands and looks around the rest of the loft room; she had expected old barrels or tangled, ragged fishing cords. But instead, just this: Jón's mattress, a small table, a chamber pot. All quite clean, quite empty — as if they are waiting to be used. She searches the shadows for any sign of another person who might have been here — any sign at all.

The loft stretches the entire length of the croft, and Rósa cannot see the far wall from so close to the door. What if Anna is waiting in the shadows? Or what if the ghost, the *draugr,* has pressed itself into the walls and is watching Rósa, even now? She takes a breath and begins to walk.

Her footsteps echo through the dark space and she hears whispering ahead of her. She freezes, halfway down the long room. When she turns to look back, the rectangle of light from the doorway seems very far away: in the time it would take her to run to it, someone could leap on her and clamp their hands around her neck. She touches her exposed throat; her pulse flutters under her fingers.

She almost turns. Almost. But she walks on.

Darkness. Silence. She is nearly at the end of the room and she inhales shakily. There is nothing here. She stretches her arms out and takes another deep breath. It must have been her imagination — all of it.

Then, suddenly, from the darkest corner, a snap of cloth. Rósa jumps and cries out.

Something alive! Someone . . .

There is a flapping again, and a flash of white. She flings herself back against the wall, away from this ghost that rustles in the gloom.

'Anna!' she hisses.

Another flutter. It sounds so much like the inhalations that Rósa had heard when she pressed her ear to the door. She crouches on the floor, unable to move. This is the *draugr* she had feared. *This* is the creature that will smother her, or seep into her body and infect her mind, until she doesn't know herself and is wandering the hills, muttering and weeping.

Her body screams at her to run, but she cannot move: her eyes are fixed on the trembling white shape.

But then, as her breathing steadies, she notices that the *draugr* isn't creeping forward: it isn't advancing on her, ready to smother her. It seems fixed, somehow, and its struggling movements look like attempts to escape.

She narrows her eyes, peering through the gloom, then gasps.

Not a ghost. No *draugr*.

A bird!

'A gyrfalcon,' she whispers, her mind reeling. All those noises . . .

The bird shifts and stretches its white wings wide. Rósa sees the cruel curve of a yellow beak, as the creature twitches its head from left to right. She straightens up and tiptoes towards it, slowly, so as not to startle it. She has never been this close to a gyrfalcon, has only seen them soaring in the distant skies — savage, beautiful murderers. The bird fixes her with a beady eye and thuds the air with its wings, bating from the perch, then being tugged back by the leather jesses on its scaly legs.

Rósa stops at arm's length from the creature. It flicks its head towards her. Its reptilian eyes remind her that it has one purpose, and one alone: to kill. It flexes its feet, fixing its hooked claws into the perch.

Gyrfalcons are worth a fortune, especially

to Danish traders. It is said that nobles in Denmark will pay the bird's weight in gold.

But, as she gazes at the creature, Rósa is struck by another thought: not of the bird's value, but of the old stories about this taloned hunter of ice.

It is said that, if a falcon is captured as a person is dying, and if the creature is held close to the body at the last breath, then the dead person's spirit enters the bird.

And behind the perch, along with the droppings and the lacework of scattered bones of tiny creatures, there is a wad of material.

Clothing, Rósa realizes with a chill. And, next to it, a bundle of paper and stones. She kneels and squints at the little pile — if only she could move past the bird to look more closely. She is sure some of those papers are her own letters. And, next to them, some other writing in a large, scrawling hand she doesn't recognize.

She leans forward and reaches out.

The gyrfalcon turns its cold yellow eyes on her and clacks its beak; she steps away from it, pressing her back to the wall. The bird inclines its head to follow her movements, then launches itself from its perch, straight at her face.

Rósa gasps and falls, landing painfully on

her wrist, but she barely notices: she is too intent on getting away from the bird, away from that merciless, searching stare.

She scrambles backwards, until the sharp yellow eyes fade into the gloom, then leans her head against the croft wall and concentrates on the rise and fall of her own chest. When she can bring herself to stand, she almost trips over something large and wooden.

She runs her hands over it. It cannot be . . . And yet, yes, it is . . . A crib.

Rósa looks back to where the bird rests in the shadows, and then to the crib before her. It is made of driftwood, which has been carefully smoothed by the mouth of the sea, then planed by hand. The edges, where the wood has been cut, have been rounded with a rough stone. It is a work of patience and love.

Her thoughts turn again to the noises. She looks at the shadowy shape of the gyrfalcon, tethered at the end of the loft. Tales of children transforming into animals fill her head. It gazes back at her, unblinking — she can just make out the yellow eyes, through the gloom — then hunches its body, as if preparing to launch itself at her again. She is far enough away that it will not reach her, cannot touch her. It clacks its beak. She looks away. It is a bird, just a bird. The old stories are simply tales told to frightened children . . .

But still . . . She looks back at the crib. Had there been a child? There had never been any rumour of a baby, or even a pregnancy — or no whispers that had travelled south to Skálholt. But Jón is so good at silencing people. She thinks of the stone-faced, close-lipped inhabitants of the village, who carry secrets in the slump of their shoulders and the narrowing of their eyes.

Perhaps there was a child and it died. What if . . . What if Anna had been pregnant and Jón had shut her away up here, after she had discovered something — whatever it was he was so eager to conceal? She studies the crib, peering closely at the wood. There are no marks on it, no signs of use.

Behind her, Jón stirs and murmurs, making Rósa jump. His eyes open, briefly, and he looks straight at her.

'Anna!' he hisses. Then his eyes close again and he is still. She watches him, heart thudding, but he makes no movement, other than the rise and fall of his ribcage.

There is a sudden crunching noise from below, and the rumble of voices from outside the croft, and Rósa remembers: Pétur will be returning.

She springs upright, darts across the loft and out the door, her damp palms sliding over the handle. She fumbles with the key, almost dropping it, and the voices from outside are louder now. She sobs as she tries to turn it in the lock, but it is stiff and sticks fast.

Pétur will find the door unlocked. She imagines the rage on his face.

Her breath comes in frantic gasps as she tries one last time. The lock shrieks, the key turns. And, as it does so, it slices into the palm of her hand, leaving a perfect semicircular imprint in the shape of the end of the key.

She curses as blood seeps down her wrist and she has to stumble down the ladder one-handed. She trips and almost falls as she races through the *baðstofa,* presses a cloth to her wound, snatches up some knitting and sits on her bed. At the last moment, she remembers the key in her pocket, and throws it into the straw where she found it. It lands perfectly but, too late, she sees the smear of her blood across the metal.

Then Pétur and Páll walk in and she forces herself to smile. Her hand throbs.

Their faces are rimmed with ice; Pétur strides straight past her, then climbs the lad-

273

der. She hears him search his pockets for the key, hears his sharp intake of breath when he realizes it is not there. She sits, frozen, and waits for him to come down. Páll looks at her, his eyebrows raised, and she finds she cannot meet his eyes, in case something in his expression breaks through the fragile skin of her pretence.

Pétur walks back into the *baðstofa* and clicks his tongue. 'The key?'

She keeps her face smooth, although her insides churn. Her throat is dry, her mouth parched, but her voice is steady as the lie slips from her tongue, like water. 'I haven't seen it.'

She watches as Pétur pats his pockets again, muttering. A strange tightness forms in her throat: she has to smother a bubble of hysterical laughter. Her hand pulses. Any moment now, he will see the wound.

'Perhaps you dropped it outside.'

He curses, then moves to the door. And she watches him go, watches as he opens the door and steps out into the blizzard, which will swallow him while he is hunting for the key that she threw on the floor, moments before. For a moment, she imagines his body, rigid and blue with cold, crushed under the weight of the ruthless snow god.

'Pétur!' Páll calls, pointing at the floor.

The key flashes in the firelight as Pétur returns and snatches it up, then claps Páll on the shoulder. 'Good man. I'd have frozen looking for it.' Pétur grins as he describes his death, and Rósa forces herself to smile along with him, even as she cannot help picturing his corpse.

Then Pétur looks down at the key and sees the blood. His jaw hardens and Rósa's throat constricts as she waits. After a moment, Pétur wipes the key on his sleeve, saying nothing about it.

Slowly, Rósa exhales.

JÓN

Killing is never an act I have undertaken lightly. If a life must be taken, it should be done with reverence and from necessity. I have heard that there are countries across the ocean where men thrill at the thought of murder. They delight in feeling the victim's heart slowing, watching the eyes clouding.

I have only ever killed when I had no other choice. Yet now I am stalking through the darkness: two knives in my belt, a sharpened piece of flint in my fist, and enough rage in my belly to drive that stone into a human skull.

Before I met Pétur, I had never slain another man — not intentionally. But knowing Pétur changed everything: suddenly, I found myself capable of murder.

Pétur became Egill and Birgit's son at

about twelve summers, though he has no true idea of his age. A merchant had found him wandering around the volcanic rocks at the base of Hekla, foraging for leaves and berries, thin as an oar, and coated in so much dirt that he might have been made of earth. The merchant used a loaf of bread as bait, coaxed Pétur to his cart, then bound his wrists and ankles and tried to sell him as a slave. No one would buy him: Pétur bared his teeth and growled, snapping his jaws if anyone came too close. The merchant brought him into Stykkishólmur to sell to one of the Danes, hoping they might take the boy to Denmark as some feral curiosity.

But Birgit was entirely besotted with him. She and Egill had no children of their own and she set her heart on caring for him. Egill was against it, but she pleaded until he relented, and they took Pétur in. Everyone in the settlement was appalled and delighted in equal measure.

I was overseas at the time, and thought little of the wild-eyed boy who could barely speak. He ran around ragged and barefoot, while people laughed at poor Birgit, who pursued him with shoes, and kissed him when she caught him.

Katrín told me that, over the next five years, the boy seemed to calm and grew fond of Birgit, though he and Egill clashed: there were often shouts of anger from their croft, then cries of pain as Egill beat Pétur into submission.

He grew more compliant with age, and, by the time he was eighteen summers, he could pass for Egill's natural son, bar his dark hair and eyes. But that particular summer, Pétur and Egill were heard bellowing, and Birgit screaming.

Then there was a long silence.

I tried not to listen to the village gossips, but Katrín told me that Pétur wasn't seen for days afterwards; people rubbed their hands in glee, agreeing that Egill had killed him. Egill, however, came to my croft, pale, saying that the boy had fled. He believed Pétur had travelled south on one of the merchant ships. Would I help to find him?

'Why me?' I asked. 'Should you not fetch your boy yourself?'

'He will not listen to a word from my lips. But you are a man of standing. And you are skilled at . . .' His mouth twisted in distaste. '. . . persuading others.'

I laughed. 'This is not a trading agreement, Egill. Pétur is not some Dane I can charm with an ell of cloth or a cut of mutton. Send one of the boy's friends.'

'He has no friends. The villagers loathe

278

him, and he them. I . . . beg you, Jón.'

Egill pleaded and bargained. He would sing my praises at the Althing. They might grant me lands elsewhere on the Snæfelles peninsula, once they heard Egill laud me as a wise and capable *goði.*

'They may allow you to trade on lands to the north too, Jón.'

I nodded. 'You make a good case, but I can't force him to return. Besides, I hear that matters have been . . . discordant between you for some time.'

Egill's mouth distorted. 'I have tried to change him — to save him. The devil has a hold on him. But now Birgit misses him.' Egill's eyes slid from mine, but not before I saw, just for a moment, a flash of something like pain. As though the boy's absence caused him genuine grief.

I sighed. 'I will try.'

It was not difficult to track Pétur down: rumours of the half-savage dark Icelander led me to the north coast. I was weighting my boat to the sand with rocks when I saw Pétur running along the beach. He was taller than I remembered, and thin-limbed — he looked half starved, like a colt that had grown too quickly.

Then I saw that two burly men were chasing after him. They were laughing and

279

shouting. At first, I supposed it was a game, but Pétur's face was taut, his eyes wide. He has the most unusual eyes: the bronze of beaten copper, fringed with long, dark lashes. But that day they were filled with panic.

'Stop!' I cried, and stepped in front of the pursuing men. 'Leave the boy be. He's terrified, any fool can see that.'

'Careful who you call a fool,' one of the men sneered.

'Cut out his impudent tongue,' the other growled, his hand at his belt.

I put my own hand to my belt, where my knife was ready.

'Wait!' called the first man, his hands outstretched. 'You are Jón Eiríksson from Stykkishólmur.' He swayed slightly — clearly he was drunk.

I nodded curtly. 'The same.'

The man turned to his accomplice. 'Jón brings good meat and grain to these parts, wood and linen from the Danes too.' He hiccuped. 'Drop your knife, Bolli.'

Bolli grunted and let his hands fall back to his sides. 'He's getting away,' he complained, nodding at Pétur's sprinting form.

'What has he done?' I asked. 'He is barely more than a boy.'

'He is an outlander — can't even name

his parents. All in these parts know he's a foundling brat,' growled Bolli.

'He is the son of Egill and Birgit of Stykkishólmur.'

'*Egill!*' the man spat. 'Worse and worse.'

'You can't beat a boy for his pabbi's crimes.'

'We don't beat him,' chuckled the first man. 'And we will feed him after.'

'Hush, Thorolf!' hissed Bolli.

'No, Bolli,' Thorolf said, a sly smile playing on his lips. 'Jón has bread — there, in his boat.' He narrowed his eyes. 'Share the bread and I will give you something.'

'Thorolf,' Bolli whined.

'Quiet!' Thorolf turned back to me, grinning. 'Jón may play the saint, but he is a man like any other.' He leaned forward, lurching a little. 'And unmarried, they say.'

'What of it?'

'You have been at sea for some weeks?'

'Why do you ask?'

'So long unmarried, Jón, there are whispers of what you are.'

I reeled and took a step back.

'No fear. We won't tell a soul if you help us catch him. We'll bribe him with your bread. It will be easier with two to hold him, while the other goes at it.'

My jaw dropped. 'You . . . I —'

'You can thank us later. And no one will know. There is a crack in the ground where we can throw the body when we're finished.'

I stepped back again, shaking my head. 'I am *goði* . . .'

I had meant it as a threat, but Thorolf misunderstood. 'Don't pretend you are pure as the snow, man. Besides, it is no more sinful than using your hand, and better than catching a disease from some peasant girl, eh?'

They laughed. In that instant, I could have slit their throats.

I drew my knife. 'Get away from me, you filth. You fiends!' I jabbed the blade at them, nearly cutting Bolli's face. They turned and ran. I stood, trembling, unable to erase the image of Pétur being held down and savaged by those brutes.

I spent the whole day searching and into the evening.

When I found him, it was the shadowy time when the sun has just dipped below the horizon. I heard the noises before I saw him.

Grunting, and a cry. Then a long, drawn-out groan.

I knew what it must be, but I was still unprepared for the horror of it.

They had cornered him where some rocks

met a deep fissure in the ground. Pétur must have tried to squeeze himself into the crack in the earth, but had become wedged, and then the two men had caught him.

Bolli was pinning Pétur's arms and held a knife against his throat, while Thorolf stood behind him, thrusting.

I was frozen in horror. Then Thorolf cried out and collapsed forward, panting. Both men laughed. Pétur lay as if dead, his eyes blank.

Bolli stood behind Pétur, untied his trousers, then spat onto his palm.

I ran forward, bellowing, and thrust my knife into Thorolf's thigh. He screamed and crumpled, clutching his leg; Bolli yelled and jumped back, scrabbling about for his own knife, but he was too slow. I stabbed hard and Bolli's shouts became gurgling yelps.

'You've cut his throat!' Thorolf lurched over to where Bolli lay gasping and holding his neck. Blood bubbled out over his fingers.

My own blood was sudden ice. Already, Bolli's cries were weaker. I stepped towards Thorolf, who wept with fear and fumbled about until he found a stone.

'I'll bash your skull in!' he snarled. Blood streamed from the gash in his leg.

I stopped short. It would have been easy, weakened as he was, to slit Thorolf's throat and let him bleed to death too. I lifted my knife, then let it drop, shaking.

I crouched next to him. 'If you live,' I growled, 'you will tell no one of my part in this. No one will believe anything you say. I will spread word that you are a sodomite — that I saw you murder Bolli. Run far away from here.'

Thorolf nodded mutely, but his breathing was shallow and rapid as he tried to crawl away. I had seen animals die from blood loss: further threats would be unnecessary.

I walked over to Pétur, who gazed up at me wide-eyed and unblinking. I reached to help him up; he growled and snapped his teeth at my hand, like some feral creature. I flinched. Perhaps he truly was more animal than human.

I eased my hand towards him, crooning, as if he were a wild dog. 'Steady.'

Pétur stared at me. 'I know you. You are Jón Eiríksson.' His voice was deep and melodious, his words perfectly comprehensible.

'I am.'

He nodded wearily, then lay again across the rock. 'Be quick. I want bread and meat. And set your knife down, so you cannot stab me after.'

My mouth dropped open. 'I would not . . .'

I raked my fingers through my hair. 'Stand up.' I turned away while he stood and pulled down his tunic.

Behind us, Thorolf breathed his last and slumped, his blood dripping off the rocks around him. My heart clamped in my chest. I had murdered a man. Two.

I swallowed, but my mouth was dry, and my heart was a clod of earth beneath my ribs. I closed my eyes and tried to mutter a prayer but could not force the words past the pain in my throat.

I felt a hand gripping my arm. Pétur's face was close to mine. 'Thank you,' he whispered.

Rósa

After Pétur has picked up the key and wiped off the blood, he turns to Rósa and Páll.

'I must give Jón more water. Stay here.'

Rósa worries that she has left some sign of her presence up there. But she cannot follow him without raising his suspicions.

He climbs the ladder and she imagines him in the dark room above, crouching next to Jón, walking over to the gyrfalcon, perhaps giving it a chick or a rat to eat.

She remembers the creature's uncanny eyes upon her and shudders.

Páll sits next to her on the bench. 'Pétur has told me what is in the loft room.'

Rósa starts but attempts to sound casual. 'Oh?'

'Some papers of Jón's concerning the farm and the people here. He is particular about keeping them private and Pétur wants to follow his wishes.'

286

She opens her mouth to say more.

Pétur crashes down into the *baðstofa*, his cheeks the colour of curdled whey. Before they can ask, he snaps, 'Jón is worse. Much worse. The wound . . .' He lets out a cry of anguish and punches the croft wall so hard that one of the boards splits.

'Show me.' Rósa stands and walks to the ladder.

Pétur moves to block her way. 'No, you cannot.'

'Show me. He is my husband. Or would you let him die?' She looks into Pétur's strange eyes, aware that Páll is standing behind her, so close his breath brushes her neck.

'Now!' she growls, in a tone she has never heard from her mouth. 'If you value his life.'

He closes his eyes, inhales, then climbs the ladder.

She follows, her legs shaking. Páll is behind her.

The loft door is open and the room is as dark as before. Pétur lights a candle and the flickering flame throws shadows up the walls. It is impossible to see into the gloom at the far end of the loft, to the crib and the gyrfalcon.

Jón's rattling gasps fill the room. His skin is paler than it had been earlier and is pulled

287

tightly over his bones.

But before she can go to him, Pétur mutters, 'Stay here.' Then he takes a woollen blanket and drops it in the corner, in the shadows beyond the candle flame, near to the crib and the gyrfalcon. The gesture seems too odd to be motiveless. She squints into the darkness. The floor, half hidden by the blanket, is scored with deep grooves. As though something has been carved into the wood.

Pétur stares at her, as if daring her to ask, then says, 'Stay in this part of the loft. No questions.' Then he beckons her and kneels beside Jón. Her husband is slick with sweat. His blank eyes roll back in his head and he whimpers.

She kneels beside Pétur. The wound seeps a pinkish liquid and bulges horribly every time Jón inhales. Páll brings fresh moss tea and linen, but they all watch helplessly as his breathing becomes more shallow and rapid and Rósa realizes that she has argued her way into her husband's loft simply to watch him die.

There is a sudden flare of white in the darkness.

Páll leaps up, wide-eyed. 'What was that?'

'Nothing,' replies Pétur, looking narrowly at Rósa. And she knows she should have jumped, should have reacted somehow, but it is too late.

'There is *something* there,' Páll hisses. The gyrfalcon flutters its wings again. 'There, look!' Páll steps further into the loft.

'Don't move!' barks Pétur. 'Rósa?' His gaze is hard.

She swallows, then closes her eyes and whispers, 'It sounds like . . . like a bird.'

Pétur leans towards her, his breath hot on her face. He whispers fast and low, so that Páll cannot hear, *'What have you seen?'*

Rósa's heart batters frantically in her ribcage as she thinks of the clothing, the letters, the stones . . . the crib. She turns to Páll, her face smooth, her voice level. 'There is a bird. A gyrfalcon. It is easily startled. You should stay away.'

'A gyrfalcon?' Páll's voice is full of wonder. 'I would like to see —'

Pétur's whole body is rigid.

'No. You will frighten it,' Rósa says. 'Now, come and help me hold this cloth over Jón's wound.'

Páll hesitates, then sits next to Rósa, casting a reluctant glance in the direction of the bird.

Pétur's body uncoils and he gives a low chuckle as he stands. 'Sensible man, Páll. It is a dangerous bird and tends to go for the

289

eyes. Valuable creature, though. I would not want it to attack you: it is more worthwhile to preserve the bird's wings than your face.' He laughs again, but Páll's eyes are flint.

Pétur's lip curls. No one moves for six heartbeats.

Then Rósa puts a hand on Páll's arm, indicates the cloth, and he takes it. His hands shudder with repressed rage.

Pétur turns away, then moves into the darkness at the back of the loft.

Rósa and Páll look at one another and listen to Pétur's crooning as he approaches the bird. Then there is the sound of objects being moved — the rasp of linen, the flutter of paper, the rattle of stones.

Páll's eyes are wide, but Rósa has no answer for his questions — or no answer that will not make him launch himself at Pétur or think her a madwoman.

Time slews past. They watch the flickering shadows and listen to the rattle of Jón's teeth, observing the judder of his muscles; they avoid looking at one another. At some point, Rósa dozes, her chin on her chest, but she jolts awake.

Pétur is standing over her, his expression grim. His hand is at his belt and, for a moment, his are the eyes of the creature that will rip out her throat. His gaze is implacable, brutal, like that of the gyrfalcon, which has no feeling but only the compulsion to kill. She shakes her head minutely. *No! Please, no!* She opens her mouth, but she can't gather the breath for speech. He watches her for three shuddering inhalations, until she looks away. Then he returns to sponging Jón's forehead.

Páll stirs, glances at Pétur, then flashes Rósa a quick smile, which she can't return: her face is a frozen mask.

Pétur rubs his face with his hands and stands. 'The animals . . . And the path must be cleared again. Páll, come.'

'I'll stay with Rósa.'

'You will come with me.' Pétur's voice is flat and hard. To Rósa, he says, 'If Jón worsens, you will find me.'

Rósa almost asks, 'And what will you do then?' But Pétur's face as he looks at Jón is so desolate that she merely nods.

Pétur throws himself into the snow again; after casting a last brief, desperate glance at Rósa, Páll follows. The world is a blizzard-blurred huddle of white drifts and blank hillocks, made of nothing more than ice and air. Everything has reduced to an arm's length away, as if life beyond the croft no longer exists. Rósa watches from the door-

way, shivering: the men are shadowy out-
lines within two paces. Within four, the
snow has swallowed them.

Rósa knits, hoping the clacking of her
needles will cover Jón's wheezing, but she
cannot stop herself waiting for every new
breath. She wants to go to the gyrfalcon
again, to see that strange collection of
objects, but her limbs are as immobile as
rock.

Jón's exhalations grate with the groaning
wind and he hunches like a child curled
around the cramping pains of a stomach
sickness. She lays a hand on his shoulder.
His flesh is scorching. She presses a cloth to
his forehead, then wipes it over his cheeks,
his chin and his chest.

There is a startling intimacy in these
movements. This is the man who has lain
atop her and possessed her. And yet it is as
if she is touching him for the first time, feeling his hot skin, examining the pitted and
knotted scars that mark his chest and back.
What made him bleed so that his skin has
never healed, but has formed these ridged
calluses?

She brushes back the hair from his face.
He looks small and shrunken.

Slowly, she presses her mouth to one of
the scars on his chest. Beneath her lips, she

can feel the strain and clamp of his heart, the heave of his lungs within the cavern of his ribcage.

He twitches. She jumps back, but he doesn't wake.

Deep in the darkness, the bird ruffles its feathers; Rósa startles again. The gyrfalcon shrieks and Rósa shivers, thinking of the other myths about gyrfalcons: once, long ago, the plump ptarmigan and the gyrfalcon hunter were sisters, but in a flash of vicious rage, the gyrfalcon murdered her flightless sister and devoured her. Then the gyrfalcon gave an anguished cry, which echoed across the land. The gyrfalcon has hunted the ptarmigan ever since. She shrieks because she cannot help but be a murderer.

Rósa's legs are stiff and she is filled with a creeping dread, but she takes the candle, stands and walks towards the bird, as if tugged by some invisible thread.

With each step, her fear blossoms. Four paces away from the gyrfalcon, she stops, looking for the objects she had seen previously.

The floor is bare.

Her brain whirrs back through the day: when could Pétur have removed everything? She remembers dozing for a short while. But where would he have put the letters?

293

Her Sagas? And those other writings, scribbled in an unpractised hand. She leans her head against the floor and closes her eyes, so weary she could weep. The wood is warm from the heat of the *hloðir* below.

It is when Rósa opens her eyes that she sees it. There, carved deep into the darkest areas of the wooden floor, dozens of angular symbols.

Runes.

Her mind hums. She sees suddenly why the loft has been locked, why her husband wants no one in the croft, why he forbade her to come here. But who carved the runes into the wood? Not Jón.

Pétur? People say he is a pagan.

They also say Anna turned to witchcraft before the fever killed her. Witches, and those who shelter them, are condemned to burn at Thingvellir. And what might Jón have done to a wife who risked his reputation by meddling with runes?

Rósa runs her fingers over the runestone in her pocket, then glances at Jón's sleeping form. He looks weak and helpless now, but the words of a sickly *goði* would still carry enough weight to condemn her.

She walks through the loft room, down the ladder, through the *baðstofa* and kitchen, then flings the door open. The blizzard whirls into the croft, burrowing into Rósa's skin and stealing the air from her lungs. She gasps, closes her eyes, then hurls the runestone out into the storm. When it is discovered, after the thaw, she can claim no knowledge at all.

Her pocket is too light and she feels suddenly exposed, but she slams the door on the snow and the cold, and huddles next to the *hlóðir.* Her hand aches to clutch some talisman for comfort, but apart from the cross in her pocket, she has only the glass woman. She clamps her hand around it and squeezes, waiting for it to crack or splinter. But the fragile figure of the tiny, perfect woman is stronger than it looks. The glass remains cold against Rósa's skin long after she has stopped trembling.

At night, the snow stops, but it lies slumped like a woollen shroud on the crofts and the hills. The landscape is muffled in ice — who knows how many corpses the snow conceals?

After digging for half a day, Pétur and Páll return, exhausted and grim-faced. They carry a rat each, to feed to the gyrfalcon, but nothing else.

Pétur swings the rats by their tails. 'Should we feed these to the bird? We may need them ourselves if we want to avoid slaughtering a sheep. Or each other.' He grins. 'Smile, Rósa. I will butcher Páll first. He is muscular and would make a delicious stew.'

She stares.

'No need to thank me for sparing you,' he continues. 'I'd be a fool to use you for food — you will fetch a high price with the Danish traders in the spring. If I can keep you and the bird alive, I will be rich. Fat too, once I have eaten Páll.'

Then Pétur hoots and, after a moment, Páll laughs uncertainly. Rósa forces a smile, even as she wants to curl up in the corner, clutching her exposed throat.

They settle into an uneasy silence and, against the backdrop of Jón's rattling breaths, they sit and knit, trying to ignore the shadow that is creeping into the croft.

They hold Jón's hand, dripping home-brewed *brennevín* onto his tongue. Breath by breath, the flesh melts from his bones. His face sharpens; his skull appears.

Rósa makes stews and holds the spoon to his lips, urging him to take a little, Jón, *elskan.* But he can't swallow and gabbles gibberish, throwing his arms around, thrashing in half-sleep, as if warding off some imaginary foe. Again, he reminds her of a child. She can barely picture his rage and his threatening glances now.

Once, when she is sponging the sweat from his face, his eyelids flicker and he looks straight at her, into her eyes. His hand paws the air. She flinches away from him and his arm drops back onto the mattress.

'He wants to hold your hand,' Pétur murmurs.

She blinks at him and Pétur nods. Slowly she reaches out and clasps Jón's hand. His lips twitch into something like a smile. Her heart clenches. She looks up at Pétur. He is watching, with a complicated twist to his mouth, but when he notes her gaze on him, he nods his encouragement.

She strokes Jón's sunken cheek, and she and Pétur take it in turns to wash the wound, which is increasingly red and swollen.

When they are back in the *baðstofa,* Rósa turns to Pétur. 'Jón needs help,' she whispers. 'Katrín —'

'Fetching Katrín would be madness.'

'*This* is madness,' Rósa snaps. 'Do you care if he dies?'

'Of course I care. But we could tunnel for days, going about in circles. Then we would die. And he would die too. So, yes, Rósa. Yes, I care if he dies. But I don't want all of us to join him.' He stamps back up the ladder, and Rósa can hear him stifling what sounds like a sob.

Outside, the wind blows. The candles gutter; the shadows stir, then settle.

Rósa had thought Páll was asleep, curled up on some blankets, but he sits up and murmurs, 'Pétur is desperate too. You must see that.' He takes her hand and they sit in busy silence.

Then there is a movement above them and Pétur is scrambling down the ladder. Rósa leaps back, snatching her hand away.

'I have a thought!' His voice is raw with excitement and he rushes through the croft, yanks open the door and runs towards the storeroom, banging the door shut behind him. He returns within ten breaths, grinning.

'Follow me!' He climbs the ladder, then produces, with a flourish, a small pouch of leaves that look like dried cabbage.

'Sea kelp. We use it on the animals' wounds.' He presses the pouch into Rósa's hands. 'Why didn't I think of it before?' He looks very young. 'You can make a tea from it too. Fetch a dish and linen, Rósa. And boil some water.'

She does as he asks and passes everything back up the ladder. Pétur kneels next to Jón and pulls back the blankets. They gasp at the wound.

It is raw and bloated; it bulges around the sewing thread — a ravenous mouth, clamouring with rage.

Pétur winces. 'Clean it and pack the kelp against it. Hold him down.' He wipes the wound.

Jón moans.

'You're hurting him!' Rósa protests.

'Better to hurt him and keep him alive.' Pétur's jaw is rigid and Páll holds Jón's arm as Pétur presses the wound hard. A stench like the guts of a rotting creature fills the room. All three gag and retch.

Jón roars and flaps and howls, animal with pain. Pétur is sweating and shaking.

They continue to bathe the wound and drip the kelp tea into Jón's mouth all day and into the night. They wipe the sweat from his brow with a damp cloth. As Rósa changes his blankets and strokes his cheek — a gesture she never would have dared had he been conscious — she feels a surge of tenderness.

Later, when Pétur and Páll are sleeping in the *baðstofa,* she creeps further into the loft, to look again for the papers and cloth that Pétur must have taken, and to examine those deep runic scratches in the floorboards. Something catches her eye: a single scrap of paper stuffed between the boards. Thinking it might be one of her own letters, she clutches it eagerly, only to find, as she pulls it out, that it is covered with an unfamiliar looping hand, not hers or Jón's.

She squints in the gloom and holds the candle closer to the paper. It is a scrap torn from a larger letter, as if someone has shredded and crumpled it.

. . . most troubling rumours involving your wife. If I refer the matter to Copenhagen, then you will stand answerable, the more so because of Birgit's death. I am sure I need not emphasize the gravity of this matter, or the mortal danger it places upon . . .

Rósa peers closely at the letters underneath, which have been severed in half when the paper ripped, but she can make out no words.

Birgit had been Egill's wife and Rósa knew she had died of sickness some time before Anna's own death. But how could Birgit's death have cast suspicion on Anna?

As she folds the paper to return it, she notices a smudge on the word *mortal.* Had it been there before? She doesn't think so. With a creeping horror, she looks down at her hand and sees a brownish stain on her forefinger where her fear-borne sweat has smeared the ink.

Dry-mouthed, she folds the paper and stuffs it as deep into the floorboards as it will go. But when she scrubs her finger against her skirt, the ink remains.

Pétur and Páll come up late that night and send her to the *baðstofa* to rest.

Exhaustion weights her limbs. She tries to mull over what the letter might have meant, but she can keep her eyes open no longer and falls into a dreamless sleep.

Suddenly, a noise yanks her back to heart-thrumming wakefulness. She bolts upright.

A footfall.

'Who's there?' she hisses.

A creak of wood, the rustle of hay, the crack of joints. Sharp tug of fear in her stomach. She scrabbles backwards on the bed, but her back is already to the wall.

There is a crash from the kitchen. Both Pétur and Páll rush down the ladder.

'What is it?'

'What's happening?'

Crouched on her bed, Rósa hisses, 'Someone in the kitchen.'

They all edge forward, muscles tense, breath tight.

On the floor in the kitchen, like a bundle

301

of rags that has been dropped next to the stove, is a body. The men spring forward and pull it upright. The figure slumps and the head lolls, hair falling over the face.

At the same time, Pétur and Rósa gasp, *'Katrín!'*

Katrín doesn't respond and, for a moment, Rósa panics, but then she sees that Katrín's chest is still rising and falling.

'*How* did she get here?' Rósa demands.

Both men shake their heads.

'Wrap blankets about her and bring her closer to the stove,' Rósa says. She boils the stew; the steam wafts around them. Gradually, as though waking from a deep sleep, Katrín revives. She blinks and gives Rósa a weak smile. 'You're alive. Thought I'd risked losing my nose to the cold for nothing.'

'How . . .'

Katrín holds up her mittened hands. 'Like a fox burrowing.' She shivers convulsively and her eyes glaze.

'Save your breath, Katrín,' Pétur says.

Katrín mumbles, 'Keep the girl safe . . . I don't want . . . like Anna . . .' Her head droops onto her chest.

'What does she say of Anna?' Rósa says. 'Katrín. *Katrín?*'

'She's mumbling nonsense,' says Pétur. 'Leave her be.'

Katrín starts and opens her eyes, then takes sips of the tea Rósa presses to her lips. They layer on more blankets and watch her.

After some time she yawns, as if waking from a deep sleep. 'Where is Jón? He will be eager to hurl me back into the snow to freeze.'

None of them smiles.

Katrín struggles to sit up. 'Where is he? What happened? He's hurt?'

'A ewe gored him,' Rósa says. 'The horn went deep and —'

'Show me.' Her voice is tight with fear.

Pétur's gaze is cold. 'You should rest. Then return home.' He glances at Rósa.

'Where is he?' Katrín demands.

Rósa looks pleadingly at Pétur. 'She could help him.'

'No!'

'He will die.'

'I have said no!'

Katrín and Páll watch them.

Rósa stands, straight-backed. 'I will not let him die.'

Pétur's expression is anguished. 'Jón wouldn't want people prying.'

'Don't be a fool, Pétur.' She flinches as soon as she says the words, waiting for his towering rage, bracing herself for his sudden violence.

But he stares at her, as if seeing her for the first time.

'The loft,' he grunts.

The tension in the room lifts, like the lid from a boiling pan.

They climb up. Jón has thrown off the blankets; his limbs are sprawled at odd angles — he looks like a carelessly dumped corpse. Stripped of his tunic, he is all shadows. Rósa cannot pull her gaze from the excavated chasm of his hollowed chest, his concave stomach, the cavernous, barred crypt of his ribs. And those raised scars that crisscross his skin. He looks beaten and helpless.

Rósa tries to shield him with a blanket, but Katrín pushes it away.

'Not with a fever. He should remain uncovered.'

'He will be furious,' Pétur growls.

'So you've said.' Katrín looks around the room. Her eyes flick over the mattress; she squints into the darkness, where Rósa knows the gyrfalcon must be sitting on its perch, as if carved out of rock. As if guarding those markings.

Pétur watches Katrín's face. His hand creeps towards his belt, to his knife.

'A fine mess!' Katrín snaps, indicating Jón. 'Were you trying to kill him?'

Pétur uncoils. His hand moves away from his knife and Rósa exhales.

Katrín kneels and presses around Jón's wound with light, deft fingers.

Pétur says, 'Don't touch him. He wouldn't like it.'

Katrín's voice is flat. 'He would like being dead less.'

'Can you save him?' Rósa asks.

'Well, he's still breathing, despite your efforts, but he's rotting inside.' She turns to Rósa. 'A knife and water. And more of the kelp.'

'Pétur?' Rósa says. 'You heard Katrín.'

Pétur doesn't move. Páll hovers behind him, face strained.

Rósa sighs. 'Páll, fetch Katrín whatever she needs.'

He hesitates, staring at Pétur. Rósa raises her eyebrows. Páll nods, then goes down the ladder and returns, moments later, with all that Katrín has asked for.

Katrín flashes a smile at him. 'We haven't spoken, but I'm sure we know each other through other people's chatter. That is what usually happens here.' Carefully she cuts each of Rósa's clumsy stitches and squeezes the wound. There is a gush of stinking yellow pus. Rósa has to turn her face away to avoid vomiting.

Katrín grimaces. 'Water.'

Rósa hands her the bowl and Katrín tips water over the wound, wiping away the weeping ooze. Jón remains unconscious. Only the shuddering rise and fall of his chest reassures Rósa that he is still alive.

Katrín douses the wound in the kelp water. 'It looks dreadful and the smell is terrible, but that's simply the poison. If he fights it off, he may live.'

She turns to Pétur. 'So. I must return to my croft now, yes?'

Pétur looks at his feet. 'You should . . . stay.'

Katrín nods. 'Folk are more likeable when they offer a service.'

No one answers.

'I will sleep in the barn.'

Rósa starts to protest but Katrín holds up a hand. 'I can tend the animals and Pétur won't have to keep clutching his knife.'

Pétur scowls and Katrín gives a low laugh. Jón moans and Rósa places a hand on his cheek. Pétur reaches out and grabs her hand — his fingers grasp her wrist so tightly that she flinches. Slowly, he turns her hand over and she sees the smudge of ink from the letter. He examines it, then looks up at her. She snatches her hand back, rubbing her wrist. His jaw clenches but he looks away, then inclines his head to Páll and they go down the ladder to dig through the snow.

The men dig the path to the barn and the storeroom again, in spite of Rósa's protests that there is too great a risk of Katrín being trapped in the barn by the blizzard. But Pétur is implacable: he will dig the path twice daily, he states, but he will not have Katrín sleeping in the croft. Rósa tries to argue further, but Katrín shakes her head.

'He'll keep the path clear. He knows I can help Jón.'

Pétur gives a stiff nod.

Katrín helps Rósa to brew more kelp tea. They burn the wool from a sheep's head, the acrid smoke stinging their eyes, and Katrín shows her how to boil the skull and weight it with a stone so that it sinks to the bottom of the whey barrel. The meat will keep for months this way. They make rye bread and, as they knead the dough, Katrín tells Rósa what has happened to the settlement.

'When the snow first started falling, people took to the hills to gather up their flocks. Then a *moldbylur* started: big drifts — you couldn't see your hand in front of your face. The men didn't return. The snow god has them.'

'The men are still out there?' Rósa clasps her hands.

'Frozen, unless they have found a cave.' Katrín draws a shuddering breath. 'The snow grew heavier — even Gudrun couldn't recall the like. Folk began muttering about curses, and that was when the roofs started caving in. Some people escaped. Others were too slow. Buried alive.'

Rósa shakes her head. 'I cannot imagine . . .'

'They were there, calling out one moment, gone the next . . . We dug and shouted. Nothing. Six people: four on the hills and two under the crofts somewhere. No bodies.'

'They must still be buried,' Rósa says.

Katrín's gaze is piercing. 'They left no trace.'

'The men who went after the sheep — you can't abandon them.'

Katrín's mouth trembles. 'So we should send more men into the hills to die? That's why I came here. We don't know what to do.'

'You were lucky not to freeze.'

'I am used to the cold. I know to keep moving and where there are caves to shelter. I often walk out in the snow . . .' She trails off, then gives a small tight smile. 'I thought Jón . . . He's the *goði*.'

Rósa lays a hand on her arm. 'Did you hope for advice? Or a prayer? You should have gone to Egill. Or has his croft been buried?'

'Egill is safe, shouting about curses and God's judgement. But I came for food. Ours is buried or ruined. It is bold to ask but —'

Rósa holds up her hands. 'Of course. We will be glad to help. We will share everything.' She notices Katrín's face. 'Why are you smiling?'

'If you are to play the part of *goði,* then you should demand some payment for your kindness. Jón will wish he had taught you better.'

Rósa flushes. 'Sometimes I think . . . he loathes me.'

'He loathes everyone.' Katrín smiles wryly. 'Himself most of all.'

Rósa waits.

Katrín digs her knuckles deep into the dough, then brushes a strand of hair from her face. A dusting of flour smears her cheek: she couldn't look more harmless. 'I could drag Jón down into the dirt, if I chose.'

Rósa holds her breath and waits again.

Katrín shrugs. 'And he thinks I poisoned Anna.'

Rósa gapes and Katrín grins. 'I made her

309

a witch, apparently.'

Rósa chooses her next words carefully. 'I had heard that she became preoccupied with . . . delusions.'

'My fault, of course. Jón likes to find others to blame and won't accept that gossip is part of being *goði.*'

Rósa presses a piece of dough beneath her fingers. 'What truly happened?'

Katrín rubs her hand over her eyes. 'Anna wanted a child. Desperately. She collected stones, started circling the croft at midnight, chanting. People began whispering and, well, Jón was frightened.'

Rósa thinks of the letter she found, which spoke of *mortal danger.*

Katrín's face is pale. 'Then Pétur came to tell me that Anna was ill.'

'After the gossip had started,' Rósa murmurs. She feels suddenly cold.

'Exactly so. Jón said it was a fever. Within days she was dead and Jón had buried her. I never saw her.' Katrín wipes her eyes on her sleeve.

Rósa reaches for her fingers. 'You don't think . . .'

'I was half mad with grief and I accused Jón of . . . many things. He called me a witch and warned me not to speak to anyone about Anna.'

'He *threatened* you?' Rósa hisses.

Katrín leans forward. 'He *reminded* me that he provides food. And that witches are burned. Anna used to say he frightened her. I had never understood why, but suddenly —'

'You think —'

'No. He wouldn't have . . . No, I don't think . . .' Her smile is thin and unconvincing. 'But the villagers talked to visiting merchants and, well, you understand how stories grow with every telling. Between the northern mountains and the southern islands, a man could turn from an angel to a monster.'

Rósa nods. Her hands are trembling.

'You've a face like milk. Let's speak of other things,' Katrín says briskly.

'Are you —' Rósa's voice sounds strained. She coughs. 'You aren't frightened of the snow?'

Katrín stares off into the distance, a faint smile on her lips. 'I told you of my daughter, Dora. She was a dreamer. Precious girl. Blonde hair, like the finest spun wool. Who knows where that curl came from? I used to wind it around my fingers.' She holds out her hand, then lets it drop.

The stillness of Katrín's face fills Rósa

with dread. She knows how this story must end.

Katrín continues: 'When her pabbi — the boat — just broken wood, no bodies. Ægir is a greedy god. He gives little back, except fish. Grief made Dora cold. She was at that age, I think. But I didn't want to cling to her, smothering her with love, the way parents can, pawing at their children, as though they are dogs.'

Rósa nods.

Katrín turns back to the dough and sprinkles some flour on it. 'Dora walked day and night. I didn't stop her. One day, it snowed — she didn't return. The whole settlement went on the mountain, calling for her until our lungs burst. But it was as if she'd melted into the air. I think,' Katrín's eyes shine, 'perhaps the *huldufólk* kept her. I like to imagine her, tucked up warm in some hole in Helgafell.'

Rósa touches her arm.

Katrín sniffs. 'I find it goes hard with me now, to see a young girl wandering into the wilderness, stepping through a strange land that could swallow her whole.'

312

JÓN

My cave is cold without a fire, but I have learned that it is wise to wait for the perfect moment before striking. I test my blades again and again. They prick bright beads of blood from my thumb.

I must stay out of sight: if the merchants have brought their tales south, then anyone who recognizes my face will try to capture me, or worse. Those who give me shelter will be exiled. Banishment is a death sentence.

The winter snows will soon cover my bones.

I sit and I watch and I wait.

I have imagined the deed a hundred times, but I find I lack the necessary courage. This may be my last act of rage, my last act of love, and I dread God's judgement. Villains and murderers are damned to burn for all eternity. And yet, after that meeting with

Pétur, I knew it was my fate.

After we had left the bodies of Bolli and Thorolf for the ravens and foxes, I persuaded Pétur to come aboard the boat. At first, he spoke very little. When we stopped in an inlet, I offered him dried fish, mutton and ale. He ate and drank as though he was starving.

Between mouthfuls, he gave me scraps of his past. Of Egill, he would say only, 'He is a small man who makes himself larger by crushing others beneath his boots. He claims compassion, but his love is a weed that strangles.'

He told me that, although he had never known his true pabbi, his mamma had cared for him greatly. They had travelled about the country, mother and son. Nowhere allowed them to settle, perhaps because of their dark eyes and hair, or simply because they were outsiders. I have seen it happen myself: travellers are shunned as strangers, so they must journey on to the next settlement. And so it continues, until they become another set of bones, rotting by the wayside.

'Your mamma died of sickness?' I asked.

'They burned her for witchcraft,' he said flatly. 'In Ísafjördur. I was twelve.'

'Oh. I . . .' I shook my head.

Pétur's mouth twisted. 'They laughed when she screamed. Offered to quench the fire by pissing on it.'

The image hung in the silence. I almost reached out a hand to steady Pétur, but stopped myself, not wanting to tug at the fragile thread of understanding between us.

I busied myself building a fire with sheep dung and scraps of wool to catch the spark from my flint and iron. 'You are shivering and will need to wash your wounds. Lift your tunic.'

His eyes flashed to my face, and I saw my mistake. 'I mean no harm.' I held up my hands. 'I'll stand here, and you can clean them. Here, water and wool.'

Pétur didn't move, so I walked down towards the sea and stood with my back to him. The water looked iron in the grey evening light. I closed my eyes, inhaling the fresh cut of salt air. Live but once by the sea, and it will never leave your soul.

The night was sharp with the coming cold. If I held my breath, I imagined I could hear the hum of forming ice, the first syllables slow, then becoming a full-throated roar. In Iceland, winter kills without hesitation.

A cry broke through my reverie. I spun around. Pétur was clutching his side, a thin trail of crimson creeping from under his fingers. 'Bolli's knife,' he gasped.

I reached out, then stopped. He nodded. Gently, I wiped the blood from the wound. He flinched, but stood still.

'I have nothing to bind it,' I murmured. 'Here.' I hacked a strip from my cloak and wrapped it around his torso.

As I worked, my eyes traced the raised marks and stippled scars covering his skin. A map of his childhood: the unknown years before he came to Egill's croft. Or perhaps Egill had made the wounds.

Pétur cringed, as if my gaze were an unwelcome touch, then pulled away.

Later, he allowed me to wash his hurts daily, to bandage the ruined left arm, where the scar broke open time and again — he never told me what had happened to it. But he stared at the scar as if he despised the limb. And watching his eyes darken with loathing was like seeing my own reflection on the surface of the sea.

It was a three-day journey back to Stykkishólmur. Every night, we moored the boat in some desolate cove; every morning I waited for Pétur to leave. I braced myself to let him go. Egill would never support me before the Althing if I returned alone.

316

The days passed and Pétur shrank into himself. I pulled on the oars, trying not to imagine his pain. Pétur was a means to an end, nothing more.

And yet, each morning when he did not leave me, I felt a lightening of my spirits; each night when I imagined him going, the thought was like darkness.

Perhaps his scars spoke to me. Or perhaps it was simply that he was the first true companion I had ever had. He seemed part of the hard land I loved, with its belly of fire and the cold wind and ice that swept across it.

Every morning, he unmoored the boat and helped me push it into the cold water. I climbed in, then gripped his hand and pulled him to join me. There was an easy silence between us, even in those early days.

He seemed to know me instantly, too, in a way that needed no words. Once, when I was looking at him, thinking of Thorolf and Bolli, and the bargain they hinted Pétur had made with them, he said, 'I have sinned, I know.'

The sea hushed around us. I gazed down at his scarred hands.

'Your face.' He smiled. 'You looked suddenly . . . disgusted.'

'No,' I said. 'I am puzzled. Why you would

317

let them —'

'It is only a body.' He shrugged. 'It must earn food somehow.'

He saw that I was shocked and smiled. 'It is not worth much to me. You wouldn't understand.'

But I did. I recognized the feeling of revulsion at one's own skin. I thought of the scars on my own body that sickened me. To me, Pétur's scars were different: they told a tale, however painful, of survival and strength.

I sometimes wish I had left him in one of those frozen bays, for Pétur was the blade that butchered the heart of my old life, and I destroyed him too. I long to return to that moment on the beach. I will watch him run past, terrified. I will watch the men chasing him, laughing. And I will turn back to my boat, back to the sea. I will tell Egill that I couldn't find Pétur. And my future will stretch before me, bright and clean as an unbroken wave.

As it was, on the morning of that third day, I found myself begging Pétur to return to Stykkishólmur as my apprentice. To live in my croft, rather than Egill's. He said yes, without hesitation.

But Pétur's return to Stykkishólmur caused

318

more dismay than I could have imagined. People saw only that he had survived alone on the land, like one of the *huldufólk,* and once again, as when he was a young child, they whispered that he was not quite human. They laughed that I kept a monster in my home.

Egill raged outside my croft, demanding that I return his son.

'He is not a cloak I have borrowed that I may give him back to you, Egill.'

'You have no honour, Jón.' Egill's mouth was a thin line. 'You must *make* him return to me.'

I spread my hands. 'How can I? He is his own man, and he chooses to stay.'

'Do you imagine I will support you before the Althing when you steal my own child from me?'

Suddenly Pétur was at my shoulder. 'I am no *child,* Egill, and I am not yours. Take your threats elsewhere. They cannot touch me now.'

Egill's expression softened and he reached out his hand, tenderly, towards Pétur's cheek. But Pétur flinched and stepped backwards. Egill's face became a mask of fury; he turned and strode away, black cloak flapping.

Pétur sighed. I felt the tension drain from

his body.

'You fear him?'

Mouth hard, he nodded.

I thought of the scars that spanned his skin and felt my heart clamp.

'He will take revenge on you,' Pétur murmured.

'Let him try.'

'I should leave. Go elsewhere.'

I remembered Thorolf and Bolli. 'You'll stay.'

In time, people grew to accept Pétur living with me; they believed I had tamed him. Pétur was a hard worker and doubled the grain and fish I gave to the village. They still told stories about him, no doubt, but he filled their bellies, so they whispered discreetly.

Sometimes I caught Egill staring at Pétur, slack-mouthed with grief. But the next moment, he would threaten both of us with Hell and damnation, and I saw why Pétur despised him: for all Egill claimed to be appointed by God, he was a small man, petty and greedy by nature.

When I first married Anna, I thought it would quell the gossip that I was too strange and aloof from every soul, except Pétur. And, for a time, it worked, but once her wanderings started, people were talking again. Chatter of a different sort: *his wife is unhappy; she is bewitched.* They looked at me through narrowed eyes and I knew they were questioning why she was so sullen and dissatisfied with me.

She started to wander by the sea. When people called greetings, she stared blankly, then returned to scrabbling at the stones, ripping off her fingernails, numb to any pain.

Katrín clucked over her and bound her bleeding hands, but there was something in her expression — a lack of surprise.

'*You* persuaded Anna to do this,' I growled.

'I did not.' Katrín's face was tight as she bound Anna's wounds.

'Scratching about for moss, and you claim no part in it? You must think me a fool. She was muttering *spells.* They'll claim witchcraft. You know Egill —'

'It is not spells,' snapped Katrín. 'Stop your yammering and *listen.*'

I leaned in close to Anna's lips, which were moving, as if she were whispering an incantation. Her eyes were clouded. It chilled me to the marrow. Her voice was like the faint crackle of the fire in the *hloðir,* but I could just discern the words: 'A child.

321

Please, God, a child. Please. Please.'

I recoiled.

Katrín's gaze was sharp. 'She can pray as hard as she likes, but she asks for a miracle, and she is no Mary to be visited by the Holy Ghost.'

'Hold your tongue! I should have you tried for blasphemy.'

'Perhaps.' Katrín nodded. 'Or perhaps you should give your wife a child.'

I tried. Many times I tried. But her face, her eyes and her body made me wilt at every attempt. And then she would weep and say that I was no true man. She was right, and I hated her for it.

I gathered driftwood from the beach and fashioned a crib, praying that the hope it offered might soothe her. But she thought the crib a cruel joke and tried to smash it.

Seven nights later, she was discovered late at night trying to climb Helgafell to recite her three wishes to the grave of Gudrun Ósvifrsdóttir. Then she began to visit Egill. He had shunned her since Birgit's death, some months before, but after Anna went to his croft, he began looking at me with gimlet-eyed glee. I knew what I must do: I sent Katrín away, accusing her of corrupting Anna's mind with sorcery. I found a lock for the loft room and said that Anna had a fever.

I did not intend to do her violence. But every time I think of our last fierce struggle, I feel sickened. When I close my eyes, all I see is her screaming face and blood. So much blood.

Afterwards, in the half-light of a summer midnight, I dug my wife's grave.

■ ■ ■ ■

PART FIVE

■ ■ ■ ■

Love flares the hottest in secret.
                    Icelandic proverb

RÓSA

Katrín is as good as her word: she sleeps in the barn and comes to the croft early in the morning and late in the evening, battling through the blizzard to bathe Jón's wound. After it has drained for a day, she packs it with linen, which she then tugs out at each cleaning. As the infection fades, the film dulling his consciousness dissolves; he whimpers. By the second day, every dressing change is conducted to the staccato chorus of Jón's howls.

Rósa can't watch; she sits in the *baðstofa,* knitting, wishing for deafness. Pétur crouches on the bed opposite, iron-jawed, fisted hands trembling. It is Páll who holds Jón down, passing Katrín the water, kelp, and the other herbs she packs into the wound: chickweed, angelica and moss.

After a particularly torturous change, Katrín kneels next to Rósa, who tried to

327

help but then huddled in the corner, watching in horror.

Katrín puts a hand on her shoulder. 'His screams are a good sign, Rósa.'

'But that *smell.* Like rotten meat.'

Katrín nods. 'It is terrible to see a loved one in pain.'

Love? Rósa has never considered it. He is her husband and she is bound to honour and obey him: the Bible commands it. She wants to be a good wife: her survival and her mamma's depend on that. But *love?* She studies his face; she knows every outline, every expression. She reaches out and touches his cheek, then runs her thumb over his lips: they curl at the edges and his face is creased from laughter past. He'd been happy, once.

When she looks up, Páll is standing in the doorway, eating a piece of dried fish and staring. She blushes. He turns away, his eyes dark caves.

And she lets him leave.

Adulterous men are hanged or beheaded; women are stuffed into a sack and pushed out into the drowning pool at Thingvellir. And the Bible says that one who lusts with his heart has already committed adultery. This is for the best.

■ ■ ■ ■

The next day, while she is cooking, Pétur shouts from the loft: 'Rósa!'

Then Pétur and Páll together, voices raw and frantic, 'Rósa! Rósa!'

Her spoon clatters to the floor. She races up the ladder, knowing she will find Jón dead. Her heart plummets, then lifts. She can return to Skálholt with Páll after all. This will feel like a nightmare. And yet what sort of monster has she become, to wish her husband dead?

She takes a breath and walks into the loft, bracing herself.

Jón is sitting upright, sipping a cup of moss tea that Pétur holds against his lips. Páll and he are staring at him, as if they have witnessed the raising of Lazarus.

'He is *thirsty,*' Pétur says, with wonder.

'Praise God!' She runs to Jón, pauses, then flings her arms around him. 'Jón *elskan,*' she breathes, 'I'm so . . . happy.' Her knees are trembling. She dares not look at Páll.

Jón gives a weak smile. 'It seems me nearly dying has made you into the perfect wife.'

If she had Katrín's courage, Rósa would reply that, when he was near death, he was an easy husband. She forces her mouth into

329

a smile. 'I have made a stew.'

From the corner of her eye, she sees Páll's shoulders slump. Then he walks from the room. She tries not to let the hurt on his face pain her.

'I feel as though I've been trampled by a herd of horses,' Jón says.

'You should rest, *elskan*. Sleep.' Her legs itch with the need to run after Páll. To take his hand, pull him in close and say that . . . What can she say?

'I have slept enough. Come here.' Jón takes her hand and kisses it. Her skin itches at his touch.

In the depths of the darkness, the gyrfalcon stretches its wings. He starts at the whisper of feathers, then turns to Rósa, squeezing her fingers harder . . . too hard.

'You will not tell anyone of the bird?'

She shakes her head mutely.

His dry claw tightens around her hand. 'Gyrfalcons are worth more than gold, Rósa. If someone in the settlement discovers I am keeping one to trade, it will cause envy and bring trouble . . .'

She swallows. 'The settlement is buried. No one has been here, except —'

'Rósa!' Pétur hisses, an urgent warning in his voice.

She starts at his tone. He is pacing the

330

room and chewing his thumbnail. He keeps pausing, then drawing breath, as if to speak, but continues to pace.

'Stand still, Pétur,' Jón croaks. 'You will wear away the floorboards.'

Rósa says, 'I must tell Katrín you have woken, Jón. She will be so happy.'

Pétur stops pacing and glowers at her.

Jón heaves himself upright, gasping at the pain. 'Katrín?' he growls.

Rósa looks at Pétur. 'You have not told him.'

'Katrín was here?' Jón demands.

Pétur's voice is low. 'Her care has —'

'Was Katrín here? In the loft?' Jón spits. 'Answer me, damn you!' His face is pale, and his breath batters from his chest — he collapses forward, panting.

Rósa kneels beside him. 'She wanted to help you.' She reaches out to Jón's face but cannot bring herself to touch him. 'She will not tell anyone anything.' She thinks of the bird, the crib, the scratches on the floor. She has no idea what Katrín has seen.

'You don't know,' gasps Jón. 'You don't —'

'I know she will not spread rumours, Jón.' Rósa takes a steadying breath and looks him in the eye. 'You must trust her — you must try —'

'Silence, Rósa.'

Rósa presses her legs together to stop them shaking. She forces her words out. 'Katrín will not say a word to Egill, Jón. You have nothing to fear.'

Jón makes a noise that is somewhere between a cough and a laugh.

'Try to understand,' Rósa continues. 'You were fading so fast. And Katrín has saved you. Hasn't she, Pétur?'

Pétur is gazing at the light from the window, which glows the colour of *skyr* in the reflected brightness from the snow outside. 'I was against her staying,' he whispers, 'but you were dying.' Rósa hadn't known Pétur could feel fear. She hears the almost-boy he must have been when Jón rescued him. Pétur's face is pale, lost. There is a click in his throat when he swallows.

Rósa forces herself to take Jón's dry hand. The bones are parched twigs with a thin vellum of skin stretched over them; blue ropes of veins bulge underneath. 'Pétur is not to blame.'

Jón is silent for three laboured breaths. 'Bring her to me,' he says savagely.

Rósa stands up. 'You will not harm her.' She looks from Jón to Pétur. 'Neither of you would harm her?'

The silence stretches.

Eventually, Pétur murmurs, 'Of course not. Fetch her.' But neither man will meet her gaze and there is some unspoken conversation in the way they look at one another.

'Very well.' She struggles to draw air. Perhaps she can tell Katrín to flee.

Outside, the sky is metallic grey-black, like a fresh bruise. The cold air slices her insides. Rósa trudges the hundred paces to the barn, each breath a cloud that freezes, fades, then is gone for ever.

Are souls like that? she wonders. *Will I disappear one day, dissolve like melting ice into rushing water?*

It is an unChristian thought, so she banishes it and pushes hard against the solidity of the barn door.

It is bolted. Everything is closed or locked in her husband's world. She pulls her mittens off; her fingers are slick with melted ice and numb with cold. She fiddles with the latch and eventually manages to lever open the door. Then she falls forward into the dank shadows and fuggy quiet of the barn.

She can hear the jostling of the animals in the darkness, their uneasy bleats and snorts.

A single candle glows on a ledge at the end of the barn, and Katrín is hunched underneath it.

Rósa starts to speak, but Katrín holds up a hand.

'Hush, listen. *There!* You heard it?' There is a strange glitter in Katrín's eyes, and she grips Rósa's arm too tightly.

Rósa listens to the groans of the landscape, the moan of the wind, the creaking of the snow outside. 'Just the wind. Don't be afraid —'

'I am not afraid. You've heard it before?' Katrín's voice is too bright. She smiles, then says, too quickly, 'Yes, it must be the wind. And yet it does sound like . . .' She stares into the distance again, head cocked to one side.

To cover her growing unease, Rósa blurts, 'Jón is awake.'

'Páll told me. Good news!' Then Katrín's face falls. 'But what is wrong? He's worsened? Or he's refusing to drink my potions?' She gives a wicked grin. 'The witch's brew.'

'He wishes to . . . speak with you.'

Katrín raises her eyebrows. 'Ah!'

'He is agitated.' Rósa picks a stray tuft of wool from where it has caught on the barn wall, and presses it between her fingers. It is coarse and greasy. She looks directly at Katrín. 'He wants to know what you've seen — in the loft.'

'He does?' Katrín looks more amused than scared.

Rósa draws a deep breath. 'The loft was . . . locked before. And now he thinks you will gossip and . . . an accusation of *seidr* would see him burned.'

'He thinks I'll try to set a fire under his feet?' Katrín laughs softly.

'How can you laugh? He is in a foul temper!'

'Oh, Rósa, I have been married and know how to soothe a man's rage. I shall be as meek and mild as the Blessed Virgin herself.' Her eyes glint and Rósa returns her smile uncertainly.

Katrín takes Rósa's hand and they walk into the blizzard, then battle through the mountainous drifts. The world is reduced — they cannot see the hills, the sky or the endless ocean, only a tiny circle of life and warmth as far as their arms can reach.

Beyond that, an unknown wilderness lies, snaggle-toothed and snarling.

When they reach the croft, Pétur is sitting tensely in the *baðstofa,* using his knife to whittle a piece of driftwood to a sharp point. He looks uncanny and threatening, like a piece of the land uprooted and set down in the warmth of the croft, but still carrying the barely cooled menace of volcanic rock.

He glances up, his gaze flicking past Rósa to Katrín. 'Jón wants you hurled out into the snow.'

'Ah, then he is a fool. You must throw a witch into water, or burn her.' Katrín says, 'Snow will be no good, especially now you have warned me, so I can steal your blankets. Besides, the fires of Hell keep me warm.'

Pétur's mouth twitches. 'I told him you are too wise to be loose-lipped.'

'I could have destroyed him a hundred times, years ago. I chose to stay quiet.'

'As I thought. Be . . . gentle with him. He is frail.'

She nods and some frisson of understanding passes between them. Then Katrín climbs the ladder into the loft.

Rósa makes as if to follow, but Pétur shakes his head.

Rósa pushes past him. 'This is my croft.'

Pétur encircles her wrist with strong fingers and, though his touch is light, she can feel the suppressed strength in his grip.

'I only stop you to spare your energy,' Pétur says. 'Climb, if you wish, but he will send you down again.'

She pulls her wrist free and rubs the skin where he touched her.

'I am not contagious.' He laughs. 'You will

336

not turn into a monster.'

Suddenly, from over their heads comes the sound of raised voices, the creaking of boards, then a single cry and a *crash.*

Rósa and Pétur scramble for the ladder. Rósa reaches the loft first.

Jón is on the floor, Katrín standing over him. At first, Rósa thinks she has struck him, but then she sees that he is struggling to stand, and that Katrín is trying to push him back down. Both are staring towards the darkened area of the croft, towards the bird and the crib and the runic scrawlings. Their faces are pinched and hard.

'Tried to stand and fell,' says Katrín, her voice falsely bright. 'But he seems all in one piece. Come, Jón.' She leans down and, as she puts her arms about him, she hisses something into his ear. Her face is savage, and Rósa expects him to bawl at her, but he nods.

'Why did you stand?' demands Pétur. 'You might have burst your wound.'

Katrín speaks over Jón's gasps as she helps him to lie back on the mattress. 'He said he would test his strength. I warned him, but he knew best, as ever.'

There is something both aggressive and anxious in her voice — she speaks as she might growl at a wild animal, perhaps to conceal the quaking of her knees.

But Jón does not look hostile, his face tallow-pale. A sheen of sweat slicks his neck and chest as he sucks in air effortfully and with obvious pain. With a start, Rósa sees that he looks terrified.

In the darkness beyond them, the gyrfalcon is bating again and again, flapping from its perch, then being dragged back by its jesses.

'Calm it, Pétur,' Jón gasps. 'Before it tangles itself and snaps a wing.'

Katrín shows no surprise as Pétur's candle reveals the shape of the bird and, below it, the crib.

Pétur approaches the bird cautiously, clutching it before it flaps away. Then he places it on its perch, where it sits, beak open and panting, its wings held a little aloft from its body. Distress is scrawled across every angle of its frame.

Rósa has heard men say that falcons hunt by sound as well as sight: that the frantic thrumming of a rabbit's heartbeat will carry to their ear. The bird must be overwhelmed by the chorus of drumming hearts in the loft.

Once Jón is settled and his breathing has slowed, they return to the *baðstofa*.

Katrín clutches at Rósa's arm and pulls

her close, so Pétur cannot hear. 'Those runes,' she hisses. 'Can you read them?'

Rósa shakes her head.

'They are deep enchantments.' Katrín's eyes are wide. 'Deception and cutting off the heart —'

'You mean —'

'Murder. Those signs were intended to bring on sickness and death.'

Rósa feels suddenly cold. 'But who . . . ?'

'The signs were not there before . . .'

'Before Anna?'

'Before, when the loft was open.'

'But who would have . . . ?'

Katrín's eyes are flint. 'The runes are those of sickness and death. And Anna . . . I can't help but think —'

'Surely Jón wouldn't —'

'No. I don't believe . . . But he seems a stranger to me now.'

'Perhaps Pétur?'

'Perhaps. But whoever made those marks, this croft is cursed and these men are dangerous. Rósa, there is more. Under the linens in the corner,' Katrín's grip on her arm tightens, 'there is a bloodstain in the wood. Someone has tried to scrub it away, but my husband was a fisherman and I know bloodstains when I see them.'

Rósa thinks of the knife, the dried blood,

the matted tangle of blonde hair. Everything suddenly fits together, like a key in a lock. 'Jón! He must have —' She claps her hands over her mouth.

Katrín's eyes darken. 'There must be some other reason.'

'You say Anna feared him?'

Katrín nods silently, chewing her lip.

Rósa's mind reels. 'I must leave. I will go as soon as the thaw permits.'

Katrín jumps away as Pétur descends the ladder. 'Why do you two whisper?'

'Women's matters,' says Katrín, smoothly.

Pétur raises his eyebrows and Rósa squirms. 'There is mutton in the storeroom, which I must prepare,' she mutters.

'I'll help,' says Katrín, rising.

'No,' says Pétur. 'Katrín, tell me how to speed Jón's recovery. Come,' he pats the seat next to him, 'sit alongside me.'

He knows what she saw, Rósa thinks, with a jolt.

'I will stay here too,' she says. 'The mutton will not spoil in the cold.'

'No, Rósa,' says Pétur. 'You mustn't neglect your duties. Katrín will stay.'

Katrín inclines her head and gestures that Rósa should go. She has no choice, and leaves Pétur with Katrín.

■ ■ ■ ■

The storeroom seems even colder than outside the croft: the door is rimed with white; plumes of frost have crept between the tiny gaps in the turf walls.

To Rósa's surprise, Páll is sitting at the table, sectioning mutton. She smiles in relief, but his gaze is icy. She remembers how he had watched her with Jón, then turned from the loft, iron-jawed.

Now he says, without looking up, 'How is your husband?'

'He is . . .' He is what? A liar? A murderer? A man who imprisoned his wife, then said it was for her own protection? Rósa draws a breath and sits. Almost imperceptibly, Páll shifts his body away from hers.

'He is better.'

'Good. I will leave knowing you are happy.'

'Leave?'

'As soon as the thaw comes.'

'Take me with you!' The words spill out before she can stop them.

Páll's eyes widen. 'Why would you —'

'I want to return to Skálholt.' She places her hand on his, trembling.

His face softens. 'Rósa, it is unthinkable.'

'I am so miserable.'

341

He clasps her hand. 'You can't leave.'

'I won't stay.'

'Only moments ago you were all concern for your husband.' He strokes her cheek.

She is so wearied by the pressure that stretches between them, like brittle ice that will shatter with one false move. She could almost wish for that ice to crack, for the black water underneath to swallow her, rather than this agonizing *waiting* and restraint that freezes her every movement.

She draws a shaky breath. 'We will go home, Páll. After the thaw.'

Páll's eyes are dark with grief. 'I want . . . But the risk to you . . .'

As soon as she spoke the words, she knew she was naming an impossible dream. She might as well have said she longed to walk across the ocean to Denmark, or to sprout wings and fly to her mamma this very night.

Páll brushes his fingers across her lips, then releases her hand and turns away. She feels the chill when he lets her go.

'I will see you again soon,' he says softly. 'I will visit next summer.'

'Yes, you must,' she says dully. When she tries to imagine the days ahead, she can see only a cavernous blackness. Next summer is a bottomless abyss.

He puts his arms around her and rests his

forehead against hers. His eyes, so close to hers, are blue and clear. Looking into them is like staring into her own soul. She puts her hand on his chest and can feel every clutch of his heart; the push and tug of his breath and hers. Which is which?

There is a sudden sharp cry from outside the door. 'Rósa!'

She and Páll jump apart, as if stung. Rósa turns away as Katrín bursts into the storeroom. Her gaze flicks from Rósa to Páll. 'The sheep are gone. The cows too.'

'*Gone?*' Rósa says.

'How?' demands Páll.

Katrín explains as they stride through the croft and out into the snow, pulling on shawls and mittens as they walk.

She and Pétur had heard a noise from outside and had rushed into the snow. 'It sounded like a voice calling, crying out for help, or in pain.'

They had thought it might belong to someone from the settlement, one of those poor men who had ventured onto the hills only to be engulfed by the snow. They followed the cries to the barn and found the doors open and the animals gone.

'But *how*?' Rósa gasps, battling the frozen wind. 'We shut the door, Katrín.'

'That is what I told Pétur, though he is

calling me a brainless old witch. The snow is churned up all around, but the tracks are fading fast.'

'They'll be buried in this before long,' puffs Páll.

'That cry,' says Katrín, wistfully. 'It was so like . . . a child shouting.'

'You think someone is out in the snow?' Rósa asks uncertainly.

Katrín's eyes are bright as she avoids the question. 'Look,' she points at a dark shape ahead, 'here is Pétur. And this is how we found the barn. Door wide open.'

Pétur's face is grim. Rósa feels her cheeks flush, even though she *knows* they had shut the door.

'We search in pairs,' Pétur says. 'Katrín with Páll. Rósa with me.' When she shakes her head, he growls. 'I won't tell Jón I have lost his wife as well as his sheep.'

Rósa opens her mouth to argue, but Katrín and Páll have already started treading a path through the snow, following one of the gashes into the blanket of white that the animals have trampled.

Pétur sets off in the opposite direction, where there is a single path, as though one of the animals has broken from the rest and charged away by itself, in a blind panic. They wade through the thick-falling snow,

344

the ice stinging their faces, but they hear nothing, see nothing, except the never-ending white. The snow is so thick that it coats Rósa's eyelashes, and when she wipes it away more flakes quickly settle. She has the lurching sensation that she is going blind, but she must continue walking. Pétur is so close, yet she can't see him. She stops and cries out in alarm.

Pétur is next to her in an instant, and, as much as she fears him, she clings to him as though he is a rock and she is battered by a stormy sea.

'Take my hand,' Pétur calls.

Rósa doesn't argue, but grips it as tightly as she can.

Páll and Katrín are nowhere to be seen. She shouts their names, but there is no response.

She is alone with Pétur and the snow god, Ullr, and she knows, deep in her bones, that one of them will kill her.

She cries out again but the snow smothers the sound. She must not weep: the tears will freeze, and if she brushes them away, the ice will flay the flesh from her face.

The cold seeps into Rósa's dress and her shawl and insinuates itself beneath her skin, settles into her bones. Her teeth rattle. This is madness. She will tell Pétur that they must return to the croft, or they will both die.

Perhaps that is why he has brought me here. Perhaps Jón told him to take me out and kill me, and he will kill Páll and Katrín afterwards.

She stops walking and Pétur shouts something indecipherable at her, but she shakes her head. Leaden-eyed, he shouts again, but she doesn't move. She will not walk to her death.

Then she hears a cry.

'Stop!' she calls. 'What was that? Páll and Katrín?' But it is coming from the other direction, from ahead of them.

'I heard nothing.'

'There!' Rósa can hear the cry again. Insistent and regular, like the bleating of a sheep, but higher in pitch. The hairs rise on the nape of her neck. Pétur is stock-still too now.

'You hear it?' she asks, putting her hand into her pocket to feel the cold shape of the glass woman. It is calming, like placing her feet on the rock, which, long ago, must have been melted to make this perfect form. It has been shaped and transformed by fire, and has travelled over land and sea unbroken. And as fragile as it looks, it remains whole.

346

The cry rings out again.

Pétur wipes the snow from his face, then points towards the sound.

They run, the wall of white striking at them. Rósa's skirts are heavy and wet; she falls, snow filling her nose and mouth. Pétur yanks her upright and pulls her after him.

'*Ég ríf ykkur í bita!*' Pétur shouts into the darkness, and Rósa's scalp prickles at his words: *I'll rip you apart!*

Silence. As if the cries have been stifled. Over and over, Pétur calls, raging at the empty blizzard, until his angry words sound like a spell in a foreign tongue. Rósa's legs are burning and she cannot take another step. She falls again and again, and Pétur half drags her, grunting with exertion.

The snow groans beneath their feet, as if the earth itself is in the throes of some monstrous labour.

Then faintly, in the distance, that uncanny cry again.

For a moment, Rósa allows herself to imagine that the sound they heard is one of the *huldufólk,* leading them to exhaustion and death. In her hand, the glass woman is like ice, the burning cold throbbing through her mittens.

The call comes again, clearer and closer.

They run again, shouting as they stagger through the drifts — it is like wading through a river. Rósa stumbles, pushes herself upright and falls again, sobbing.

Pétur turns and scoops her up. 'I will carry you.'

'No! Put me down!' Rósa tastes the sour metallic tang of blood, and her muscles blaze but she will not let this man — this monster — carry her. She forces herself forward. Just when she is about to collapse, Pétur stops.

'There!'

A dark shadow stands in the veil of white. They could have run past it a hundred times, obscured as it is by the falling snow.

'What is it?' Rósa hisses. The figure is the height and shape of a man, but looks too wide to be human — it bulges alarmingly in the middle.

'Þú ert dauður!' Pétur says. *You are dead!* Rósa's blood ices.

Pétur leaves her and approaches the figure warily. It doubles over, and howls. He pounces on it, wrapping his arms around it. It collapses, as if it were a spirit composed only of air. He scoops the figure up, grunting because his arm pains him. Rósa sees a spill of yellow hair, and a pale face, blue eyes half closed.

348

A woman.

She stares at Pétur in horror, because she knows the answer to the question that dies unasked on her lips. She knows the name he will say.

'Anna.'

JÓN

Near Thingvellir, December 1686

Sometimes, violence produces itself, like spores of mould that lie dormant, then multiply and consume. Anna invited her imprisonment, as surely as if she had put her hands in chains and locked herself into my loft space.

Every month I did not put a babe into her belly, her resentment grew. Katrín believed she longed for something to nurture after the wasteland of her own childhood. I knew better. She craved a creature she could rule entirely.

I *wanted* to love her. I tried so hard to make myself sit with her, hold her hand, embrace her. But the longer I lived with her, the more I saw touches of cruelty in her nature. So often damaged people turn their rage upon others, as if the years of fear fill them with a poison that slowly infects all around them.

I saw the swift kicks Anna aimed at the sheep, the way she tugged on the hens' tail feathers when she thought no one saw. She would have held our children close and kissed them, even as she pinched the soft flesh on their fat little legs.

I do not believe she was wicked, only that she knew no other way to show love than by causing hurt, then trying to soothe it.

At first, I did not mind her wanderings, solitary as they were. I would have allowed her to circle the settlement all day, had it brought her some comfort, but her behaviour as she walked grew strange. She carried a staff and muttered under her breath. People stared, then ran to tell me that my wife was summoning spirits.

My guts roiled. Egill would destroy me if he saw but a trace of the old ways under my roof. Already I could feel the heat of his gaze, like an open flame beneath my feet. I knew he was spreading word in the village that Anna had cursed Birgit somehow, causing her to sicken and die.

When I asked Anna what she had been whispering as she wandered the land, she said, 'Oh, only a song I learned from Katrín.'

Katrín swore blind she hadn't taught Anna any spells. That woman could teach the changing moon to lie.

I took Anna's hand. 'You must not go out, *elskan*. It is dangerous for you . . . for all of us.'

But Anna wandered further still, and left little piles of herbs in mounds, next to pieces of driftwood arranged in patterns.

Egill delivered her to my door, a triumphant smile stretching his mouth wide. 'Runes!' Egill crowed. 'The *goði's* wife is muttering spells and covering the land with runes. I will ask the Althing how we can follow a man who cannot govern his own wife.'

'How like you to delight in misery, Egill. Anna is . . . unwell and needs to rest. But she is a godly woman, and would not dabble in witchcraft.'

'I see runes, Jón.'

'And I see them not,' I snapped. 'It is your imagination.' I tried to smile; my jaw ached. 'Why does *your* mind see runes? Perhaps we should ask the Althing *that.*'

Egill glared but said no more — that day, at least, although the next morning Olaf delivered a letter from Egill, threatening to report Anna's behaviour to the Althing and telling them that she had cursed Birgit.

I tried again to explain to Anna the danger she brought to us all.

'Egill will watch you burn, Anna *elskan,* if you but give him the chance. He will be

352

crueller to you because he seeks to harm me — you must see that.'

I took her hand, those little fingers, her bones so delicate I could have snapped them. 'Stay in the croft. You are safe here.'

She snatched away her hand, as if my affection seared her skin. 'You care nothing for me,' she hissed, her eyes burning. 'You want to keep your name pure.'

'Be careful, Anna. Don't say what you may regret.'

'If your precious people knew that you are a shrivelled worm . . .'

I drew back my hand, imagining the thud of her flesh, the hot burgundy of her blood — I stopped myself, horrified.

'Strike me,' she sneered. 'Perhaps you will feel more the man for it.'

I turned away, slapping my palm against the driftwood walls, time and again, so the whole croft rang with the sound. I did not even feel my hand bleed.

Afterwards, as Pétur bound my hand with linen, he murmured, 'She is dangerous, Jón. She will destroy herself and take us with her. And she will laugh as we all burn.'

The next night, Pétur found Anna wandering on Helgafell, chanting her three wishes to the grave of Gudrun Ósvifrsdóttir. He

353

returned her to the croft, grim-faced. 'She says she wants to talk to Egill. Alone.'

Pétur helped me fashion a lock from smelted pieces of bog iron; we settled Anna in the loft, with a mattress and a chamber pot — she was like a lost child, allowing us to lay her down and swaddle her in blankets.

I agonized over whether to leave the crib in there. Surely the sight of it would taunt her. But then I decided that taking it from her would be a final blow: confirmation that I would never get her with child.

Despite her protests, we sent Katrín away 'in case of infection' and told her to tell the village that Anna was ill. 'It would shame her to be seen like this,' I said. 'She is not herself.'

In truth she was not: once her reverie had broken and she found she was confined, she clawed at her face and growled like a savage animal. Then she beat at the door and howled to be released. Whenever I felt I might relent and let her go, Pétur was quick to remind me why I could not.

'Egill would warm his hands on the fire he made of her. And us.'

When she ceased shouting, I thought she might grow calmer and more biddable. I hoped we might be able to free her.

But when I opened the door, I found her

sitting in the corner of the loft, scratching the wood with a stone. She did not stop when I called; I had to clutch her arm before she would look at me. Even then, she only stared at my hand around her wrist, as if both belonged to other people.

'How are you, husband?' She wore the same fixed grin I had once seen on the face of a hanged man.

I studied the marks she had made in the wood. Bile rose in my throat.

'What have you done?' I gasped. Was this a curse upon me? An incantation to summon dark spirits? Or had she scrawled secrets of mine upon the floor?

'What does this say?' I demanded.

'Only the truth,' she whispered, a faint smile playing on her lips — and I knew then that she would kill all of us. Containing her here wasn't enough. She would destroy everything. And Pétur? The villagers would blame him for witchcraft without hesitation.

I could not help thinking how much easier it would be if she . . . ceased to be. I loathed myself for the villainous thought, which must surely come from the devil. Yet there it lodged, in the corner of my mind: the desire to snuff her out like a candle.

The next morning, when I entered the loft,

she was squatting against the wall; she smiled at me and looked almost peaceful. My heart lifted. I crouched next to her and stroked her cheek. 'You seem better, my love.'

'I am much better, Jón.' She leaned close to me, still smiling. I went to stroke her hair and she turned her face to nuzzle my palm, then shifted her whole body so that she was sitting in my lap.

'Anna.' I tried to shift from under her and push her away. 'I cannot, while you are so . . . You are still unwell.'

She snaked her arms around my neck and put her lips on mine. 'I am much better. You have said it.'

'Anna.' I tried to push her away again. 'Anna, stop, I cannot —'

She fell from my lap onto the floor, then leaped up, her eyes flashing. 'No, you *cannot*! I want a child and you *cannot* give me one.'

'I will not take you while —'

She screeched with uncanny laughter, lay down on the mattress and spread her legs. 'Take me, Jón. I am yours.' She laughed again.

I shook my head and turned away, sweating.

'No.' She jumped up. 'I know what you

356

are. Egill suspects, but he will be happy to know what I have seen.'

'You have seen nothing,' I gasped. 'You would not —'

'I have seen the look on your face. I see where your eyes go, and they do not fall on me.'

'Damn you, woman!' I lunged at her, but she stepped backwards out of my reach, then yanked her shift over her head and stood naked before me.

'Come, Jón.' Her voice was suddenly soft and lilting. 'Show me I am wrong.' She stepped towards me.

I turned away. 'Cover yourself! I will not lie with a madwoman who —'

'You will not lie with a woman!' she spat. 'I will tell the whole village that you are a miserable worm. You and he both! You are a big man, but your neck will snap just the same as his when I tell the Althing —'

I grabbed her by the throat and lifted her off her feet. She gasped and choked and raked her nails down my arms. I dropped her, then stared at my hands, shaking.

She sprawled on the floor, spluttering and clutching her neck.

I knelt and embraced her. 'Forgive me, Anna. Forgive me, I . . .' I kissed her cheeks, her eyelids, her lips '. . . I wouldn't hurt you, but you must understand —'

She turned to me and, with her naked body in my arms and the heat of fury still humming in my veins, for the first time in so long, I felt . . . aroused.

I lay on top of her and she kissed me. I closed my eyes and tried to maintain my desire. She wrapped her arms and legs around me. I kissed her neck.

But it was no good. Before the end, I felt myself shrivel inside her. I pulled away from her, slumping onto the floor.

I felt sick to the pit of my stomach. She crawled away from me and curled in the corner, trembling. She had cut her lip when she fell from my arms. Now she touched it and smeared the blood over the runes, then reached for me and painted it over my lips.

I flinched.

'You are a monster,' she whispered.

I retched, then spat out blood and bile. I wanted to beg forgiveness, but how could such a thing be forgiven?

We sat in the *baðstofa* all that day, Pétur and I. What could be done? I couldn't confess to him how I had used her, only that she was truly mad and daubing the loft with her blood. Pétur was in favour of returning her to Thingvellir.

'I cannot take her back to her uncle, as if she is a horse I have purchased, then discovered to be lame.'

'No,' agreed Pétur, bleakly. 'A lame horse would present an easy resolution: slit its throat and hang the meat in the storeroom for winter.'

Neither of us laughed.

That night, my dreams were sweat-rimed, full of whispering: I was a monster. My pabbi's face hung before me; his laughter filled my ears as he hissed, *Miserable worm.*

I woke early, my eyes gritty, my thoughts clear. I would unlock the loft. I would return Anna to her uncle, no matter the gossip.

But when I climbed the ladder, I found the door open, the room empty. The only sign that Anna had been there was the scarring of the runes, scored deep into the wooden floor. And, glittering in the dim light, I saw the tiny figure of the perfect glass woman I had once given her as a token of my love.

Pétur swore blind he had no knowledge of when she had disappeared, or how, or where she could have gone. He set off on Skalm and searched the settlement and hills, trying not to draw attention.

For two days he searched, but she was

nowhere to be found.

'Perhaps she drowned after all,' he said, taking a long draw of ale. 'Tried to swim to one of the islands, and the sea took her.'

'She could not swim,' I answered. 'She would not have risked herself so.'

'Pity,' Pétur muttered.

But, watching Pétur gulp his ale and eat, as if the land had not seemingly consumed my wife, I could not shake the conviction that he knew something more of Anna's whereabouts. I was *certain* I had locked the loft door. I remembered doing so.

After three days with no reports of Anna, Pétur suggested we tell people she was sickening.

Katrín wanted to see her, of course.

I tried to keep my voice steady. 'Pétur and I have both felt unwell. We fear smallpox — Anna has a terrible rash. Do not risk yourself.'

Katrín's mouth folded tightly. I remembered her lost daughter, Dora, and felt a twist of guilt.

'Here.' She pressed a bundle of herbs into my hands. 'Make sure Anna has these, and I will gather more for you and Pétur.'

Two nights later, I dug Anna's grave.

RÓSA

As soon as Rósa says Anna's name, the woman's eyelids flutter. She has wide blue eyes and is full-lipped — she should be beautiful. But her sunken cheeks are blackened with mud and her blank eyes roll in her head. She coughs and Rósa flinches.

'Rósa, take her arm,' Pétur puffs. 'We will take her to the pithouse.'

Rósa feels simultaneously rooted to the spot and overwhelmed by a dizzying vertigo — as if the world has been yanked from under her feet and now she is dangling over the edge of some yawning precipice.

'Now, Rósa!' Pétur snaps.

She shakes her head. If she touches this *thing,* it will all be true, all real. The *draugr* from her dreams: this thing that has haunted her and stood over her while she has slept. This is the spirit that has driven her to the point of madness: it will devour her soul,

361

leaving the hollow coffin of Rósa's body for the ravens.

'She is human,' he growls. 'Now, help me lift her.'

Anna collapses again, nearly dragging Pétur into the snow, and it is this movement, and the grunt of pain the woman gives, that breaks through Rósa's reverie. She rushes to support her head, and Pétur puts one of Anna's arms around her shoulders.

Rósa exhales to steady herself, then concentrates on placing one foot in front of the other. Too many thoughts clatter in her head. When she was a girl in Skálholt, a travelling trader had juggled onions while everyone watched, agog. He added more and more onions, until eventually, to the children's delight, the vegetables rained from the sky, smacking him on the head. Rósa feels that the spinning revolution of one more fear might cause her whole world to collapse.

As she walks, she risks a glance at Anna's grubby face, barely inches from hers. It is smattered with bruises. The woman seems asleep; her pale eyelids flutter disturbingly, as though she is experiencing a convulsive fit. Just then, Anna doubles over and howls, clutching at her belly.

She falls to the ground. Pétur curses and

tries to pull her up, but she squats in the snow and growls.

'She is cursed!' Rósa cries. 'Some spirit . . . The devil!'

'Rósa, you're a simpleton!' He grimaces and turns back to Anna. 'Up!' His voice is flint but his touch is light. Rósa draws comfort from seeing him rein in his anger.

Anna's fit subsides. She allows her arms to be laid over their shoulders and they trudge onwards. Twice more, she convulses and nearly falls, and twice more Pétur cajoles her forward. Only his gritted teeth betray his mood. Rósa has never seen him so outwardly gentle when his thoughts are in such obvious turmoil.

Suddenly Rósa stops. 'Surely we should go to the croft. It will be warm.'

'The pit-house is closer.' Pétur uses the long-suffering tone one might direct at a petulant child. 'There is food there, ale and blankets. But no! Let us drag Anna two hundred paces to the croft. She will have a comfortable place to die and we will hang her in the storeroom with the sheep carcasses, until the thaw.'

Anna gives a throaty snarl, which Rósa realizes is a tiny chuckle.

'Pit-house,' she gasps.

Rósa nods. They do not say another word

until they reach it.

Pétur digs the snow away from the doorway and they tumble into the darkness. He lights three tallow candles and, as Rósa's eyes adjust, she notices that the single room is perfectly kept. It is laid out with two straw mattresses and some benches. There are flagons of ale on the table and pieces of dried meat hanging from the rafters. There is even some half-finished knitting.

'Who lives here?' Rósa demands.

'No one,' Pétur answers. 'Jón and I use it, if we return late from fishing.'

Rósa stares at him but he says no more.

Anna crawls onto the bed, then gives a long moan. Pétur barely looks at her but pours ale into three cups, made from sheep horn.

'We must stop these attacks,' cries Rósa. 'She will die!'

'This is no *attack*,' says Pétur, taking a long draught of ale. He passes a cup to Rósa. 'And now she can rest, she will not die.'

'But you said —'

'There is nothing wrong with her that many women do not endure.'

Rósa puts a hand to her mouth. 'She is . . .'

'Yes.' Pétur draws aside Anna's many cloaks and tunics; the swell of her belly is tight as the skin on a ripe apple.

Rósa draws a sharp breath. 'Oh!'

Not just his wife then. His *pregnant* wife. Rósa's thoughts whirl.

And yet she is winded by pity for this fragile creature. Her body is tiny against the rise of her belly; her arms and legs are sticks of driftwood.

Rósa reaches out to Anna; the other woman pushes her away, spitting curses. Rósa keeps her hand outstretched, as if offering it to a wild animal to sniff. She looks into Anna's eyes and sees, beneath the rage, a terrified child.

Rósa smiles, lips trembling. 'Let me help you.'

Anna collapses forward into her arms. Rósa cradles her, then shifts her gently onto her back and peels off layer after layer of Anna's clothing, until she lies in just a shift. Her body is bruised and mud-blackened.

'You have lived in the hills?' Pétur asks.

Anna stares at him. 'Katrín . . .' Her blue eyes light, then shine with tears. 'I want Katrín.'

Rósa strokes her grubby cheek. 'Katrín is . . . close. She will be here soon.' Her lie sounds unconvincing, even to her own ears.

Pétur scowls and turns away.

Another pain shakes Anna and she cries

out, then lies back against Rósa, panting. Her eyes are huge and pitiful. 'Will I die? Don't let me die.'

Rósa clasps her cold fingers. 'Hush, no. You won't die. Here, sip this ale.'

Anna mutters over and over, 'Don't let me die, don't let me die — I won't die!'

Pétur turns back to Anna. 'And where have you lived these past two seasons?' She recoils from him.

'Leave her be,' says Rósa. 'Fetch me a cloth and some water for her face.'

Pétur does as she asks.

Rósa gently wipes her face and arms. Anna's face is blank. 'I was frightened. I'm so . . .' She trembles then moans, a drawn-out, wordless cry that scours the walls of the pit-house and makes the hairs rise on the back of Rósa's neck: for a moment, it is as though she is looking into a mirror. She sees the same torturous rift that has ripped her in two these past months.

Anna's body shudders again and her belly tightens; she clenches her teeth and snarls. Once the pain has passed, Rósa strokes her hair and holds the ale to her mouth.

'You told everyone she was dead,' Rósa murmurs, glancing up at Pétur.

His eyes flash. 'What else could we have done? She . . . escaped,' he mutters, staring at the floor.

'Run away,' Anna murmurs. 'Run far, far away.' She sobs, then cringes as Pétur glowers at her.

Rósa stares at Pétur and he flushes, drops his gaze, then looks back at Anna. His lip curls and he takes a step forward, but Rósa puts herself between him and Anna. 'Don't touch her! *You* did this.'

'No!' Pétur reddens further. 'Not mine. I wouldn't . . .'

Rósa narrows her eyes. 'What did you do?'

'I . . . I have never hurt her.'

Anna sighs and murmurs, 'Run away, run away,' in a sing-song chant that fills the room, so it seems as if the walls themselves are whispering.

Rósa's legs shake but she forces herself to face Pétur, to look into those predator's eyes. 'You *made* her leave!'

'It was better. With her gone —'

'But Jón —'

'He *knew* it was better. She would have ruined him.'

Rósa shivers. They had preferred the thought of Anna's death to the story of her flight. Jón had played the part of the respectable grief-stricken widower.

Pétur turns to Anna. Contempt twists his face. 'And now you come to stir trouble.

Perilous travel, but worth risking yourself and the babe, just to wave your belly —'

'Pétur! Enough!' Rósa leans forward and strokes Anna's cheek. But Anna makes no response except to hiss.

She lies quite still between pains, panting. Her sweat-sheened face looks like a grey, river-wet stone, and Rósa can feel the shape of the other woman's fear as if it is her own, as if it is the darkness that has swallowed her these past months.

'We should fetch Katrín,' she says.

Pétur shakes his head, but Anna's eyes are suddenly sharp. 'Katrín,' she groans, her voice cracking. 'Bring Katrín.'

Another spasm bends Anna double, and she howls.

'She seems weaker,' Rósa mutters, sponging Anna's cheeks and forehead. Another cramp grips her and her whole body is shaking. Rósa's legs quiver too, as Pétur watches her, but she is tired, so tired, of being afraid. She grips Anna's hand.

'Go! Now!' she says to Pétur. When he doesn't move, she adds, 'If she dies, I will tell —'

'Enough, woman!' Pétur groans. 'I will look for Katrín.'

He slams out into the cold and then the air is quiet and still, apart from Anna's laboured breathing and the heavy thud of Rósa's blood in her ears.

Rósa squeezes Anna's cold hand. The tips of her fingers are laced with blue. She gazes mutely at the straggle of roots in the turf roof.

'Did you come in here,' Rósa murmurs, 'when you were . . . when you lived in Stykkishólmur? I was forbidden.'

Again, Anna doesn't answer, but she is suddenly still, her breathing quiet.

'I saw the runes,' Rósa whispers. 'In the loft. And the . . . stain. He hurt you?'

Anna looks straight at Rósa and then she screams — an uprooting sound that makes Rósa recoil and want to cover her ears.

When the pain has passed, she wipes Anna's forehead and whispers, 'The blood in the loft. Did Jón harm you? Or did Pétur?'

Anna's gaze fixes on Rósa — those eyes, like the azure in a glacier, where it is coldest and most dangerous. 'They take everything. Men take everything.'

Rósa opens her mouth to argue, then shuts it again. She remembers what Pétur had told her: how the Vikings claimed the land by chopping down the trees and tilling the soil until it turned to dry dust and barren rock. Men desire everything. Women's bodies are part of the land they claim. She clears her throat. 'But they didn't try to . . . They didn't hurt you by —'

'I wished for a baby,' Anna gasps. 'Wishing is dangerous.' She wraps her arms about herself and laughs, a high-pitched sound, like splintering glass. Then another spasm takes her breath; the laughter becomes a moan.

Rósa feels a chill. It is as if she is looking at the snarled mess of what her own mind is becoming: a tangled skein of rage and fear and loss. She presses her lips to Anna's forehead. 'You are safe now,' she whispers.

Anna's eyes are dark caverns. 'You are a fool.'

Rósa inspects the area under her skirt often, but there is no change. Between spasms, Anna seems to sleep, her breath puffing lightly from between her parted lips.

Rósa reaches into her tunic pocket to run her fingers over the shape of the glass woman. But her pocket is empty, the little figurine gone. Rósa imagines it lying outside in the snow. She shakes her head to rid herself of a stabbing sensation of loss. She had somehow tied her own fate to the ornament: this thing that seemed so breakable yet remained unmarked, even when she tried to crush it. Jón had thought it an apt gift because it was humble; Rósa loved it because, though it appeared no more substantial than ice, the glass woman had survived. And, in the face of Jón's stifling expectations, survival itself had seemed an act of rebellion.

She wipes away a tear, then strokes Anna's damp cheek and rubs her stomach. 'Does this help or pain you?'

Anna's eyes roll and she moans. Rósa tries to quell her rising panic.

Pétur does not return. The tallow candles burn low and gutter. Rósa manages to find two more before the light disappears completely.

Rósa opens the door to see if she can make out Pétur's shape, but is blinded by the dizzying shatter of snowflakes reeling through the grey air. The shadows howl; she cannot even tell whether it is day or night, and she slams the door.

Anna is weaker still, her breathing shallow. She barely regains consciousness, even in the throes of the pains, but writhes on the bed, groaning.

Rósa whispers meaningless words of comfort into her ear, but Anna's skin is as slick as wet obsidian, and her eyes are dull.

Rósa lies next to her on the bed, hoping that her own body might somehow take

371

some of Anna's pain. But Anna's lips draw back in a rictus and she snarls. Rósa crushes her own fear and revulsion: this woman needs her.

Anna's teeth are chattering, and Rósa bends to pick up the woman's discarded dress to lay it across her. And that is when she feels it in the pocket: a stone. She reaches in and draws out a flat runestone with the sign for protection scrawled upon it. It is flatter than the one Rósa threw into the snow, and darker, but still, it offers her some comfort. She presses it into Anna's hand and whispers the words of protection, lines from the Sagas, phrases from the Lord's Prayer, all jumbled together.

The sound must soothe Anna, because her breathing lengthens and, between pains, she seems to doze.

Then a spasm grips her and bends her body almost in two. She screams and suddenly Rósa sees a dark pool of blood inching across the blankets beneath Anna's shift.

'Blood everywhere!' The horror knocks the breath from her: she has seen this in ewes. The afterbirth is blocking the birth canal and has come away from the womb. Anna will bleed dry.

Rósa feels a crushing pressure in her chest, as if someone has bound her with ropes and is pulling them tighter. She knows what she must do. The baby might still survive . . . But it will have to be cut from Anna's belly.

Anna will die.

Rósa's breath is tight. For a moment she feels paralysed. Then she thinks of the baby and she draws a shaky breath. The decision is as clear as a drop of meltwater in the palm of her hand. A life may still be saved; some good can come from this. Watching Anna bleed to death would itself be an act of murder. She is growing paler; her hands, lips and nose are tinged blue, as if she is already becoming ice.

Even as panic grips her, Rósa realizes that fear is useless, like lighting a candle to melt a snowdrift. She knows what she must do, and bites her lip until she tastes metal. She picks up Pétur's knife from the bench, turns to Anna with shaking hands and draws her shift up over her belly.

Her mind searches blankly for a prayer, a spell, a line from the Sagas. She can only whisper, 'Forgive me,' her voice fracturing as she presses the blade to Anna's bulging abdomen.

A tiny bead of blood appears on her white skin. It is nothing against the puddles and spatterings of gore that cover her legs, the mattress and the blankets, but still Rósa retches and stops.

She floods with the overwhelming caged-animal terror that has plagued her for months, the knowledge that there are duties she must fulfil, orders she must obey.

Then she thinks again of that tiny baby who has never known the world, has never drawn breath to do anyone harm. Purest of beings, yet the life is draining from it, before it has had a chance to blink, and bawl at the cold misery of living.

She sets her shoulders and squares her jaw. She *must* do this. It is a choice, and she will grasp it with both hands. As she looks down at Anna's body, it is as if she is seeing herself, the pain that has gripped her. And here is a chance to conquer it.

She starts to cut.

The blade is sharp. Sudden blood. Anna screams.

'I know! I know! I'm sorry,' Rósa sobs.

Anna groans.

'It will be over soon. You will hold your baby. I promise.' She presses the runestone into Anna's hands.

Her flesh is cold as the sea, her eyes wild. Rósa clutches her icy fingers and the stone with one hand, the knife with the other.

But then she meets resistance, something

hard — the womb. She jerks away and rubs her fingers reflexively to rid them of the sensation of cutting *someone.*

Anna moans, and Rósa thinks of the fox pup, of the trust the little animal placed in her.

She strokes Anna's cold cheek. 'You are safe, I promise.' Her voice trembles but the lie is necessary. Sometimes deceit is kinder than the truth.

So much blood. Sticky and hot and stinking of metal. Rósa wipes the wound. A tear falls onto her hand.

Anna lies still now, breath barely puffing from between her slack lips.

Rósa takes a breath and cuts. Another gush of blood. She braces herself to hear an infant howl.

Silence. Rósa reaches into Anna's body and tugs. Like a miracle, a tiny body emerges, whole and intact.

Rósa gasps. 'Beautiful!' But then she turns the baby around, and her breath catches in her throat. Its skin is bluish; it shows no sign of drawing breath. But more than that: it is like a little sea creature that has been ripped from the ocean too soon. Its skin is iridescent and the eyes, half open, are utterly black. There is a smooth bulge of skin, where the genitals should be.

Rósa presses her fingers against its chest, willing it to rise and fall, but the baby remains lifeless. She blows on its face, even turns it over and slaps it. She kisses its pale cheek.

'Breathe. *Breathe!*'

Nothing. A gaping silence where life should be.

Rósa cradles the limp little thing and presses her lips to its cooling forehead; she caresses its webbed feet, its small pointed chin, its delicate tipped ears, like an elf's. She thinks of the whispers about *huldufólk*.

Rósa draws a shuddering sigh and wraps the blanket around the tiny creature, concealing the hands, the ears, the point of the chin. It looks like any other newborn, sleeping peacefully.

'Anna. Your baby. It is . . . perfect, see.'

Anna's eyelids flutter and Rósa lays the baby on her chest. There is a shadow of a smile on Anna's lips. 'A girl?' she murmurs.

Rósa draws a shuddering breath. 'Yes, a . . . girl.'

'Give her to Katrín.' Anna's voice is barely more than a breath.

Rósa leans in close. 'Anna. Whose child is it?'

'Call her . . . Dora,' Anna whispers, then shudders. Her face falls slack.

'Who is the pabbi, Anna?'

'Tell Jón I forgive . . . Oddur Thordson was —' Anna gasps, then her breath catches.

'Who is Oddur Thordson?'

Anna's eyes are blank. She does not make another sound.

Rósa waits for a word, a movement, a breath — anything to show that she lives, or that she is passing the threshold into death. But there is nothing so momentous. No marker to show when she exists or when she is no more than a bloodied husk upon the bed. Death, when it comes, steals her with a whisper and silence.

Rósa feels hollow and tearless, a dried-out shell. She lifts the tiny dead child from Anna's chest and arranges it in the crook of her arm. Then she tugs Anna's shift down and layers the two of them in blanket after blanket, mother and child. At a glance, they could be tucked up in bed together, sleeping.

After what seems like half a day, the door bangs open and Pétur gusts in with a sweep of frozen air.

Rósa turns. 'Katrín, I . . .' The words die on her lips. Pétur is alone. He stares at the bed, at the bodies, at the blood that spatters the walls and has dried over Rósa's face and arms, so she feels she is encased in a solid mask of gore.

'I tried . . .' she whispers, and suddenly she cannot stop her tears.

Pétur is grim-faced as he draws back the blanket and gazes at the tiny misshapen baby. 'She was doomed, Rósa. And see the size of the infant. It was born too soon — a mercy, perhaps.'

'Katrín and Páll?'

Pétur shakes his head, and grief hits Rósa, like a balled fist in the guts. She weeps as Pétur rewraps the child and places it back in Anna's arms.

'It looks like . . .' Rósa cannot choke out the words: that it looks like a monster.

Pétur is hard-jawed. 'Not Jón's child . . .' He trails off and there is silence.

Rósa whispers, 'She said the pabbi was . . . Oddur Thordson.'

Pétur's head jerks up and he stands trans-fixed. 'Oddur Thordson?'

Rósa nods.

'You are certain? She said Oddur Thordson?'

'Yes. Who is he?'

Pétur is muttering the name, like a spell.

'Pétur! Who is Oddur Thordson?'

Pétur's face is sharp with sorrow and something else. Dread? Revulsion?

'Oddur Thordson,' he rasps, 'is Anna's uncle.'

JÓN

It is dark and Oddur will be sleeping. I imagine him, drowned in drink, lips slack, every breath a puff of stinking fumes.

The door to the croft is ajar. I slip through the gap like a shadow.

Inside, the tiny croft is almost bare: a single room with two beds. He is lying on one, insensible. Everything is grubby, with a sticky patina; the table and bench are littered with half-eaten crusts. The open fire is nearly burned out, surrounded by weeks of accumulated ash. I find a pile of sheep dung in a corner and heap a little on the embers, then blow until an orange glow fills the croft.

He stirs and moans in his sleep, but does not wake. I work around him, taking the thick rope from around my waist — Danish, strong enough to truss a bull — and bind his legs together, then his arms, plac-

380

ing his hands in front of his chest, so that he could be praying. He twitches, grunts, then continues to snore.

I position my bench in front of the bed, beyond the stretch of a swung fist.

Then I fill my cup with *brennevín.* I sit and wait.

Pétur fetched me from the loft in the middle of the night. 'Jón! Jón!' He shook my shoulder.

I pushed him away. 'Let me rest. My stomach feels all fire.'

Pétur put his face very close to mine. 'I have found Anna.'

'Anna! How? But she's —'

'In the pit-house.'

'That cannot . . .' My thoughts reeled. 'Take me to her.' I tried to scramble up, then sank back, coughing, pain knifing across my side.

'Steady.' Pétur put an arm around me and eased me upright. 'She is —'

'She is *what*?' I tried to stand, then fell back, clutching my belly: it felt as though my guts might spill out. Something in Pétur's expression gave me pause. 'What?'

'Anna is . . . she is — dead,' Pétur croaked.

'Show me.'

He leaned down and lifted me, as if I were

381

no heavier than a child, though I knew his arm hurt him from his sharp intake of breath as he bore my weight.

'You are in pain,' I protested. 'Set me down.'

'My pain is nothing,' he said, then put me across his back while he descended the ladder. He cradled me against his chest while he struggled across the snow. Every jolting step was a blade in my side; the breath whistled through my teeth.

I leaned my head against his warmth and tried to mask my agony.

Anna was laid out on the bed, the babe wrapped up next to her. Rósa knelt on the floor beside them, holding Anna's hand. Her shoulders were shaking.

I put my hand on the back of her neck. I could feel every one of her fragile bones. She recoiled, then scrabbled backwards.

'I'm not a monster,' I said, but it emerged as a growl, and she flinched again.

'Of course not, Jón,' she whispered, her eyes large. I could see her frantic heartbeat in the delicate hollow of her throat.

I tried to smile, but managed only a grimace.

Then I sank onto the bench, wheezing — every inhalation was a tongue of flame licking across the wound.

In death, Anna was beautiful. The mouth had lost its stubborn petulance, and her face held none of the tense anger that had shadowed her every glance in life.

Pétur murmured, 'She was always doomed. And, look, she is all bones. The Lord knows how she dragged herself here.'

She has her baby now. I would not speak such a brutal thought aloud.

I reached out towards the tiny shrivelled thing. 'Mine, poor child.'

Pétur shook his head. 'Not yours.'

I frowned. 'But —'

'It cannot be yours, Jón. You know it cannot . . .' He trailed off and I put my head in my hands.

Rósa and Pétur exchanged a glance; Pétur shook his head at her.

'What is it? What did she tell you?'

'It is of no matter,' Pétur said.

'Tell him.' Rósa's voice was stiff, as though the past week had hardened her.

Pétur groaned.

'Tell me!'

They were both silent.

Then, 'Her uncle,' Rósa whispered. So quietly that I thought I must have misheard. I asked her to speak again because surely, *surely* not.

Pétur scrubbed his hands through his hair. 'Oddur Thordson is the pabbi.'

'No!' I reeled, remembering the man Anna had lived with when I met her first, the drunken fool who had raised her half wild. I recalled how she sought to avoid him, and spent so many days wandering the hills. I remembered her eagerness to wed me: she had been so desperate to escape Thingvellir. I thought of her dissatisfaction in our marriage bed, and how, when I lay atop her, she stared at me with a contempt and hatred that made me wither.

I closed my eyes. She had been a drowning soul and I had watched her sink beneath the surface again and again. Nothing I had done had pulled her from the water.

I spoke slowly. 'I'll cut Oddur's throat.'

'Jón, you will not,' said Pétur.

'I can't let this stand.'

'And yet you must.'

'*Why* would she return to him?' I looked down and found my hands were trembling. 'Why did she not go elsewhere?' I demanded.

Pétur averted his eyes and, once more, I was struck by the suspicion that he had threatened her. And yet I could not ask him. To confirm my fears, I would have to confront him, to condemn him.

'Oddur!' I muttered. 'I will throttle the miserable wretch.'

'No!' hissed Pétur. 'You will change nothing by bringing the law upon your own head. In the spring, we will seek justice through the Althing.'

I gave a vicious bark of laughter. '*How? How* can I condemn the man who violated my wife when I have told one and all that she is in her grave?'

Silence settled between us. Outside, the snow dropped through the darkness, muffling and concealing everything. Rósa still held Anna's hand, and was stroking the lilac fingertips. She must have sensed my gaze on her because she looked up, eyes hard. 'I suppose you must lock me away now, to silence me?'

I stared at her. 'Rósa, I —'

'I will not tell a soul about the child,' Rósa interrupted. 'Not for your sake, but for hers. People are cruel.' She stroked Anna's pale cheek. 'I would not have more whispering about her.'

Pétur was watching Rósa, his body tense; he exhaled slowly and leaned back against the wall. Even so, I knew his thoughts must be running ahead, as mine were: Anna's body in the pit-house was a danger. The ground was too hard to bury her, but the sight of her and her poor deformed bastard child would whip up a storm in the settlement. Certainly I would be *goði* no longer: Egill would accuse me of murder.

Pétur squeezed my arm. 'We must do it tonight.'

'The ground will be frozen for weeks,' I muttered.

Rósa ceased her whispered prayers and turned on me. 'You would bury her now? Hide her, unmourned?'

'Who would mourn her?' Pétur snapped. 'You did not know her, Rósa. She had no friends —'

'Katrín loved her,' Rósa said.

'Katrín has mourned her once.'

'Without a proper burial.' There was a new defiance in Rósa's voice, a challenge in the angle of her jaw. 'Katrín loved her like a daughter. And she lost her, like her daughter. You say you are no monster, but you deny —'

'I would *deny* Katrín *nothing.*' My tone must have been more ferocious than I intended, for Rósa cowered.

'I would spare her this misery,' I said, more quietly. 'Will it lessen your sorrow to have Katrín share it? Will her grief raise Anna from the dead?'

Rósa's head was bowed and a tear

splashed onto her hand.

I drew a breath and spoke more calmly. 'We must protect Katrín from this. Surely you see that telling her would be cruel.'

Rósa said nothing, but brushed the hair from Anna's forehead.

'We will bury her tonight,' I said.

Rósa bit her lip. Rebellion glittered in her eyes, but she remained silent.

I rubbed my eyes. 'A fire to soften the soil will draw too much notice.'

'Let us hope Egill lies crushed beneath his croft,' Pétur muttered darkly. He paused. 'If we took her up onto the hill,' he said, 'nature would do its work.'

'*No!*' Rósa and I spoke together. She rose to her feet, mouth twisting in revulsion. 'You would let the foxes feast on her? On the child? You heartless —'

Pétur held up his hands. 'It gives me no joy, but what else?'

'I never believed those who said you weren't human. But now —'

'Pétur would not do it,' I said, putting my hand upon Rósa's shoulder. 'We only seek some way to bury her that will cause no more pain.'

Rósa shrugged off my hand and strode to the fire, stiff-backed. 'I wish . . .' She stopped, and I saw her angrily wipe her cheeks, then kick one of the hearthstones with the toe of her boot.

I suppose she wished herself unwed, that she wished herself back in Skálholt, that she longed to be anywhere but here. I could read her regrets and yearning in the shuddering of her shoulders, in the way she held herself apart and rigid, like a trapped animal. But I did not ask what she wished for. I could not trust myself.

Pétur watched her too, his body rigid. I caught his eye and shook my head.

He sighed. 'We can't bury her at sea.'

'She would remain there until spring, floating under the ice.'

Rósa muttered something.

'Speak up,' Pétur demanded.

'The hearthstones,' she whispered, and the look of self-loathing on her face could have cracked my heart.

We wrapped the bodies separately in linen sheets, layering stones in the material.

I swaddled the child with a stone next to its heart. I whispered my longing for forgiveness to Anna's cold body and pressed my lips to the crust of dried blood on her forehead.

My wound pained me as we began to carry her down to the sea ice — I struggled to hold myself upright. Pétur tried to persuade me against it. He could manage alone, he insisted. But I couldn't allow Anna such a lonely leave-taking. She had always made me feel so small, but looking at the softness of her face in death, I could see only the terrified child who had crouched behind her fury.

As I held Anna's body close, Rósa stepped forward to help.

'And what if I forbid you?' I asked sternly.

She raised her chin and gazed directly into my eyes. 'And what if you do?'

Her face was hard, her eyes unreadable, and I was suddenly struck by how, in that moment, she reminded me of Anna.

We cradled Anna's body between us. Pétur and I bore the brunt of the weight, carrying her legs and her shoulders. My breath whistled from between my teeth.

Pétur stopped. 'Rest, for God's sake.'

I shook my head. 'Walk on.' I clenched my jaw. Every step gave something back to Anna.

Rósa walked between us, clasping the swaddled child, no bigger than the span of my outstretched hands. Her face was pale and tense, like one of the waxwork death masks they make in foreign countries.

Lord, what have I done to these women?

The snow grew deeper as we laboured down the hill. The land was a flat white pall, spread out like rumpled wool.

Into the distance stretched the solid sea, sullen and murky beneath the ice.

The sea will trick a man, seeming frozen and steadfast on the surface, but under the white crust, the black water gulps greedily at the breathing world above.

In time, I knew, despite everything that had happened, the sun would rise and the light would glitter off the ice, like shards of glass. The world would glow.

Walking downhill jolted my wound. Every step echoed through my body, the pain as exquisite as cut crystal. My gift to the woman whom I could not save.

A chill wind blew across the frozen water. There was no marker to show where the land ended and the sea began, except for the blocks of solid sea, where the water had frosted over, shifted, then frozen again. Tiny slabs of ice squatted, stacked like tombstones.

We walked out onto the crusted water. The ice groaned under our feet, the rumble of an Arctic bear, warning as the dark water beneath shifted. We stopped. My heart beat in my throat. I waited for the crack of the ice, the roar of the water.

The world held its breath.

I turned to Rósa. 'Stay here. Give me the child.'

'I will come too.' Her mouth was stubbornly set, but her lips trembled.

'Don't be a fool,' I growled.

She dropped her gaze. I felt a flood of relief.

I took the little bundle and Pétur and I walked onwards, feet crunching on the ice, which whined beneath our weight. Anna's cold head bounced on my shoulder.

I closed my eyes and imagined, for a moment, that I had been able to reach her. That my gifts of warmth and clothing and ornaments had been enough to soothe the poison that Oddur had dripped into her before we met. I wondered if Pétur felt the same grief but, as ever, his true feelings were a mystery. Had he truly chased her away — condemned her to death? I would not — could not — ask.

We reached a point ten horse-lengths from where the white ice ended in ragged circles, and the black open sea stretched beyond.

'We go no further,' Pétur muttered. 'I do not trust it to hold.'

He took a stave and jabbed at the ice. It splintered, and black water bled hungrily to the surface. Wasn't it the greatest sin of all, to hide her body? She would rot in the sea, fish-nibbled and unknown. I stared into the chasm of darkness. It seemed I was gazing at the hollow void of my own future: by burying the truth, I was stepping into the shadows, walking away from God.

It was too late: Pétur released the baby, then Anna, feet-first.

The stones in her shroud dragged her away, a fading smudge of white in the drowning darkness. The water consumed everything. Her quick, wide smile that I had seen so rarely. Her flashes of rage. The way she tensed her jaw and glared. Her longing for a child. Her capacity for love, so thwarted from the start. Everything disappeared with the speed of a breath. The sea monster gulped her down, then yawned, insatiable.

I tried to mutter a prayer, but my mind was like a blank sheet of vellum. In the end, the only words I could think of to say were 'Forgive me.'

From behind my shoulder, Rósa's voice: 'Amen.'

'When the storm abates, the waves roar,' Pétur muttered. Beside me, Rósa shivered, and I could see why: over the grating ice and the vanished body, Pétur's words

392

sounded like a prophecy. We did not say *Amen.*

The ice moaned.

We walked back to the croft in silence. The witnessing moon sailed above, wide-eyed and watchful.

In Oddur's croft, memories and the *brennevín* have lit a fire in my belly. I am ready. My wound throbs with every thud of my heart, as if the thin layer of new skin that holds me together may tear apart at any moment. Ten breaths more, and it will not matter. This vengeance will be my last gift. Then I will crumple around my guts and sleep.

Oddur still snores before me on the bed, limp as a dead man. I draw out my knife and prick his finger, hard enough to draw blood. He grunts and starts, blinks blearily in the firelight. Then he sees me, sees the blade in my hand. 'Christ!' he yells, and staggers upright but, trussed as he is, falls heavily to the floor. 'I have no coin.' His voice is blurred with drink. 'Take the pewter plates.'

'I do not want your plates.' I smile. I am not a cruel man, but he looks ridiculous, half naked, sweating and wheezing. Anna would have laughed to see him.

'You want gold?' His tone is wheedling

now. 'I will show you Gunnar Arnason's croft. He has gold. And a red stone the size of a man's fist.'

'A red stone?' I have no interest in such things, but I would like to know if Oddur is a liar as well as a villain.

'Huge. We can take it together. Gunnar is a fool and will not suspect me.'

I lean forward on the bench so that my face is inches from his. His eyes are still wide and fearful, but there is a glitter of hope there too. And greedy cunning. There is no stone, I would stake my life on it. If I let Oddur go, he would knife me and steal my coin purse as soon as he could.

'So, you are a liar and a thief, as well as a lecher?'

Oddur frowns and tries to focus his gaze on me. 'I — I know you. Who . . . ?'

'You don't remember me, Oddur?'

His face registers horror, which he covers with a cry. 'Jón! My dear kinsman Jón!' He laughs too loudly. 'But so filthy and wild-looking. A fine trick. But these ropes pain my wrists. I cannot fetch you ale if my hands are numb.'

I lean closer. 'I have come for Anna,' I growl.

'Anna? Ah. She is . . .' His eyes dart left and right. Sweat glistens on his forehead. 'I don't know where she is.' Too late, he adds, 'There was talk she had died this last summer and you had buried her.'

'You know that was not true.'

He licks his lips. 'Not true? Then she is alive?' He eyes the knife. 'But you are angry. You must not shout at me, Jón, if you cannot keep your own wife.'

'She appeared in Stykkishólmur.' I watch his face. 'Some weeks past.' I pause. 'Do you not wish to know where she has been between times?'

His hands clench, but he says nothing.

'She had been here, in *Thingvellir,*' I hiss, watching his expression carefully. 'All that time, I thought her dead. Yet she was sheltering here. With *you.*'

His eyes widen. 'She was not! I have not seen her since you married her.' He is a skilled storyteller, his face full of shocked innocence. 'Believe me, Jón.'

'Lies!' I put the knife to his throat and press inwards, hard enough that I can feel the hammer of his pulse echoing up the blade and into my hand. 'God hates liars, Oddur. Will you die with the burden of deceit to add to your other evils?'

His eyes roll and his breath comes in gasps. 'I swear I have not seen her.' He gulps. 'The knife . . . it pains me.'

I press harder. 'Who fathered that child?'

He blinks and stares, so I increase the pressure on the knife again. I feel his skin break, and a drop of blood trickles down the blade.

'*Who?*'

He gulps. 'What child? I know nothing of a child. Don't hurt me, Jón.' He begins to weep.

I slump and drop the knife. 'She was not here?'

Oddur rubs his throat. 'She returned to you safely, you say?' he whispers. 'And . . . the child?'

'They are both dead,' I snarl. 'The child was crosswise in the womb and misshapen. It had to be cut from her. Anna bled to death.'

'Oh . . .' His face sags and his voice cracks. 'Did she suffer?'

'Yes.' A fierce rage bubbles up in me — I see no need to spare Oddur. 'She was fearful and in agony.'

'I had hoped . . .' He draws a shuddering breath.

'How do you dare to weep for her? You made her miserable and desperate.'

'Do not try to blame *me*.'

'You poisoned her childhood.' I indicate his broken-down croft.

'If you must place fault, then look to yourself, Jón.'

My mouth drops open.

He leans forward, his pouchy face eager and sweating. 'What sort of man makes his wife so desperate that she abandons him?'

I shake my head. 'You neglected her.'

'*I* neglected her?' He laughs. '*You* did, Jón. She longed for a child, but —'

'Do not push me, Oddur.'

'You want truth?' he sneers. 'You drove her from your bed because you are no man. I hear you cannot have a child because your eyes look elsewhere. I hear —'

I strike him before the thought has even occurred to me. His head snaps backwards and my knuckles sting. I expect rage, but he smiles, and I long to punch him again and again, until his face is a bloody pulp.

But my old restraint takes over. I steady myself and force out a slow breath.

Oddur chuckles quietly. 'Your blood is too thin for violence, *goði.*'

I imagine taking my second knife from my belt and slitting the man's throat. But before I can move, Oddur surges forward and knocks the knife from my grasp; it clatters into the dark. Then he launches himself at me. His bulk sends me crashing to the floor, and before I can draw breath, he is atop

397

me, grunting.

He brings up his bound hands and fixes a meaty paw about my throat. I cannot breathe. I try to clout him, but it is like lifting the crushing weight of the ocean. Every movement threatens to rip open my stomach wound.

The strength drains from my muscles; darkness creeps into my vision. I buck my whole body in one final, desperate attempt to shift him. The wound in my stomach radiates pain. My world shrinks, then dims. I know that I will die with Oddur's face filling my gaze. I try to pray, but God is silent.

Then, suddenly, my scrabbling hand finds my belt — and my second knife. I use the last of my strength to roll a little to one side and grab it.

He leans in close, his expression one of growing menace as he feels me weakening. And his face, in that moment, reminds me not of my pabbi's but of my own: haunted, terrified and distorted with hatred. From deep within the heart's still pool, I feel the twist of that frayed old rope of revulsion and fear.

'You are as weak as she said.' Oddur laughs. 'A miserable worm, that's how she said you were.'

The words ring through me. The same

words Anna had used: *miserable worm.* But how had he known, unless . . . The knowledge sinks into me like a sharpened blade: she *had* returned here.

My rage gives me the sudden strength I need to force him off me. He rolls to one side, his trussed hands underneath him. He is laughing still. I press my blade against his neck again.

'She was *here*! Admit it, or I stab you now.'

He hesitates then nods. 'She crept into my croft one night, not long after the Solstice.'

'And you hid her?'

He nods again.

'Why did she leave?' A creeping dread prickles my scalp. I can already imagine what Oddur would have demanded as payment for shelter and silence.

His eyes flick left and right and his tongue wets his lips. 'I don't know.'

'Liar!' I cuff him about the head and he grunts. 'You wanted her. Did you force her?'

He shakes his head, but not before I see his eyes widen and, in that moment, like a glimpse into a stinking crypt, I know I've seen the truth.

I collapse back against the wall, retching. My wife so feared me that she had returned to *this*?

I look up at him slowly. 'When you saw

she was with child, you sent her back to me?'

'How could I have kept a child hidden?'

My thoughts unspool. He had sent her out into the snow, weak and with child as she was. He had sent her to her death.

He smiles at me. It is like a gaping chasm opening up in the earth. 'She is better off dead, Jón. You must know that. You are safe from rumours, and I am free from whatever poison the little slut might have whispered.'

I roar and cuff him. His head snaps back and I hit him again. And then again.

He laughs.

After confessing to his villainy, then learning of Anna's death and the baby, he *laughs.*

Some age-old savagery surges through me and, suddenly, I cannot stop. I pick up a hearthstone and slam it into his face.

There is a crunch and his laughter is cut off. I pound the rock against his skull and am filled with a fierce, wild exultation, as if I am God's own hand, beating down the devil that has plagued the world for so long.

I throw the rock to one side and stagger backwards, away from his bleeding, twitching form. My wound has broken open and my seeping blood mingles with his. I lean against the wall, shaking, and watch him until he stops moving.

My veins buzz with fierce life and I think

of Anna's smile, half-wild, as she was when I first met her. And over the sound of my ragged breathing, I think I hear the sound of her laughter.

'God speed,' I whisper.

I sit with Oddur until his body is cold, until my muscles have stiffened and I can see the black imprints of his hand burgeoning under my skin.

A grey, gloomy light seeps into the room. I stand and stretch my aching limbs, then walk back up towards my cave. My body is racked with exhaustion but my thoughts soar above, weightless.

Someone will find me, Egill's men or the outraged people of Thingvellir. And I will lay my head upon the block without protest.

RÓSA

Stykkishólmur, November 1686

In the days after Anna's sea burial, a muzzled, threatening peace encloses the croft. Pétur and Jón talk in strained whispers, falling silent if they note Rósa listening.

Jón sees her watching and raises his eyebrows. 'You know how to be silent, Rósa? If they return? The danger otherwise. For all of us. For you . . .'

She nods. *If.* She tries not to imagine Páll's body, frozen and ice-laced in the snow. Every time the thought comes to her, she feels she might vomit.

She cooks and sweeps and knits in a daze, unable to forget the slick heat of Anna's blood, the way she had writhed and groaned in pain, the terror that had made caves of her dark eyes. She struggles out of shadowy dreams, sure her arms are weighted with the shrivelled little thing she had pulled from Anna's body.

402

When Jón notes her weeping, he squeezes her shoulder. Once, he kisses her cheek. But her soul is a stone, sealed within the rigid shell of her grief.

Pétur says, 'You did well, Rósa. She could not have been saved.'

The words seem muffled, as if she is underwater, listening to his voice echoing from fathoms beneath the sea. His attempt at kindness cannot touch her.

Outside, the snow continues to blow lazily from the sky and the wind sweeps over the croft, piling the whiteness into strange shapes: a mountain range of ice is growing up around them. Once, she would have marvelled at its threatening beauty; now she sits and imagines Katrín and Páll, freezing and starving in the blizzard.

On the third day after Anna's death, the snow stops, the wind drops, and the sun glows through the clouds. The world is bathed in an eye-stinging, orange luminosity.

Rósa stands in the doorway, squinting at the bright beauty of the land.

'They may yet be alive,' Jón says, behind her.

She turns, and he takes her hand. His rough fingers feel clumsy, but she does not pull away.

'Remember, I warned you. If they return, you must . . .' He sighs and his mouth crumples. His cheeks are sunken, his eyes red-rimmed. 'You should not tell. It would distress Katrín and —'

'I am not a fool.' She turns away.

All day, she stares out at the flat blank of snow, and all day it remains as empty as a sheet of parchment. Darkness drops early, and then she hears a cry from outside.

Pétur and Jón both rush to the door. Then Pétur gives a shout of laughter. 'The Lord bless that meddling old witch!'

Rósa strains to see past them and, dimly, through the gloom, she can make out the shape of two people on horseback. Before them bustles a flock of bleating sheep and a herd of cows. Rósa's whole body is suddenly numb. She cannot move and grips the door to stop herself falling.

Jón and Pétur stride out to greet them, laughing.

'How did you find the animals?' Jón shouts. 'Is that all of them? Are they un-harmed? And the horses too! You will have people accusing you of *seidr*!'

As they draw closer, they dismount. Katrín leans on Páll's arm: she is limping and Páll has to half carry her. They are both haggard and gaunt and, in the spill of light from the croft, look like translucent spirits that have wandered from the hills.

Rósa ushers them inside while Pétur shoos the animals into the barn.

They sit, blinking at the orange warmth of the fire, flinching at the light.

'It's a miracle,' Rósa chokes, pressing bowls of stew into their hands. They are shivering and their hands seem too stiff to hold the bowls. Rósa shakes Katrín's shoulder. 'Can you eat? Are you hurt?' She can't look at Páll's drawn face. She recalls stories of people who return mad from the hills.

Katrín coughs. 'I can conjure myself a new leg.' She directs a crooked smile at Jón, who rolls his eyes.

Breathlessly then, between sips of stew, which Rósa spoons into their mouths, Katrín and Páll explain how they survived. They had started searching for the animals, and found them all together, far up on the hillside. It was already dark and they were exhausted, so they drove the animals to a cave Katrín knew. They ate strips of dried fish and smoked mutton, and the beasts licked the moss from the sides of the cave.

'They were so hungry, I thought they might turn carnivore,' Páll says.

He is safe. He is alive. Rósa's legs are shaking. She almost reaches out to take Páll's hand, but Jón is watching them thoughtfully.

Pétur is standing in the doorway. 'You are as strong as the ice, Katrín — stronger.'

Katrín's expression is suddenly calculating. 'We thought we saw you, Pétur. On that first day, when I feared we would become lost and freeze. Do you remember, Páll? I saw a figure, broad as you are, Pétur, dark and tall. But when we called, the man turned back down the hill.'

Pétur's face is smooth. 'The snow makes all manner of monsters appear real. Still, you are safe now. Have more stew. You must warm your bones.'

He ducks his head and busies himself filling their bowls. But Rósa is suddenly wary. She remembers the time that she was alone with Anna, while Pétur was out on the hill, searching for Katrín and Páll. Surely he would not have left them to freeze.

Pétur glances at Jón and inclines his head. The briefest of expressions, yet it sends Rósa's heart thudding into her boots.

He saw them! He saw them and walked away.

If Pétur had been happy to watch Katrín and Páll walk to their deaths, then what would he do to them if they learned of

Anna's fate? She must never let them suspect the truth.

And now, with the knowledge she has, Jón will certainly never allow her to leave. He wouldn't be happy to pretend that she was dead, as he had done with Anna. He would hunt Rósa down and make sure of it.

The day after the thaw begins, Jón and Pétur go to the barn to feed the animals, and Páll comes to find Rósa in the kitchen. He smiles when he sees her, but she turns away and his smile fades.

'Let me help,' he says, trying to take the dough from her.

'No.' She snatches it away. 'You should be with the animals.'

Go! she thinks. *Please go.*

He stands dumbly, as if she has struck him.

'Go to the barn, Páll — the men have need of you there. I have none.'

She lets him leave, the sensation a rending of her own skin. And yet she cannot risk his kindness. She imagines Jón's hot rage if he knew she had told him anything about Anna; she remembers the clench of his jaw when he'd reminded her of the need to be silent.

This distance from Páll is for the best.

Anything closer will crack her resolve.

She pounds at the bread dough and draws a deep, shuddering breath.

On the fifth night, Rósa is alone in the croft. Katrín and the men are in the barn. Tomorrow they will deliver food to the settlement and help to rebuild the crofts. Rósa is exhausted after spending the day baking loaf after loaf of rye bread. Their flour is almost gone, but Jón seems unconcerned. Rósa wonders if his generosity is born of guilt or the desire to increase the villagers' debt to him.

Rósa pulls the last loaf from the *hlóðir* and sits down with her knitting. She hears footsteps outside the door. She expects to see Jón or Katrín, but it is Páll again.

'I have finished,' she says, before he can speak. She expects him to leave, but he stays in the doorway. 'What is it?'

'Don't.' He walks towards her, then stops in front of her.

She raises her chin. 'You must go.' A burning measure of empty air separates her body from his. Then he takes her hand and pulls her close, leaning in so that his eyes are all she can see. 'I . . .' She pushes him away. 'Please . . .'

He releases her, then rubs his hands over

408

his face. 'I remember when I knew.' His voice fractures. 'When I was certain . . . that I loved you.'

Her mouth is dry. She should stop him. If anyone overheard, these words would cost them their lives.

Páll strokes her cheek. She flinches, but does not — cannot — move away.

'We were twelve,' he whispers.

Twelve? He has loved her since then? But then, looking at him, she feels she has always known. He stares at her steadily.

'It was the summer before I was to begin roofing with my pabbi,' he says. 'You were to stay at home with your father. You remember?'

She nods and closes her eyes. A summer spent in the open, beneath the watchful sun, circling high above. Endless light; the gaping blue of the sky. And Páll. Swimming. Collecting bog bilberries — he had sneaked some into her tunic, then squeezed her so the purple fruit burst between them.

They had pretended she was bleeding to death.

We thought it funny for me to feign being stabbed, she thinks wryly. 'It was perfect,' she whispers. His face is close again. The set of his mouth as he smiles; the stubble on his chin; his warmth. Her skin tingles with it — her whole body hums, like one of the seashells she sometimes finds upon the beach. At first glance, they seem empty, but hold them to your ear and the echo of your throbbing blood will make them sing.

He pulls at a strand of her hair. 'You remember what it says in *Laxdæla Saga* about Gudrun Ósvífrsdóttir — *the most beautiful woman in Iceland, and no less clever than she was good-looking.* The Saga is wrong. You are.'

'I am . . . what?'

'The most beautiful woman in Iceland.'

'It is cruel to mock.'

His face is grave. 'And you are twice as clever as you are good-looking.'

She turns her head away. 'I am not. And *you* are a flatterer.'

'I am an honest man.' He leans towards her.

She pulls away. 'I am —' She is what? Married? A deceiver? A killer?

Her stomach jolts as she remembers Anna's blood. So much blood. 'I can't —'

'I know.' His voice is heavy, wretched.

She can feel his breath on her skin, can feel the thrum of his heart. It would be the most natural thing, to hold him. Falling is easy — the constant pull of the earth tugs her ever downwards. She should leave. She should make him go. She should cry out for her husband. She reaches for his hand, holds it against her cheek and closes her eyes. 'I am so sorry.' And she barely knows to whom she is apologizing, or for what. But those words crack something inside her. She lays her hand upon his chest.

Under her open palm, his body vibrates with life.

And his breath is hot. And he kisses her mouth, her cheeks, her nose, her hair, her eyelids, her throat. Between each kiss he says, 'Never . . . leave . . . my . . . side.'

She laughs and kisses him back. His touch seems to strip her of everything so that, clothed as she is, she feels raw and exposed. He tastes of salt and heat. But her kisses are fuelled by a growing terror.

She gasps and pushes him away. 'No! I am —'

'You are truthful.' He sighs, then kisses her forehead. 'Fear not for your chastity, fair maid. I will sleep at your feet, like a faithful dog.'

'Fool!' She laughs. 'But, *dog,* I suspect you will try to crawl beneath my blanket in the night. Hounds must sleep on the other bed.'

He pretends to whine, then darts at her, as if to lick her cheek.

'Off!' She shoves him across to the other bed. He gives a growl of frustration and then she hears him stretch out.

She knows by his breathing that he is still awake. And she still shivers at the burn of his lips on her skin. But she will not court death. So she lies awake in the dark, skin aflame.

Eventually, sleep claims her. Outside, the wind drops.

Sometime in the shadow between night and morning, the earth shifts, and the sea ice breaks. And a body comes bobbing to the surface.

Arm aloft, as if waving.

■ ■ ■ ■

PART SIX

■ ■ ■ ■

Men shall be beheaded, women drowned.
And he who has taken a life will be
subject to lifelong outlawry.

Grágás Laws

RÓSA

The sight of Anna's face, after her body has been pulled from the sea, is horrifying: the translucent skin with a map of blue veins beneath. Her blackened lips; her eyes, half-open and blank as the sky. Worse than her face, though, is the livid rent across her stomach, but no one peers closely enough to see that, underneath the wound, her womb has been torn open and emptied. Rósa's breath is tight in her chest as Jón carries the body into the *baðstofa;* the villagers follow, buzzing with excited dread.

Rósa can remember the smoothness of the warm skin beneath her knife. The resistance of flesh, then the sickening jolt as the blade punctured the body. Her stomach convulses.

Katrín sobs and kisses Anna's pale cheek again and again.

Old Gudrun steps forward, eyes wide with feverish horror and excitement. 'No smell

415

of rot — she's not been in the sea long. Anna died months ago . . .'

Pétur and Jón exchange a glance. Then Pétur bustles people from the croft, pushing them out the door. The *goði* must have time to grieve, he declares.

'This smacks of murder!' Olaf cries, as Pétur herds them into the chill night.

Pétur holds up his hands. 'We will root out the wrongdoer, have no fear.'

The wrongdoer. Jón will never confess that his first wife abandoned him, then returned with another man's babe in her belly. With a shiver, Rósa realizes they will need a villain. She looks at Jón's face for reassurance; he will not meet her eyes, but gazes at Pétur. His eyes flick towards Rósa and he raises his brows. Jón nods, slowly, tight-lipped.

Rósa steps backwards until she feels the hard turf of the wall against her back. Where is Páll? He must be outside with the others. She thinks of Sigridúr, far away in the tiny pinched croft in Skálholt. She stifles a sob.

Katrín is still hunched over the body, weeping and clutching Anna's cold hands. Rósa would like to embrace her, but guilt and shame pinion her to the spot.

'How?' Katrín whispers, without taking her gaze from Anna's body. 'She was . . .

416

Jón, you told me she had died months past. A fever. But . . . Who? *How?*'

A leaden silence weights the air. The men exchange glances. Then Jón looks at Rósa again. Their language of raised eyebrows and tightened lips opens an abyss inside her.

Finally, Pétur sighs. 'It is baffling.'

'You *claimed* she had died,' Katrín hisses. 'Two months before the Solstice.'

'I . . .' Jón spreads his hands. He doesn't even blush.

'You *buried* her. You dug her *grave* out on the hill. I laid flowers —'

'She left,' interrupts Pétur. 'She abandoned her loving husband —'

Katrín snorts.

'— and we couldn't find her. What else could we think, but that she had died?'

'*If* you had loved her,' Katrín growls, 'you would never have stopped searching. *Never.* And you, Jón, seem not to grieve at all.'

And Rósa thinks of Katrín, trudging through the blizzard every year, scanning the snow for any sign of Dora, who must be dead, devoured by the land years ago.

'It was easier to believe Anna dead,' Katrín hisses. 'Did you rejoice when —'

'What would you have me do, Katrín?' Jón asks wearily. 'Would it breathe life into Anna if I howled and tore at my hair? Such shows

417

are only for the living. They give nothing to the dead.'

Katrín dashes away her tears with a hand, then nods curtly. 'She must be avenged, Jón. To savage an innocent girl, and bundle her into the sea — what butcher would do it?'

Butcher. Rósa's mouth trembles.

'How will we ever know?' Pétur shrugs. 'There are a thousand darknesses in men's hearts that the world never sees.' His voice is smooth. His hands don't shake.

'The settlement must know the truth,' Katrín says, 'even if her own husband doesn't care to.'

Again, Jón's eyes flick to Rósa. Then he stares morosely into the distance. She can feel her life being tested, like a loose thread.

Finally, he stirs, blinking slowly, as if waking from a deep sleep.

'Egill,' he murmurs.

'Egill would not stoop to murder,' Katrín scoffs.

'No. But he will be rubbing his hands at the chance to use this against me.'

'You think he will accuse you?'

Jón shakes his head. 'He is too clever to attempt it. He would aim for someone close to me — someone the villagers might easily distrust.'

His gaze rests on Rósa. Pétur looks at her

418

too, and something like pity clouds his expression. Then Katrín stares up at her and brings her hands to her mouth.

Rósa raises her hands, as if she can ward off the maelstrom that will devour her.

'You can't think . . .'

Jón's face is grave. 'It will not matter what we think, *elskan.*'

'But no one would believe —'

'Egill will persuade them that you stood to gain from Anna's death,' Jón says. 'He will slander you to blacken my name. Who will respect a *goði* whose first wife deserted him and whose second wife murdered the first, then hid the body?'

Rósa clutches the table. It is as if her whole world has tilted, yet someone is attempting to convince her that it is perfectly logical to be standing on her head.

Katrín holds her. 'We will protect you.'

Rósa watches the men for a sign that they agree, but they stand fixed and staring at one another. Their faces are chiselled stone.

None of them leave the croft that night. Rósa feels the urge to weep and howl at the cage that is growing around her, the bonds that seem to tighten with her every thought and word.

But tears change nothing, so Rósa remains

dry-eyed, holding Katrín as she sobs. They wrap sheets around Anna's body, as if cocooning a sleeping child.

She tries not to think of the baby, resting on the seabed, alone and unknown, lullabied by whalesong.

The next morning dawns blackly: the sun barely rises from the belly of the sea.

A steady rain skitters on the turf roof, echoing Rósa's scrabbling thoughts — an itchy tension kept her wakeful all night and still hums beneath her skin. Jón was restless too — he feigned sleep in the bed opposite; she heard his anxiety in the staccato rhythm of his shallow breathing. But now he yawns and stretches.

'The rain will start the thaw. I'll begin repairing the people's crofts.'

Rósa sits up. 'You can't. Your wound . . . and . . .'

'What better way to earn trust? I am *goði* still, Rósa.'

'They will expect you to be grieving.' How can he be so dull-witted? If he begins rebuilding the crofts the day after his dead wife has been dragged from the sea, with her stomach laid open, people will think him callous. Worse, they may believe he knew she was dead. All suspicion will fall

420

upon his croft, and it will be easy for him to direct it towards Rósa. 'You mustn't do it.'

Jón grimaces, but then Pétur enters the *baðstofa*, his expression dark. 'Egill has ridden past the barn twice today and has been talking in the village.'

'So he spins the tale of Anna's death already.'

'Not her death. He is calling you . . . an adulterer.'

'And wants to see me beheaded at Thingvellir? Egill is nothing if not predictable.'

'Predictable, yes, but he's also as persistent as the stench of shit on a boot. He called for your croft and buildings to be examined for more evidence of your dishonesty.' Pétur coughs. 'They stopped alongside the pit-house too.'

Jón's eyes widen and Rósa gasps. 'They didn't . . .'

'It is locked,' Pétur says. 'But still . . .'

Rósa has a sudden flash of the carnage: the bloodstained floor and bed. 'I will clean it.' Her stomach twists at the memory of the thick, metallic odour, but if the blood is discovered, it will stand as evidence of her violence.

'It is no work for a woman.' Jón scowls.

She raises her chin. 'You wanted a wife to

scrub and sweep.'

Jón sighs. For a moment, Rósa feels a surge of pity. Perhaps Jón is also crushed by guilt and anxiety. But then his gaze goes to Pétur and she has that lurching suspicion, once again, that her husband would feed her to the fire to keep himself from being burned.

Jón presses his fingers to his eyelids. 'If the rain continues, we can bury her.'

Rósa nods. 'Perhaps once she is . . . After the burial, the talk may cease?' Rósa can imagine the flames licking at her feet. She looks at her husband.

Jón's smile is taut. 'These people are carrion birds. They will feed upon this story for years.'

Later, Rósa watches from the doorway as Pétur, Katrín and Páll walk down the hill.

Jón stands at her side. She can feel his gaze on her face; she freezes.

'You have done well, Rósa,' he says finally. 'You have not breathed a word.'

'And you . . . You will not say anything?'

His face is grave. She exhales, then holds her breath.

He steps closer, locking his fingers lightly around her wrist. Her skin is cold and pale. She thinks of Anna and shudders.

His skin is the colour of old wax. 'If you spoke to Egill, he could have me killed. If I spoke out . . .' He doesn't need to finish the sentence. The shadows under his cheekbones give him a skull's empty glare.

She pulls her wrist away. 'I wouldn't see you killed.' And as she speaks the words, she thinks they may be true.

His face softens and she catches a glimpse of a lonely boy, shouting into the darkness to scare away the night. Trembling, she places the palm of her hand on his cheek. It is like stroking the muzzle of a half-tame wolf.

He takes her hand, then clasps her in a quick, tight embrace, squeezing her until she can barely breathe. She stays absolutely still in his arms. Eventually, he releases her. 'Go. You must scrub the pit-house.'

She takes the pail and brush and walks down the hill. She doesn't look back, but she can sense his eyes upon her. She can still feel, deep within her chest, like the grinding hum of shifting glaciers, the echoing tremor of his limbs as he held her.

The pit-house is chill and empty. It has not been touched since that night. There is more blood than Rósa remembered. It has frozen, forming perfect iced puddles of gore, filigreed with ruby crystals. But now, with the thaw, the dark pools are turning to liquid, as if the floor itself is bleeding.

It smells too: sour copper. Rósa's stomach clamps; she fights the urge to retch.

She works quickly, sluicing the bed and the mattress first, then scrubbing the floor. The water dilutes the blood and she mixes it with the mud and straw from the pithouse floor, then sweeps it into a pile. But how to move the grisly mess outside? Perhaps she should have used less water. Then she might have burned the straw.

In the end, she gathers armfuls of it and heaps it back into the bucket, then carries it down to the stream, where she stamps on the frozen surface until the ice fractures, then feeds the foul mixture into the water.

She is covered with the blood-black paste, so she splashes water over her chest and arms, wiping the muck from her tunic as best she can.

At least the smell in the pit-house has faded. Only when she holds her fingers very close to her face can she catch the faintest scent of something . . . *raw.* Rósa closes her eyes and swallows until the painful constriction of her throat eases.

Suddenly there is a cough behind her. Rósa whirls around.

Páll is standing in the doorway, panting, as though he has been running. He blinks at her wet clothes, then shakes his head. 'People are talking,' he gasps. 'In the settlement.'

Her stomach lurches. 'What have they said?'

'The old woman — Gudrun? She says she knows who must have killed Anna.'

'Then she has the gift of prophecy.' Rósa feels sick: she knows what Páll will say next.

'They say that Jón's second wife, *you,* stood to gain from Anna's death.'

A peal of laughter bursts from Rósa's mouth. It surprises her as much as Páll, but she cannot stifle it and bends double. Even as she laughs, she can see how it will unfold: they will take her before the Althing and they will hang her. Men, they behead for murder, but women are hanged — Pabbi told her so. The bodies of the dead are left to rot as a warning to others. Their bones are picked clean by ravens.

Her laughter becomes a ragged gasp. Jón will not allow it. Yet . . . if her guilt proves his innocence . . .

'I will keep you safe.' Páll holds her.

'No!' She pushes her hands against his chest and backs away. She cannot risk him, cannot allow him to step into a marsh that will swallow them both.

He moves towards her again and she holds up her hands, as if warding off an assailant. 'I'm married, not yours to save.'

He stops then, and the pain in his eyes is almost enough to make her relent and rush to him again. She draws a breath. 'I must . . . I must tell Jón what they are saying.'

He nods tightly. 'May I come with you?'

'Of course.' It is like speaking to a stranger.

She walks ahead of him up the hill, the stinging rain turning the beautiful swathes of white into a sludgy grey mire. If the rain continues, the settlement will be in more danger from flooding than it was from the snow.

Something gleams in the mud in front of her. Rósa stoops. It is the little glass woman. One arm has broken off, and, when she peers more closely, Rósa can see a deep crack running through the very centre, as though a boot has crushed it. It is ruined and useless now. She stuffs it into her tunic pocket, the fragile thing she had so treasured for being unbreakable.

Páll and Rósa are more than ten paces from the croft when they hear the commotion: men's voices bellowing and a woman shrieking.

For a terrifying second, Rósa imagines

that Anna has risen, unwound her shroud, and now stands in the croft, screaming murder.

But as she runs closer, she recognizes the woman's voice. The door is flung wide and Katrín's words gust out. 'I *know* you, Jón. I see the shame in your eyes.'

'Hold your tongue, woman,' Jón snarls.

'You are a monster to stand and let them accuse her.'

Rósa freezes outside the croft door.

Jón's response is slow, his voice quieter. 'Idle chatter is not the same as standing before the Althing.'

'But one may lead to the other. And if you let harm befall that girl —'

Rósa enters the kitchen and Katrín falls silent. She and Jón stand at either side of the *hlóðir,* red-faced and scowling. Pétur glowers in the corner.

'Rósa!' Jón folds her in his arms. 'I will not let them harm you. You must trust me!' His face is earnest, as if he believes his own words.

'Their whispering *harms* her,' Katrín says.

'What can I do? I don't know what befell Anna!' Jón's tone is harsh but he sounds full of conviction — there is no hint in his voice of the lie on his lips.

'Then why don't you seek her killer?'

427

Katrín demands. 'The people expect you to be raging, determined to find who slit your wife open like a fish. Why don't you scour every cave in Iceland? Unless . . .' Her eyes widen. 'You know!' She claps a hand over her mouth. 'Lord! You *know* who did it!'

'Of course I don't! But I do not see how my rage would lead to confession. I must bide my time, not scare the villain away.'

'And while you wait, the people have decided Rósa's guilt.'

Rósa feels her life slipping between her fingers, like melting ice. It would be so easy for Jón to paint her as the murderer. She readies herself to confess. Perhaps Páll and Katrín will understand: she was not trying to kill Anna, only to save the baby, the shrunken little creature that never drew breath.

'Katrín is right, Jón,' Pétur murmurs. 'If you do not find some culprit, then the settlement will name their own. Egill will delight in —'

'*Egill!*' Jón spits. 'Egill be damned. I will not let him accuse Rósa.'

'And yet he will,' says Pétur, firmly. 'You know he will.'

They both seem entirely earnest, utterly convincing in their desire to protect her. Yet Rósa cannot escape the suspicion that this

428

is a performance and that their true desires lurk in the twin darknesses in their eyes. Still, when Jón looks at her now, his face seems shadowed with grief. She dares to allow herself to hope.

She holds her breath. Outside, the rain drums down. Beyond the wall, in the storeroom, Anna's body warms.

'You could accuse me.' It is Páll, standing behind Rósa, grave-faced. 'Say I did it.' He shrugs, as if he is suggesting that they light the fire to keep warm, or that they eat to ward off hunger.

'No!' Rósa gasps.

Jón shakes his head. 'It is a great risk, Páll —'

'No one need harm me.'

Pétur gives a shout of rough laughter. 'Jón *must* harm you! He must string you up by your bollocks and leave you to rot on top of Helgafell, if you confess to killing his wife.'

Páll spreads his hands. 'I need not *confess*. I will flee, which will suggest my guilt. After I am gone, you may say that you believe I . . . murdered Anna.' His eyes, on Rósa's, are wide and clear.

'No!' repeats Rósa, trembling. 'They will hang you and —'

'They will not find me,' he says, his voice gentle but firm.

429

'But you would never be able to settle anywhere. You would be an exile. You would live in fear, or freeze to death. You could not —'

'I could not live, after watching you hanged.' His voice cracks, but his gaze is fixed and steady. She knows the expression from childhood races when he had decided to win, no matter the cost. He once ran until his legs gave out and he vomited.

'No!' Rósa turns to Jón. 'Tell Páll he can't — he must not do this.'

Jón sighs, then looks at Pétur, who folds his arms across his chest, closes his eyes and briefly inclines his head. 'It may save your life.'

'No!'

Jón turns to her. 'Rósa, I will not accuse him. We shall let the settlement gossip, and draw attention from you. Páll will hide for one winter. The rumours will pass. He could make a life elsewhere — in the east, perhaps.'

'It is not right! And they wouldn't believe it, surely.'

'What choice have we?' Jón takes her hand between his own.

You could tell the truth. But he will not. And her own fear silences her.

She snatches her hand away and stalks

from the kitchen, out into the icy wind, into the needling rain that falls slantwise from the sullen sky.

She gasps lungful after lungful of cold air, yet still she feels she is drowning.

There is a call from the croft behind her: 'Rósa!'

She runs down the hill, then ducks into the warmth of the barn. The horses are chewing contentedly on the hay. They raise their heads at the sight of her, then resume eating. It is comforting, their peaceful indifference to her tears. She puts her arms around Hallgerd's neck, allowing the mare's warmth to seep into her.

When the barn door creaks open, she doesn't move. Páll does not say a word, but wraps himself around her and holds her, swaying gently back and forth. The movement is soothing: like the pulsing swing of water, the hushing of the waves; the rhythmic rocking of the heart in the body, counting out unravelling time.

She wishes she were braver. *I thought I was doing the right thing,* she would say. Perhaps he would believe her.

And yet what if he does not? What if her confession makes him see her differently? As a woman capable of violence. A woman skilled in the art of deception.

It seems the worst kind of cowardice: to abandon what she knows to be right, simply to retain the faint hope that, miles away as he will be, Páll will still love her; that, though he may leave her in body, his heart will still long for her. She should have the strength of will to confess and so salvage Páll's good name, but she cannot risk saving him only to have him look upon her with contempt as they hang her. And perhaps, if he leaves, he will be safer, far away from this murderous place and the vicious people in it. So she says nothing, but stands in his arms as he rocks back and forth, back and forth. When she looks up, his cheeks are wet — from the rain outside, perhaps: she cannot tell.

'I'm sorry,' he whispers.

She nods against his chest.

'I hoped . . .'

She knows. She had hoped, too. But hope has long since had its guts pulled out and scattered for scavengers to feast upon.

'I will go to Skálholt first,' he murmurs, into her hair. 'I will find your mamma and tell her you are well. I don't want her to believe . . .'

She nods again.

'I will move on after three nights. Egill may send someone after me. But I shall stay there for three nights, Rósa. Do you understand?'

She raises her head and presses her lips to his. It is a kiss of desperation, not desire; she understands perfectly what he cannot say — what he will not ask her to do.

He will wait for her in Skálholt. He will give her three nights to decide if she will leave her husband to follow him.

JÓN

Thingvellir, December 1686

I run from the croft as the flush of dawn
creeps across the skies. I take the bloodied
rock and one of my knives, leaving Oddur
slumped on the floor, an empty sack of
flesh; he will never harm anyone again. As I
walk back up the hill, the sky is incandes-
cent. I close my eyes, stretch my arms wide
and draw the light deep into my lungs.

The cave is dark and cold. I set about
rekindling the fire. As I kneel I notice a boot
print in the ash. Large. A man's.

Someone knows I am here.

I feel none of my earlier dread and horror
when I imagine Olaf capturing me. I have
twined the snarled wool of my own fate so
tightly about myself that my only remaining
hope is that I may still retain the power to
choose my own death.

Egill needs me arrested. He wants my

434

humiliation: a public trial, an edict from Copenhagen, the shame of a villain's execution — a sharpened blade and a bloodied block. Perhaps, if I struggle violently enough, I can speed my own end — a quick death in a dark cave, rather than public disgrace.

I unsheath my knife. It glitters in the moonlight, pointing the way to the path of escape within myself that I could open. But no. I squat in the entrance of the cave, at the point where the light turns to shadow, and I wait.

Páll fled Stykkishólmur that night, just as he had promised.

The next morning, I watched Katrín's face as she returned from telling the news in the settlement. She nodded grimly. It had worked: gossip had Páll as the villain: the outsider who had stalked Anna, stabbed her, then hidden her body under the sea ice.

I watched Rósa listen, pale-cheeked, then turn away.

When I asked what troubled her, she said, 'It will not stand. Even they, who do not know Páll, must question it. He did not know her, had no reason to harm her.'

'They have a man who behaves as if he is guilty,' I said. 'And they know men commit

435

evil acts if the devil grips them.'

'They are fools,' Rósa snapped savagely, and stalked to the barn.

Pétur came to stand at my side. 'She is right,' he murmured.

I nodded. 'I know. But we must hope that Páll's seeming guilt will be enough. We may have some hope, if Egill has been deceived.'

But, even as I spoke, I knew they were both right. Egill would not stop until he had destroyed me. And accusing my second wife of murdering the first would fit his purposes perfectly.

We had decided to bury Anna upon the hill. I had hoped for a small private burial, where I might grieve for what had passed, without the feel of eyes on me, weighing my every expression. But every soul in the settlement plodded up to the hill, even those who had been injured when their crofts collapsed. The funerals for the poor souls who had died would take place over the coming days.

Pétur suggested that he and I should carry Anna up to her burial, but the thought of it sickened me — the memory, perhaps, of the night when we bore her bloodied body out across the ice. I could still recall the sensation of her cold cheek against mine, like some perverse lovers' embrace.

436

So when Katrín argued that Anna should be borne to her resting place by women, I agreed. Pétur and I walked up the hill to wait with the rest of the settlement.

'Let us hope this is an end to it,' he murmured.

I gave him a tight smile, and saw, in those strange wild eyes, so like those of a hawk, the same foreboding I felt. Pétur had his knife in his belt, as had I.

The rain had stopped and the clouds lifted; a smear of unseasonal sunlight flooded the sea. I watched the straight-edged rays showering down, as if the light itself were liquid dropped from Heaven.

A muttering from the crowd drew me back to myself. The women were bringing Anna up the hill. I didn't know Katrín had rewrapped the body, until I saw that Anna had layers of the finest linen from my croft wound about her. For a moment, it was the expense that rankled. Then I saw the women's faces, and the implications of what Katrín must have seen struck me.

That gaping wound, like an open mouth. Her emptied belly. Her ravaged womb. With more time to examine the body, Katrín would have seen all that grief had made her miss when Anna had first been found. What had Rósa told her? Pray God she had

fabricated some story, or else feigned igno-
rance.

Both women had tear-stained cheeks. I
cursed. Rósa had told Katrín everything.

The shame of what I had done flooded
me. Katrín's gaze was scorching and I
looked away. I knew she must be imagining
Anna wandering alone across the land:
starving and freezing because I had spread
the fiction of her death.

And Katrín would need only to say a word
for the blame to fall upon Pétur and upon
me also. The village would know of our lies
and deceit. It would be easy enough for
Egill to twist that tale into one of murder
— of Anna and her child both.

Katrín stood, tight-lipped, watching as we
lowered Anna into the ground. Her fisted
hands were trembling. Pétur's hand was on
his knife.

After Egill had prayed over the body, I
stepped forward and spoke the words of the
funeral blessing; the crowd murmured the
correct responses. I measured my breaths to
stop my voice cracking. I must not break
now.

Do not look at her body. There was a
viscous silence. The waxy light made every
face seem drawn and skeletal. *All flesh is as
grass.* I closed my eyes and muttered,

438

'Amen.' Katrín wept and clenched her jaw.

Then Egill stood forward and held up his hands. 'This is a dark day.'

'I have said the blessing, Egill, and need no other man to add words to mine.'

'And a darker day still when the suspicion falls on the croft of the *goði*.'

'Peace, Egill,' I growled.

The thin smile on his bloodless lips unnerved me. 'A black day, indeed. And we shall remain in darkness, until we find justice.'

'We will have *justice*,' I snarled, 'when we know the wrongdoer.' I flicked my gaze to Katrín.

She stood poised, mouth open.

'A man has fled. Is that not confession enough? You should pursue him,' Egill said.

'I do not think it would stand before the Althing.'

'Then you will not hunt the villain down?'

'I will hunt no man down when I am not certain of his guilt.'

'Jón!' Pétur called. But too late.

'You do not believe him guilty, then?' Egill crowed.

'I do not know,' I muttered, praying that Katrín would stay silent. Her face was hard, her eyes bright with tears, but she said nothing.

Thank you, I thought.

I started to walk back down the hill. The villagers turned to follow, muttering excitedly.

'The boy had no motive,' Egill called from behind me.

Pétur hissed. I knew that, like me, he had read Egill's intentions. Páll's guilt did not serve his purposes. He needed another villain, someone closer to me, someone people distrusted, and who had had reason to harm Anna. His gaze flickered between Rósa and Pétur. I tensed. Pétur folded his arms and raised his chin. Katrín stared at me.

Rósa stood with her fingers knitted into her woollen skirt, leaning against Katrín. I had thought her fragile when I first met her, but now I knew that, beneath her quiet curtsies and modestly lowered gaze, she was fashioned of flint and steel.

Still, her eyes widened when Egill turned to her. 'Páll is your kinsman, Rósa?'

Rósa looked Egill in the eye. 'And what if he is?'

Inwardly, I rejoiced at her insolence. Perhaps she might best him after all.

But then Rósa said, 'He would not have harmed Anna.' She paused, then finally whispered, 'He did not harm her.'

I tensed, waiting for her to explain how

440

Pétur and I had wronged Anna, had lied and deceived everyone.

Already I could imagine how Egill's eyes would light when he heard the tale. I could picture the people's excitement at the confirmation of Pétur's barbarism and his savagery — they would believe he had corrupted me too. We would both lose our heads.

'Páll did not harm Anna.' Rósa's clear voice swept over the hill with the whirling wind. 'And I did not mean to . . . I never intended . . .'

The people drew closer to her, sharp-faced, and formed a ring around her. It was like watching a pack of circling wolves. I threw a desperate glance at Katrín, but she had been pushed to one side.

'Speak up, girl!' Egill said, his eyes suddenly bright.

'I know what happened.' Rósa drew a shuddering breath. Her voice faltered as the villagers stepped in, waiting to do Egill's bidding.

'I tried to save her,' Rósa said. 'I did not intend —'

'Rósa, no!' I called. But my call was lost in the excited cries of the villagers.

'*You?*' Egill said.

No! I couldn't allow it. No matter the

441

cost, I couldn't let her confess for my crimes.

But it was too late. The people had surrounded Rósa. I could barely see her and, though Katrín was trying to push past, they had closed around her. I could hear whispers of 'Murder'.

Njáll Agnarsson called, 'She killed Anna! You heard her say it.'

Rósa cried out, her voice tight with fear.

'No!' I called, trying to drag them away. But they were huddled together and it was like pulling at a rockface.

Egill folded his arms and watched.

Katrín was shouting and trying to fight her way through. There was a thud and a cry as Pétur punched someone. His face was desperate.

I struck out, but before my fist could connect, I felt Olaf's meaty hands around my throat. I scrabbled at his fingers, but his hands were like iron on my neck. I couldn't breathe. The blood thudded in my skull.

I saw a hand reach down and fumble for a stone, then hurl it. I heard Rósa shout. Katrín shrieked — she was weeping and clawing at the backs of the villagers, crying out their names, pleading, but they ignored her. Rósa screamed as more stones flew through the air. I saw her face emerge from

442

the huddle of bodies briefly; then she was dragged back under and engulfed in a sea of tearing hands and pummelling fists.

Pétur bellowed and hurled himself into the crowd, but was thrown backwards.

Rósa cried out again, her voice raw, then cut off, mid-scream.

I kicked back as hard as I could and threw my body forward, loosening Olaf's grip. Then I swung around and punched him in the stomach. He doubled over.

The idea slid home with the ease of a sharpened blade. There was one thing I could do to prevent this wave from crashing over Rósa and swallowing her. I gasped a lungful of air and roared, 'Stop!' But they ignored me.

'Stop! I did it!' I bellowed. 'It was me.'

The crowd froze, fell silent and slowly turned.

'It was me,' I repeated.

Every eye was upon me now. The crowd moved away from Rósa. She huddled on the ground, whimpering, her arms curled around her head and face. Katrín rushed in and cradled her. I caught a glimpse of her torn lip; one of her eyes was bloodied.

'I did it,' I repeated, more quietly.

Egill's face was lit. 'Did what?'

'Jón, no!' Pétur cried.

'I killed Anna,' I said calmly. 'I am the guilty one.'

There was a collective gasp. Rósa moaned. Pétur cried out and cursed at me, but Egill's voice was louder, his excitement almost palpable.

'*You* killed her! How? Why?'

'The events are between my soul and God. I'll not name them for you. I give my confession to the Lord only. But know this: Anna died because of me. Now move away from my wife.'

And, as I said the words, I knew them to be true. That poor crosswise thing buried in her womb was my fault. Her madness, her desperation, her wanderings: all my doing. I did not wield the knife, but I killed her, as surely as if I had. And I must finally repent and pay the price of murder.

They closed around me and I let them. I allowed them to drag me away, to spit at me. Olaf punched me in the stomach twice, but I barely felt it.

They dragged me towards the pit-house, despite Rósa's tears and Pétur's rage. I knew I should feel a crushing terror, and yet I was strangely triumphant, as though I had stripped off layer after layer of clothing, only to find that underneath, where I had expected to see scarred and shrivelled flesh, I had discovered feathers and a rich plumage. People might mock me, but my thoughts felt winged and soared above the pit-house. Rósa would be safe now. Pétur, too. I smiled, then laughed.

Olaf punched me again and again, but the laughter bubbled from my mouth: suddenly thawed ice that had created a torrent after the years of frozen stillness.

Just before Olaf pushed me inside, Pétur grasped my arm.

'Why?' he demanded.

I gripped his arm, hoping that somehow the force of my hand around him might tell him everything I could not voice aloud.

Then Olaf bundled me inside and slammed the door. I heard the key scratch in the lock. Olaf's bulk cast a great shadow between the wooden boards. There would be no escape.

RÓSA

Stykkishólmur, November 1686

Rósa can barely stand and she collapses into Katrín's arms. Her face is bleeding from a cut above one eye, and her arm is numb where someone had grabbed and twisted it. Her whole body is shaking. She had never imagined that such a thing would be possible, that people could turn into a many-clawed monster, deaf to its victim's pain and pleading, intent only on destruction. She had thought they would rip the flesh from her bones.

Now they do not look at her, but slink past and walk back to the village in a tight-knit huddle, whispering.

Rósa sobs and Katrín holds her upright, stroking her hair, then guides her over to the stream, where she sits her on a rock and washes her wounds, repeating, 'Hush now, you're safe. They can't hurt you now, *elskan*. Hush, Rósa.'

Eventually, Rósa's tears subside.

Katrín kneels next to her and holds her face in her hands. 'You are safe,' she says. 'But Jón is not. Do you feel strong enough to walk?'

Rósa nods. Katrín takes her hand and turns towards the hill and Egill's lonely croft. He had walked home while Olaf was beating Jón, his mouth twisted downwards in distaste, though he did nothing to halt the violence.

'Quickly,' Katrín gasps. 'Before it is too late.'

Rósa's eye has swollen shut and her breath still comes in ragged gasps; she cannot order her thoughts into speech, but she is aware that Katrín's lips are pursed and her face hard as she knocks on Egill's door.

'Stay quiet and look penitent,' she murmurs.

Rósa wipes her eyes, but Katrín stops her. 'No, leave your tears. And the blood.'

Katrín pushes the door open. Egill is kneeling on the earthen floor, praying. And behind him, sweeping, is Gudrun. She glances up and her milky eyes glint.

'You!' Katrín hisses.

Gudrun's shoulders stiffen, but she says nothing, merely pats her hand on the table to find Egill's Bible, then holds it out to

447

him. He takes it from her, with a nod of thanks, and she returns to making slow, shuffling sweeps across the floor with the brush.

'Katrín, my child.' Egill smiles. 'And Rósa. Such confusion today, but I am glad you are safe, now Jón has confessed, praise God. His villainy nearly killed you — imagine! Do you seek counsel or a prayer?'

'I seek mercy.' Katrín looks narrowly at Gudrun, then casts her eyes down. Rósa copies Katrín and drops her gaze to the floor.

The wind presses itself against the walls of the croft; the wood groans.

'Mercy?' Egill's gaze sharpens.

Outside, a raven caws. Rósa draws a steadying breath.

A muscle is working in Katrín's jaw. She swallows, then clasps her hands before her, as if in prayer or supplication. 'I come to plead for your mercy upon Jón.'

Egill raises his eyebrows. 'He has confessed. The Althing will judge him, not I. If the thaw continues, we may send a messenger south tomorrow.'

Gudrun continues sweeping. The room is stark and chilly as a burial mound.

'But you could plead with the Lawspeaker . . .'

The wind insinuates itself through the gaps in the turf. The tiny fire flares, then gutters. Rósa shivers.

Egill smiles. 'Why would I do such a thing?'

'I do not believe he killed Anna.'

Gudrun coughs. The raven shrieks again.

Rósa closes her eyes. How is it possible to prove Jón's innocence without her own confession? She remembers the villagers' hands on her. They would tear her to pieces.

'His guilt is for the Althing to decide. His case may go to Copenhagen.' Egill is almost smiling, as if he relishes the excitement.

The lungs of the wind exhale. Rósa stares at him and feels her lip curl.

He spreads his hands. 'Why would I plead for such a sinner? His death will cleanse this village.' Egill's cold smile widens. He will gain so much: Jón's croft, his land, his sway in the settlement. Egill will be a great man now, able to dictate who stands as the next *goði*. Rósa can guess at the argument he will put to the Althing: there is no one else in the settlement with the power and wisdom to hold that title. Egill will argue that he should stand as both *prestur* and *goði*.

'Go now,' Egill says. 'I must thank God for His justice.'

Katrín gives Gudrun a final dark look, then curtsies. Her hand, when she grasps Rósa's arm to pull her from the croft, is hot and dry. They stumble down the hill, towards the sea, blinking tears.

The sea ice has started to thaw, and the water gulps under the blackening glass. A chill wind winnows in from colder lands to the north, plucking at Rósa's cap, whipping Katrín's grey hair into her face.

She squeezes Rósa's hand. 'You cannot confess.'

Rósa allows the squally breeze to encircle her, gasping as the ice burrows into her bones.

Jón will die.

She hears a shout from behind her and turns to see Gudrun battling into the wind, struggling not to be blown over. When she reaches them, Katrín looks at her with contempt. 'I should push you onto these rocks. Go back and tend Egill.'

'Egill!' Gudrun sucks her teeth, then spits.

Rósa raises her eyebrows. 'You dislike *Egill*? I thought Jón was the villain.'

'Egill seeks to profit for himself, but calls it God's work. And he'd have watched the village crush you, young Rósa.'

'I didn't notice you trying to help, Gudrun,' says Katrín, sourly. 'You were sitting on a rock while they threw stones at her. She's bleeding.'

'A nasty thing to happen.' Gudrun nods. 'But Egill might have stopped it. What sort of man would watch a woman being attacked? *He* is the true villain.'

'So now you say Egill should not be *goði*?' Rósa says. 'But you are content to sweep his floor?'

Gudrun blinks her cloudy eyes against the wind. 'Everyone must earn food somehow. But now the villain speaks to us of tithes . . .'

'Ah! Tithes. The *villain.*' Rósa laughs bitterly.

'You may mock an old woman. But Jón never demanded what we could not afford. He sent Pétur to help to rebuild my croft and has not asked for a single ell in return. Egill would have us half starve ourselves and call it worship. And *you* . . .' She turns her rheumy eyes to Rósa. 'Jón is a good husband, is he not?'

'I . . .' Rósa bites her lip. 'He is —'

'Pah! Young people expect the world on a platter. He's never struck you?'

'No.'

'There! A fine husband. Besides,' Gudrun continues, 'my eyes may be weak and my ears may fail me, but I heard Jón's confession. His voice was full of lies. He confesses

451

falsely to hide something, is that not so? Whom does he protect?'

Rósa examines her mittens and Katrín looks out at the blank of the sea.

'No matter. It is a dishonest confession and now Jón is a dead man.' She sucks her teeth again.

Rósa turns into the wind and allows it to gust the tears from her eyes. She can feel Gudrun's silence, like a threat. Then the other woman leans forward and clasps Katrín's and Rósa's hands. 'Dead bodies should be removed through the walls. Remember that.'

Then, still scowling and muttering, Gudrun turns and struggles back up the hillside.

While Rósa is considering Gudrun's words, she walks back up to Jón's croft, limping. She is still unsteady and the wound on her head throbs, but she needs a moment alone to reflect on what she must do next.

Inside, she fingers the soft homespun that covers the beds in the *baðstofa,* and opens the Bible with its fine vellum pages — it must have cost a fortune. All Egill's now.

She closes her eyes, imagining Páll journeying south across the thawing land. She must let him go. He should return to Skálholt, free of the misfortune she carries within her. She squeezes the glass woman in her pocket until the fractured edge of the shattered figure pierces her skin. Broken. She has broken everything.

Suddenly purposeful, she picks up a blanket and spreads it flat on one of the beds. In the centre, she places the Bible, a pot of honey, and the whalebone knitting needles that an ordinary farmer could never hope to buy. After a thought, she takes the runestone from her pocket and folds that into the blanket too. She bundles it all together.

She searches about. What else can she take?

There is a loud scrabbling from overhead. Rósa startles. Some spirit in the croft must see her thievery. Then she remembers and her heart slows: the gyrfalcon. She lays her little bundle down on the bed and climbs the ladder.

The loft is dark, but the white-barred shape of the gyrfalcon, huddled in the corner, seems to emit a light of its own. It is worth a hundred cows, a thousand ells of cloth. Men kill and are killed for this bird of kings, this frozen hunter.

The ice-people from the snow lands to the north have another name for it: they call it *the grasper.* Rósa can see why: its feet are long and scaly, the black claws curved and vicious. They grip the perch with a strength that promises impalement.

She reaches out to touch it, and, for a moment, lays her fingers on feathers that feel softer than the finest linen. Then the bird bates, flapping and hanging upside down, twisting on the jesses until Rósa worries it will fracture a wing.

She remembers how she had feared the bird contained Anna's spirit. It cocks its head to one side and stares at her, unblinking.

As she stretches out her hand, Rósa begins to whisper her favourite passage from *Laxdæla Saga,* when Bolli kills his best friend, Kjartan. She and Páll used to recite it together: *'Then Kjartan said to Bolli, "It is an ignoble deed, kinsman, that you are about to do; but I would much rather accept death at your hands, cousin, than give you death at mine."'*

The bird's body is rigid and trembling.

Rósa whispers, 'After Bolli stabbed him, Kjartan fell and died in Bolli's lap. Bolli wept and repented. But weeping gives nothing to the dead.'

The bird flaps its wings, as if in agreement.

'Still,' Rósa continues, 'there is a differ-
ence between murder and . . .' She pauses.
Is there a name for what she did? She had
known Anna would die when she cut her.
That is murder, certainly. But she had
meant to save the baby. Katrín had understood, when Rósa told her. 'Intentions
matter,' she'd said, her eyes bright with
unshed tears.

Now Rósa creeps forward and eases her
arms around the gyrfalcon. Fear throbs
through its whole body, but it doesn't
struggle. It is as if it is used to human kindness. Rósa imagines Jón capturing the bird:
he would have been careful and gentle as he
pinioned it. He would have fed it daily,
nurtured it, even as he kept it prisoner.

She remembers the whispers she had
heard at night from the loft room. What
secrets does this bird know?

Its eyes are golden and merciless: the eyes
of a being whose sole purpose is to hunt
and kill.

At first the bird panics and strikes out at
her, but gradually it stills. Its body is lighter
than she expected, as if it is a ghost after
all. She makes her way slowly down the ladder, careful not to jolt the gyrfalcon and
mindful of the curved beak and talons.

Back in the *baðstofa,* Rósa searches for

something to use as a perch. Finally, she snatches up the Bible from the bed. Then, with the bird under one arm and the Bible under the other, Rósa strides out of the confines of the croft and into the chill sea air.

The night is falling fast, blackness seeping up from the horizon. The stars are clear as candles: it will be a cold night. High overhead, the wind tugs a ragged scarf of cloud over the frozen-faced moon. Rósa holds the Bible in one hand, then carefully sets the bird's feet along the spine. It instinctively perches on the leather covering, and digs its sharp claws into the surface, puncturing the soft calf-skin.

Rósa waits until the bird has stilled. Then slowly, slowly, she reaches out and unties the leather jesses on its feet. It is a fumbling struggle, and she worries she will hurt the bird. But it waits, frozen and trembling, as though it knows what she intends. It stretches its wings and gives a sharp *caw,* as if to hurry her. Its yellow predator's eyes flash: fierce and furious.

As she tugs on the cord, the gyrfalcon flaps its wings: they smash bruisingly against Rósa's face and she flinches — how can something that seems made of air be so strong? Her fingers are clumsy, but finally the cord loosens and drops to the ground.

The bird perches on the Bible. It is unfettered. It spreads its wings, but doesn't take off. It gazes at Rósa, sharp-eyed, waiting.

'I know,' she whispers. 'You're frightened. But you have been made for this.'

Rósa turns to the mountains, raises her arm, then flings the Bible and the bird into the air. The book crashes to the ground, but the gyrfalcon beats its wings and rises. In the thud of three heartbeats, it is high overhead. Within ten breaths, it is a tiny black outline against the white fang of Helgafell.

The power of the creature's flight — its freedom — leaves Rósa breathless. Suddenly Gudrun's words make sense.

Dead bodies should be removed through the walls.

Jón is a dead man. Egill's judgement has pronounced him so.

JÓN

Thingvellir, December 1686

I sit in my cave, staring at the boot mark in the ash and waiting. When I touch my tunic, I find it soaked, and my fingers come away black with blood.

If Olaf does not arrive soon, he will find that time has made a corpse of me. I close my eyes, willing my body to continue. It has served me well, even when broken.

After throwing me into my pit-house, Olaf bound my wrists and ankles. I waited for hours, a fierce energy throbbing through my veins, expecting Egill to come to gloat.

I was woken some time later by a boot thudding against my ribs. I groaned and Olaf hauled me upright.

Standing before me was Egill. He smiled. 'You look very ill, Jón.'

'You must be sorry to find me still breathing.'

His smile faded. 'Remember, our suffering brings us closer to God.'

'My suffering brings you more sway, and that is all you —'

'Not everyone has your grasping heart, Jón.'

'You are a bitter old man, Egill.' I sighed. 'Go away, so I can sleep.'

'Would *you* not be bitter?' he hissed, leaning in close. I could see every wrinkle in his skin, leprously pale. 'Wouldn't *you* be filled with hatred had a man stolen your child, made your wife sicken and die with grief — and if the man's own wife cursed yours? Wouldn't *you* despise the one who mocked you before your people? Who *poisoned* your son's mind —'

'Pétur is not your son!' I roared. 'And you were a tyrant.'

'The boy was full of the devil!' Egill cried. 'I had to purify him and —'

'Beat him?' I spat. 'A grown man beat a boy until he bled? Did it make you feel stronger? You *coward*!'

'I should have beaten him harder, to save his soul. To save him from your sin.'

I strained against the bonds at my wrists, imagining the satisfying thud of my fist against Egill's skull. 'You tormented Pétur, then threw him out into the cold, and demanded that I bring him back so you could torture him again. Tyrant!'

Egill flinched. 'I did everything to protect him. I *loved* him. I . . . love him still, but he is . . . lost.' His mouth crumpled; his eyes shone.

I almost felt pity then. I softened. 'Pétur is a good man. Talk to him. Be reconciled.'

'You are a fool, Jón. You would sacrifice yourself to save Pétur's body, rather than strive to redeem his immortal soul.'

'And *you* are saving his soul?'

'You mock me. But God Himself cast Adam out of Eden and allowed him to choose the path of righteousness or of sin.'

'Pétur has no more sin than any other man.'

Egill knelt next to me and put his lips close to my ear. I could feel the dry heat of his skin, as though his fervour was a fire within him.

'He is depraved,' Egill whispered, 'as *you* are depraved.'

I couldn't draw breath to speak.

'Anna told me what you are. None would have believed it before. But now you are a murderer. You killed Anna to silence the truths she spoke. Soon all Iceland will know of your other perversions. The Althing will take your head. Your name will be a pollutant on every tongue.'

The walls compressed around me. All my vision seemed filled by Egill's burning gaze.

He continued: 'And as your soul is twisting in the eternal fires of damnation, men will speak of your acts and curse you, until you pass out of living memory.'

I tried to speak but could gather no breath. It wasn't true. I had never allowed myself to do more than think . . . to wonder in the darkest hours of the night. Had Pétur ever thought of me? Had he suspected? I shook my head, then retched.

Egill leaned in close again. The sudden darkness in his eyes was all-consuming. 'So, I see what must pass for Pétur to be free, for him to be pure and upright, as I taught him. He must be without any friend or comfort in the world, save the Lord. Then he will turn back to God. Then his soul will be saved. But you will die. And you will burn.'

I stared at him.

'And Stykkishólmur will be transformed after you are gone,' he hissed. 'It will be a place of the Lord's at last.'

I looked deep into those dead eyes. 'You disgust me. Had you been *my* pabbi, I would have stabbed you while you slept.'

Egill recoiled, drew a deep breath, then

461

turned and pounded on the door. Olaf opened it and Egill swept out. The door banged behind him; the darkness settled.

In the dark bowels of the night, I was woken by a scraping on the wall next to my head. I bolted upright, wishing I had a blade: I had neither eaten nor drunk in so long, and a creature of any sort might have quieted my raging hunger and thirst. But as the scrabbling continued, I realized it was too deliberate and rhythmic to be that of an animal.

Someone is trying to get in! One of the people from the settlement, perhaps, determined to deliver a quicker and more violent punishment than beheading. The scratching grew louder still, and I suddenly understood that someone was *cutting a hole through the wall*! I felt a cold rush of night air and readied myself to pounce, but then a voice hissed, 'Jón!'

'*Rósa!* How —'

'Hurry!' She reached through the hole and, in the darkness, I could just make out the glint of her eyes. There was the sudden flash of a knife and I recoiled, until I understood that she intended to cut my bonds. I drew the rope across the blade while she held it and, once I was free, rubbed the blood back into my wrists before

462

cutting the rope binding my ankles. 'Take my hand,' she whispered.

I obeyed and scrambled through. The sudden slap of the night air made me gasp; the splash of rain on my face was like stepping into the chill of sea, hoping for my boat, and endless miles of unbroken time. I felt dizzy.

'How have you . . . What of Olaf?'

There was a low laugh, and my heart clenched at Pétur's voice. 'We planned to give him a concoction of Katrín's,' he said, 'but she couldn't find the herbs she needed.' He chuckled. 'So I smacked him over the head with a rock.'

'Is he . . .'

'Still breathing. Leaning against the door, like a sack of dead fish. But I will not stay for when he wakes. I'd rather not share your executioner's block, Jón.'

'There will be no block.' Katrín's voice was hard and, even in the darkness, I could feel her anger. 'By morning, you will be miles away.'

'I . . . Where could I go?'

'Don't tell me,' Pétur said. 'If I am found, I don't want the knowledge of your whereabouts to be cut and burned from me.'

'You won't travel with me?'

'My face would be our death warrant. I

will always look too much like *that villain Pétur, from Stykkishólmur.*' He grinned at me, a quick flash of his teeth in the darkness. 'Alone, with a longer beard, you may survive.'

'But you . . .' My stomach dropped. His face would be his own death warrant, after what he had done for me. 'I cannot let you —'

'It is done already. Rósa and Katrín will claim innocence and will be ready to attend to Olaf and feign concern when he wakes. It will seem I sneaked you out through the wall while they were distracted at the door. And Katrín will happily send Egill's men hunting after me rather than you — is that not so, Katrín?'

I did not want this for him, but I could not possibly voice the despair I felt, at thinking of him being hounded across Iceland because of me.

'Now we must part ways,' Pétur said. It was impossible to decipher his expression in the darkness. He pulled a cloak about my shoulders and pressed a sack into my hands. 'Some things Rósa took from the croft for you.' Into my belt and my boot, he placed two knife blades.

'You must have a weapon too,' I protested.

'I have four.' I saw the gleam of his teeth

again in the dim light. 'Now hurry.'

I pulled Rósa into a quick, tight embrace. 'Forgive me,' I muttered in her ear.

Her face was damp, from tears or the rain, and she nodded silently.

'There is coin in the loft space,' I said. 'Enough silver for you to return to Skálholt.' She stiffened slightly in my arms, and I quickly added, 'Only if you wish. The croft is yours. Egill will try to take it from you, but you can defend your right to it before the Althing. You may stay or go, as you please.'

'I . . . Thank you, Jón.'

I forced a smile. 'See, I am the broad-minded husband now!'

She gave a choking little laugh, then pressed a stone into my hand. I glanced down at it and, in the spill of moonlight, could just make out the trace of a runic marking. 'For protection,' she murmured.

I nodded and turned to Katrín: the set of her jaw betrayed her simmering rage at how I had wronged Anna, at all the many ways in which I had been unable to save her, and at the lies I had told. But she clasped me tightly and muttered, 'You can make this right. There is a debt owed to Anna in Thingvellir.'

'I know it.'

465

'Hurry, before Olaf wakes,' Pétur urged, tugging at my hand. We began to run up the hill, towards Helgafell, towards the open heart of the country.

The pain in my side slowed me, and Pétur slackened his pace to match mine. We said nothing. What words for such a moment?

I wished I had revealed my longing years ago. So many breaths of buried silence, painful days, filled with yearning and fear. And even now, knowing I would never set eyes upon him again, I could not lay my heart bare. Better never to speak, never to know.

I could not name my soul and watch it trampled by the sickened contempt on his face.

I once saw a winged insect — it looked like a moth, but was more delicate and of gorgeous colour, as though it had been painted by a monk who had tired of illuminating manuscripts and decided to decorate God's other handiwork. It fluttered onto a nearby bush. I watched it for breathless moments as it trembled, then flew again. I longed to examine this marvel more closely, so I picked it up, with the gentlest of fingers, only to find that its fragile wings ripped under my touch. When the creature tried to fly, it floundered to the ground,

where it lay, beating those beautiful, broken
wings. Finally, I had to stamp on it — it
seemed cruel to watch it suffer. But ever
after, I wished I had left it alone to fly
unscathed.

I would not speak my heart, only to grind
it beneath my heel.

When we reached the top of Helgafell, Pétur stopped and turned to me. 'I know you
will go south. I don't want you to tell me
more.'

'Nor I you. Although,' I could not look at
his face, '*nothing* could make me betray you.
Not torture, nor death.'

He sighed, then wrapped his arms around
me and held me close — close enough for
me to feel the thud of his heart in my own
ribcage. His solidity was like the muscular
curve of land. He touched his forehead to
mine; we stood still for the span of four
breaths. I closed my eyes, took the clean
smell of his sweat into my lungs.

My heart was a shard of glass in my chest.

'Fare you well, Jón,' he said.

'Fare you well,' I whispered.

Now, squatting in my cave, waiting for my
executioner to arrive, I am glad, so very
glad, that I stayed silent. My last thought
will be of that embrace, of the delicate-

winged longing that hung between us. I am thankful I did not crush it with words.

There is a sound from the mouth of the cave. I tighten my grip on the knife and squint into the darkness. Is that a blacker shadow moving? I blink, but the dimness only deepens.

Then I am certain I hear it: the whisper of a muffled exhalation. I do not wait, but leap forward, knife blade ready. My hands grip cloth and skin; I wrap my fingers around a throat. I draw my knife back to strike.

'Stop!'

I hesitate. The voice is familiar, but it cannot be . . .

'Let me go!' the man wheezes.

And I do. And I fall to the ground.

The knife clatters onto the floor. It is impossible. And yet . . .

'Pétur?'

There is a cough and the scratch of flint, then a spark in the darkness.

Pétur's face appears. Like me, he is bruised and bloodied and, when he smiles, I notice that one of his teeth is broken.

'Let it be known,' he mutters, 'that I don't wish to die by strangling.'

I launch myself at him before I think. I don't care if he pushes me away. But he wraps his arms around me, as if he, too, is a drowning man, and I am a spar some kindly soul has thrown into a treacherous sea.

When he pulls away, his face is sober. 'I see you have visited Oddur's croft.'

I know that he is remembering the other two men on the beach all those years ago. And that Oddur's murder reveals me as a vicious and violent thug, barely better than the men I have killed. I cannot meet Pétur's eyes.

But there is no reproach in his voice, only tender concern. 'Your face . . . Those wounds must be washed.'

I try to wave away his hand, but he draws out a small bottle of liquid — *brennevín,* by the smell of it — tips some onto his cloak, then dabs at my face. When I flinch, he holds my jaw with one hand. 'Heaven's sake, sit still, man.'

Pinioned so, I feel utterly safe.

'I can't tell you how I have longed to see you,' he whispers, so faintly that I wonder if I have imagined it. But his words are the axe that shatters the ice within me. A tear trickles down my cheek. He brushes it away, then touches his finger to his lips.

'You taste of the sea. And dirt.' He grins, then gently cleans my wounds.

After he has finished, I use my cloak to clean his injuries. The worst is a livid cut above his left eye. I wash it tenderly — the thought of his pain hurts me.

He notes me wincing. 'I cut the fingers off the man who did it.'

I cannot tell if he is serious. I don't ask.

'Can you walk far?' he asks.

I shake my head. 'The struggle with Oddur tore open the wound in my belly.' I lift my tunic.

He draws a sharp breath, swallows audibly, then cleans it with the last drops of *brennevín*. As he wipes, he says, 'We must leave. You have trampled a path from Oddur's croft to this cave.'

'*You* must leave. I haven't the strength.'

He nods slowly, then settles himself back on the floor, locks his hands behind his head and closes his eyes.

'What are you doing?'

'Waiting to die with you.'

I argue and curse him, calling him a fool and begging him to go. I almost weep as I try to push him from the cave, but it is like shoving the earth itself.

'I will leave with you, or I will die with you,' he says. 'You choose.'

I hold my head in my hands, then exhale slowly and limp to the mouth of the cave.

He claps me on the back. 'I was beginning to think you'd left your brain in

470

Oddur's croft, next to his.' Pétur gives a wicked grin. Then he puts my arm over his back and, together, ruined and hobbling, we stagger up the hill, away from Thingvellir.

'You are a good man,' I murmur.

'I am a devil. Haven't you heard?' The smile curls at the edge of his voice.

I stop and turn to face him. 'Be serious. I am proud to have known you.'

Pétur purses his lips. 'If you continue to speak like a man on his deathbed, I will have to beat sense into you. Don't make me strike you, Jón — I am tired.'

As I turn to smile at him, I catch a movement from the corner of my eye. I squint into the distance. Two men, travelling this way.

Pétur follows my gaze. 'Come. We must move faster.'

By mid-morning my wound throbs. I keep tripping and falling to my knees. Occasionally, we lose sight of our pursuers, but then they reappear. Each time, they are closer.

Finally, Pétur stops. For a moment, I think he will go on without me. But he lifts me, wordlessly, into his arms and continues to walk, cradling me. It must be agony for him. He counts through clenched teeth, as if try-

471

ing to outstrip the pain.

'Put me down,' I gasp. 'Go on without me.'

He shakes his head.

He has to stop often. Every time, I argue and try to walk, then stagger or double over with pain. Pétur picks me up and carries me, time and again.

And *this* is love, I realize. This broken-bodied stumble forward, one carrying the other in spite of exhaustion, pain and the glare of the outside world.

In love, every one of us is a cross, every one of us a Christ.

The thought is blasphemous, but I cannot find it in myself to care. I am suddenly awake. After a lifetime of floating frozen under the sea ice, I feel warm and alive, dragging myself forward, and being dragged, through the darkness.

Pétur carries me through the night. When we stop, a grey light is unfurling on the horizon. We can no longer see our pursuers, but they are out there still, closing in with every breath.

■ ■ ■ ■

Part Seven

■ ■ ■ ■

Bare is the back of a brotherless man.
                              Icelandic proverb,
                          from *Njáll's Saga*

Rósa

Rósa reins in Hallgerd at the top of the hill and gazes at the gaping stretch of land that she once called home. It seems smaller; the crofts are shabby and shamefaced.

Páll will have journeyed onwards days ago. When she tries to imagine her future without him, it is like staring out across an ice sheet. Perhaps he will have gone east. Perhaps he will return one day. Perhaps . . .

She closes her eyes and listens to the birds circling overhead. Ravens chattering — they will be ravenous after the freeze, but the thaw will reveal rich pickings.

She should have left Stykkishólmur sooner, but she had stayed for three nights after Jón fled, trying to summon the courage to tell Egill about Anna's true fate. Maybe then Jón could return. Briefly, Rósa had imagined she could rewrite the past and the future, simply by telling the truth. She

475

had pictured the quiet marriage she'd once hoped for: the gentle drudgery of daily tasks, of waiting for her husband to return home after a day in the field or at sea. She dreamed of a life that was dull, and uneventful, and safe.

'Egill would not hear you,' said Katrín. 'It would not suit him to find that Jón did not harm Anna. He has ears only for Jón's guilt.'

And she was right, Rósa knew: Egill had been furious when he discovered Jón had escaped, and had denounced both her and Katrín, refusing to believe that they knew nothing. He even offered to grant Rósa Jón's croft, which was hers by right anyway, if she told him where Jón had gone. But she kept her lips sealed. Stykkishólmur was nothing but darkness to her now.

After three long, lonely nights, she decided to return to Skálholt. She was going home. To Mamma. She dared not hope that, one day, she might see Páll.

Rósa had tried to persuade Katrín to come with her.

'My place is here,' was all she would say.

And in the silence between the words Katrín would not speak aloud was the longing for her daughter, Dora, and the hope that she would return.

Rósa remembered the light in Katrín's

eyes when she learned that Anna had, however briefly, risen from the dead, emerged from the belly of the land like an elf. She knew it was not from Katrín's hope for Anna alone, but the never-ending longing and the tiny grain of faith that any parent must feel for a missing child.

One day she will return.

So Rósa kissed Katrín's cheek, saddled Hallgerd and rode south to Skálholt.

At night, she begged for shelter in barns, curling into the mare's body for warmth. She ate dried fish in the saddle and drank from streams. Under the open eye of the arching curve of the sky, she felt very small and entirely free. It was as if she were watching herself from years hence. She could see the tiny speck of life travelling over the hills, could see her insignificance within that fractured world, the land that could conceal bodies, or spew them up, like a magician's ruse.

As she travelled, she wondered: would Páll have waited the whole of three days, or would he have gone? Perhaps he would have told her mamma where he planned to travel. Perhaps, if she waited in Skálholt long enough, he would return. The pull of duty she felt towards Jón was an anchor: she was tethered, but secure. The uprooting hurricane of her desire for Páll left her dizzy and exposed.

Dangerous as it was, she couldn't let him go.

Some loves are deep enough to dive into, deep enough for the total submersion of the self. Around Páll, Rósa knows that the rest of the world becomes a blur of velvet shadows and murky echoes. Yet she also knows that the love that cradles her body would steal into her mouth and nose and throat, filling her lungs until, mid-laughing breath, she would suddenly discover that she had long since drowned and was sitting on the seabed, staring up at the light, but anchored for ever by the size and weight of her longing.

As she travelled south, she ran her fingers over Hallgerd's mane, and tried not to think.

And now here she is. *Home.*

And yet it feels so different, as if the shape of everything has changed in her absence. Or as if, like a stone that has been dragged free of the rockface, she has been battered by the suck and pull of the current and, returning to the rock that shaped her, finds herself too broken to locate the space that once enclosed her.

She digs her heels into Hallgerd's flanks

and the mare trots down the hill.

It is early and quiet; she reaches Mamma's croft unseen.

Sigridúr is still sleeping; her snores fill the small *baðstofa*. In repose, her face seems old and frail: her mouth sags open and her skin is like crumpled parchment. But her breathing is easy, and her lungs no longer rattle on each inhalation.

Rósa feels a rush of relief and affection. She sits on the edge of the bed that once was hers, and presses a kiss into her mother's wrinkled cheek.

Sigridúr's eyes flutter open in alarm. Then she gasps and holds out her arms. 'Rósa!' she cries. 'My child, I thought . . .' And Sigridúr kisses her again and again, her frail hands trembling. 'Why?'

'I — I was afraid . . . for you. After the snow.'

There are too many other words and too many stories, but for the moment she closes her eyes and inhales safety. One day she will tell the truth, when she is sure that Sigridúr's face will not harden — when she can be certain that Mamma will not think her a different person.

Some stories she will not tell. She will choose, day by day, which truths to reveal. And, gradually, the tales she tells will

479

become truth. In this way, she will live with who she has become. She is a woman capable of violence. She is a woman who did what was necessary. She is a woman who has survived.

But the truth isn't solid, like the earth; she knows that now. The truth is water, or steam; the truth is ice. The same tale might shift and melt and reshape at any time.

At this particular moment, Rósa simply fetches a bowl of meat stew to share, then climbs into bed next to Mamma. They huddle together for warmth, just as they used to.

That afternoon, she goes in search of Páll. Sigridúr said that he had returned days earlier, but that he wouldn't tell her anything, other than that Rósa was safe.

He is still here! Rósa daren't allow herself to hope for more than to see his face. But, still, a painful, burning anticipation shifts inside her as she searches for him.

She finds his croft empty, the rooms darkened, as if he has already left. With a lurch, she runs back out into the cold. She calls his name. The sound bounces off the mountains; they are remote and uncaring as she runs towards the river Hvítá, calling for him again and again.

People put their heads out of their crofts, whispering and nudging each other as she runs past; she doesn't care. Because it is a raw hunger she feels for him. Not love, not want, but *need*. Like the desire for food, it is uncontainable. And she feels his absence as a blank white space on every breath as she calls for him: as if his name had been written alongside hers on some page in the Sagas, then scrubbed out, so that no trace remained.

She runs to the Hvítá, because he must be there, surely, at the place they used to sit, when she used to read to him, and where he first looked at her as though she were the only thing in the world.

And then, as if the heat of her desire has created him, there he is, staring into the swirling river. She is struck by the slump of dejection in his shoulders. He is as easily read as a well-known parable. Her heart thuds in her chest. She stops running, smooths her hair, gathers her breath.

'It would be a cold drowning today,' she calls.

'Rósa!' His eyes light. He holds out his arms and she reaches for him. All her worries are suspended: her fears of his judgement, her own guilt. Thoughts of her husband and all that happened in

Stykkishólmur are distant and ice-covered. They belong to another life. For now, this closeness, this comfort, is all that exists.

'I was afraid you had left,' she mumbles into his chest.

'I would have waited for ever here, for the hope of you.' His words rumble through her, like the first stirring of the current under the frozen ice.

And he holds her to his chest and kisses her hair, her cheeks, her forehead. And she meets him, kiss for kiss, messy, mismatched kisses, until they are both giggling and she is inhaling his laughter deep into her lungs.

The next day, Snorri Skúmsson hobbles up to her and takes her by the arm.

'Your husband knows you're here, then, Rósa?'

Once, she would have flushed, jabbered an excuse and scurried away. Now, she looks the old man straight in the eye. 'That is not your concern.'

Snorri's bushy grey eyebrows waggle. 'Oh, but it is. Your husband sends food here. And if you're seen wandering about, fluttering your eyelashes and flicking your skirts, then it puts all of us in danger.'

Her stomach lurches but she manages to say, 'Gossip is a sin, Snorri. You want to stay in the bishop's good graces.'

He spits, 'There are other sins, worse than gossip, and worth gossiping about.'

Rósa strides away, but she can hear him shouting after her about modesty and adultery.

She wonders where Jón is, if he is safe. Out from under his shadow, she is able to see her husband for what he is: a terrified man, fighting to survive in a world that would rip him to pieces. She hopes he has found peace.

Rósa runs her fingers over the little glass woman in her pocket. It is all she has left of Jón. The glass is sharp where the arm has shattered. She presses her thumb against it, hard enough to draw blood. She wonders at the fragility of the body, and the fierce resolution needed to survive.

When Sigridúr isn't looking, Rósa rubs her hand over the skin of her stomach, which aches more every day. She has not had a monthly cycle since she shared Jón's bed in September. One day soon her secret will be written on the swell of her belly. For now, the knowledge is hers and hers alone, safe from the world of gossip and sly glances.

One cold morning, just after they have

celebrated a sober Christmas, eating *skyr* and dried fish, on a day when the sun barely seems to stir behind the crypt of the clouds, a merchant rides down over the hills.

His saddle is weighted with bags of linen, knives and plates fashioned of metal and soapstone, wooden spoons and other luxuries. The villagers crowd around, either pressing cut-off pieces of silver coins and ells of cloth into the man's palm, or bartering: this chicken for that plate; this wool for that tiny pot of salt.

As coin and goods change hands, pieces of news are traded also. Rósa discovers that the coastal ice floes have grown larger; the Althing will meet early; harvests have been poor across the land, so people are starving and dying.

The villagers sigh, shake their heads and turn away, clutching their trinkets.

Rósa hangs back until everyone has gone and the trader seems about to move on. In her pocket lies a single silver coin, whole and heavy.

'What is in that bag?' she asks. Perhaps, while he lingers, she can discover news from Stykkishólmur.

The trader grins, winks and unties the cord, then tips something gleaming into Rósa's palm. At first, it is so cold she thinks it must be water. But it is solid and she sees a dark, ovular shape squatting in the centre of it.

It is a piece of glass, roughly shaped into the form of a woman — Rósa can make out the streaks that represent her long hair. But it is the dark object *within* the glass that makes Rósa catch her breath.

A tiny piece of wood, lovingly carved into the shape of a baby. It has perfect little legs, pulled in close to its chest, and it has one hand against its face, sucking the thumb. Its miniature eyes are closed. The glassmaker must have squeezed the glass woman at the neck and the legs, so that the tiny baby sways around inside her hollow belly.

'It is beautiful,' Rósa breathes. 'How came the wood to be inside the glass?'

'Couldn't say,' grunts the trader. 'Picked it up off a fellow further north and he didn't know either. Doesn't seem possible.'

'No,' she whispers.

Glass and wood: one hard and easily shattered, the other pliant, but stronger. It shouldn't be possible to fit one inside the other. Yet here they are, the hollow glass shielding the wood from the damp and rot of the world. If the figurine shatters, the wood inside will decay, but as long as the glass woman remains intact, she will keep

485

the wooden baby safe.

Rósa pulls her coin from her pocket. The man blinks at the large piece of silver, but accepts it with a nod. From his broad smile, he thinks he has done well.

'You said you travelled from the north,' she says lightly. 'Did you go towards Stykkishólmur?'

He shakes his head and her heart sinks. 'I avoid those paths. Superstitious people, strange ways. They keep separate and are wary of traders they don't recognize.'

She sighs and is about to walk away, the little glass woman clasped in her hand, but then the merchant calls, 'I heard something, though, from another merchant. Just gossip, I suppose.'

She turns. 'Yes?'

'They found a man on the beach. A great man in those parts — I forget his name. Had one of the *huldufólk* for an apprentice, they say. There was some story that he had murdered two wives, and was fleeing.'

Rósa feels a chill, imagining Jón captured and awaiting trial, or Egill commanding Olaf to mete out a brutal justice. 'Where did they take him? Where is he now?'

The merchant squints. 'Why, he's dead. Was found so — I thought I'd said as much. They think he'd drowned. He was just lying on the beach, and his boat was gone. Stolen, probably. He was laid out under a blanket, not a mark on him. Sounded odd to me. Jésu, are you well? Here, take my hand.'

He holds her arm, while she tries to catch her breath, squeezing the glass figurine until she is sure it must shatter.

'I didn't mean to shock you. Sometimes I forget women are fragile.'

She shakes her head. 'I am . . . well. I . . . I must go.'

And she turns from the merchant and runs, her breath coming in ragged gasps, until she reaches the Hvítá. The water thunders past; the cold spray settles on her cheeks and insinuates into her lungs, creeping into her bones, until she feels she is slowly freezing from the inside.

Rósa bends double and howls. She clutches her belly to bring some warmth to the fatherless child within her. But she feels like stone, like ice — like the glass woman clutched in her numb fingers. She clasps it tightly, this ageless fragment from the heart of the earth, which time has crumbled and fire has transformed into something beautiful and impossible, and nothing like the crumbled stone it once was.

Later, when Páll finds her, it is dark. Her

whole body judders with cold.

The river thunders past, promising a moment of violence, followed by icy silence.

She turns away from the water. Her husband is dead now. For the first time ever, she belongs to herself. She stretches her arms wide, feeling the sudden reach and weight of her limbs. She draws a shuddering breath, then wraps her arms around herself.

Páll brushes the tears from her face. 'Your skin will freeze,' he says, with a small smile. 'Don't weep yourself to death, Rósa.' Then he lays his warm hand upon her cheek, leans forward and kisses the tip of her nose.

At that touch, something inside her shatters.

She finally looks at him. And the swooping, dizzying jolt of staring into his eyes leaves her dry-mouthed and silent. She winds her arms around his neck, his hands go about her waist and her whole body lifts itself to meet him — her blood, her bones, her heart, her breath. Her muscles, like sudden water.

He leads her further down the path, to a tiny cave near the river, where no one from the village ever goes. He spreads out his cloak on the ground; she lies down and he lies next to her, cradling her head. And she thinks she might be weeping, or perhaps they are his tears, or drops from the river cooling on their bodies. And then there is only the blur of sweat and heat, and the weight and shape of him over her, and his open-mouthed gasp as he moves inside her.

He pauses, presses his forehead against hers; his eyes, staring deep into hers, are smiling. And that wordless moment of being truly seen, of being *known,* runs through her. She gasps and kisses him again and again, absorbing his shout at the last, against her open mouth, so that it echoes through their bodies.

Afterwards, shaking, Páll lays his hand on the slight swell of her belly; she lays her cheek on his chest. Every plane of his body is as familiar and grounding as the land beneath them.

He kisses her again, strokes her hair, then lies on the ground so he can wrap the cloak around her. 'Don't want you to freeze.'

'I'm not cold,' she whispers.

'You're trembling,' he says, and pulls her close.

It has taken her so long, but now she knows it: they are interwoven threads from the same cloth — she would unravel without him.

As she presses against him, something

sharp digs into her skin. She reaches into
her pocket and pulls out the broken glass
woman Jón gave to her. The crack within it
has grown; the face is chipped. It is impossible to discern the passive, downcast eyes
and humble expression.

'What is that?' Páll asks.

'Nothing.' And Rósa tucks it back into her
pocket; it clinks against the rounded glass
figure she bought from the trader.

Rósa breathes in the fresh mist of the
gathering night and winds her arms around
Páll again; his body fits against hers, like
the runestone fits the contours of her hand.

The body remembers love, as rock remembers the heat and compression that formed
it. It waits, buried under the earth, cold and
longing, until it is freed. Then that same
rock can skim across a river, travel an ocean,
be carried across strange lands until it finds
its way home.

Rósa closes her eyes. When she opens
them again, it will be morning, and the
thick-breathing air that has surrounded her
— the weight of the ocean that has crushed
her — will have lifted.

Her swelling body will be her own, at last.

And on another morning, not too far
away, the ice will melt. The land will stir,

and new life will quicken and flourish under the rising arc of the sun.

■ ■ ■ ■

ONE WEEK EARLIER

■ ■ ■ ■

Fear not death, for the hour of your doom
is set and none may escape it.

Icelandic proverb,
from *Volsunga Saga*

JÓN

We are fools for returning this way, I tell him, but Pétur will not listen. His plan, I admit, is a good one: we will find a boat and row out to one of the islands in the bay, far enough away that no fisherman will ever find us. There we will live, he and I, on fish and rainwater.

Both of us could navigate those thousands of islets as well as we might trace the map of the vicious scars and livid lines that mark the other's skin. Yet even I agree that we could become lost among the islands, if we wish, so we may still hope to find peace and silence there.

The thaw continues; the rain patters down daily, making the land as slick as a seal. I half wish for the snow to return and coat the earth in its harsh shroud. Everything — even death — glistens with beauty.

But the thaw is the breaking of the earth's

waters: everything smells of salt, of the sea, of new birth. We travel to the coast, where we will find my boat. I can almost taste our new life — fresh and clean as melted ice. When I catch Pétur's eye, he smiles.

Our journey here was treacherous: we travelled for nearly a week, following the rivers north from Thingvellir. Pétur had a fishing cord with him, and his usual charmed luck meant he could pull three fish from the water within the space of a hundred breaths.

'I could have you burned as a witch,' I called.

He grinned. 'Who would conjure fish from the water for you then?'

After dark — once we had eaten and Pétur had quenched the fire, kicking turf over it so that it wouldn't reveal us to any pursuers — we walked and found a shelter. Sometimes this was a clearing in some bushes, at others a cave. Once, it was no more than a hollow in the ground.

There, Pétur pulled my tunic over my head, washed my wound and rebound it. I tried not to wince, though it was agony, searing to the touch.

He tore strips from his own shirt to bandage me, and helped me to dress again, as tenderly as if I were a child. As he worked, I saw the clench in his jaw from the pain in his arm, but when I asked if it hurt him, he shook his head.

'It is nothing,' he growled. 'Now keep still.'

The thought of living without him was endless nightfall. *My heart. My soul.*

Once I was dressed, we would lie, face to face, almost touching in the darkness. Pétur, exhausted from carrying me, fell asleep quickly, but I lay still, sensing his breath on my cheek, watching the movements of his eyes under their lids. I felt, always, a wonderful stillness and anxiety in watching his restless dreams.

Take me with you.

My whole life was in those moments. I felt able to breathe, at last. My devotion, when I watched him sleep, was stronger than my own breath, my own skin.

Sometimes we woke in the night, huddled against the cold. Then, in the darkness, the world and everything in it became as skinless as water, no boundaries to show where one wave ended and the next began, our bodies like paired oars, each movement driving us further into the unknown. Time and sensation blurred. Tiny moments of golden brilliance, gossamer-thin and stretched to breaking, in a life otherwise steeped in grim shadow.

I did not simply hold Pétur in my arms; I embraced him with blood and bone, clasped him with muscle and spirit, everything that I was and hoped to be.

God might strike me down, but I felt saved and whole.

Afterwards, we fell asleep intertwined. In those last moments of wakefulness, blinking up at the stars, as I sensed Pétur's sweat cooling on my skin, I felt utterly human and fallen, and utterly content. And in those heat-soaked rags of time, I wished for every mountain in Iceland to shudder down rocks upon us, concealing us for ever from the gaze of the world. If we were ever found, our bodies would be dragged from the rubble together: tangled, knotted — inseparable.

But such moments of savage contentment are as fleeting as the reflection of the swelling moon blinking upon the surface of the sea. Only ever minutes old, they dissolve with a passing cloud, or a gust of wind.

In every human heart glows a tiny flame of hope that tomorrow will bring a love that might satisfy the smouldering yearning to be known. In some hearts, that fire is greedy and becomes a devouring inferno. It leaves only dead ash and dry dust behind. The wind whirls it into emptiness.

But there is such heat while it burns . . . And the light is infinite.

We have followed the arterial seam of the river to its destination: freedom and the sea. We will wait on the beach until nightfall; then I hope we will find my boat and we will row. Pétur has washed my wound and rebound it and, despite the shiverings of the growing fever in my blood, I feel peaceful.

The darkness is smothering, but I can hear the inhalations of the waves and smell the salt. The sea has been present all of my days, like lifeblood.

Suddenly in the black sky, beneath the stars, there is a whispering, muscular swathe of light. I nudge Pétur. We watch the rippling ribbons of colour unfurling across the horizon. It is like a sign from God. I grip Pétur's hand; it is as solid as the earth. We watch until our eyes sting, until the lights fade and the sun pushes a sulphuric glow over the horizon.

And then, as if one miracle was not enough, a tiny bird flits overhead, in defiance of the black-winged ravens that croak and swoop around it. It is a delicate thing, the sort that should have migrated south months ago or perished. But here it is, alive and winging a frail flight across the restless waters. It will never survive in this savage climate but, still, it labours onwards.

Out of the corner of my eye, from the sea, I see a flash of white. Even though I have not imagined it in days, I could swear that a pale hand is waving. I shake my head, and the vision fades.

We begin to scramble over the stones that lead down to the beach and, I hope, to my boat — if it is still there. Pétur grips my hand when my stomach pains me. I pull him upright when his arm cannot take his weight. Neither of us will let the other fall.

I look back at the land. The hills of Stykkishólmur are so close. I can see, through the gloom, the outline of the croft I fought for. And it seems, for a moment, that I see a shadow moving, or perhaps two, something flapping among the rocks. The tail of a long black cloak? But, although I blink and squint, it disappears. Perhaps it was the wing of a raven, after all.

I turn back to the sea and continue to heave myself painfully onwards, following Pétur over the rocks. Every step is a stab into my side. My breath whistles from between my teeth. Pétur holds out a hand; I force myself to smile, to wave him on. I move more and more slowly, stumbling

500

often. My limbs feel all fire, though my skin is as dry as bone. Finally, I collapse onto a rock, panting.

I call Pétur back. 'Leave me here.'

'Don't be a fool.'

'You must go. They will catch us.'

'You —'

'Pétur . . . I am a dead man.'

'You are *not*. Don't say that, or I'll kill you myself. Come, up.' There is a tremor in his voice and he clenches his jaw as he struggles to heave me upright.

I swat him away. 'Let me die. Take the boat. Wait on one of the islands for a trading ship, then go to Denmark.'

'You are coming with me.' The pain in his eyes is unbearable.

I shake my head. 'It will comfort me to know you live. They will treat you better there, not like some monster. You can make a life there, free.'

'I will not leave you —' His voice fractures. I have never seen him weep. He dashes away the tears savagely with his palm.

'You must,' I say gently.

'I would rather die.' He speaks from between gritted teeth. I know that look: he will not change his mind. So I nod, slowly, and agree to rest, to sleep. We curl up together, his arms strong around me. His whole body shakes, whether from cold or grief, I don't know.

He will never be free while I am with him. And I will bring death for him.

I rise in the dark belly of the night, when only the stars blink down. I press my lips to Pétur's mouth. He stirs and reaches for me. I kiss his hand and place it on his chest. From around my neck I take the strip of leather, on which dangles a tiny figure, made of glass. St Jude, the trader had said, the Catholic patron of lost causes, but I didn't care: it was beautiful.

I fold it into Pétur's palm. Then I tie my cloak about my neck, forming a pouch — the sort of sling in which a mother might carry a child — and fill it with stones, starting with the runestone Rósa gave me. Every time I bend, the pain knifes through my side; the makeshift sack grows too heavy for my fever-weak limbs. I worry that the stones will not be sufficient. Still, I have seen enough men drowned to know: one good breath will do it.

Pétur sleeps on. I lift the sack over my head and walk forward.

The sea is cold.

I cannot.

I turn back to Pétur . . . He will hate me, curse me.

502

Then I imagine him rowing out across the water. I see him aboard a trading ship, the wind whipping the hair from his eyes, chasing away years of fear. I picture him in Copenhagen, moving through crowds, like any other man. He will never again hear the whisper of *huldufólk* or *monster.* Without me, he will be free.

Love opens us, as an earthquake opens the earth.

I turn to face the sea and I walk. I am overwhelmed by the sensation of lightness, as if the stones weigh nothing. It is a return to the still waters, after a lifetime of currents and drift.

And, beneath the breathing sky, I have never felt more alive.

GLOSSARY OF
ICELANDIC WORDS

baðstofa — A living and sleeping area, often with beds along the walls.

Bless — A greeting (less formal than *'Komdu sæl og blessaður'*).

brennevín — A clear schnapps, made from fermented grain or potato mash.

dagverður — Daytime meal.

draugr — An undead creature or an animated corpse. Plural *draugar.*

elskan — A term of endearment, like 'darling'.

ginfaxi — A runic sign for victory in battle.

goði — The chieftain of a settlement.

hloðir — An open hearth for cooking, constructed of large stones over a fire.

huldufólk — The 'hidden people' or elves.

Komdu sæl og blessaður — Formal greeting to a man.

Komdu sælar og blessaðar — Formal greeting to a group of women.

505

lifrarpylsa — A sausage made from chopped liver.

moldbylur — Snow so heavy that it is impossible to see an inch in front of you.

nattverður — Evening meal.

seidr — Witchcraft (punishable by death).

skyr — A protein-rich fermented yoghurt.

prestur — A village priest or minister.

vegvísir — A runic sign for protection and finding one's way.

ACKNOWLEDGEMENTS

People believe that writing is a solitary activity and that writers are private beasts, but I couldn't have written this novel without constant support, encouragement (and gentle criticism) from a whole host of individuals. I am so thankful and so indebted to so very many people.

Thanks first to my wonderful, fearsome and fearless agent, Nelle Andrew, whose uncompromising perfectionism guided me through countless redrafts, revisions and deletions. I couldn't have hoped for a more talented and supportive champion for my book and my writing. You're a phenomenon. To Marilia Salvides for all your hard work and support, and to Laura Williams for your last-minute cheerleading. Thanks to all the team at Peters Fraser and Dunlop.

Thanks also to my brilliant editor, Jillian Taylor, who fell for *The Glass Woman* at the first reading (and wrote the loveliest letter I've ever received). Your fierce belief in the novel and in my writing has been as invaluable as your insightful editorial instinct. To my exceptional copy-editor, Hazel Orme, whose sharp eye was so key in refining the novel. Thanks also to Bea McIntyre and her wonderful proofreaders, Eugenie Woodhouse and Kathryn Sargent, and to Katie Bowden and Laura Nichol. To all the team at Michael Joseph who have thrown themselves behind the novel: thank you.

Huge thanks to Sigurður Gylfi Magnússon and Árni Daníel Júlíusson at the University of Iceland, who were so willing to meet with me and discuss the minutiae of Icelandic life in the seventeenth century. Thanks also to Regina Hrönn Ragnarsdóttir for her advice on the layout of crofts and turf-houses.

To my family: thanks to my sister Annabelle, who read and loved a scrappy first draft and offered such great and perceptive ideas. To my lovely mum, for listening to me and supporting me, for loving everything I write and for buying me *so* many books. Posthumous thanks to my brilliant, misanthropic dad, whose abrasive intolerance of all noise encouraged me to read voraciously. To my sister Sophie, for her love and her special blend of sarcasm and support.

To the wonderful people who read and offered advice and feedback on drafts: thank you to Bill Gurney for your wonderful eviscerations of early drafts (most notably, for your comment that some of the first draft was 'Like being in Iceland: the supermarket . . .'). Double thanks, Bill, for reading and commenting on *two* drafts. To Nettie Gurney for your wonderful reading recommendations and insights into my short stories. Thanks to Sachin Choithramani for your discerning eye and to Robert Ward-Penny for your perceptive comments and humbling praise. To everyone else who was kind enough to read and offer thoughts on early iterations: Penny Clarke, Nicky Leamy, Adele Kenny and Katie Purser. To Cathy Thompson for talking through an early idea over wine, when I'd only written the prologue.

Thanks again to the great teachers who inspired me: to Graham Crosby, who first told me I could write; to Maureen Freely and David Morley — I'm so delighted to be teaching on the Warwick Writing Programme, which gave me such a great start.

Thank you to John Wood for support in spite of tricky circumstances, for lifts to the station and for being flexible with book-induced changes of plan, even though it drives you mad. Thanks, too, for printing off research articles and sending through useful links to interesting websites.

So many thanks to Liz Day and Doug Day for your endless support, enthusiasm and cheerleading, and for looking after my two small boys, who, rightfully, adore you. You're both wonderful.

More than thanks to Roger Dix for everything and for being *all* the things. Let's not fuck it up.

To my two wonderful sons, Arthur and Rupert. Thank you for your endless patience and love, and for sharing me with imaginary people. Every day, you make me laugh; every day, you make me proud. Every day, you teach me things about myself that I really didn't want to know. I love you more than words can say.

AUTHOR'S NOTE

Seventeenth-century Iceland may seem an unusual choice of setting for a writer from Jersey, but as soon as I started to read about the country and the period, I found myself enthralled. Geographically isolated, Iceland has a rich cultural history and set of beliefs, which are as distinct as its compelling landscape. I was fascinated to discover that, even in modern Iceland, it isn't uncommon to believe in the *huldufólk* and that people still sometimes simply 'disappear' — one look at the wild landscape of volcanoes, ice floes and geysers and it's easy to see how someone in Rósa's time would have believed in the power of the land. Increasingly, as I wrote and immersed myself in Rósa and Jón's world, I discovered that the landscape itself was becoming a character. I was struck by how terrifying it must have been to live in a place where the very surroundings that sustained you one summer might kill you during the winter. I was also fascinated by the Sagas, which formed some of the earliest western literature. Unlike Greek and Roman myths of gods and goddesses, the Sagas are often stories about real men and women and their very human struggles — although, appropriately, they also contain references to the supernatural.

I found a number of books very helpful when researching both the place and the history: *Names for the Sea: Strangers in Iceland* by Sarah Moss is wonderful and compelling and proved inspirational for its sense of landscape and exploration of culture and history. Kirsten Hastrup's *Nature and Policy in Iceland 1400-1800* was a constant point of reference. *Wasteland with Words,* by Sigurður Gylfi Magnússon provided some useful insights, as did Gunnar Karlsson's book, *Iceland's 1100 Years: The History of a Marginal Society.* Similarly, *Romance and Love in Late Medieval and Early Modern Iceland,* edited by Kirsten Wolf and Johanna Denzin, was very useful. I enjoyed reading Halldór Laxness's *Independent People* and *Iceland's Bell* and also loved Sjón's novels *The Blue Fox* and *The Whispering Muse.* Hannah Kent's novel *Burial Rites* was also superb for its sense of place.

The short time I spent in Iceland was both enlightening and inspirational. It is a wonderful country: the landscape is breathtaking, the sense of history is mind-boggling and the people proved incredibly welcoming. Two Professors of History from the University of Iceland, Sigurður Gylfi Magnússon and Árni Daníel Júlíusson, happily gave up their entire afternoon to discuss what Rósa and Jón's world might have been like. It was refreshing, too, that in response to one of my questions about possible attitudes to a woman knowing how to read, both professors agreed that, while they didn't know the answer, that shouldn't matter, because I was, after all, writing fiction, wasn't I? I used that thought as a touchstone while writing: all novels are invented — even non-fiction books often contain elements of fiction and interpretation. I've tried, where possible, to adhere to my research, but have unashamedly resorted to invention in instances where the facts weren't readily available or would have impeded the story. All mistakes are very much my own.

I loved exploring the idea of what it would have been like for a woman in this time, especially one who, like Rósa, is torn between the old beliefs and the 'new' religion, who is divided in her loyalties to her family and her husband, and who finds herself isolated and terrified. Even with my modern privileges of education and financial autonomy, I've still found myself in circumstances where, in the face of a man's assumed dominance and entitlement, I've felt small and scared and have, in some instances, doubted my own sanity. In this way, at some points, Rósa's story didn't feel very far from my own, despite the distance in time and space. Like many women, and like Rósa, I remind myself daily to be brave. I hope for a future where my sons won't behave as though their various privileges entitle them to everything, and where my nieces won't have to check their armour before they leave the house.

Caroline Lea
June 2018

ABOUT THE AUTHOR

Caroline Lea was born and raised in Jersey in the United Kingdom. *The Glass Woman* is her second novel. She lives in Warwick, England.

The employees of Thorndike Press hope you have enjoyed this Large Print book. All our Thorndike, Wheeler, and Kennebec Large Print titles are designed for easy reading, and all our books are made to last. Other Thorndike Press Large Print books are available at your library, through selected bookstores, or directly from us.

For information about titles, please call:
(800) 223-1244

or visit our website at:
gale.com/thorndike

To share your comments, please write:
Publisher
Thorndike Press
10 Water St., Suite 310
Waterville, ME 04901